34 Seconds

Stella Samuel

34 Seconds

Copyright © 2015 by Stella Samuel

www.stellasamuel.com

Line and Copy Editing: Melanie Glenn
Editing: Dark Star Publishing
www.darkstarpublishing.com
Formatting completed by Rik Hall
www.WildSeasFormatting
Cover design by John C. Harman
www.johncharman.com

ISBN: 978-0-9968088-0-4

This book is dedicated to
Jeff, Arwen, Zoe, and Nolan
and written for Daddy.

Erin,
I'm going to miss you and your beautiful family. I do hope you come to visit. Thank you for always being there.

Stella

Samuel

Fifteen Years Ago
Deltaville, Virginia

My heart was beating so fast and so loud, I was certain it would soon leave my chest and bounce itself right out the window, down the street, and into the Piankatank River. Will not only asked me if I wanted to come over and listen to his new song, but he also invited me into his bedroom and then closed the door. He was sitting knee to knee with me, only his guitar separating my heartbeat from his body, his soul, his voice. His entire being.

We met three days earlier, late at night in a neighborhood pool. I knew I wasn't naïve enough to think I was in love, and I also knew *I was absolutely in love*. I knew it wasn't lust, because I thought I could live forever with him without ever touching him. Well, maybe I would touch him. But before I do, I would melt in his voice. I'd be like little written notes on a musical staff melting across the lines with each strum of his guitar. I was sure it was love. I was absolutely in love with Will. William or just Will? Shit, I didn't even know his full name yet, but I could draw the coffee stain like birth mark on his left leg by heart. I could die in his eyes. I could give a name to each ringlet of hair that fell around his face. Those spiral curls were what started my heart beating to begin with. Will didn't have surfer hair like so many of the boys who swoop into town, but instead medium length blonde hair with spiral curls any girl would kill for. And those curls weren't something unnoticed. I noticed his hair, his sense of humor, his confidence, and his voice; oh I could see all of it exuding from him the night he took off all of his clothes and jumped into the pool.

Two days later, after the evening Will and his best friend, Brian, spent a few hours swimming naked with me and my friend, Liza, in the dim hours of an early summer evening, Brian asked me to join the two of them at Will's house to hang out. I can still feel girlish embarrassment because I misunderstood something Brian had asked me. Or maybe my embarrassment was because I was naked when we all first met. I stayed in the deep dark waters; it was night time. I'm fairly confident I was able to be modest, as modest as a naked person could be.

"Wanna do something later?" Brian asked.

"NO!" I said with confidence and the vigor of someone proving a point. There wasn't much to do in Deltaville, Virginia. I didn't even know anyone with a trampoline or anything else exciting near my house. There was the pool, but it was really only fun if we were sneaking in at night. I hadn't been back since the night Brian and Will jumped in and scared Liza and me while we were having our late night swim.

"Whoa, there's no need to get mean about it, we just wanted to know if you wanted to do something later. We were thinking maybe you can get the girl who was with you in the pool the other night to come over and hang out with us, maybe take the boat out for a spin around the creek after the sun goes down. It's not the best time to sail, and we probably won't get far, but we could grab our guitars, a couple of cute girls, and see if the jelly fish are swimming," Will said.

"Oh," I said, averting my eyes. "I thought you asked *if* I was doing anything later, and I was just thinking there's just nothing to do around here. You don't know this area like I do. There really is nothing to do around here; especially after sundown." I said. "So I said, 'No', as in no, I'm not doing anything later."

I'd screwed it up; I just knew it. "Sorry," I said, feeling my face growing hot. "I would love to do something with you, and I'm sure if Liza's not working, she'll join us." I could feel my stomach tighten into one huge knot, but I almost felt saddened by my own embarrassment. Finally, two cute boys with personality and great hair come into town, and I blew it. In Deltaville, boys came each summer to visit, sail in regattas, and make the local girls feel out of place in our own town. The population in Deltaville tripled in the summertime, but most of us knew it was just summertime visitors, all just staying for a short time. No one made friends with those summer folk beyond the summer, but our local marinas, restaurants, and little bed and breakfast joints lived out the year on the business summer brought. Those boys felt different to me. They seemed to really like me and Liza. They sailed, but they didn't care about sailing. They weren't at the Yacht Club at 6AM in their Docker shorts and button down shirts with their boat shoes, pouring coffee and talking about the wake in and out of the creek. They had guitars, liked to have fun, and didn't seem to care what other people thought. As an artist myself, a painter in fact, I gravitated to other artists and stayed far away from the Yacht Club sailors. Yep, I knew I was in love.

We did go sailing. Well, we floated. There wasn't a breeze felt all evening; the night was still and humid. And I'm sure Will wasn't supposed to be in any boat without his grandfather knowing and possibly even helping. Will wasn't an established sailor, and the boat wasn't even his. I'm not even sure the boat was a sailboat. It wasn't the catamaran I'd seen at the dock at his grandfather's house earlier. It was not much bigger than a wooden dinghy with a bright sail that didn't move. There was no wind. Brian and Will were able to row it out away from the houses, so we wouldn't bother anyone around in the early evening hours. In the small, quiet town, everyone seemed to know everyone else's business and make it their own, so being away from the houses was a great idea. It was probably the best night of my life. We floated in the middle of the creek after the boys rowed us out a bit, and then we sat still and quiet for a while. The moon was waning into a perfect crescent. The small sounds the water made were soft and romantic. Every now and then we'd hear a big fish jump, but other than the sounds of nature surrounding us, it felt as if we were the only four people in the entire world. There was a moment sitting in the boat when I knew I would fall in love with Will. We were sitting side by side with his guitar next to us, and he started humming. After a few seconds of humming, Brian started humming, and after Brian started, Will broke out into full singing. It was a comical moment. My heart melted further.

"I can't feel the air, I can't see the sky, but I have you near, so I think I might fly." It was a silly little ditty, but he sang it with the seriousness of someone singing the national anthem at a Super Bowl. I melted in the sound of his voice so much in the moment, I wasn't even sure what he said. I just didn't want him to stop singing.

"Did you just say you'd fly because we are near?" Liza asked. I came back to reality. Liza had the ability to see through guys and their tricks to get attention from girls. Usually, I was never interested enough to care what a guy said to try to get our attention. My heart sank. What was Will saying? Did he mean he didn't want to be near me? Oh, how could I fall so quickly for someone I didn't even know?

"What?" Will asked. "No, I could fly, as in I feel so high to be out here with you two, and my good buddy, I feel so high I could fly," Brian started humming, and Will finished off the tune by singing, "I can't feel the air. I can't see the sky, having you near; I'm so high I could fly."

"Yeah, man, did you bring your notebook. We need to write that down. This is good. We could make it a song." Brian said. He picked up Will's guitar, and started lightly strumming a few chords while humming the tune Will just sang. I didn't want the night to end. But there I sat knee to knee with Will, alone in the room. And I knew I never wanted our second night together to end either. I was certain it was the way I would always feel.

Being alone with Will for the first time, I could feel the heat from his knees touching mine. I could feel the earth move as he sang the song he started to write on the boat just two nights earlier.

Will chuckled his own unique chuckle. "Huh hehe, I need a break from this," he said as he put his guitar down. He took my hands and held them up in the air between us. Then he let go. I dropped my hands back into my lap. He picked them up again, but when he let go this time, he held his in front of mine, very close to mine, but not touching. We sat still for a few moments. I could still hear my heart beating and was sure if he looked at my chest, he would see it thumping. Keeping one hand up near mine, he moved the other hand to my cheek, and with the back of his finger, slowly followed my cheek bone down to my chin, and then put his hand back in front of my two hands still hanging midair.

"Do you feel it?" he asked me.

"I'm feeling a lot of things right now, Will. Which it might you be speaking of?" I asked trying to portray a calm my body was far from feeling.

"The heat. Can you feel the heat from my hands flowing into your hands?" he asked.

"I'm not sure if it's heat from your hands, Will. It might be emanating from me. I gotta be honest with you. I'm a little heated right now. I'm not sure what to do about it, but I'm a ball of tight nerves, energy, and hmmm, I think there's a bit of desire somewhere in there." I didn't plan on being so blunt with him, but all of those

4

things were entirely true. I guess my body needed him to know even if my heart and mind didn't know if it was a good idea.

I could barely breathe.

"Then it's both of us. We're both emanating this heat. Can you feel it?"

"Yes," I whispered. More of my heart slid down the inside of my chest, fully melted.

"I felt it on your face as well. You are hot," Will whispered back to me.

"I hope I don't start sweating. The humidity is uncomfortable enough," I said before pausing. "And this moment isn't easy either. Will, I'm starting to feel uncomfortable. And nervous. I'm still very, very nervous," I said the last in barely a whisper.

"I don't want to make you uncomfortable, my dear, Nikki. What's uncomfortable?" Will asked.

I paused for a moment, shook my arms out, leaned back, and put one hand in my lap. Will quickly took my hand, kissed my palm, put it back next to his lingering hand, and tilted his head in a questioning look. I stared for a moment at the hand Will just kissed. He had kissed me! Sure, just my hand. But a kiss was a kiss, and I had received one. I didn't know how I was supposed to speak.

After a long pause, I just let my thoughts run out of my mouth. "I'm eighteen years old. I've never been in love before. But I've also never felt this way before. I'm usually in control of my feelings. I can usually tell what a guy is thinking. And I can usually set him straight before things get out of hand with anything I might feel." I looked down at his knees which were touching mine. When had I missed that? "I don't know what this is for me, but I'm nervous to be near you, and being nervous makes me very uncomfortable. I like control. I like having control of me, myself, my emotions, and my actions. I don't feel like I have a good grip on myself at this moment."

Will backed up, leaving my knees cold and my palms suddenly yearning for the heat between us.

"Why did you do that?" I asked, almost too quickly.

Will just looked at me for a minute, then scooted back towards me, so we were knee to knee again, and placed both of my hands inside his. "You said you were nervous to be near me. I don't want to make you nervous. And if you'd like control, baby, you can do whatever you'd like to do to me," he said in a near-whisper.

Baby! Had he just called me Baby? First he slipped in a palm kiss and then threw in the word, "Baby," like we were a couple. I didn't know how I was supposed to function, breathe, or speak. The way he tossed out such sweet gestures made me want him more.

"Oh," I sighed. "I'm nervous to be near you, and I'm nervous to not be near you. It's a scary feeling for me. I don't know what it says about me. I'm confused, I figure. If the logical part of me took control, I'd walk away, but I think I might die if I walk away from you." Oh, shit, what kind of thing was that to say? I sighed again. If this was love, which I knew it was; I was confused. I would laugh at anyone who told me they were in love after just a few days, love hurt, and hurt felt so damned good.

"Nikki, the heat you feel from my hands and from my knees is cycling through my whole body. I'm nervous to be near you too. I'm scared to be too close to you, but I don't want to be any further away from you," Will said with a smirk.

"I think this is what they call an impasse," I said, looking down at his crossed legs.

Will leaned into me, took my hands, and held them on our ankles between us. He then placed his lips next to mine. He didn't dare touch them; he didn't dare touch anything except my hands he was holding down. He seemed to be taking the control I couldn't muster. Time seemed to stop for a moment as we lingered there almost lip to lip. I held my breath, as time seemed to stand still. And in a split second, he lifted my hands, dropped them on his crossed legs, cradled my face in his warm hands, and pulled my lips onto his. It took him three days to kiss me, and I don't think it could have been more perfect. There was heat. There was passion. But there was no tongue, no thrashing, moaning, or groaning. It was just a simple kiss, one that would linger on my lips waiting until he planted the next one on me. One kiss spoke words to me. It said, 'Do not be afraid. Let go. Trust your gut. Net the butterflies. Enjoy the moment. Don't linger too long in one moment or you will miss the next. And allow yourself to fall for this guy. He is the one. And it is okay.'

I knew when he did his "huh hehe" chuckle it was time to open my eyes. I didn't even feel the warmth of his hand rubbing my knee until I opened my eyes and realized I was still leaning toward him, lingering in a kiss that was no longer taking place.

***

Their tune did end up as a song for the amazing duo. They spent the summer writing music, and I spent the summer listening to them, floating on fluffy clouds, kissing Will *a lot*, and falling in love with the most amazing man I had ever laid eyes on. Liza and Brian didn't hit it off like Will and I did, but we were a good foursome. Brian and Liza made decent friends; they acted a lot like a brother and sister might, arguing a lot, but with kindness and respect and some weird understanding between them. When Will and I began to take nights to ourselves, walking the beach or riding around in his Camaro, Liza decided to pick up more hours at the restaurant, and Brian spent more time helping Will's grandfather around the house and just hanging out enjoying the country life.

***

It was the best summer of my life, with romance, joy, music, carefree days, and evenings spent naked in a pool with a man who had the utmost respect for me as a young woman. I couldn't have been happier and willed time to freeze for Will and me and our young love. But time didn't freeze. Time marched on; time tore us apart. Time willed strength to ooze from our bodies in places where love had previously flowed.

June 2014
3:34 pm
Deltaville, Virginia

Thirty four seconds is all it took to realize I had just watched Will's last breath. Will was thirty-four years old. Thirty four seconds passed in time standing still, in a breath held waiting for the next to inhale. Only another breath never came for Will. Thirty four seconds took Will away from me.

Part one

Boulder, Colorado

May 2013

Chapter One

I sat with my knees on top of the bed, legs behind me, chest rising and falling as my breathing grew more rapid. I could see my face in the mirror in front of me, but I wasn't looking in the mirror. He was standing in front of me, naked and ready for me. I watched him flex his stomach muscles, and as he did so, the tip of his hard penis touched his stomach. Even before he relaxed, I could see just how ready he was. The throbbing was visible from where I was sitting. I felt more excited and ready for him, just watching him. I was enjoying the view as he stood in front of me. He wasn't posing by any means. I can't say what exactly he was doing; I just wasn't paying much attention to details. There were enough details in his body and his intentions to keep my mind busy. It was a moment which only took a few seconds while he did some mundane task, but my memory of it seemed to linger. When he was ready to move, he turned slightly toward me and took the three steps it took to get to the edge of the bed where I was waiting. Placing his hands on my shoulders, he gently laid me down. I could feel his lips on my neck and shoulders. Then he found my ear, my second favorite place to have his lips. I let him linger for as long as he wanted. Tongue in my ear, teeth slightly nibbling on my lobe, I almost didn't feel him enter me down below, but only because I was in such a trance. I was almost always in a trance when he was naked anywhere near me. It was a pleasant surprise when I felt his hard body press down on my stomach as he entered me, filling me with warmth and joy. I could feel his hands slide down my sides to my hips as he helped himself to the treasure we both wanted him to find. Gliding in and out, I started to think sex hadn't ever been better. This is what we needed. What I needed. I needed him. And I needed a good orgasm. Chris felt so good inside me, and I was so ready; but I wanted to wait to feel the infamous rush…

The screaming woke me. A thought tugged in the back of my

sleepy mind; I shouldn't have waited.

"Ma Maaaaaa Ma Ma Maaaa," a tiny voice said. I opened my eyes, searched for the clock, and moaned. The moaning may have been a remnant of the pleasure I had just given up in my unfinished dream, or it may have just been the disappointment in not seeing any sunlight while hearing the cries of my thirteen month old daughter. She was the light of my life. Her big sister filled a lot of space in my heart as well. It was dark out still, but the full moon shone through the large arched picture window in my bedroom. It was a great view anytime of the day or night. In the winter time, it seemed to settle in the window much of the night. It was getting into late spring, and I knew my view of the moon would start to change from my bedroom, making this too-early awakening much tougher on me. If I had to wake so early, I preferred to have a good view or at least some natural light. I didn't need sunlight when I woke to a bright and smiling face that only wanted to see me each and every day at five in the morning.

It seemed the actions my husband and I were going through in my interrupted dream were just memories now and only appear to me in dreams. Life with two small children had taken over, and the actions it took to create those beautiful little lives were something we only saw in movies. Who was I kidding? I couldn't remember the last time I had two hours to devote to a movie. If I had two hours to do nothing, I was sleeping or lying awake thinking of all the things I should have been doing. But I never really had two hours to do nothing.

The screaming ceased, but she was shaking her crib rail and muttering, "Uh Oh. Uh Oh," which meant she'd dropped something out of her crib, and anything in her crib was probably important since it just spent the entire night keeping her comfortable and safe. I knew I should probably go get it for her.

"I'll get her," I mumble to the snoring lump beside me.

I was kidding myself again. Not only did he not hear me volunteer to get out of our warm cozy bed to rescue our daughter from her little jailhouse, but he never heard her sleep piercing scream. Though I felt very safe around this man I loved so dearly, I was convinced our house would implode around him, and I'd have to wake him to tell him to go into the light. This is what our lives had become. The kids woke up; I tended to them. Motherhood had become my life. I knew he would, if he could hear them in his sleep. While he slept, I managed their every need. Once awake, I figured I should just get up and deal with it. I was too tired at night to stay awake much past the sun going down. He was too overworked to go to bed early, so I let him sleep during most of our early mornings. However, he usually tried to get up so I could sleep, and I just got up anyway. I had been losing the battle for sleep more often than not.

In the hallway, I almost bumped into my three year old in the near darkness. She was bright eyed and cheery in the moonlight coming in through the window of the guestroom. Another beautiful view. Where was the sun? Why were they awake this early?

"Mommy, Bella woke me up. She bloomed. You have not bloomed yet, Mommy. Can I eat all my oatmeal, and then I can have a lollipop." No, I hadn't bloomed yet, but maybe morning blooming would come with the intake of coffee. Wiping my eyes, I wondered if she asked a question or gave me a detailed plan of action for her early morning. I couldn't begin to think of lollipops yet, and I wasn't even sure if we had oatmeal.

"Emily, I need to go get Bella, and then we can talk about breakfast and candy when we get downstairs. And after I have something hot and caffeinated in my body," I said quietly, thinking about the other hot thing I'd rather have in my body, bringing my mind back to my unfinished dream. It was only a dream. I needed to wake up and get into *Mommy* mode. "Go on downstairs, and I'll be there in a few minutes," I said to her, trying to sound authoritative and all-knowing but wondering how I would lift a sixteen pound baby out of the crib without dropping her while half asleep in the dark.

"Good morning, my little butterfly, flutter by, flit flit flutter bug butterfly. Good morning," I whispered to my youngest daughter. It didn't matter how tired I was; the sight and smell of my babies would wake me and fill me with smiles. A wonderful and warm feeling washed over me. As hard as it was, it was life.

We met Emily downstairs. I managed to scrounge something healthy for my children to eat for breakfast. It turned out we had oatmeal after all. And fresh strawberries. Bonus, I thought to myself, having passed the Mommy test for the day. As I sipped some very hot Breakfast Blend, I began to come to life. I doubt it was the actual caffeine that woke me, but rather the idea of a stimulant and something hot in the morning. It could be only hot water; it would wake me up just the same. But I did love the taste and warmth of coffee.

As the kids ate, I turned on the laptop I kept on the island in the kitchen and checked my email. I stayed at the kitchen counter, checked on the status of our flight, and looked for any news regarding our planned trip out to Virginia. I didn't know what I was looking for, but I was disappointed when there was no news to be read, like maybe a cancellation. I did, however, manage to drink an entire cup of coffee while standing there. While my attention was on coffee consumption, my girls managed to eat about half of their strawberries and oatmeal, and Bella managed to smear the rest on her jammies and high chair tray while Emily's bowl was upside down on the floor.

"Emily, do you have your books packed yet? We are leaving tomorrow," I said to my three year old as I read the email confirming our flight out to Virginia the next day. She was only three years old; I couldn't exactly expect her to pack her books, but I had asked her to pick out a few favorites to take on the airplane. I knew I'd end up reading Cinderella over and over again for three hours straight, but I was also hoping the new movie I picked out would keep them both busy on the cross country flight. I remembered getting a deck of cards and wings when I flew as a small child. Today, parents take an entire playroom to entertain our children. But these are the days of sitting on tarmacs for hours and hours without knowing why the plane is not in the air, so we have to be prepared for anything. Especially with kids.

"Mommy, I just want to take Cinderelly," Emily replies. This much I knew.

"Okay, sweetie, but maybe we'll take some extra books just in case we decide we want to read something else, too." Or in case we lose 'Cinderelly,' I thought to myself, imagining the fantastic story in a nice big trash can sitting at Gate B32 at Denver International Airport. I was a little tired of Cinderella. Maybe I knew a girl couldn't dance with one man for an entire evening with a bunch of other women standing around watching, and then marry him the next day when his aide brings her the shoe she just happened to leave at his house. I'm cynical. Fairytales didn't impress me much, but I'll let my girls live them until the day I bring them into the real world.

14

They could live in their little fairytale bubble, and Cinderella was a favorite.

With the children fed and hot coffee in my tummy, I headed upstairs to shower. I met Chris, my husband, on the stairs and told him my plans, asked him to check the flight plans one more time, print our boarding passes, and keep an eye on the kids, so I could shower without little hands all over the glass trying to touch Mommy through the shower door.

"Remind me to tell you my dream later." I snuck in a little grab as we passed on the staircase. I may have felt older and unattractive being a mother of two little girls, but I still liked to flirt and play. I couldn't find time or energy to actually complete the task of lovemaking.

We built our dream house two years earlier. I was reminded of how much I loved the house each time I walked into any room. My bathroom was not huge, but it was beautiful with seventeen foot ceilings and mirrors I couldn't even reach without a ladder. I always felt like a princess when I was in our Master Bathroom. When I was there, I wanted to pamper myself and not just pee or shower. I was a housewife though, and I was reminded of my non-princess status when I had to pull the ladder out to reach and clean the mirrors. The windows were so high only soaring eagles could see my post baby naked body walking around. And of course they were so high, they never got cleaned, so it was not a worry anyway. I was not going to bother with cleaning either the mirrors or windows though. I planned to stand in a hot shower, shave my legs, and maybe sit on the built-in bench while the hot water ran down my face and back, waking me up even more. I needed all the rejuvenation I could get. Our shower was a great place for a lot of things. The bench was great to sit on, great to put my feet on while I shaved, and I thought it was a great place to connect with my husband. But usually his showers were at five in the morning, and my showers were spent with little hands all over the door and conversations I couldn't really hear with a three year old. Chris and I didn't really have time to connect in the shower or out.

The shower was a great place to think. In less than twenty four hours, I would be flying back home. As each year passed, it grew harder to go home. This time it was almost frightening. So much time had passed between me and home. The place, the people, the lifestyle. So many things had changed over the years. The water running down my neck and face was hot and hid the tears running down my cheeks. The shower was also a good place to cry. And think. And cry. And wonder why I was crying.

My mind began to wander to another time, another place. Another song. I'd never forgotten the lyrics. A song written for me by Will, in a time when we knew we loved one another, but he was backing away and beginning to withdraw from me.

> *Another place, another time*
> *You would have been so good for me.*
> *Another you, oh it's in your sign,*
> *you could have been, oh so good for me.*
> *Your lost soul,*
> *searching me,*
> *finding me, longing for you.*
> *Oh, another place, another time,*
> *I would have been so good for you.*
> *Another me, oh it's in my sign,*
> *I could have been, so good for you.*
> *My lost soul,*
> *it is searching you,*
> *found you wanting me.*
> *Oh another place, another time,*
> *oh you know, I would, would you?*
> *Ohhhh, Another place, another time.*
> *Would you-oo?*

Will sat in a rickety little boat with his old guitar singing to all the people lined up on the beach awaiting the start of the regatta. His new song, 'Another Place, Another Time,' was written about us. I sat near some tall grass almost hiding from the crowd enthralled with the sound of his voice, his talented fingers running up and down the neck of his guitar. I had given him a new, beautiful guitar, and though I wanted to see him play it, and I wanted to take offense because he wasn't playing it, I knew he'd never bring it on to the boat where it might get damaged. He did cherish his Takamine guitar I had given him. I wished he'd cherished me as much. I sat there with sand on top of my toes and grass tickling my cheeks wondering why, if we were so perfect, we'd only be a great fit if it were another time. When would it be time for us?

I picked myself up off the shower floor. There were times when I needed water to drench my tears, hide my emotions, and swallow my sorrows. I just sat right on the drain where I felt like I was in a warm rain. I wiped the tears from my eyes, reeling from the memory of the beginning of the end with Will, and tried to shake off the hurt, sorrow, and questions I still had after all those years.

I was a happy person. I felt lucky. I was Nikki Ford, formerly Nikki Jackson, before I married my wonderful husband, Christopher Ford. And he was wonderful. I loved him, and I had loved him for many years. Nikki Jackson once loved a man named Will Westerly. The one who got away, so to speak. The Romeo and Juliet summer love which didn't last. It lasted more than a summer. It lasted two years, actually, and those years were the best of my life. They were a time in my life when I was who I wanted to be. I was a free spirit, happy, and young. I was a songwriter, an artist, a painter in love, with dreams and hopes. Will was the great guy who *never* wanted to get married and never wanted kids. After two years of bliss, we had to walk away. From each other. Our hopes and dreams were different. He walked away from me. He walked away from my dreams. And then left me with a broken heart.

My family and I had been invited back home, to Deltaville, Virginia, to attend his wedding after all these years. The wedding of the man who never wanted to get married. I was happy for him. And for her. And I wasn't sad it wasn't me; I was already married. It was just bittersweet; I guess. And for it all, I cried. Or maybe I cried because I was so tired and couldn't seem to sleep for more than a few hours at a time. Maybe I was crying because I missed sex, and I didn't know how to get it back. Maybe I was crying because I was going back home. Home was always hard for me to envision. Home was Colorado with my husband, my children, and our cat. But home was also eighteen hundred miles away where I grew up. And it tended to stay the same while I grew and changed, but it also changed each year in ways that hurt my heart. Even without a wedding, change is tough to look at in the face. The shower was a place to let it all out and cleanse my entire system. When I exited the shower, my body and face were both red from crying and from the hot water running down my soft skin. I was glad to not only be free of little hands all over the shower door, but also free of Chris for the moment. I would have hated for him to see me cry. I think he would have hated to see me cry, and not because he'd want to hold me and sooth and comfort me, but because he'd be uncomfortable, would wonder what he did wrong, and turn and walk out of the room anyway. I was glad to not have to face him. I was pleased to have an alone moment. More tears were freed from my eyes.

The rest of the day rushed by in a blur. Getting to the other side of the country alone was a lot of work. Dragging two kids along was next to impossible. There were a lot of things to pack and prepare before getting two small kids to the playground or the mall. To get on an airplane or in the car for a long trip, we might as well take the entire house. My day was spent packing it all up, arranging and rearranging suitcases and carryon bags, and negotiating with a three year old over what could and couldn't be taken and with my husband over what was needed and not needed. He was an extremely grounded person and traveled often for business. He told me to leave the kitchen sink at home and reminded me entire wardrobes were not necessary because laundry could always be done while visiting my family in Virginia. I still managed to sneak some extras into the luggage because it's what mothers do. I tried to come and go prepared. It was the least I could do to feel prepared for the trip.

Chapter Two

They say you can't go home again. I managed to do it about once a year. Each time I did, I was astounded at the change. Boulder changed each year with more and more people moving in, old neighborhoods falling down, and eight thousand square foot homes peppering the Front Range. But for me, coming back to Virginia and noticing the amount of change was almost painful. There didn't seem to be much progression in the area where I spent my childhood, just tree growth and age. It was the aging all around that pulled at my heart strings. We are all aging, I knew, but Deltaville seemed to be on warp speed for aging but not for growth.

The Richmond International Airport had changed over the years. It was bigger and maybe even better. When we got off the plane, we followed the signs to baggage then to car rentals, spent the next thirty minutes loading the car, before finally leaving the airport. For an airport, it was actually a fairly easy and quick process. I was grateful for efficiency with our children tired and hungry after the long flight. The drive down interstate 64 east towards the Chesapeake Bay was uneventful but served as a reminder that the few trees in Colorado were planted generations before, keeping the views lingering forever and the skies vast. The skies in that part of Virginia weren't visible beyond the tree line. Nothing was visible. I could feel claustrophobia settling inside my stomach once we were in the car. The interstate was a tunnel of tall, skinny pines. I could only see about a quarter of a mile ahead of myself. After years of growing up in the area, I knew what lay beyond the trees. Deltaville, the town where I moved when I was only six years old. The place where I spent my childhood, staying out in town until sundown, or when my dad whistled to let my sister and me know it was time to come home. Deltaville, the boat builders' capital of the world, or so I thought when I was growing up. They did have a sign at the entrance of town touting they were the boat building capital of the

Chesapeake Bay. At a mile wide and three miles long, surrounded by water, it sure was a beautiful place to spend a childhood, but driving down the interstate heading toward the exit that would take us to Deltaville, I felt a sense of dread. This wasn't just a visit home to see my family. This was a trip to say goodbye to someone I once loved; goodbye to a love which was never allowed to flourish and grow. This was a journey of acceptance where the past met the present. Where Chris and Will would maybe shake hands. Where Will could look at my daughters with wonder. Maybe I was hoping for too much there; he never wanted children either.

We pulled into town, and I felt as if the past thirty years hadn't passed. Not much had changed. The once neatly trimmed yards on either side of the road were ridden with weeds, and moss was sweeping into the street bearing small pebbles which flew up and hit the windshield with each bump. There were mailboxes at the end of each driveway. When I was growing up there was no post to the house. We had to drive into town to pick it up at the post office. I dropped Chris and the girls off at my sister's house for a quick visit while I met Dad at his house about two miles away. I could see my father's garage peeking through the thick trees and fallen limbs. There was a thick film of mildew and mold growing on the outside of the white siding. My dad's green Thunderbird was parked in the garage. I remember the day he bought it. I was still in high school. It was a great car, but it was showing its age, with a small dent in the front fender and paint fading in the light shining through the double door pass-through garage.

It had been more than ten years since I left. I'd been home at least once a year in all those years, and each time I saw just how quickly time was slipping away. This time was different. This time I was discovering myself in many different ways through the girl who once lived here. And this time my grandfather is gone. He would be working in his work shop in his back yard making a wooden calendar or a clock or sitting in a lawn chair in his driveway which connected to my father's driveway making two half circles meeting at the property line; if he were here. It had been three years since he passed away. I still expected to see him, and I waited a moment to hear him calling me to come look at his latest project. Dad's overly adored adopted dog, Bernie, was also gone. I realized when I get out of the rental car just how much I missed his lopsided run to greet me as I pulled into the driveway. He'd been gone for a few years. It was all really just hitting me then. Every time I visited there I thought I was still the young woman who left so many years ago. I'd locked up certain pains into little compartments inside my heart and inside my mind, and some of them tended to pop open like a Jack in the Box when I set foot onto my father's property. I forgot just how many years have passed. I forgot how much can change yet still stay the same.

My eyes begin to tear. Home was different. I was different. Everything had changed. Life had moved at such a quick pace, and I was only just then realizing how quickly and how much change had taken place. A town seemingly lost in time, with no stop lights, businesses closed on Sundays, and ladies walking to church every Sunday with baked goods in their arms; seeing the way the area had aged became almost heartbreaking.

"Nikki!" My dad came out with his arms wide open ready for a hug from his baby girl.

"Daddy! You look so good. How are you?" I said while holding him as tight as the little eight year old girl did when he would come home from work. The adult in me looked for signs of change in my father since he began getting older. Each time I came home I tended to look for sure signs of aging or change in his weight. He did look very well and seemed to be handling aging with grace. I had worried about him for years. Since he and my mother divorced, he'd been all alone. It really hit home for my sister and me when we both moved out or got married, and for me, when I moved to Colorado, deciding to live so far away.

"Oh, you know, baby girl, I'm hanging in there. It's humid, and the knees ache a little bit, but life is good. Isn't it, Nik? Life is good. Where are the girls? Chris is here, isn't he?" Dad asked while holding me in his arms. I felt so safe.

"Yes, Daddy, they flew in with me, but they wanted to go see Natalie and the kids. I think they'll be here in about an hour." Natalie was my older sister by four years. She had three kids, all boys and all under the age of six. Their oldest was almost six years old, and the twins were four years old and were the best surprise for our family. I'm not sure my sister and her husband always agreed, but like all children, they were instantly in love once they arrived. They continued to surprise us all each day, and my kids adored them.

Emily was always talking about how much they looked alike but were not the same person at all. It was fun to see the world from the eyes of a three year old; especially since they didn't look much alike at all. One was very blonde; the other had very dark, almost black hair. It was even more fun to see two little people who looked so different, but were the same size and same age, shock and confuse a little three year old who was trying to learn about the world around her. I knew soon enough she would understand just how different they were and just how much they were alike as well. Natalie was always telling stories of how one would do something crazy like climb on the roof just to pee off of it, and she and her husband didn't bother trying to stop him. They could only focus on getting the other boys to not climb on the roof and pee off it. I couldn't imagine having my own babies climbing a roof at all, but Natalie said they would do anything their big brother could con them into doing. She also said I'd understand it more if I had boys. Natalie once told me boys were different from girls because you could give them the same toy, and a boy would take it apart, put it back together, and maybe even pee on it before he was done playing, but a girl would give it a name, a blanket to keep it warm, and tuck it in at night with butterfly kisses. I guess I still had a lot to learn about parenting altogether. Each year my only hope was that we could continue to come home often, so they would remain in our lives. Anytime I felt overwhelmed with parenting, I called my sister and laughed until I cried. She taught me so much about motherhood; when to take it seriously and when to relax.

Walking inside Dad's house was usually exciting. My eyes first found the picture of my sister and me hugging before school one day when we were very young. Then I noticed change again. A knot formed in my chest. I felt myself start to cry again. The baseboards were almost yellow. There were cobwebs in the corners and on picture frames. The once blue carpet was now a dull gray. The house looked tired, and I was saddened by this. But I knew I was not the little girl who used to live there anymore. Many years had passed, and things had aged. I'd aged, but this would always be my home. It was home. Not my home, but it was a place where my heart still dwelt.

"The phone has been ringing off the hook, Nik. I guess word got around you'd be coming home. You know it's been a year already.

Amy and Eliza have called three times looking for you. They both seemed surprised you are going to Will's wedding," Dad said with a smirk on his face.

I don't think anyone was really surprised I decided to go to Will's wedding, but many, including my father, were not exactly happy about it. He never liked Will. Once Will and I broke up, Dad told me he'd always thought something was off about "that boy." I always figured it was because he was from Richmond and only came to town to visit his grandfather before he moved to Deltaville permanently. I never thought Dad minded the fact I dated a boy from the big city as much as he was bothered by the fact it was a boy from the big city who came to our town to visit. He never much liked the tourists who came to town every summer. But I never really knew why Dad never clicked with Will. Maybe as a strong adult male who had lived through a broken heart and barely survived, deep down he knew Will would just end up breaking my heart. If that was his reason, he sure was right. And he was there for months after Will and I broke up to wipe each and every tear and give me all the fatherly advice he could cram into a heartache session.

The only person who actually had nothing negative to say about me going to the wedding was my own husband, and personally, I found it sort of odd. "I'll call them when we get settled. Will you help me unpack the car, Daddy, before Chris and the kids get here? I'd also like to go see Nana for a bit before they get here. I forgot to send her a card for her birthday, and I could use a big hug." My Nana gave the best hugs. Everyone loved Nana's hugs, but we knew we all hugged her each time we saw her because it was the best way to measure how short she was becoming. It seemed each year she lost at least an inch. When I hit my peak height at a whopping 5'2", I was the same height as Nana. I would have guessed that day she was about 4'10". It was a long running family joke I was not sure she had ever understood. For that and so many other quirks about her, I love her more than the moon. She had been such a rock in our family, yet she had always been the one in the family we laughed at more than anyone else. She was a smart woman and had not forgotten a thing her entire life, except our names, of course. I kept thinking someone needed to sit down with her and get the history of our family because I knew it would die with her one day. She knew everyone in town and who was related to whom and how, and I had confidence her knowledge of the locals went back at least five generations. But the woman couldn't remember a name to save her life. I'd been called Lori almost my entire life. Lori is my dad's sister. Natalie had been called everything from Nikki (how she could be confused with me, I'd never understood) to Danny, who is my dad's younger brother. Yep, Nana wasn't prejudiced to gender. You could be a girl, and she'd still call you by a boy's name.

Caught in my daydream, as I was, Dad had to repeat himself again. "Nikki? I said I don't think we have to go to see Nana; she's on her way over here now."

Sure enough, I could see all 4'10" of her walking across the yard from her house next door. She was the only constant for me at home. I knew she was going to have aged each time I saw her, but she always looked solid, young, and the same as she did years ago. The family rock. Strong and sturdy. Even at four feet tall - maybe.

"Nana!" I called to her as I ran out to greet her in the yard. Wrapping my arms around her, bending down further than ever before, I smiled my little girl smile. I was home! It did feel good. Bitter sweet, but good. Good like Nana's fried chicken and apple pie good.

"Oh my soul," Nana said pinching my stomach. "Where did you go? You lost weight, Lori." Lori, Nana had said, almost never Nikki. "How ya been? Where the girls? They came with ya, didn't they? Dan come too? How was the flight? You know when I used to travel with your Pop, it didn't used to take all day to get somewhere. I don't know how in the world you travel like that today." Dad and I ignored the reference to my husband as Dan. Chris was used to being referred to by another name. It was funny because it didn't start happening until after we were married. I've told him it's a sign he's accepted as family. When we were dating, Nana always called him Chris, but after the wedding, he'd been Dan, Sam, Eric, and Steve, but almost never Chris.

"Nana, the world has changed, security lines are long in airports, more people are flying than did thirty years ago, and it's just something we are used to. Chris travels a lot for work, so it's a way of life for him. It's tough with two little kids, but it's a lot easier than driving thirty hours in a minivan and stopping every hour for snacks and potty time," I told Nana after our embrace. We were standing under the enormous cherry tree that divided the property line between my dad's house and Nana's house. This was the very cherry tree which held three rope swings when I was a kid. I would climb up the tree, jump out while grabbing onto the rope, and swing my short little legs around a small log my dad had tied into the bottom of the rope for a seat. I was always a little shorter than my sister and all my cousins, so when I jumped, I was swinging for about three seconds with just my hands on the rope before I was able to wrap my short legs around the log. I remembered the tree being the biggest thing in the yard growing up, but it never reached the house. I looked up to see a branch overtaking my dad's roof. It was light in color and without the leaves the rest of the branches showed.

"Daddy, have you thought about cutting that cherry tree branch? It just might wrap itself around your whole house soon if you don't cut it. It even looks as if it might be dying. The rest of the tree is okay, right?" In the moment, I noticed how big all the trees were. When my parents built the house, the lot was a soybean field. Now, the holly trees we planted when I was a little girl were taller than the house and wrapped around each corner of the house in giant prickly hugs. The maple tree I ran over with the lawn mower as a young teenager looked to be about thirty feet tall; and to think I was afraid I had killed it summers long ago when it was barely a twig.

"I trimmed it about two years ago, Nikki, but the past two years I've had to get Nana's yard cleaned up from the tornado, so I haven't had time to work much on my yard," Dad said. A devastating tornado had ripped through the little town and dropped the tops of dozens of trees close to homes and cars just after it had torn apart one of the many beautiful local churches. The whole town spent the summer cleaning up after the tornado. Many were still rebuilding more than two years later. From our home in Boulder, I watched the news and saw reports of all the damage in the area. I remember feeling helpless seeing images of people I had once known and buildings where I had once played falling apart. When I came to visit months after clean-up had begun, it still resembled a weather war zone. It always amazed me how such a beautiful place could be so unknown or so forgotten in the big world. It was where real life happened. Those of us who live and work in or near cities have no clue what country life is really like. Those people worked their land, traded for food, and drove fifty miles to fuel their cars and gather a few groceries. Those were the reasons I left, but there was still a beauty to it, to which I find myself attracted. But I was always quickly reminded of what I didn't like about it on my third trip to the grocery store fifty miles away. Life there was not about convenience, it's about living, sailing, fishing, and gossip. I found it fun about one to two weeks a year.

An hour later, we had the car unpacked and had heard all the latest gossip from Nana. I found her gossip was true since she knew everyone and usually got it all firsthand. I could be away from this place for years, spend an hour with Nana, and be caught up on everyone in town over a couple of cups of hot tea. Chris called to let me know he was on his way with our children in tow. Everyone was worn out and hungry, so I started rummaging through Dad's cabinets and fridge for food with an ounce of nutrition. One thing I've noticed is when men are alone for too long, their diets turn to frozen food, chips, and soda. Vegetables and fruit can spoil, so they tend to not bother buying them. I made a note to drive the several miles to the grocery store and stock up for the duration of our visit. My kids would love eating junk food, but I could only handle them on junk food for about one meal. After one meal, they could quickly become grumpy and downright mean. Many three year old kids throw tantrums, but mothers would agree tantrums are so much worse when their little bodies are filled with sugar and junk.

Minutes later Emily and Bella came running up to the house; Bella walking fast, dragging her blanket along the dirt mumbling something that resembled MeMe MaMa. At her age, she was sometimes confusing. She knew to call me Mommy. But sometimes I was also known as MeMe. Her blanket was MeMe, too, and milk was mostly known as MaMa. I was convinced this was a result of nursing her for thirteen months bundled in her same, now very dirty, blanket. Mommy equals milk. Milk equals comfort. Comfort equals blanket. Many times we are all under the same umbrella.

"Hey, hon," Chris said to me as he placed a hand on my shoulder. "Natalie gave me the car. Not enough car seats to get the bugga bears and her kids down here, so you'll have to get the car back to her later tonight. I guess we can blame a long flight with two little monsters on not thinking about you taking the rental with the car seats and all the room." Chris winked at me. Why hadn't I thought of switching cars when I dropped Chris and the girls off at my sister's house? Chris finished, "Also, Liza stopped by while we were there. She must have been watching the road for an unfamiliar rental car in the area, because she showed up almost as soon as you left. It would seem you have some kind of girls' night you need to attend tonight at her new house. Or her grandmother's house? I'm not sure. Welcome home. It's not a vacation unless you have to visit twenty people before you change your underwear, right?" He handed me the keys to my sister's car and walked over to shake my dad's hand. He was a good man. After all our years of marriage, he still showed respect to my father, yet was comfortable enough in my father's home to let me go out with the girls our first night in town.

"The bags are in the house, Chris. I found a frozen pizza and some apples for the girls. I'm sure they will be ready for bed soon after the trip we've all had. Maybe you and Dad should order steamed shrimp from Molly's once the kids are down. I'm gonna grab a quick shower if I am to be presentable and at a girls' night." I knelt down, hugged my girls, and hyped up the exciting meal I had cooking for them inside.

Walking back into my father's house brought back a memory of an argument my parents had when I was about eight years old. My mother had come back from her home in Florida. I never knew why or what she wanted, but she showed up, argued, and left again. I found myself staring at a spot on a door that seemed to have a burn mark on it. I think it was ketchup years ago, a bottle or a dinner thrown out of anger so long ago. It was barely there, but I could see it as clear as it was almost twenty-five years ago. A pillow flying through the room, a TV tray getting tossed aside, doors slamming, and some sit-com on the TV. I didn't know what the argument was about. I didn't care. But I did know I didn't want my kids to be in a house with emotional pain. No one is perfect, but I could try to be perfect around my children. It was them who brought me back to the present. "Mommy, is it pizza night? Pop-Pop always has pizza night on Tuesday. It's pizza night, Bella. It's Tuesday!" Emily said with great excitement. It was actually Friday and just so happened to be pizza night because it was quick, easy, and available. I shook my head thinking I wasn't sure Pop-Pop actually had a designated pizza night, but if Emily thought it was Tuesday, and if she thought her grandfather had a designated pizza night on Tuesdays, then I was sure they would enjoy it all the more.

When I left for Liza's an hour and a half later, they were both on the floor giggling as Dad tickled them with his beard. My grandfather used to tickle my neck with his beard until I laughed so hard I would pee. I smiled as I watched them, wondering if my own mother felt the warmth I was feeling when she would hear me giggle as a child. I knew the girls would be safe and have fun while I was gone though I wasn't so sure how I would fare. I took my sister's car, so Chris had the car seats, just in case there was an emergency or suddenly something fun to do in town. I was sure they would play tickle bug until bedtime.

Chapter Three

"Nikki Jackson Ford in a Mercedes Benz! Get your tight ass in here, and do it quick! Do you want wine, beer, or a hurricane? Howya doin', doll? I knew 'dat dern boy'd get married some day. I just knew he'd breaka your heart. You doin' okay? Lemme make ya a hurricane, I make 'em strong, honey. Strong enough to give any cheatin' heart a makeover." Liza's voice filled the humid air around me, and I instantly felt a headache coming on. Each year since marrying, I got a different car attached to the end of my name, but it was seldom my actual last name, Ford. Liza was very southern and very smart, but with her, for some reason, the smart often got lost in the southern. The southern was a bit much; I could tell she had been drinking for a while now. Without the help of rum, she could lose her drunken southern drawl. With the help of rum, it always seemed to get a little worse. But it did provide some good comic relief.

"Just a beer, thanks, Liza," I said after putting my sister's car keys in my coat pocket and finding a chair to drape the coat over. "Will didn't cheat on me, Liza. We broke up years ago. I am married with two wonderful children now. Will and I have remained good friends, and I'm happy to see him happy." Smiling and saying it out loud, I really did believe it. Or I thought I did, anyway.

I'm not sure what happened to the beer I asked for, but next thing I knew I was drinking a bright red drink resembling what I remembered of hurricanes but with tons of rum and an extra shot of vodka. Within minutes, Liza was explaining her cheatin' heart comment, but instead of a cheatin' heart makeover, she now had mascara smeared across her cheeks. She told me all about the boy who broke her heart after a year of dating and promises of marriage. I could tell all the talk of Will's wedding was upsetting for her. I had no idea she was going through so much pain. I knew they broke up, but I hadn't expected tears and heart wrenching stories of dreams being ripped from her soul.

After dumping the rest of my drink down the sink drain and grabbing a Corona from the fridge, I realized I was in for a night of consoling and listening, and I needed to stay sober to get through it all. This was not a girls' night for us to laugh, have a drink, catch up, and talk of old times. This was a vent about men night. I didn't have anything horrible to say about men. I had a wonderful husband who was sitting in the house where I had grown up, taking care of our children, and listening to my father talk about politics while I sat here listening to broken dreams. All the while my ex-boyfriend from many years ago was down the street getting ready to wed a woman I'd never even met. Not that it really mattered much, but my secrets included wondering who she was, what she looked like, and if she was anything like me.

"Dreams. Shattered dreams, I tell ya. He took my dreams away from me there. In my heart I knew he was gunna break it. I knew it in my dern heart. Knew I shouldn't a loved 'im like I did. Shouldn't a let him think I was ready for a house. Kids. Marriage. Nik, how are the girls? They doin' good? We were gunna have kids a our own. Did I tell ya that? Yep, he was gunna marry me. I should a gotten knocked up. Then where'd he be? Tell me that, Nik...just where would that dern bastard be then, huh, if I were knocked up?" Liza wasn't stopping. I guessed she didn't really want to know about my children, even though she had asked. This was a true bitching session, and my job was to make sure she stayed up right, hold her hair if I needed to, and listen and nod my head at the right moments. I knew not to really answer any of her questions about this heart breaker, and I quickly learned she had been drinking long before I knocked on her door. I wondered if she was this noticeable when she saw Chris and our children earlier and hoped she walked or had ridden her bike at least to Natalie's house when she was looking for me. Natalie lived almost a mile away, but even if Liza had ridden her bike it would have been safer than driving. I didn't have time to mother my oldest friend, though.

"Liza, let's go outside and get some fresh air. Is the pool still down the road? The one where we used to meet Will and Brian?" I started to guide Liza to the back door. The pool, if I remembered correctly, was another five or six houses away. It was a great pool when we were kids. Filled with saltwater to match the bay surrounding us; it was always warm and soothing. We used to sneak in after it had closed for the day. I didn't think I'd even been there during open daytime hours. We'd all walk down the road from Liza's grandmother's house, where Liza lived, climb the fence, take off our clothes, and dive in. At first taking off our clothes was a matter of not getting busted. If we had dry clothes to put on when we were done, we could explain to anyone who might ask that we weren't swimming in the pool, just hanging out around the pool. Years later, it didn't make much sense, but I guess it was a good thing we never got caught naked in the pool. Well, by our parents at least. After a few times skinny dipping, it became a fun event, and as we got older, it added some erotica to our evenings. Especially when Will and his best friend would come out to play with us. I fell in love with him in that pool.

"This way, Liza. Just how much have you had to drink today? Let's get some fresh air. Yeah, this way, babe," I said while guiding her down the steps. My mind wandered to the first night Will and his good friend, Brian, showed up at the pool.

***

It was the start of summer after graduating high school. Liza and I were both eighteen. She and I were already in the pool and already naked, just starting our nightly swim. It was just the two of us. Our dry clothes were waiting on a plastic lawn chair someone had left at the pool. Of course we never thought anyone would ever notice wet hair, because we never did anything to make ourselves actually look like we weren't just swimming. But we also never got caught. At least not by adults. We didn't hear them come up at first. I think we were gossiping about the yacht club boys who visited each summer. Liza swam down to the deep end giggling over some guy who won the regatta earlier in day. Not wanting to talk about boys anymore, I stayed in the shallow end bobbing up and down, my perky little boobs barely moving as I jumped in the water. I heard a squeal and Liza yell something unintelligible before going under water. Then I saw two figures run through the dim light with bundles of clothing in their hands. They had taken off with our clothes, and we didn't know who they were or where they were going. After doing the teenage girl freak out, we realized at least one of us could get back to Liza's grandmother's house without neighbors seeing us, but we had to wait until about midnight, after the nightly news was over, and the neighbors went to bed. Until then we'd just swim. On edge.

We stayed huddled together in the deep end where we felt nearly invisible in the dim light of the moon. It only took about fifteen minutes for the two clothes stealing boys to come back to the pool. Only when they walked through the gate, they were stark naked too. They stood there in the moonlight with their treasures hanging loose. It wasn't a well-lit night. The moon was almost a half moon, but it was quite cloudy. We couldn't really see anything. Neither of us knew what to say to them or to each other. After standing on the edge of the pool for a minute or two, I heard one say, 'Ready?' and then they both cannon balled into the saltwater pool. I wondered if and how much it would hurt a naked boy. Liza and I were back in the shallow end, and when they came up, we both started cussing at them. Being naive teens, we certainly weren't thinking any harm could come of us. We were trying to sound like we were really upset, but really wondering what fairy godmother had come our way and sent the two gorgeous naked guys into our pool.

We spent the rest of the evening in the middle of the pool. Away from the shallow end where shadows hide, and boobs can be seen clearly by the soft light of the moon. They were both from Richmond. Will's grandfather owned a house on the Chesapeake Bay nearby, and he decided to spend the summer at his house to help out with the maintenance. Brian was Will's best friend and was here for the week. After spending the evening naked in the pool with two local girls, he decided to stay the summer with Will. I guess there was too much to do around the house for one cute boy. Watching them do the yard work was a fun and exciting past time for Liza and me all summer. It always meant they would be shirtless and sweaty.

"What do ya'll do here during the winter months? My grandfather lives here all year now, but I've never stayed for more than a weekend. It seems most of these houses here are summer homes. I don't think I've ever seen a local outside of the cashier at the Stop and Shop," Will said, talking of the old lady who usually forgot to put in her teeth before heading to work at the local super market. I was never sure how that place had stayed open this long. No one who lived locally shopped there. There was a Wal-Mart fifty miles away, and locals usually shopped there about twice a month. If you were out of milk and were in desperate need, you'd go to Stop and Shop and pay six dollars for a gallon of milk which was sure to

expire the next day. The locals all knew only the summer vacationers shopped there.

Liza spoke up. She was never very tolerant of the summer folks and the ignorance they brought with them each year. "We may not be a thriving metropolis, but I'll have you know we have a few hundred people who live here year round. We could all live just fine without all you summer folks coming in and filling our streets with big Suburbans, expecting to get your big ass boats down our little country roads. At least us locals don't go around stealing clothes from a lawn chair late at night."

Brian spoke this time, but I could tell Liza was just getting more and more irritated by the minute, "Whoa, he's sorry, girlie. Don't go flying off the handle there. Your clothes are not far away. All you have to do is go get them."

"Girlie! Did he just call me girlie?" Liza climbed out of the pool ready to join a fight. Only then she realized she was naked, and her boobs were exposed. In haste, she found her footing on the concrete and delicately placed an arm in front of her chest, leaving the rest of her totally exposed.

"Yes, he did, Liza, but he also said our clothes are close by, so don't piss him off until we know where they are. And, by the way, covering only your boobs while standing naked outside of the pool defeats the purpose of covering anything at all," I whispered to her. "How about we get off the local talk, and you two tell us what you're doing out here at a private pool at this hour?"

"It may be private, but I know it's open to anyone who lives here in Stingray Bay Hills and their guests," Will said swimming a little closer to me. I felt my hand touch my stomach as he got closer. Not exactly hiding from him, but feeling a little self-conscious, I kept my hand on my belly in an effort to calm the butterflies taking flight.

I don't remember many details of the conversation after he moved closer to me the first night we met Will and his soon to be best man. Once the ice was broken and we were laughing, it wasn't long before Will and I were in the deep end getting to know one another a little better. My memory of it could still generate a nice tingling sensation in my groin, but he was really very respectful and didn't even try for a simple kiss. Instead he flirted a lot, making me think he was as interested in me as I was in him.

***

"Ow!" Liza brought me back to present day as she moaned when she tripped over a tree root. There was another sign the world around me, the world was once so clean and pure from a little girl's eyes, was changing. Tree roots were jumping above the ground, poking through grass and causing grown women to catch themselves before falling flat on their faces. It was then I noticed a new street light near the pool, along with the same old wooden short two-rail fence and a new lock on the gate. I guess over the years there became a need to secure the pool from intruders who would jump the fence and swim late at night. Someone put a lock on a gate only about three feet tall. Anyone could just as easily climb the fence and still get into the pool. The only deterrent today was the mold and moss growing on the wooden fence, making it a bit slippery. I almost fell onto the concrete climbing over the fence.

"There it is, Nikki. There is our pool! Hey, you know it's not salt water anymore, right? Some loony local made it a chlorine pool. Said something about if you want to swim in salt water, the bay is right there. No one argued, so it's chlorine now." Liza walked ahead and sat down on a bench and took her shoes off. She threw her head back and started to breathe in the salty air. Salt from the bay, not from the pool. More change for me to process.

Chlorine. No salt water to taste. No salt to feel on my skin. *If* I were to get in. I hadn't even thought about swimming at all, but when Liza told me it was chlorine, I suddenly felt like I had to get in and swim. Suddenly I really wanted to feel and taste the salt water. And I was upset it wasn't there. I may not have wanted to swim at all until I saw another piece of my past change for the present. Tree roots above ground, mossy fences, and chlorine. What else could be happening to my world there?

Then I saw him. Will. Standing there against the fence, with his curly locks hanging slightly in his eyes, shorts, and a cotton button down shirt, fitting just loose enough to look sexy. Sexy. Holy shit. I could have been looking at the man I loved so many years ago. I think it is marriage and parenthood which ages us so fast. Will hadn't been down the road of marriage yet, of course, so he was still as hot as ever. I thought about telling him before he took the fork in the road. I had paused long enough, letting my mind wander to the last time I saw him here. We had decided to meet up, and we simply sat on the cliff just on the other side of the pool playing guitar and singing songs. It was so fun and so romantic. Several people on kayaks and row boats stopped at the bottom of the cliff, listened, and applauded when we were done. I knew no one was applauding me. I had stopped singing long before the boats showed and became once again mesmerized in his reedy, deep voice. The voice which could melt my heart within the first few words. That was the last time we'd made love. Our evening on the beach was spent discovering each other again, years after our loved ended, with sand fleas jumping on the blanket we tried to stay on while rolling around, exploring our bodies as if we'd never touched before. It was the last time I had sex with someone other than my husband, since we started dating just after I returned back to Colorado. And it was the best sex I'd had in years. He held me like he never had before. Touched me with similar emotion. That was the night I learned love making could be about the other person enjoying you as much as you both enjoy the orgasm. Even earlier in our relationship, we were so young and naïve, the sex was good, but it didn't have the emotion behind what I had experienced with him later. His tongue explored my body, tasting me as I yearned for more. He moaned and looked up at me saying something, making me giggle. I tried to pull him up, but he said he wanted to lick more, taste more, and feel more. Then his fingers alone drove me into an orgasmic frenzy. His tongue and fingers together, the emotion with which he touched me, the way he seemed to want to please me more than have sex for himself; those are the things I remember about our last day together, long ago. Selfless love and amazing sex.

I knew this couldn't be healthy. I was married. I was a happily married woman, and he was about to be married. And there I was not speaking because I was thinking about the great sex I had with him almost ten years earlier just feet from where we stood. I had to say something, and I had to say it quick. And whatever I came up with couldn't reveal my thoughts or my surprise at seeing him here. I felt butterflies releasing and taking flight in my stomach. It was such a familiar feeling around Will. I absently put my hand on my stomach to calm the butterflies and acknowledge the growing familiar knot.

"Will!" I thought I was doing well so far. "How are you?" I walked over for a gentle hug. I reminded myself to hug with the shoulders, not with the waist. And don't linger. I didn't need to feel him against me right then. That would not be good at all. Don't hug with the waist, I kept telling myself. Then I realized, we'd been hugging a few seconds too long. My hips were suddenly aware of his body touching them. I had given him a purely natural whole body hug, and I didn't want to let go. Whole body hugs or simple shoulder hugs are no different if they linger.

"So, how's Rebecca? Is she ready for the wedding?" Rebecca was the fiancé of course, and I was astounded I could remember her name at all in the moment. And to say it without spitting was a bonus for me.

"She's good, Nik, real good. I think she's nervous about the wedding, but only because she has a bunch of family she hasn't seen in years coming in from Maryland. Something her mother insisted on since we went with the small beach ceremony instead of the huge church wedding she'd always planned for her little girl. You know how it is." His voice trailed off like he was leaving something out. I imagined he was feeling his own bachelor days ending, pre-wedding jitters himself.

Yes, I knew how it was. Wait. What? No, I had no idea how it was. Chris and I got married in Las Vegas in a little chapel with a few family members, and everyone was very happy for us. It was like a planned eloping with guests. But I guess pre-wedding jitters are normal, and anything with a large family is nerve wracking anyway, so I guess I could relate a little. I couldn't relate to the nerves she might be feeling about saying "I do" to Will because I never got the opportunity to feel those particular jitters.

"Will, what are you doing here? Shouldn't you be at some bar watching some scantily clad woman perform a last dance with a rose between her teeth and a few drinks in your hands?" I asked Will, wondering how he ended up at the same dark lonely pool I did on the same night two days before his wedding to a woman I didn't know.

"Well, Nikki Jay," Will said, backing away from me on heels teetering close to the pool's edge. Nikki Jay was a nickname he gave me years ago, short for Nikki Jackson. He's the only one who had ever called me Nikki Jay. More butterflies took off in my stomach. "You know I've never been one for roses and scantily clad women. I'm more of a beer in a can by a pool kind of guy. Besides, I figured you'd be hanging out with Liza, and when you two get together, you usually end up naked in this pool. So I thought I'd get lucky and swing by." I could see a smirk crossing his face even in the low light of the pool. Or maybe I just imagined his beautiful grin melting my heart as it crept from one side of his mouth to the other.

"Didn't you just say you're not one for scantily clad women, Will?"

"Naked isn't scant, Nikki Jay. It's naked. Where is your man tonight, Nik?" Will asked me with a curiosity which told me to back away, and go home to my man, and to my children, and stay as far away from getting naked and in the pool as I possibly could.

"Chris and the kids are at my dad's house. And I don't think I'll be getting in any pool tonight, Will. I didn't bring my bathing suit," I said as I took a step back and almost stumbled on a tree root sticking above ground. "Besides, Liza told me it's chlorine water now, not salt water. If I come half way across the country to swim, it will be in salt water. I think it's best I leave soon anyway. I'm feeling a little…uncomfortable." I couldn't believe I had just said it out loud. Uncomfortable? Was that what I felt? Or was a better word vulnerable? Or maybe it was questionable. I was feeling all those things because a part of me was angry at Will for suggesting we get naked and in the pool. And part of me was angry because I really wanted to get naked in the pool with Will. But I also knew what I wanted was to be eighteen again. I didn't want to be a married woman in a pool with an old boyfriend who was about to be married. I didn't want to be there with a new gate and moss all over the fence and chlorinated water with over grown trees and bushes that hadn't seen a set of trimming shears in many years. I didn't want to accept life moving on too. Had moved on rather. I could accept I was older and married with children, but I expected the world around me to stand still and wait for me to be ready for growth and change. It turns out life doesn't wait for us to be ready.

I walked over to Liza about the same time our other oldest and dearest friend walked up to the pool. We grew up with Amy at our side, car dancing with Liza and me. Car dancing was an old favorite when there was nothing else to do. When we weren't sneaking into the pool, we were cruising along the three miles of beaches dancing in the car, on top of the car, and outside of the car. It was a pastime favorite of the Deltaville country folk. The three of us walked down the aisle together to get our diplomas, and then Amy split to Mexico for a few years to study ancient Maya lands and Latin men. I think she studied mixed drinks and bartenders more than anything, though. She came back with four tattoos, several piercings, and a baby. The baby was about ten or twelve years old, and Amy would tell anyone who would listen that men are disposable. She was the best person to be with Liza right then. I think she could probably tell Liza all she wanted to hear about how horrible men were and how she didn't need them. Amy was the person who introduced me to something called The Bullet. I never tried one because she said she couldn't orgasm without one when she was with a man, but she also said because of it, she would never need a man. I wasn't sure if I'd ever be there in my life. I loved being with my husband, and I liked that he could bring me to orgasm without ammunition.

"Nikki Jackson Ford! How the hell are ya, girl?" Amy yelled at the top of her lungs as if we owned all the houses on the street. The mom in me immediately thought of all the sleeping children in those homes who were just woken by the strident sound of Amy's voice. Then I remembered most of the houses were empty much of the year. This time of year there were probably just the retired locals and the vacationing grandparents in town. It would still be a few weeks before summer and before the accompanying summer tenants hit Deltaville. And if my memory served correctly, most of the year round residents on this street wouldn't hear a bomb if it went off in their own backyard. I remember hearing the sounds of TV news coming from all those houses in the summer time growing up. We'd all laugh at how we didn't have to watch the news; all we had to do was walk down the street to hear it. Once the news was over, the street was silent; except for the giggling and splashing down at the pool of course.

"Amy!" I said, walking over to hug her. "How are you? How is Adelaide? What grade is she in now? I haven't seen her in what seems like years, she must be close to middle school by now."

"Addy is in eighth grade. She starts high school next year. I can't believe it myself most days. She's a handful. She's not into boys, thank the Lord, but she does have a girlfriend who hangs around a lot," Amy winked at me. "I wonder sometimes if they aren't, you know, getting to know each other a little better. There's been rumors about this friend being gay, but I just don't know. I want Addy to grow up not depending on men, but I'm not sure if I

38

want her sleeping with women either. Shit, we are more whack than most men are." Amy seemed to almost laugh off this new revelation about her daughter. Knowing Amy has experimented with a few women herself, I knew she'd be open minded about Adelaide dating a girl. I just wondered about the family she had there in the little Southern town.

Instead of saying what I was thinking, I simply stated, "Well, she's too young to date anyone right now, so you can't worry about who she may or may not pick for her future. She'll be fine. Just don't tell her men and women are disposable; she's got to be open to loving someone," I said with a smile. We all need someone to love. Though for some, one person is often too much.

"Nikki. With all the right things to say. She's too young. Don't worry. Do right by her. How'd you get so smart anyway, Nikki?" It was Liza who spoke this time, and she was oozing sarcasm. I felt like I was stepping out of my boundaries with my old friends, and I was about to be called out on it. But Liza continued, "Amy, I know men are not disposable. I think you really want to find someone to love, but you spend so much time jumping away from relationships, you wouldn't know a good guy if he bit you, because you'd be running from him after you put your bullet to work." I could tell Liza was sobering up because her southern slurs were starting to diminish, but I could also see an argument coming on.

"Men are disposable, Liza. When you learn that, I won't have to listen to you cry for months on end over a loser who led you to believe he was your knight in shining armor when all along he was just a silly pirate. And I don't need a man for sex, that's exactly what the bullet is for. Men are no good at it anyway. It really takes a woman to show a woman how to feel good. But women are too emotional for me, so for me, it takes a little steel. I'm not going to argue with you, Liza, you are too emotional for me, and I'm sure you started drinking early this morning, so there's no reasoning with you anyway." Amy walked away.

Will came over at the most inopportune time. "Did I hear someone talking about doing some girl on girl action over here? Now this is the bachelor party of my dreams. Maybe Nikki and I can watch from the pool where we can get reacquainted. Whaddya say, Nik? For old time's sake, the two of us in the pool, and to celebrate all of us moving on, maybe the two lesbos over there can get it on."

"Will, they are not lesbians. One doesn't like men. One hates men. But it doesn't make them lesbians. It makes them angry at men. If you try having a bachelor party with them, it may end in you hanging from your balls on the light pole. And I'm not getting naked in the pool with you. I am married. You are about to be married. I'm going home. Now. Before anything crazier happens here. Maybe you all need to think outside this town, put the bottles down, and look at your lives here. Will, you are to be married. What would Rebecca think if she knew you were out here hitting on your old girlfriend? Don't make me regret coming home. Now, I'm going down to my dad's house. We are taking the girls to Williamsburg tomorrow. I will see you all in two days." I gave Amy and Liza hugs, whispered "I love you" to them both, and glared at Will for a moment, then smiled. I had to smile. At least I hoped it came off as a warning glare and not a look which said, "Never mind, take me here and now, dear old soon to be married boyfriend. Let us pretend we are not who we say we are and lose ourselves in one another for the next few hours before our real lives call us back." My warning glare and my own thoughts were giving me mixed signals. I grabbed Will's hand, in an effort to hold on to something, even insanity, reached up, kissed his cheek, and told him I loved him before walking back to Liza's house for my sister's car.

Stingray Bay Hills Road has a speed bump every few hundred feet. I think the speed bumps were the only hills around. As a kid on a bicycle they were a blast. We'd try to get our speed up and jump them. I still had scars on my knees from falling off my bike onto those speed bumps and the gravel surrounding them. As a driver, the speed bumps were just a huge pain in the ass. You can't go fast enough to actually drive over them without bottoming out because they are so tall and so close together, and when you go slow enough to manage them, they hit so hard your head practically hits the ceiling of the car. It takes about fifteen minutes to drive the mile long bumpy stretch. I could walk it faster. I remember spinning out of Will's driveway a few times, wishing I could speed away in anger, only to have to come to an almost complete stop before each massive bump in the road. I couldn't imagine living in Stingray Bay Hills and ever being late. I was sure I'd lose my transmission trying to get anywhere on time, and then I'd be left stranded without a car anyway.

It took me almost twenty minutes to drive the few miles to my father's house. When I got close, I ended up in the neighbors' driveway because my father's driveway was so overgrown with grass and weeds, I couldn't see it in the dark. It was only when I drove past the fence post on the neighbor's property line, I knew I had passed Dad's driveway. I guess some things change and grow and some things don't change. The chlorine in the salt water pool really bothered me, as did the weed ridden driveway, but when I saw everyone, I really felt blessed to be away most of the year. It was always nice to come home. I wouldn't want to have a reason to not go there and never return, but each time I returned, it was all a little older, and I was further reminded I was better off not living there.

I left Natalie's car on the grass still showing a bit of gravel underneath. I was sure it was where the drive way once was. I yelled a little "Fuck!" when I ran into a spider web walking to the house. As soon as the expletive came out, I saw a little orange glow coming from where I remembered a chair once sitting on Dad's deck.

"Did the spider getcha? She builds 'em big, that spider does," Dad said to me, puffing on his cigarette. I should have known he'd be sitting outside in the dark. It's how he always greeted me when I was growing up. I would only know it was him when I saw the glow from his cigarette.

"I don't know how you still live in the middle of the woods, Dad. This is a little too much nature for me. Don't you have motion lights on the garage? I couldn't see the driveway and... shit, do you think she's in my hair?" I suddenly put my hand on my head, feeling for what I just knew would be a big hairy spider with a million little spider babies on her back. I was not sure if those wolf spiders built such large webs, but out there in the woods, a hairy baby-carrying momma wolf spider was always what I imagined. And now she'd be in my bed. If not in my bed, then in my dreams. And when I was dreaming of a spider, I may as well have been sleeping with her too. There is a little eight year old girl who still lives somewhere inside me, and she hoards this memory of a giant black widow coming to get her while she sleeps. It's a memory I have from childhood. When I was about eight years old, my father caught a massive black widow spider and put her in a jar in the kitchen window. That night I had a dream. I knew it was just a dream, but I thought I was lucky because she was so large she couldn't fit down the hall to get to my room.

Otherwise, the little eight year old girl I used to be may have become spider food instead of the mom and wife she became. Inside me there is a small child who is dwarfed by the red hourglass spot on the spider's belly. Inside me is also a little girl who can't seem to remember she is bigger than the spiders. I fear any and all spiders, especially if I have walked into one's web.

"Look up at those stars, Nikki. You can't get sky views like this in Boulder. Do ya'll even have stars out there?" Dad was laughing at me. He grew up in Colorado and knew just how vast the skies are. Sure, we have city light pollution, but with very few trees, we can see for miles and miles.

"Yes, Daddy, we have stars. And we can see them each night. Emily even has a little telescope of her own. What we don't have are huge spider webs sitting in the middle of a huge pocket of air, seemingly connected to nothing. Is it black widow season? Do I need to worry about those yet?" I was sure Daddy could hear my concern.

"They're out there, honey, but no, you don't have to worry about them. They don't build webs up high. Only Charlotte builds them that high up. Check the girls' hair for ticks each night. You'll be fine. Go to bed. I'm sure Chris is up waiting for you to get home." Dad took one last puff of his cigarette, and I could see the red glow flickering and falling to the deck as he pressed and rolled the remainder between his fingers until it was out.

"'Night, Daddy. I'm going to check on the girls and get some sleep." I walked away, aware of every patch of air around me. I knew Charlotte was waiting, and she was probably pissed because I had ruined her web.

I found Chris on the couch with his laptop in his lap reading some research papers. He told me the girls missed me but were worn out; they were both asleep before he finished reading their second book. Then he tossed me a sheet of smiley face stickers and told me he'd see me in the room in a few minutes. I crept into the room my daughters were sharing; Bella in a crib and Emily lying sideways in a twin bed with her feet hanging off the front side. I took a purple and a pink sticker from the sticker sheet Chris gave me, placed one sticker on each of Emily's hands, and then straightened her out, tucked her in, and kissed her soft cheek. Bella didn't need a sticker to know I checked on her after she was asleep, but I found her blanket in her crib, and I tucked her in the best I could. I still had to brush my teeth and get dressed for bed, so Chris beat me to our room. But when I finally made it, he was eager to hear all about Liza and her love crusade. Well, *eager* is not the really the word. He just wanted to laugh at her and her troubles. I guess he could tell she wasn't quite sober earlier in the evening after all. Being a typical man, he didn't want the details, just the funny highlights.

"Has the prince returned to Love Lorn Liza?" He asked in a fake British voice with a chuckle.

"No, she's smitten with the joker and doesn't seem to get his funny costume gives him not royalty, nor loyalty. She thinks now he wants to be a pirate. And a pirate is not someone who wants to settle down with just one wench. Right, me love?" I crawled into bed next to Chris and noticed he wasn't wearing boxers. Usually the lack of clothing in bed meant he was ready for our own business. And of course asking about my love sick friend was his way of showing he cared about me and could be emotionally attached to me as well as physically in need of me. It's a man's way of foreplay. We were in my childhood bedroom, so odd, but even if quick and quiet, I'd take it when I could get it.

"Well, Nikki, my dear, you can't worry your pretty little head with all of this prince pirate nonsense. What you need to worry about it is that pretty little neck of yours." Chris started to kiss my neck. His touch was so soft and gentle. We have both always loved the energy we get from sex in taboo places; like my childhood bedroom at my father's house or the cab of his truck on the side of a mountain road on the way home from a ski trip where we had a beautiful hotel room with a huge bed and huge bathtub in which to enjoy each other over and over again, but chose the side of the road as well. The naughty sex on the side of the road was so much more pulsating than any sex we had in the hotel. And sex at someone else's house was always exciting. His kisses worked their way down to my breasts. They arose to the occasion rather quickly. He lingered there for a few moments and then moved south. He really had my attention then. For the first time since arriving in Virginia, I felt myself truly relax. I moved my hand out to him and rubbed his back. Then I slowly felt his back turn into the top of his head as his mouth found my stomach. I flinched when he tickled my side with the bit of scruff growing on his face. He was tender and slow, and I felt as if I was sinking into the mattress with each exhale. The tenderness quickly turned to rapid lust when I felt his tongue heating me up, and with a few quick flicks, I gasped so loud I grabbed the pillow from under my head and put it over my face. The taboo of sex at a parent's house had so much to do with noise levels, and there was no room for squeals of pleasure. I knew what was coming next, so I had to prepare my loud mouth with some sound insulation. The rhythm of his tongue grew faster and faster, and I could hear one or two moans coming from below. I felt him throbbing against my leg. He wanted in, and he wanted in badly. With my back arched, pillow over my head and my breath held, he used two fingers and a fantastically talented tongue to bring me to a meadow of flowers in sunshine. A meadow, where behind my closed eyes, I was eighteen with Will's face touching mine. I'm not sure why I had visions in my head during sex, but this time, as the breath was released from my lungs and blood rushed through my body, visons filled my head. As my muscles contracted and released several times rapidly in a matter of about sixty seconds, I could see hills, green grass, white puffy clouds, and flowers behind my eyes. And Will. I sighed, "Oh My God!" into my pillow and felt my wonderful, loving husband suck juices from me once more before he brought his mouth back to mine and slid right into my meadow scene. When I opened my eyes, the flowers were gone. Chris was with me instead of Will, and the orgasm I just had was still vibrating through my body, and the thrust of my husband sent me to an oblivion I have wanted to feel for so long. I was having a connection with my husband in a moment important to no one but us. He moved fast, whispered a few short moans, then said, "Oh, God, Nikki," thrust once more and stopped. There we were hip to hip, him pulsing and shooting stars into the night. We were both still, and for a few seconds our bodies were so in tune, our throbbing became one. Then he collapsed on top of me, whispered something about great into my ear and laughed quietly.

"Laughing after sex is never a great thing, honey," I whispered back.

Kissing my ear he said, "I wasn't laughing at you, I'm sorry. I was thinking about what we were talking about before. Liza's loser becoming a pirate. What the hell does that mean; she thinks he's a pirate?"

"Yeah, it is kind of funny. He does reenactments of pirates, I guess. And the pirate group he's in all hang out in their pirate garb at the bar and pretend to be pirates together. It could be sexy, you never know."

Chris chuckled again. "Sexy, I'm not sure about. Silly ass grown men dressed as pirates hanging out at the bar is not what I would think of as sexy, but I guess if you are Johnny Depp, you can be sexy wearing anything." He had a point.

"I don't think he has to be wearing anything to be sexy. Johnny Depp, I mean, not this loser pirate guy. But I'm sure for me he couldn't do what you just did," I said as I gently massaged his shoulders.

"So what else did you all do tonight besides fantasize about sexy pirates?"

"We went to the old pool I've told you about near her house," I paused. "And Will was there." I told Chris every immature thing Will had said to me and how uncomfortable I was. Chris was so secure in our relationship, he'd always been fine with the friendship Will and I had over the years. But since I lived halfway across the country, I almost never saw Will, even if we did talk on the phone weekly. I'm sure if I saw him more, Chris might not have understood why we remained close friends. I knew I wouldn't want Chris to be close to an ex-girlfriend.

"Nikki, I'm sure he was just playing around and joking with you. Did he even get in the pool?"

"No, he didn't, but men should know not to even joke with another woman if they are in a committed relationship. I mean he's about to get married! It's just not right. I'm sure Rebecca's not out hitting on old boyfriends. I'm not even sure if I should go to this wedding. I don't want to make her uncomfortable at her own wedding. I know Will doesn't love me anymore, and I'm not a threat to their relationship. But I wouldn't have wanted an ex of yours at our wedding." My thoughts drifted to our wedding. Chris drifted to sleep. We got married in Vegas. In a sleepy state I remembered the dress, the minister, and my father walking me down the aisle. There was no rehearsal, so we practically ran down a twenty five foot aisle, and within ten minutes, Chris and I were married. We celebrated our wedding evening with lots of sex, on the couch by the window, on the bed, and in the shower. I guess we made up early for the years of parenting that would come later where sex only happened in taboo places or not at all. We never saw it coming. But it happens to many married couples with kids; or at least it's what we hear. Who knows, really? Maybe all of our friends are getting it every day and laughing at us because we always talk about how we don't have the time or energy. Sleep came easily for me, but I was starting to feel a bit down and yet nostalgic at the same time. I had dreams of rope swings tied to big trees, small twigs sticking up from the ground becoming trees tall enough to overtake an entire house, a hammock tied between two pines, and a little girl watching the birds eating seeds from the pine cones above her. Meadows, blue skies, and flowers turned to salt water pools and naïve girls giggling. My mind was opening and letting in the past.

Chapter Four

The next day was a blur. Chris and I took advantage of the beautiful weather and took the kids to Williamsburg for a history lesson not quite at the level of a three year old and a thirteen month old, but they both enjoyed watching the Clydesdales. Chris even splurged for a carriage ride for us all. If anything, we got some great pictures for the scrapbooks I thought I might actually have time to work on one day.

The wind howled, and in the afternoon, dark clouds covered Williamsburg and turned it into an eerie place full of ghosts and unspoken history. We left after a quick lunch and a trip into the candy store for salt water taffy and headed back to Deltaville. Our life was back to normal; we were on a family vacation. I was feeling a bit more settled. Though with each new look around, I'd see more change. A house a friend from school lived in while growing up was now an insurance office; a tiny grocery store that had been around since the early 1900s had burned to the ground; and there was still a burnt wood pile on the ground. Back at the house, the walls in my father's home hadn't been painted in many years. The carpet needed to be replaced. Nana had a huge pile of ants living in her family room, and no one seemed to notice until I saw them crawling around and followed their trail. Things seem to be aging because time moves on and because people don't have the time they once had to fix things as they break. It was very hard for me to get past. I loved the trees in Daddy's yard. They were beautiful. Back home in Colorado, I took photos all the time of huge hardwood trees that had been standing tall for more than a hundred years. I was always making up stories surrounding the unknown history of an old tree. I usually guessed where property lines were many years ago before Denver took off; back when it was farmland and one family owned and farmed the land for miles, or at least until the next big tree line. Back in Colorado it was fun to imagine the history of old trees, and I had so much fun looking into the life and history of them. But back in Virginia, I knew the history of the trees, and it made me feel incredibly sad for some reason.

Sunday came quickly. We had to be at the beach for the wedding at one o'clock. I decided to take the kids with us to the wedding. It's hard to tell a child they will miss an opportunity to play on a beach on a beautiful Sunday afternoon. Especially if those children are used to flat lands and "play sand" in the middle of the country nowhere near a beach. I figured if they became unruly, Chris could always take them for a walk down the beach, and they could skip rocks into the York River. It took us about forty five minutes to get to the beach, after the two hours at Dad's house getting the girls dressed and ready to leave the house. It took about twenty minutes to locate Emily's favorite stuffed bunny she had named *Goon Goon.* We got the bunny for her when she was four months old at her pediatrician's recommendation. She had not been sleeping through the night. She was awake about six times a night wanting me to nurse her each time she awoke, so we got her something to hug and hold throughout the night. The idea, of course, was she would wake up, find her bunny friend in the crib with her, and the warmth and comfort her bunny friend offered would help her drift back to sleep. What really happened was she would find her bunny friend in her crib, hold it up in the air, and scream until I came into the room to get her. Then I'd have to nurse and rock baby Emily while trying to keep the bunny from falling away from her little body. I learned several tricks to catch the bunny or grab the fallen bunny with my feet and bring it back to where she lay against my breast. For almost two years, we just called the little pink thing Bunny. When Emily was a little over two years old, she started calling him Goon Goon. When Emily turned three; Goon Goon went through the change and became a girl bunny. Chris and I still called it he, every so often, and Emily was always there to correct us. Goon Goon went everywhere with us. And we were lucky she made it everywhere. She was under the bathroom sink lying under a towel. When we finally found her, I was very close to telling Emily Goon Goon would have to stay at Pop-Pop's house while we went to the beach wedding, but Chris lucked out and just happened to look in the cabinet. As soon as he found her, Emily came running out with Goon Goon and said, "She was sleepy, so I tucked her in the towels, so she could get a little rest." She said it like she knew where the bunny was the whole time, and Chris and I were playing a little game of hide and seek with this stuffed bunny. It was those things which made life with a three year old so frustrating and yet so damned cute and sweet at the same time.

Bella managed to get dirt on her pretty dress as we were getting in the car, but she didn't mind. Wiping out on what was once the driveway upset her more than the bit of dirt on the front of her dress. I wondered why I couldn't get my family out of the house in one clean piece without some trauma. The whole forty five minute drive to the wedding, Emily had to watch *Cinderella* on the iPad in the car. I'm not sure what life was like when I was a kid without all these great tech toys to play with. I remember sitting on the floor board of my parents' car, pushing on their seats and talking with them while playing BINGO on the floor. Today, kids are strapped into some kind of car seat until they are almost in junior high it seems, so they have activities they can do sitting still and confined. Mine watch TV if they are in the car for any length of time. And because we were going to a wedding, Emily had to watch 'Cinderelly'. She was so excited to go to the ball after the wedding. Yep, she was three and believed after every wedding there must be lots of people dancing at a ball to welcome the new prince and princess, the wedding couple, to their castle. I wasn't sure if she would be disappointed when she saw two pretty normal people standing on a beach for a few minutes and then a big beach bon fire party afterwards. I did promise she could dance, and hopefully the beach would excite her enough to forget the castle we should be in.

"Daddy, will you be my prince?" Emily asked from the back seat when we were driving over the York River Bridge. "I can see beaches, Mommy! Beaches there and over there and lots of beaches. Bella, that's a beach." Emily, having given up the movie, was excited about the beaches she could see from the top of the bridge.

"Maybe Daddy will let you dance on his feet," I said, looking at my husband, silently saying, you must dance with her, and her standing on your feet would be the best way.

"Yeah, we can dance together, Emily. Will you be my princess?" Chris took my bait and let his little princess know they could dance off into the sunset if it's what would make her happy.

I pointed to the road Chris needed to take to actually get to the beach. We could see the beaches from the bridge, but they all seemed impossible to get to. I noticed new condos near the beach and directed Chris to the one hotel on the beach.

"Will said to park at the hotel, and they will direct us to the area of the beach where the wedding will be. But my guess is it will be right there, under the big tent," I said to Chris as I pointed to the hotel.

People were gathering around the large white and blue tent. "Not exactly what I think of when I think of wedding, but at least it's not green like at funerals," I said quietly.

The service started within minutes of our arrival. We took our seats on the groom's side, we assumed since it wasn't as full as the other side of the aisle. Will looked stunning at the edge of the water in cream colored linen pants, no shoes, and a light cream colored button down shirt. His bride met him wearing a long cream colored linen dress flowing behind her with the help of the light breeze. She, too, was shoeless. And she fit Will perfectly. She was pretty, yet simple, earthy yet pure, and clean. I wanted to watch Will say his vows, to see how he looked at his bride, to see the love in his eyes, but I couldn't keep my eyes off her. Will's bride. The woman Will was marrying and pledging his love to for the rest of his life. There was something so innocent and pure about her. I was creating closure somehow, watching her. She looked like she could be a friend, someone I could talk to, share with. I felt a peace wash over me. I was happy for Will. And I was okay being here. Finally, okay.

It was a beautiful and short beach wedding. I held Chris' hand tight when they said their vows. He was watching Emily and Bella playing in the sand at his feet and didn't notice the tear run down my cheek when I heard Bo, the man standing in front of Will and Rebecca, say the words, 'let no man put asunder.' I'm not sure if I was crying because I cried at my own wedding, I cried at commercials portraying weddings, or because I knew the groom was a man I used to love. I did love. I loved dearly, but in so many different ways than the man whose hand I held while he gently made our children quietly giggle under the chairs.

So many years ago, Yorktown Beach saw a lot of Will and me. We explored the water, the rocks, the sand, and each other many times on this beach. We broke up on this beach, we made up on this beach. He poured his heart out to me, describing the emptiness he felt when he saw a beautiful red hanging moon and the fullness he felt when he thought of me and of our love. I remembered sitting on the beach pushing sand between my toes resting my chin on my knees listening to him, loving him more with each word. In his poetic way, he often tried to tell me he could never be who I needed and wanted him to be. He knew I wanted to be married with children. He knew I wanted a home, security, and stability. He knew he couldn't provide any of those things playing music for a living, and he knew he never wanted to be married. Now there he was marrying a woman who filled the emptiness he must have felt.

My thoughts were interrupted by the cheering. I missed the first kiss gazing into the past, and when the present hit me, it hit me with a pile of sand on my feet. Emily was building a sand castle, and I was in the way. I wiped a tear from my cheek, smiled down at her, and regained my composure. Chris looked at me, and knowing me as well as he did, put his arm around my shoulder, pulling me close to him, and kissed the top of my head. I was sure he did so to offer comfort for me, but also to protect me from my own pain. Maybe it was my husband's way of staking his claim to me. Chris knew I loved him. Will and I had had a strong friendship over the years since breaking up.

It was another thirty minutes before we saw the bride and groom. We spent the time dancing barefoot in the sand with the girls, taking pictures of Emily and her Daddy Prince dancing feet on feet and collecting pebbles and small shells from the beach. Bella was such a little doll walking while holding my hand across the slippery sand, falling down, and trying again. At thirteen months old, she wasn't the best walker, but she had such a great spirit and would try and try again until she was exhausted. Then she would usually wail until we could soothe her with her 'soft blankie,' as Emily calls Bella's fluffy pink baby blanket. By the time Will and Rebecca came around to say hello, we were all ready to get the kids in the car and head back to my dad's house. I hugged Will, mumbled something about being very happy for them, shook Rebecca's hand, forced an obligatory hug, and told her what every bride wants to hear about her beautiful gown and ceremony.

"I love you, smallcakes, my Nikki Jay," Will whispered into my ear. "You deserve the best, and the best wasn't me. But I love you so much, and I will always need you. Please remember that. I will always need you." I managed to wink at him, fighting back a tear or two, and gave our excuse for leaving so early, and then walked away without feeling a thing. Nothing. Numbness was a new emotion for me. Or maybe I was feeling things I didn't want to feel. Sadness is an overwhelming emotion. I've heard people say they see their life flash before their eyes in times of fear like a car accident or a sudden heart attack. I was feeling the loss of my life at a young age. Coming home again to see grass grown too long, moss on the side of houses, paint peeling from years of neglect, old friends getting older but not wiser, and facing the realization I just can't go back. Not back home and not back in time. The realization that I was on a path I loved but was completely different and far from this place I used to feel was home was overwhelming. On top of feeling nothingness surround me, I also felt I couldn't breathe. The world so vast surrounding me, the sky, the birds, the York River within reach was all closing in on me. Luckily, I was able to sink into the car, though I have no idea how I even made the walk from the beach.

Chris navigated away from the hotel parking lot, put his hand on my knee, and squeezed my leg in a protective fashion. "Was it as hard as it looked for you?" Chris asked me with a curiosity I'd never felt when talking about Will.

"Yes, it was hard. But I don't know why, Chris. A combination of being home, Will acting the way he did the other night, and being at a wedding I probably shouldn't have come to. I don't know. I didn't invite him to our wedding. I'm not sure it was the best idea for me to come to his. It just feels weird." I put my hand on his. "Hon, don't get me wrong. I'm not feeling this way because I have feelings for him. It's just odd; that's all. I can't explain it any further than that." I blinked back more tears.

I closed my eyes, and memories rushed in. Suddenly, I was eighteen again. All those times I sat on this beach waiting for the moon to shine over us, wanting to be as close to Will as possible, absorbing every word he said. Going back in time is impossible, yet there I sat with no children, no husband, and naïve to the loss love eventually brings.

***

Will was sitting with me, looking nineteen again, handsome with a face filled with wonder and innocence. This was the time in life when things were simple. Will touched my hand and asked me if I could find pictures in the stars above. I looked up and was surprised to see a dark sky. Looking back at him, I nodded.

"Come on, Nikki. Pictures in the sky. Don't you see them? There's an elephant there, and over there I see a turtle. And can you see the moon? It's reflecting red on the water," Will was sitting closer to me, leaning into my shoulder and pointing up to show me his findings in the night sky. He always had a thing for red colors found in the moon and the sky.

For a brief moment I looked for Chris and Emily and Bella, but then I felt Will touch my cheek, and my heart sank to my stomach. I swallowed hard and turned to him just as his lips touched mine. They were soft and tender. They were young. They were searching my mouth just as I opened to let them in. It had been almost ten years since I had touched these lips, and they hadn't changed one bit. Unlike the rest of us, they still had the warm softness of youth. I reached up and grabbed hold of Will's spiral curls around his face, and pulled him closer to me. After a long lingering kiss, Will jumped up and took off down the beach leaving me yearning for his touch. I had to chase him. It was a game he often played with me, but I was a good player and always caught him. There were even times I made him chase me, but I would never hold out as long. One day I found him in a clearing in the tall grass away from the water. Stubby hard beach grass would poke up out of the sand and surprise the bottom of my feet with sharp pains. Will was lying in a small clearing, one without all those painful blades. He was stark naked and ready for me to just climb aboard and take him. We often made love on the beach. Looking back, I'm sure it was about the only place young adults could be alone. I'd still lived with my Dad, and Will was staying at his grandfather's house. The beaches quickly became one of our favorite places. In the winter months we'd park and stay in the car, but even the really cool nights with salty winds blowing in from the seas were heated up with our lovemaking. Will ended almost every one of those nights with his infamous words to me, "Nikki Jay, I will always love you and no matter where life takes you, I will always need you."

"I miss you," I told him.

***

"I do too!" Then I heard giggles. I opened my eyes to brightness

I hadn't expected and Bella laughing and mimicking her big sister. I was jolted back to reality. I was a thirty two year old married mother of two sitting in a car with my family, not a young woman falling in love all over again. "I need a break," I thought to myself. I had needed some space for a while now, and I thought life was starting to break me.

Chris was pulling into a fast food restaurant, and when I gave him the wondering look, he told me Emily had to go potty. It took me a bit to realize we were far from Dad's house, and on the wrong side of the river to be heading back. I was so tired, I was sure Chris had just driven around to let us all sleep a bit.

Several minutes later, after a quick potty break, we were driving back over the York River Bridge, and from the corner of my eye, I saw two white doves soaring above a small crowd with Hawaiian leis waving in the air. The only thought that came to me was whether or not the bride and groom had worn leis during the reception. I clearly wasn't there, but on the same beach many years earlier instead. Chris grabbed my attention when he asked if I wanted to grab a coffee and drive. I turned to see two quiet little girls with their heads tilted toward one another sound asleep. Goon Goon was resting in Emily's lap, and little Bella had her soft blanket pulled up to her chin. Coffee and a drive would be nice. A drive back home to Colorado would be better, but I didn't think those little girls would stay asleep for thirty hours. I just nodded and put my hand on Chris' leg in a loving, 'no, I'm not pining over my ex-boyfriend from so long ago' attempt.

Businesses along the route home to Dad's had grown over the years as well. In my state of mind, I wasn't sure if I was excited to see a Starbucks in Gloucester next to new commercial growth, but it was a welcome and much needed commodity. Chris and I didn't speak much on the ride. We drove in a peaceful silence. Chris was probably wondering why I was so upset, and I was trying ever so hard not to seem upset while wanting to break down and cry at the same time. The problem with crying around men is they expect women to tell them what the problem is so they can fix it. As women, we don't always know, but we know a good cry will make us feel better, even if the problem isn't solved. Chris is a problem solver, and if he can't solve problems, then they must not exist and therefore don't need attention. It's how he treated a lot of our marriage. So there were times when we just need to ride in silence. When I felt sad or worried, I worried those silent moments would break us. I was certain those moments when I feel so alone, when we were sitting right next to one another would prove to be our downfall. I was sure in those moments Chris couldn't possibly love me, much less even like me. Sitting there in the car I wondered what he was thinking, and if he was wondering what I was thinking, and would we ever be thinking the same thing at the same time? And if we did, would it even matter, or would it cause the tears to flow? I hadn't even noticed, with all the thoughts swimming in my head, Chris had missed the turn back to Deltaville and was heading into Mathews. He and my dad had taken motorcycles down here last summer, so maybe he had a plan and maybe he didn't; but either way I didn't even notice until I could see tall marsh grass passing us as we were riding down an old country road. Chris stopped at a beach, turned to check on the sleeping beauties, and then leaned over and gave me a soft and gentle kiss.

"I know the wedding must have been hard for you, but I don't understand why you are upset. And quiet. You haven't been with him in over fifteen years. If this was going to be so hard…"

"I was with him ten years ago. We met less than fifteen years ago. But we were together for over two, then together once again, just before you and I started dating. About ten years ago. And I know ten years is a long time too," I responded defensively, but quietly. I felt guilty after I spoke. Sure, I was with him ten years ago, but it was a day of fun, laughter, and carefree sex. We were free spirits enjoying our past, letting go, and loving one another again. We had an understanding. I would go back to Colorado, and he would stay in Virginia, unmarried, playing music in bars, and living his life while I continued to search for my dreams of having a family. Chris and I started dating just a few weeks after I returned more confused than I had been when I walked away from Will and my dreams of our future together.

"I thought he was your high school boyfriend," Chris pulled away from me.

"He was after high school. We were together in college and…you know, we've never been apart. We've always been friends, but back then we couldn't find our way back to one another either. So ten years ago we were both single, and we spent a day at a beach playing guitar and singing and then spent the night together. But, Chris, it was so long ago, too. It's not Will I'm upset about."

"No? Just that he married another woman, right?" Chris' voice went up slightly in tone. I could tell my worries and thoughts were more visible than I thought, and he was growing weary of them.

Bella woke up crying and asked if we were home yet. Short car naps are not the best sleep for our little ones. Chris put the car in park, opened the door, waking Emily too, and left for the beach. I watched him walk away from me while both of our children cried to go home. As Emily became more awake, she noticed we were at the beach and wanted to go look for shells. I got out of the car, unbuckled Emily, and told her she could go look for seashells while Daddy and I sat on the beach and talked. Once I got Bella out of the car and set her up with Emily on the beach, I found Chris sitting on an old log nearby.

The beach was public but no one was around. Chris and I could sit quietly and talk while watching the girls collect oyster shells, which they seemed to think came from the depths of the exotic ocean. "Make sure you stay out of the water, girls, please don't get those dresses wet and dirty!" I yelled down the beach. My two little girls went running, flinging up sand as they went.

I sat down next to Chris just a few yards away and asked him to talk with me.

Silence. Again.

After a minute of turning my head back and forth, fighting the breeze pushing my hair into my face, I finally looked at my husband and said, "I don't think you get it because you never left home. You grew up in Colorado, and you still live there. Your family is there, and you get to see them often enough, you don't notice the change taking place over the years. I know we've seen change and growth there, but it's just not the same as coming back here to see odd growth, yet almost no change. In many ways, the change is good where it's allowed, like Starbucks," I said lifting my cup and handing him the cup he'd left in the car. "But in many ways, the change is depressing. It's a sober reminder for me. I am not a child anymore. I didn't lose a childhood boyfriend, Chris. I feel like I lost my childhood. And it took many years, but this whole trip home, it has hit me like a ton of bricks. Did you see my dad's house? There is mold or mildew, or whatever it is, growing on his siding." My voice raised an octave as I was finally getting excited over something and beginning to feel less numb. "That doesn't just happen one summer. It's taken twenty or so years to build up, and suddenly to me it looks like a worn slipper that needs to be tossed. But he can't toss the slipper because it's his home, and you know, it used to be my home too. But it doesn't feel like home. It just feels like a lost dream, something I forgot coming to the surface just now." I started talking faster and going in circles and coming back to points I had left behind just moments before. I knew I wasn't making any sense to Chris, but I was getting it all out and trying my best to communicate with him. I always seemed to think because he was my husband, he would know to expect me to just spew information that would make no sense to him and would only offer cleansing for me.

"Nik, Nik….Nikki! Stop! What are you talking about, slippers and mold…I'm not following you, Nikki. I just thought you were upset about Will getting married. I know you love him; I know you care for him. Remember I was in my thirties when I married you. I loved before you. But I was never invited to their weddings once we broke up. Not only was I never invited, I wouldn't have gone to any of them even if I were. But that's the difference between you and me. Once I break up with someone, it's over. You, on the other hand have remained friends with everyone you've ever known." Chris took my hand, kissed the tips of my fingers and said, "But that's what I love about you. You have so much love; you love everyone you've ever known. At times, I wonder if there is enough for me."

I turned to watch the girls. I didn't want Chris to see me cry again. Emily was piling shells into a part of her dress she had turned into quite the basket. Bella was sitting on her knees with her dress gathered around her waist digging a hole in the sand. I thought, at least they listen. Those dresses might be dirty, but they didn't get in the water.

"You know I love you, Chris," I said. "Don't you?" Chris put his arms around me in response. "You know what an emotional wreck I am, right? I can't keep things straight. I worry about you. I worry about us. I worry about what the moms I see at the playground each day think of me. I didn't lose Will. I gave Will up years ago. I decided what I wanted. He wanted something else. I have a wonderful life with you; I'm just having a hard time realizing life is cycling so quickly, I guess. Members of my family are dead or dying; my dad's house looks as if it's dying. My sister is divorcing a man I met when I was ten years old. I always thought of him as a brother to me, and now, I don't know if I will see him anymore. I guess I need therapy. Can we go shopping?" I forced a smile as I tried to lighten the mood with a joke.

Chris chuckled, put my face in his hands, and kissed me. "You and your sister go shopping. That's girls' therapy. Me, I like to sit right here in nature and watch the bugs crawl all over your dress. Now, that's therapy."

I jumped up. "What!?" Chris was laughing. Frustrated and pretending to be furious with him, I walked down the beach and told the girls to gather three of their favorite shells and get in the car. Pop-Pop and his aging mother and greening house were waiting for us, after all. So was the silly life Chris and I had together. Chris could almost never have a serious conversation. I'd walked away from tear jerking moments wondering if he heard me at all or if he was trying to think of his way out of the conversation the entire time I was pouring out my heart.

Chris stopped at Natalie's house. Clearly, Natalie was waiting for us to arrive. She had a look on her face that said she was hiding something.

"Nikki! Chris! Emily and Bella! How was it? Was it beautiful?" She asked these questions not really expecting an answer because she kept talking. "Nikki, I've got the girls' things gathered already, you can pick them up tomorrow afternoon when you return."

"When I return? From where?" I asked looking at both my sister and my husband.

Chris is the one who spoke up. "Thanks, Nat, I haven't told her yet. I'll just need the directions, and we'll be on our way."

Chapter Five

It's never easy to leave my children; especially when I'm not aware I am leaving them. But a few bribes to bring them something special, and the promise of a fun living room camping trip with their cousins at Natalie's house made heading to the bed and breakfast much easier for us all.

"When did you plan all of this?" I asked Chris once he put our overnight bag in the car. We were on our way down the dirt road leading away from my sister's house where we left all the kids with Popsicle smiles and faint laughter. I glanced at the road leading to Will's house as we passed it.

"It was actually Natalie's idea. She offered to take the kids, so we could have a night alone. We figured today would be the best day, so I could work on showing you how much I love you and remind you what we have together."

I couldn't help it, but this comment made me mad. "Chris, are you looking for an argument? Are you telling me you planned a night for the two of us on the day Will got married because you thought maybe I'd be so sad and upset and wallowing in my past, you'd need to pull me back into our life?" I could feel my face getting hot. No way was I going to enjoy our evening out if Chris planned it all around the fact an ex-boyfriend got married. I kept thinking how insecure he must be feeling, and for some reason, I was angry and feeling guilty. I just couldn't get the past off my mind, and now I knew it was affecting my family and obviously, my marriage.

Chris pulled into the parking lot at the ABC store just outside of the little Windmill Point town. He parked the car, turned to me, put my face in his hand, lifted my chin, and said, "You worry too much. I don't want to argue. I want you to relax. I want you to recognize no matter how you feel about this man of so long ago, you are with me now. And I feel a need to show you how much I love you. I want to share a bottle or two of wine, lay you down, and make love to you in a little room overlooking the bay. If I could do this every day, I would, but our everyday life doesn't work in such a way. Today is a good day. Just relax." He touched his index finger to the tip of my nose, winked, and got out of the car to buy a bottle or two of wine. As soon as the car door closed, I sank further into my seat. I was embarrassed because I immediately got defensive and on a night when Chris had put forth extra effort to make me feel special. There were so many times I've sabotaged myself focusing on the wrong things. How could I possibly be thinking of a newly married man who touched me long ago when I could not focus and relax like Chris told me to most days? I should have been focusing on Chris and how wonderful he was to me and to our family. I needed to hold him as close as I could and let go of the past. All of the past. I wasn't even sure I was holding on to any past, but I definitely didn't need to be thinking of it at all. Especially on a night when Chris and I could be so close. Without children.

Chris got back into the car with a large brown bag, leaned over, kissed my cheek and said, "It's time to relax, sweetie, just you and me. Oh, and two bottles of Virginia wine. Did you know ABC stores don't really sell wine, and the only wines they sell are made here in Virginia?" I smiled. I had forgotten. Nothing compared to our Colorado drive thru liquor stores.

It took about five minutes to find the hidden drive to the bed and breakfast once we were in the area. There were trees everywhere on the winding road, and we couldn't see more than a few feet in front of the car. Coming from Colorado, we were used to seeing for a hundred miles without trees in our way. I felt claustrophobia sinking in. Chris asked me to stay in the car while he checked us in. I found this odd since it was a bed and breakfast. When he came back with a key, I was surprised again to see him follow the dirt road behind the bed and breakfast house. About a quarter of a mile down the dirt road sat a little summer home located on a sandy beach. Chris parked the car on the dirt road where it ended alongside the house. We got out and saw a quaint little cottage amongst the tall pine trees with a screened in porch overlooking a private beach touching the Chesapeake Bay. Chris moved the eye hook to unlock the screen, opened the door, picked me up in his arms, and carried me up the steps, over the threshold and onto the porch. Before he set me back on my feet, he kissed me hard. I could feel the heat from his chest against my own and his tongue searching my mouth. When my feet touched the floor, I could barely stand. He'd always affected me with his pleasant and sensual surprises. It was nice to be reminded.

Once inside the little cottage, we saw fresh fruit and vegetables on the counters in the little kitchen, a new bag of coffee, and a corkscrew sitting near the two cup coffee maker. "I have a feeling we'll need more than two cups of coffee in the morning," Chris said to me, "But if they got everything I asked them for, there should be two steaks in the fridge and some bath oils near the tub." He grabbed my arm and pulled me to him again, kissing me harder and deeper than before on the porch. I could feel his excitement growing against my body. He whispered in my ear, "I think we may have some time to get reacquainted before we have to do anything else."

Kissing him back, I laughed and whispered back, "We're in the middle of the woods next to a beach with water filled with jellyfish, what else could we possibly have to do?"

"Exactly my thoughts," he said as he unzipped my dress and started kissing my neck, lowering his lips with each kiss until I felt him nibble on my shoulder.

"Relax, Nik, it's me. There are no children here. We have a whole night all to ourselves. You know I won't last long, but hey, maybe you can sleep all night after I'm done with you. How long has it been since you slept all night long?"

Yep, my husband, always letting me know he'd have sex with me, but ultimately it was sleep he yearned for. I tried to relax. Chris was trying, but part of me thought he was trying too hard. It felt a bit too unreal for me. He started kissing my neck again. If anything, when he was assertive, I responded. I needed him to be assertive. We walked slowly to the couch located in the little sitting area where he took off the rest of my clothes before taking off his clothes and silently made love to me. It was gentle, it was loving, and it felt so wonderful to be on this path of continuing to connect with my husband. Despite the world aging, overgrowing, and becoming too much for me to handle, I was starting to feel whole again. I did have a wonderful life, a wonderful husband, and two beautiful and hilarious girls – whom I missed a lot.

After short and simple sex on the couch, Chris checked the refrigerator for the food he'd requested be available when we arrived. There were two steaks, two potatoes, broccoli, eggs, cheese, four apples, and a bottle of wine. Virginia wine! What we were going to do with three bottles of wine in one night was beyond me, but maybe we could take some of it back to Colorado where it would be a rarity.

"They remembered the wine! I wasn't sure if they'd be able to get us anything with alcohol. With so many bottles, we'll have to be sure to put it all to good use. Let's get cookin'!" Chris said, while wrapping his arm around my waist and kissing my forehead. I could be good with this, I thought. He was happy and excited to be there with me.

Chris cooked the steaks while I made our salads. It almost felt like those early dating days. We worked so well together; we laughed; and we went through an entire bottle of wine just while preparing our dinner. Bella had just stopped nursing a month earlier, so the wine hit me pretty fast. But it was so good! We ate dinner and drank another bottle of wine on the porch of the quaint little cottage. Chris must have apologized forty times for not having any steak sauce. He liked his meat rare with a bit of seasoning, and I liked mine almost well done and covered in steak sauce. Still trying to relax more, I kissed the tip of his nose and told him not to worry. Dinner was wonderful, and the company was great. Our conversation turned to his work and our children. When we found alone time and could focus on having adult conversations, we usually talked about what we knew. For me it was our children, and for him it was his work. As mundane as it might feel, it was actually very nice and comfortable. I didn't want to talk about the sadness I felt just being back home and seeing all the change but no growth around the area, so staying within my comfort zone was good. Being in the little cottage on the south shore, a river away from my dad's house, my aging grandmother, my sister, and my children, I felt like I was on the other side of an ocean. I felt at peace. But I missed my children. A lot.

***

Chris brought a blanket out to where I was sitting on a little country porch swing singing a song I remembered my uncle singing to me when I was little. I couldn't seem to get away from nostalgia. Chris wanted to know what I was singing, but I couldn't remember the whole song, just the line about swinging on a front porch swing.

"It was a song about falling in love, young love, on a front porch swing. You don't remember that song? It was country, early '80s maybe, but I don't remember any more of it," I told Chris.

"In the '80s, I was listening to heavy metal, Nikki. Do you really think I knew any folk, country, or porch swinging songs back then?"

"I don't think I knew the song either, but my uncle used to sing it to me all the time. Funny, I don't think I knew what it was about back then, but the one line in the song stuck with me all these years. Now that I think about it, it was about a boy falling in love with a girl on her parents' front porch swing. Life was simple then, wasn't it?"

He wrapped the blanket around me and pulled me into his arms, and there we sat, just swinging. I'm not sure how long it took, but we both fell asleep right there on the swing. Parenting can be harsh. Stress is tiring. Traveling is exhausting. For the first time in a few years, we both found ourselves without responsibility, without children needing a cup of milk, a snack, a bath, a bedtime story, or just a hug.

At some point I woke to the sound of Chris snoring and roused him awake. The two of us crawled into bed. I lay there awake for some time, listening to the sounds of nature, the water's soft waves hitting the beach, the wind blowing through the trees, and the countless bugs singing a nightly tune. I'm not even sure Chris was aware he had moved to another room. His head hit the pillow, and he commenced his snoring sequence. After waking every hour for three years to nurse one baby or another, once I woke in the middle of the night I found it hard to get back to sleep. I couldn't turn my mind off once I was awake. I lay there hoping the girls were sleeping soundly, thinking of my sister and her kids, and of her husband sleeping in a rental house two miles away from the house they'd built together. I knew I didn't want to be there, in a divorce, waiting for my kids to come and visit me or driving them to their dad's house for a sleepover. I had to fix myself, heal my thoughts, stop focusing on the past, the things I didn't have, and start focusing on how wonderful the man lying next to me was. And he was wonderful. He was just not always checked in; into the marriage, into the family. I often felt like he was somewhere else, and I wasn't sure how to handle it. But then I'd also spent a lot of time inside my own past lately.

I watched my husband's chest rise and fall as he slept, then left the room. I walked through the cottage and headed for the beach. Before children, before marriage even, I would have been more assertive. I probably would have climbed on top of him, enticing him in his sleep. I didn't have any assertiveness in me anymore. Instead, I found myself alone in the middle of the night wondering why he got to sleep, why I was awake with my thoughts, and wondering if we were missing the important things in life. Or maybe I was acknowledging the important things in life, like letting my husband sleep when he could because he spent his days working so hard he only slept four or five hours a night.

I sat on the beach, pushing the sand onto my feet, watching the moonlight sparkle on the water. I did love Colorado, but peace could always be found for me on a quiet beach. A real beach with real beach sand, not the crushed rock and hard pebbles Colorado beaches had. I'd been to many Colorado beaches over the years, and I couldn't get used to the ice cold fresh water from snow melt, nor the pebble beaches. Nothing spoke calmness to me quite like a real beach. Chris and I honeymooned in Kauai, Hawaii, and every night I walked down to the beach to sit and stare at the vast nothingness. Chris felt obligated to come with me and keep up with the romance of the standard honeymoon, but after the third night, I told him to stay inside. It was just something my body, mind, and soul were connected to, and he didn't have to come with me each night. For the next five nights, he stayed in the condo we were renting and watched TV while I walked our private beach and put my toes in as many sandy holes as possible. Chris even joked about all the butt prints I'd left in various sections of the beach each morning. I sat there at the beach near our Windmill Point cottage thinking of the many nights Will and I sat on a beach. We sang songs, wrote songs, talked, laughed, played, and fell in love more with each trip to a beach. I remembered a night the first summer we met.

***

Brian was still visiting with Will and his grandfather. Will was trying hard to spend some time alone with me, but Brian always seemed to be near. We were sitting on the beach in front of Will's grandfather's house talking about our interests, favorite bands, favorite books, what we wanted to be when we were truly grown up, where we wanted to live, and all those things we had in common. I was feeling so connected to Will, falling for him more and more with each word coming out of his mouth. By then I had memorized each mannerism, each unique sound, and couldn't wait to explore more. Will started to tell me this story about a young girl whom his grandfather knew who had drowned on that very beach. He was such a fantastic story teller. I was enthralled within moments. Before I knew it, I was sitting on the beach in the 1950s with Will's grandfather, a much younger man than the one I had met, and this beautiful girl thrashing in the shallow waters. I had no idea Will was just tricking me and roping me into falling into the story through his voice until Brian jumped out of the boat sitting on shore next to us. Before I could ever get a scream out, Brian was throwing buckets of water on the two of us. Will jumped up, tackled Brian to the sand, the two of them laughing while I sat still, mesmerized, not even certain of what was going on. Brian yelled something to me about the story not being true. Will was laughing, telling Brian he was just talking to keep me there longer, since we were alone. I could see the bond between the two friends. Neither were angry; they laughed while they wrestled down the beach, and no one seemed to notice I was sitting there soaking wet. So I stood up, peeled off my wet clothes, leaving on my underwear and bra, and started walking into the water. I got Will's attention. Brian even joined us in the water, dunking us both and laughing at Will's attempt to scare me into his arms by telling a ghost story on the beach.

***

I don't know how long I was out there on the beach by the cottage reliving the past, but eventually my body found exhaustion again, and I crawled back into bed with my snoring husband. It was after nine o'clock the next morning when we both woke. It was only just after seven in the morning back home in Colorado, but it was the latest we'd slept in for years. For the first time in a long time, we were able to lie in bed and talk for a while. Once the guilt of responsibility set in, we headed for a couples shower, where we made love for the third time in two days. My heart was filling again. I felt I was needed, wanted, and desired again. I felt a connection with my husband again and recognized this was the break I needed. I realized for the first time, my standards for what I considered a break were too high. What I needed was time with my husband without our children, without our home, and without all the lists of things to get done looking us in the eyes. I needed to live in the moment, without the thoughts of noticing anything around me except for the love my husband had for me and the wonderful life he'd given to us. I felt whole again. We moved the love session back to the bedroom where I became the assertive woman I used to be. And I focused solely on my husband. For the first time in a long time, I didn't think of my children, or how much laundry was piling up, or whether or not I had to take the girls grocery shopping, where I could probably forget at least one key ingredient for each meal. I didn't even think of Will.

***

About three hours later, we were driving across the Rappahannock River Bridge on our way to pick up our girls. I missed them so much but felt rejuvenated and connected with my world, with my husband. Life was good again. My heart was filled with love. I was recognizing struggles within myself, and instead of pushing them away, I was learning to address them, stand up to them, and face them down. I decided I would move forward in a positive way, continue to love my life, what I have, what Chris and I have made, and raise our beautiful family. I felt connected to Chris in ways I hadn't felt in years. I felt connected to Will in ways I hadn't felt in years either, but I realized it wasn't a bad thing. I wasn't losing Will. I had already lost him years ago. We would still be friends moving forward. I would continue to love him as well, and he would still love me, but in the same ways we have loved one another for the past several years, not the ways we were in love so long ago. That was how it was meant to be.

Chapter Six

We arrived at Natalie's house and saw five children playing well together in her backyard, tucked in amongst tall but thin pine trees. They were playing on a play set her husband had built sturdy, but crooked to look as if children built it. It had a fourteen foot long slide standing seven feet off the ground. The kids loved it. In the summer time, Natalie hooked a hose up to the top, and the hose sprayed a mist, wetting the slide just enough to get a good speed going. Once they hit the bottom of the slide, the kids found themselves sliding across the yard on wet tarps sudsy and slippery with dish soap. She had the best back yard for kids. I'd tried it once and learned more body weight sends one quickly down a wet slide, and onto a soapy surface leaving them in the mud beyond the slippery tarps. I never tried again. But it was only early May. Her water slide hadn't been set up yet, so the kids had to settle for sliding down fourteen feet into dirt. They looked like they were having the time of their lives. I hugged Natalie and gave her many thanks for taking our children and helping Chris set up a wonderful night away. Then we sat on her deck and watched our children play. I didn't want to ask about her divorce or husband unless she brought it up first. I had learned many years ago when they were trying to get pregnant not to mention any issues or touchy subjects unless she brought them up first. She eventually got pregnant after all kinds of fertility treatments and, oddly enough, the other pregnancy with the twins followed very quickly, very naturally, and came very much as a surprise.

She started the conversation on her own with, "Can you believe the bastard wants to take the play set to the house he is renting?"

I knew it wasn't going to be a conversation filled with positive energy and moving forward. It was going to be an "I married an asshole" conversation. I knew I'd started a few of those myself with her, so I had to go along, especially since she kept five kids overnight and helped Chris plan such a great evening for me.

"He couldn't possibly move it without causing structural harm, making it unstable, could he?" I asked. "How could he break it down and put it back together with the same integrity it has now? Yep, he's a jerk." I could tell Natalie wanted to vent. Chris got up and walked inside, probably to give us some girl time.

"Oh, you should hear all the stuff he expects now. He says I should pay him alimony and child support. He wants me to keep the house, but he wants everything from outside. He says I'm not using any of the outside stuff. What the hell does that mean? I'm not using any of the outside stuff? He's just an idiot and being spiteful. I told him when we started this whole damned process to take the house, but he wanted to move closer to his Mamma. So he took all the cookware, dishes, anything of value, and moved to be closer to his Mamma. I say let him stay there, and she can buy him all of his outside stuff. He already has all the inside stuff!"

Yep, like most women, Natalie venting was just that. Many men don't understand when a woman wants to vent, she doesn't want anyone to talk unless you plan to verify she is in the right, and if you can't, you just don't say a word. Venting sessions also do not have endings with solutions. Many men don't understand that either. They want to jump into the conversation with a solution. I am a woman, so I understood. I just sat there for the next fifteen minutes, and let her vent. Every now and then I would nod or moan along with her resentment or with compassion, but basically I just let her talk. My heart broke for her. The conversation left me reminded of just how much work my own marriage needed.

She finally ended with, "You hang on to that one, Nikki. I'm telling you. He's a good one. You keep him, and you keep him happy; and you make sure he keeps you happy. You have a good thing going. I'm sure you don't want to be here where I am, fighting over home movies and pictures." Natalie wiped a tear escaping her eye before it started trailing down her cheek.

She was absolutely right. It was another sign I had to get myself straight. I had to fix these problems in my marriage, give it up to my husband more often, find the assertive woman I was before having children, and show him I love him. I was recognizing things in myself I hadn't seen before. Men are all about solutions; I knew. The solution had to be to tell him my issues, and tell him what I need from him. Figuring what my issues were was the problem. Being in my hometown was one thing. Ex-boyfriend's wedding, no salt water pool, crooked play house, trees blocking every corner, all added to my heartache. Being back in Colorado was another matter. Soon enough we were going to have to flip our lives and mindsets back to real life. Chris would be working all the time, children and their needs, not connecting together, no sex and no sleep, not connecting with adults, not connecting with myself or the passions I once held dear to my heart like music and painting. I wasn't sure if I was looking forward to the shot back into reality.

We only had two days left in Virginia with my family, and we had more plans, people to see, and many things still on the to-do list needing to be accomplished. I hated coming home to the depressing sights, the reminders of time marching on. Not only does it leave wrinkles on our faces, but it also wrinkles our childhood memories. But worse than facing the reality that lay at our feet in a beautiful area of the world was only staying for a few days. I hadn't planned on spending a whole night alone with Chris, so we missed a night with my dad, Nana, and other family. Chris came out of the house with the girls' overnight bags and started packing the rental car with their things. He gave Natalie a hug, thanked her, and told me if we wanted to spend some time with my dad, we should be heading back to his house. Natalie said Dad would probably order shrimp from Molly's, and she and the kids would probably join us for dinner. We grabbed our two kids who didn't want to leave the play set, the slide, or their cousins and headed to Dad's house.

I was quiet on the way there, and I'm sure the few miles felt longer for me than it did for Chris. There were times he seemed so oblivious to the things around him, and there were times when he was in tune. My challenge was recognizing he couldn't be in tune all the time. His challenge was knowing when he needed to be and when it didn't matter so much. This was one of those times we weren't connecting. Even after the amazing night we had together the night before reconnecting with one another, I wasn't sure why, but the air just felt uncomfortable. I figured it was simply tension I felt after talking at length with my sister. I knew he didn't hear all the things my sister said about her failing marriage. I knew he wasn't privy to all the information about the children and how difficult it was on them moving from home to home, having their things split up, not having everything they own in one place at a time, nor did he feel the pain I felt for my sister and her children. I couldn't possibly expect him to connect with me at the moment, but I wanted him to just reach out, take my hand, and promise me we wouldn't be there. I needed him to tell me he loved me and assure me we wouldn't fail because our ties were strong. He just drove. I stared out at the empty fields, watching a few tractors here and there plow or till the crop. Part of my healing, moving on, and part of my growth as a wife, a mother, and woman was telling the people in my life what I needed. Chris, for some reason, was the only person with which I couldn't seem to fully accomplish that. His hand was on the gear shift inches from me, and I wanted to reach out and tell him I loved him. I was uncertain as to why I was sad about Will getting married. I wasn't even sure why we came to his wedding, or why I drove through Virginia and thought only of depressing things. I wanted to tell him I was committed to our lives and our marriage, to our family, but I couldn't. I just watched the little town go past, wishing Chris would just reach out for me and provide me with comfort and understanding. I wondered if he knew, even if only a little, we might be in trouble, or if I was over thinking, over analyzing, and worrying for nothing as I often did.

When we got back to Dad's house, I had to put a smile on my face and be the strong wife and mother it seemed everyone expected me to be. I had to believe my life was wonderful because I had this strong and supportive husband who just didn't know when I simply needed a hug. I got out of the car, and before helping the girls with their things, I stood on the uneven driveway, closed my eyes, inhaled, and felt butterflies in my stomach as I remembered Chris pulling me close to his body earlier. Immediately I felt guilt. He was such a wonderful man. He had shown me how much he did in fact love me when we were alone, and he could focus his attention on me. I just needed to figure out how to get him to dish out those hugs when I needed them. One more quick breath, a small glance at our beautiful daughters, and another small memory entered my mind.

**

Chris and I left the shower after steaming up the small bathroom in the cottage. I had a towel around me and dripped water on the cold tile floor. Chris stepped out of the shower after me and walked up behind me, placing his hands on my shoulders. He started to kiss the back of my neck, licking up the water standing on my shoulders. I could feel his body against my lower back. I pressed my backside against him, and he moaned in my ear. Chris was so seldom ready for round two, but the shower episode wasn't exactly completed for either of us. As he continued to press his body against mine and kiss my neck and shoulders, he reached around and pulled at the towel I had tucked in between my breasts. As the towel dropped, I turned around, placed my hands against his face, and accepted his lips against mine. Our mouths opened, and we both moaned as we stumbled onto the bed. Chris leaned his body against mine again, and we fell together onto the unmade bed. Chris placed his hands down on the bed near my sides, lifted his body up and kissed my breasts. Within a moment, he had his hands on my thighs, pulling my body closer to his own. I arched my back and my neck as he kissed my body, his hands moving to cup my bottom, breaking the tension our bodies had created and causing us both to shudder.

***

As I stood in my father's driveway thinking of those moments, I felt myself grow excited, with a warm and pleasing sensation approaching my lower body. I stretched up into the air, inhaled again, and grabbed Bella as she started to jump out of the rental minivan. Again, I was reminded how much I needed to figure out what was important; a hug and some nice words, or a great sex life every few months. Then I wondered why I couldn't have both. At the same time, I realized Chris didn't communicate at all during sex these days, and communication was just one more thing I needed from him. Goodness, I thought it might be a good thing to keep inside. It's almost depressing. Focusing back on my family and getting everyone out of the car, I addressed all the issues at hand, the important issues.

"Bella, where is your soft blankie?" I asked. Emily immediately jumped up and told me she had Goon Goon safe and sound. "Great job, Emily. I'm so glad we didn't accidently leave her at Aunt Natalie's house." I took notice the word Aunt came out as *ant* instead of with the letter *u* pronounced like all the people in the area said. Another reminder I didn't belong there. I had to get back to real life in Colorado.

"Poppy!" My girls yelled for my dad at the same time. "Can we watch Cinderelly on your big TV, Poppy?" Emily was eager for some down time. She wouldn't admit it, but an afternoon movie really meant naptime for both girls. They cuddled in blankets, ate a small snack, and fell asleep before the cat and mouse chase began in the movie.

**

A few hours later Dad, disappeared and returned with steamed shrimp, french fries, two house salads, and a big greasy paper bag filled with hush puppies from Molly's. I only ate about four shrimp but lots of hush puppies and a salad. It felt like we'd eaten nothing but seafood the entire trip, but I knew it wasn't true, since I'd just had steaks with Chris at the cottage. I felt so detached from our time together. My mind had been reeling with thoughts, questions, negativity, and heartache. I knew I was feeling some of Natalie's sorrow, some of my own insecurities, and something or another from watching Will commit his life to a woman I didn't know. Or rather, a woman who wasn't me.

The girls fell asleep on the living room floor cuddled together with their lovies. Chris and I moved them into the room they shared and settled on the couch to watch a movie with Dad after Natalie had taken her kids back home. We talked about our plans for the remaining days in Virginia, and I quickly fell asleep on the couch. I didn't even make it past the first twenty minutes into the movie.

**

The next two days were a whirlwind of temper tantrums, tourist traps, and Chris and I talking around my family like we were one strong married couple. It all left me wondering if there was ever any substance to any of those conversations. I noticed he never once touched me, hugged me, or kissed me any of those days. For Chris, his moments of showing me love and affection went away once we checked out of the Bed and Breakfast. For me, it felt like his obligation to me, his wife, had ended. I started to lose the positive feeling I had gained after our evening together at the cottage, but I kept reeling myself back and telling myself I was seeing or worrying about something that just wasn't there. Our marriage was strong, and people could see it. Even if Chris' hands weren't all over me every second of the day. That would be too awkward around my family anyway.

Our final day we actually spent a few hours with Will and Rebecca. They had decided not to have a honeymoon away, but instead spend some time at Will's Deltaville home, his grandfather's old house in Stingray Bay Hills. Will called my dad's house looking for me and sounded frantic when I got on the phone.

"Nikki Jay! I'm so happy I caught you."

"Hey, Will! How's married life?" My heart sank a bit as I asked the question. "Shouldn't you and your bride be off on some exotic beach somewhere soaking up the sun and getting drunk?" I asked to lighten my mood a bit. I didn't want Will to hear my nervousness over the phone.

"Nah, babe, we decided to stay here in Deltaville, at the Bay house and celebrate the quiet life. You know the quiet life. Don't you? Or do you not have a quiet life in busy Colorado?"

"I live in a fairly small town, Will, and it's transient enough to feel quiet at times. What's up? Are you okay?" Again, my nerves were starting to show. What a stupid question it was. Of course, he was okay. He had just married a beautiful woman, and they'd locked themselves in a beach house to make love twenty hours a day until real life called.

"Yea, Nikki, I'm okay. Becca's okay. Hey, we'd like to see you and Chris and maybe the girls before you leave if you have time to fit us in. Can you fit us in, Nik? Can I see you again before you head back to big, bad, beautiful Colorado?" His tone seemed to change with his last question. He almost seemed too eager, desperate even.

"We leave tomorrow, Will. I guess maybe we can do something tonight if you'd like." I looked at Chris, almost apologetically. Chris nodded his head, started to roll his eyes, but opted for placing his hands on my shoulders and standing behind me in a manly protective way. "How about if Chris and I come over to your place tonight after we get the girls to bed? I'm sure you'd love to see my beautiful babies. But really, they are tired, and an evening with Pop-Pop would be better for them than rushing them around anymore."

"Okay, Nikki Jay, we'll see you tonight. I can't wait to see you again. Buh-bye." And Will hung up the phone.

That evening, or afternoon rather because Nana always serves dinner at 4:00pm, my dad, Chris, the girls, and I ate dinner at Nana's house. It was probably the best evening we'd had since arriving in Virginia. Nana served a spread fit for a king and large enough for a king's court. She had her famous southern fried chicken, hamburger steaks, macaroni and cheese, three different vegetables, causing Emily to ask what okra was and then give her famous "ewww gross" look, dinner rolls and loaf bread with butter and jelly on the side, just the way my grandfather had always expected it, and ice cream with handmade whipped cream. Nana spent most of the dinner addressing us all by the wrong names and telling us what's going on with everyone in church. None of us knew anyone she spoke of, but it didn't stop her from trying to jog our memories with their parents' names or siblings' names or who they had married or where they had lived years ago. We still didn't know who she was talking about, and we were never sure she had the names right anyway, but she sure acted like she was telling of her adventures with the queen, and that's what made it so much fun. Even Chris laughed and didn't once correct her when she called him Dan. When I wasn't laughing and feeling connected and relaxed with my family, I wasted my mind on thoughts of Will.

Nana had always called Will by his name. I was always surprised she never even tried to turn him into a William since he was just Will. Always looking for signs of The Fates working for or against me, I took it as a good sign Nana seemed to know and remember Will's name every time she spoke to him or about him. I thought she might have been about the only one in my family who actually liked him and approved of us being together. I also thought she was certain I had done something horribly wrong to lose him.

After a fun dinner, clean up filled with laughter, and lots of questions from Emily, our little girls were so sleepy they could barely keep their eyes open, but it was only 6 o'clock. Early dinners make for early sleepers. Dad told us to go on over and meet up with Will and Rebecca while he read books to the girls and got them off to bed. With a long travel day in the morning, we weren't worried about keeping them awake.

***

Chris insisted on putting his hands up in the air with every speed bump. "Wheee," he said and then laughed when I mentioned that the girls did that on bumps or hills on the road. Before we were half way down the road and halfway over all the speed bumps in the road, Chris was thinking of ways to avoid them, like driving in circular driveways to avoid one bump, or taking out mail boxes and riding in yards to avoid them. "That yard animal wouldn't give the fight these fucking bumps do!" I laughed the whole way down there and then became quiet as we came up to the pool near Will's house.

Rebecca was standing in the front yard watering some potted flowers when we arrived. She put down her old fashioned metal watering can, and walked over to us. She grabbed my hands in a very loving way and said in a Southern accent, "Nikki! And this here must be Chris. I think I may have said hello the other day, but you looked real busy with those beautiful girls of yours. Come on in, will ya? Will is waiting in the sunroom."

She led us into the house. We walked through the foyer where Will's grandfather had displayed his great boat catches over the years, through the living room with a painted white brick fire place and two white couches I couldn't bear to look at, and into the sunroom built onto the back of the house. Will was standing at a bamboo Tiki bar I had never seen before. But everything else looked about the same in the sunroom too. I felt flushed suddenly. Will walked out from behind the bar with two bottles of beer in his hands. He handed one to Chris and offered his hand for Chris to shake. "Chris, it's so nice to finally meet you. Thank you so much for coming to our wedding. And for allowing my little Princess, well I guess she's your Princess now, here to come see me off to the other side of life." He put his arm around me as he called me a Princess. He didn't even skip a beat before pulling me into a warm whole body hug. "Nikki, I can't tell you how much it means to me that you are here, that you were at beach to see me wed my new bride," he moved over to Rebecca and put his hand on her shoulder. He'd put his whole arm around me but only placed a hand on his wife's shoulder, and it didn't go unnoticed to me. I paused a moment and wondered why I had even noticed such a thing. He'd be making love to her later, so I was sure she wasn't bothered because she just got a hand gesture while I got a hug and an arm wrapped around me. I looked at Rebecca and saw her looking up at Will with a concerned look upon her face. Maybe she did notice the little details I noticed.

Chris broke the icy moment with, "Will, it was a beautiful wedding. Emily and Bella just loved the beach, and I'm honored you would have us, all of us. Thank you."

"Yeah, man, that beach is one of my most favorite places on Earth. This house is probably a close second." Will looked at me and winked. Most of our memories together were in those two places, that particular beach, as well as many other beaches, and this house. I hadn't been in this house for so many years. I looked around and noticed the one thing I had wanted to see: little to no change. The Tiki bar was new, but everything else still looked the way it had so many years ago when Will's grandfather lived in this house. There were no cobwebs, no dust even, nothing looked old, worn or broken. Time had seemingly stopped in this house. A sense of peace came over me. I sat on a flower covered wicker couch. After all the years, I'd almost expected the wicker to fall apart under my weight, but it looked the same as it did so long ago and was just as strong. In that area, humidity and salty air were brutal, rusting metals and breaking down fabrics in no time. I wasn't sure how this place had survived so many years, but Will had done a fantastic job caring for the house and for his grandfather's belongings.

Will took his bride's hand and sat on a bar stool. Chris joined me on the wicker sofa. None of us appeared very comfortable, but Will broke the ice.

"So, Chris, has Nikki Jay shown you all the fun things to do in this town over the years?" He looked as if he were stifling a giggle.

"I guess some of the fun. I've seen all the beaches, we've ridden around town, and I've eaten at Molly's. She is the reason I've eaten a…what's it called, hon, the little fried balls of dough?" He looked at me for support and to answer to the same question he asked each time we visited.

"Hush Puppies. They are called Hush Puppies. Or little fried balls of dough works too." I laughed. I hated taking punches at my own husband, but it was not only a funny story, but also a great ice breaker to get our awkward conversation going. "The first time I brought him out here to meet the family, we went to Molly's, you know to show him the finer side of life." Will and Rebecca laughed. "Dad ordered hush puppies for an appetizer and of course, you know, they come with every meal anyway. About half way through the appetizers, Chris looked up at us and said, 'What are those little fried balls of dough? They are like magic! I've never had anything so tasty!' My dad and I laughed at him. He really had never had hush puppies before."

Everyone laughed, and the air in the room lifted as if any tension we'd been carrying was sent off with the breeze.

Even Chris was good with laughter at his expense. He chuckled and said, "Hush puppies. Yes. Little fried balls of dough. I'm good with either, though I guess balls of fried dough sounds too much like donut holes, which I'm also good with." He took a sip from his beer bottle, nodded to a guitar in the corner of the room and asked Will, "You still playing?" Chris knew Will played guitar. He knew we'd written songs together, and I'd learned to play because of Will.

Will got up and grabbed the old, but familiar, guitar. He winked at me as he wiped it down and ran the tips of his fingers along the bronze strings. I knew that guitar, but if he wasn't going to point it out, I wasn't going to either. I smiled at the beautiful red surface, the white ivory pegs and was about to look at Will when he started singing.

Do you think of me in the morning?
In the morning, think of me.

And do you think of me when you're sleeping?
When you're sleeping, dream of me.

And do you wonder
How I'm doing?

How are you
Just how are you?

And you'll tell me
That you'll call me
But my phone,
It doesn't ring

Now if I told you that I want you
You would run away from here
But if you told me that you want me
I'd be here to let you in

And if I told you that I love you

You would run for a million years
But if you told me that you love me
I would cry one million tears.

Now do you think of me
When you're working?
When you're working,
Think of me

And do you think of me
When you're walking
When you're walking
Walk with me

And do you wonder
Where I'm going?
Where are you?
Just where are you?

And I'll tell you
I won't wait long
So I sit here
And I dream

Now if I told you that I want you
You would run away from here
But if you told me that you want me
I'd be here to let you in

And if I told you that I love you
You would run for a million years
But if you told me that you love me
I would cry one million tears.

Oh I would cry
Oh I would cry
One
Million
Tears.

"Wow." Chris, was the first to speak. I was floored, but I had always been floored when Will turned his voice into something magical.

"It's not a fantastic song, but being here, this time of year maybe, a wedding...my wedding, I don't know, just a few words I put together a few nights ago while sitting on the beach reflecting on life." Will looked at Chris the whole time he spoke, leaving me to wonder if those words and his reflection were about his new bride. Or me. I couldn't even believe I would even think he could write a song just a few nights ago about me. Of course the song was about his new love, his new bride, Rebecca.

Will put his guitar on a stand and flipped on a portable stereo sitting on the Tiki bar. I couldn't get my head out of the clouds. The song Will had just played for us ran through my mind over and over. His voice, those memories, the mention of our beach. A wave of emotion washed over me. If I let them take over, I knew I'd be the one crying one million tears. I took Chris' hand and squeezed it. He needed to be my rock, and I needed him to step up and sweep away the raw emotion filling my mind and heart. But he didn't. He squeezed my hand back, then leaned forward on his elbows and spoke to Will instead of truly knowing my needs for him.

"How long have you been playing, and do you play in a band or out in bars or something?" Chris asked Will.

"Oh, I've been playing since I was about thirteen years old or so. When my Mom died, I was sent to live with my grandparents. My grandmother was sick and my grandfather was caring for her. He played and had lots of guitars lying around. I tried to teach myself, but he stepped in, played old gospel tunes, and taught them to me. When my grandmother died, he moved into this house. It was their summer house. He asked me to move with him, but I stayed with friends and other family in Richmond until I graduated high school. It was real selfish of me. I couldn't see myself in this Podunk town with nothing to do. But now I wish I had come earlier. My senior year in high school I played with a few guys, including my best friend, and got better and better. Then I came here to live with my grandfather and played for him a lot."

"You didn't come here to live with him!" I said it so quickly, I wasn't even sure it was me who had spoken.

"Well, I came to help him over the summer and decided to stay.

It was just so beautiful. The sights, the sounds, everything was so beautiful." He said the last few words slowly, and I picked up on the meaning of all of them. I knew he'd stayed in Deltaville so long ago because the two of us were inseparable. He had found me beautiful.

"Right," Chris said, finally showing me some affection by placing his hand on my knee as he sat back. "Do you play out in bars today? Do you play around here?"

"Not these days. I spent a few years playing. I spent a few years working at the sailing school during the day and the yacht club bar at night, but I don't know. I guess I haven't played there in a few years now." Will looked sad suddenly. I knew how much music meant to him, but I also knew he'd never really tried to make a full career out of it. He loved doing it but never wanted to commit to anything. Until Rebecca anyway. He sure did commit to Rebecca.

"Are you all hungry? We have some cold shrimp, cocktail sauce, and I bet I could round up some other goodies. We tried to stock up here knowing we wouldn't be going anywhere for a while." Rebecca didn't sound at all cheerful about spending her honeymoon in their house. But I guess if they are stocked up on food and the Tiki bar is well stocked, a newlywed couple doesn't need to steer too far from the bedroom anyway.

"We're good, Rebecca. Thank you. I think I'm about done with shrimp and crabs. I've had enough crab cakes and fried shrimp or steamed shrimp on this trip to last me a lifetime." I said, smiling at Rebecca. I was sick of seafood. Living in Colorado all those years had turned my tastes away from seafood. "Chris loves salmon, but I don't even cook seafood these days. I only get it when I'm here in Virginia."

We exchanged a little small talk for another twenty minutes, but I never felt a reason for Will's almost frantic voice on the phone when he called and asked to see us before we left. A quiet lull in a short conversation about fishing gave Chris an opportunity I'd been thinking about myself. Chris spoke so loudly I almost jumped. "We probably should be heading back though, Nikki. We have an early flight tomorrow and I guess a long drive to the airport, huh?" Chris stood up in effort to get me moving.

"Yeah, I guess we should." I yawned. "I'm looking forward to getting home, but not so much to the trip there. I hope the girls make it easy for us."

Will got up quickly and moved toward me. "I'm so happy you all could come out here for the wedding. All of you." He looked at Chris and took both of my hands into his. "Nikki, we go way back, and you being here really means the world to me. I will always need you, Nikki. Always. I will always need you in my life. You are still, after all these years, the best friend I could ever ask for." As he said this, he squeezed my hands tighter into his. Will looked as if he could cry. I didn't know what to say. Part of me wanted to ask why, if he needed me so much, he let me go so long ago. And the other part of me wanted to tell him I needed him too. I wanted to ask Chris if he was okay with our dependence on one another. The friendship we were able to forge after our hearts were broken was worth the broken hearts and the tears. After all the years passed, Will was still in my life, and he was making it clear in front of my husband and in front of his new wife that I mattered to him – still after all the time gone by.

I hugged him. "Will. You mean a lot to me too. We've been through a lot together and we've always been there for each other. I'm so happy for you. You have found something – someone – I wasn't sure you'd ever find." I smiled at Rebecca. I wanted to tell him how much I loved him, still, even if in a different way, after all these years, I still loved him so much. But I just held the hug a bit longer instead.

Rebecca smiled at us both as we embraced. Will found my neck and lightly kissed me. I heard him whisper, "I love you, Nikki. I will always love you. I will always need you." Then he pulled away and kissed me on both cheeks, shook Chris' hand, and backed away from us both. Rebecca took her turn hugging us both and led the way to the front door. I imagined she was eager to be rid of guests, old friends or new, so she could spend time with her new husband.

"I'll call you when we get to Colorado, Will. Take care, my friend." I said as we were getting in the car.

Chris waved and pulled the car door shut. "That was nice," he said. I couldn't read his tone.

"Yeah, I guess it was. It was weird in some ways. You know, he sounded so frantic on the phone. Like he had to see us. Like he'd never see us again or something. It was weird. I was almost expecting news of some sort when we got there, but I guess they just wanted to hang out." I paused thinking to myself. "Or maybe he really wanted me to get to know Rebecca a bit."

"If you ever tell me you want to move to Deltaville, please never try to sell me on this road," Chris said taking the third of many mountain high speed bumps.

I just laughed. I didn't think I'd ever want to live here again. Odd. For years, I saw myself on that very road, in that very house, with that man back there. Things sure did change over the years.

Chapter Seven

Leaving Virginia was hard, as it usually was. It seemed to take hours to get our things together and out the door to head back to the airport. With the rental car to return, car seats and luggage to check, and kids in tow, we tried to give ourselves extra time and left really early. Saying goodbye to Dad and Nana was very difficult and sad. I knew the next time I saw them they would be older, as would I of course, but with children to keep me young, or on my toes at least. But we gave lots of hugs, promises for long talks over the phone and visits to come more than once a year, and drove away with me in tears and the girls wondering why Mommy was crying. Once we got to the airport and managed our way through security without soft blankie and Goon Goon in our daughters' hands, we learned our first flight was delayed. One thing Chris was really good at was fixing problems. He left us at Applebee's while he went to rebook our tickets going through Dulles instead of Chicago. As a mother, I knew my girls would be disappointed to miss all the lights in the tunnels O'Hare had to offer, but I also knew the shorter trip to Dulles might mean a long nap on the plane to Denver. Or four hours of whining, other passengers looking at us like we are either the worst parents in the world because our children spoke, or like we are the purple people eaters just waiting for a moment to devour them and their suits and laptops the second they turn away from us.

"Mommy," started Emily. "Can I make the airpane fly?"

"Airplane, honey, and sure, I'll show you the button to push to make the plane fly and when it's time to push it. No, Bella, no sugar, please. No, Sweetie, please don't open the sugar." I said while taking three sugar packets from Bella's little hands. She made it clear she wasn't happy without them. As her mother, I struggled for a moment with allowing her to have the three things in her life that would bring her joy and giving into her wants simply because we were in public, and she wanted everyone around us to know just how unhappy she was without sugar packets. I went for option number three: to lecture. It's the one thing I knew I shouldn't do, but did anyway. And once I started with my children, I couldn't stop. But as often as it didn't work, it also shut them up, even if only because they couldn't get a word in.

We sat there for about fifteen minutes discussing why Bella couldn't eat straight from the sugar packets, and I learned all sense of logical reasoning was long gone. This was going to be a long travel day for all of us, no matter which airport held our connection. My mind crawled in circles; Will getting married, Nana aging just as much as the area, and Dad's house covered in a thin layer of green moss and years of cigarette smoke on the walls, leaving home again and questioning the strength of Chris and me and how well we fit together those days, I knew I wouldn't be able to enjoy even the most pleasant trip home.

Bella had two sugar packets open and she and Emily were dipping their fingers in the sugar, eating, and then painting it on the table. So much for listening to Mommy. Chris walked up just as I was about to wipe all the sugar from the table and gave me our new flight information.

"The plane leaves in forty minutes, so we'll have time to grab a quick snack, but they'll be boarding in about ten minutes," Chris told me.

"I don't need to eat, but we should skip Applebee's and grab some fruit and plane snacks somewhere for the girls."

We decided I would do a bathroom trip with the girls, change Bella's diaper, and try to get Emily to understand she needed to try to go. We needed to get through those moments when we couldn't get up and rush to the potty on the airplane. Chris grabbed snacks and drinks to get us to Dulles.

We met at the gate just as they were boarding the second zone. Chris took the stroller from me, took Emily's hand, and jumped in front of the bunch of people. I'd always been undecided about the early boarding, which we missed, for parents. If we got on the plane early, the kids had much longer to sit still, which was next to impossible, but if we got on later, we tended to lose space for all the stuff we parents thought we just might need on an airplane, and we also had to walk down the aisle of shame. Everyone watching with looks that say, "Oh, great, kids on the plane, fan-fucking-tastic. This won't be a fun ride, and it's entirely your fault!" I once told a man next to me in First Class when Emily was three months old that it was three hours of his life, and he could suck it up or move to the back of the plane. I was certain he was just angry because he thought my infant didn't deserve to ride in first class. On the flight I learned to keep her close to my breast and each time she cried, I'd nurse her to sleep. I spent those entire three hours with my boob hanging halfway out, but also with my child sleeping. At the end of the flight the man next to me gave my daughter quite the compliment, something about being such a great baby and handling the flight so well. I was sure he enjoyed the view, because he certainly got a glimpse of my boob at one point or another. Now when I was on a plane with my girls, I had to tell myself it was only three hours of my life, and there would be thousands of hours that would be tougher for me as a mother.

Chris dropped off the stroller and grabbed his carryon bag, leaving me with my backpack, the girls' shoulder bags stuffed with their lovies, books, crayons, the iPad, and the girls and found our seats for us. We weren't all together, but we at least had two seats together in the same row, opposite sides of the aisle. This meant two things to me; one adult per child, and one child with the iPad. The good and the bad of travel; there was always give and take with children.

The flight to Dulles was pleasantly uneventful and after barely making our connection, we settled onto the larger plane where all four of us sat together in one row, Chris and I on either side of the girls, with our books, crayons, iPad, Goon-Goon, and soft blankie all in between us. We were ready for the four hours to Denver.

The first thirty minutes of the flight were filled with passing out snacks, picking up dropped crayons from the floor, teaching how to share headphones so they could listen and watch the videos they wanted to see, and keeping them happy and somewhat quiet. There was one child a few rows behind us who kept screaming, and I could tell the mother was at the end of her rope before the plane even left the ground. I was ready to toss her a few books but imagined she was just as prepared as we were but wasn't having the bit of luck we were having with our girls. After about forty five minutes, Emily settled down with her head on the arm rest and Goon-Goon in her hands and fell asleep. Within a few more minutes, Bella followed her sister to dreamland. Chris and I glanced at one another with unspoken accolades as if we had accomplished something Nobel Peace Prize worthy, and I watched Chris tip his head back and close his eyes. He would and could sleep anywhere without worry or the time needed for the sandman to sprinkle magic sleeping dust or sheep to count. I put my head down close to Bella's and snuggled close to my babies. I knew I wouldn't be sleeping on this flight, mainly because the irrational mother inside me wouldn't allow me to drift off with my children left unwatched. I wasn't sure what could happen to them or who could steal them with all of us thirty five thousand feet in the air and with Chris and me on both sides of them, but I was unrelenting when it came to my children. One day I would sleep, but it wouldn't be anytime soon, I was sure.

I did manage to close my eyes and, though I was sure I wasn't sleeping, I found myself in a dreamlike state with visions of Deltaville while growing up. The water, the beaches, and the big rocks I would climb up. From the sandy beach to the dirt surface where The Old Red Barn used to sit. When I opened my eyes and looked at my watch, twenty minutes had passed. Maybe I had been sleeping, but I wouldn't let it happen again. I did close my eyes again and allow myself to think of all those images my subconscious brought up. Growing up in such a small town was tough. As a kid, there wasn't much to do, but we managed to do it all. We'd fish, drop crab pots, climb trees, dance on the beach, build bon fires, and play from sun up to sun down without our parents ever knowing where we were. When the sun went down my dad would whistle, and no matter where we were in town, we'd come running home. I felt my eyes well up with tears. Not only could I not go back to being a child, but the day was coming when I wouldn't even be able to hear my dad's whistle, and my own children wouldn't know the freedom of growing up in a small town. We have a great life in Boulder, but in such a large city, even with its beautiful neighborhoods, great family life, and endless things to do, I felt so vulnerable when it came to my children. They wouldn't grow up playing around town all day by themselves. They would grow up doing family things with Chris and me. As I sat there, I realized it was not the life my children would have that made me sad, it was the life I no longer had. I'd moved a lot, started over a lot, but would never actually go back "home" to stay, and that was proving difficult to face. I knew when I was just over twenty years old and left an area where I would never return to live, to love, and to raise a family, but I was a mother, approaching my mid-thirties, and I was starting to realize what my decision truly meant so long ago. Each time I went back, it was only going to age more, just as I would age. With time passing, I would go back to my Nana gone, another family living in her home, my sister divorced from a man I knew as my brother, and, one day, even my own father and our childhood home would be gone and not accessible in my life. Once my father was gone, and my sister had her new life, with a man I wouldn't know, or once her children were grown and living their lives, my connection to my hometown would be gone. A tear left my eye and fell on Bella's head. My whole life I had put various pains and heartbreaks, heartaches, questions, and problems in neat little boxes and stored them away like old China you know you'll never need again. I felt my attic getting full. I had to learn to process some of this clutter in my head. I had to wish Will and his new bride a happy life filled with love, joy, and laughter. I had to enjoy my family while I still had them in my life. I had to figure out what wasn't right with Chris and fix it. Right then.

The flight attendant interrupted my thoughts when she offered snacks and beverages. I declined for all of us. My hope was everyone would stay asleep, and I could just stay there with my thoughts for the rest of the flight. Maybe I could start opening some of those boxes I'd stored in my mind's attic and start tossing the old crap to make room for new hope.

The night Will and I broke up the first time, we were sitting in his old Camaro on the same beach where he just recently vowed to live the rest of his life with, well, with someone else. His father had just passed away and he was feeling numb. Numb because he never really knew his father, but he'd always had a picture of him around the age of two and his dad sitting under an old oak tree framed in his bedroom. He never talked about his father much, but that night, he told me everything he knew. The man was an alcoholic, verbally abusive, and never wanted children, but he fell in lust with Will's mother. She got pregnant, and he tried to do the right thing. Whatever it was for them, it only lasted about two years, and he left Will and his mother, saying goodbye just before heading to work one morning. He never came home that evening and, after five days, he called Will's mother to let her know he was alive but not coming back. Will always said she never healed. He didn't remember his father, and he never remembered his mother when his father was around, but he knew she never got over him or the way he left. She would often talk to herself as if he was still there. Will recalled a time, while we talked on the beach, when he was about ten years old when his mother was in the kitchen screaming when he got home from school. He thought someone was there with her, but he walked in for his usual after school oatmeal cookie, and she was screaming and throwing dishes. He silently walked out of the house and went to a neighbor's house. After about an hour, he called her to tell her he had just gone to a friend's house after school. She yelled at him for not coming home and told him to get home right away. As he walked down Sleepy Hallow Lane, he could see her walking to her car. When she saw him, she told him to get in the car. That night they ate at McDonald's, words left unspoken, and bought new dishes at Montgomery Wards. When they got home, she told him to do his homework and get to bed. They never spoke of that day, and he assumed she never knew he saw her breaking every dish in the house that afternoon.

***

"My dad never wanted children. And my mother knew it. Dad had this..." He sat for what seemed like hours in silence.

"He had this what, Will?" I asked.

"Nothing, never mind."

I put my hand on his shoulder, ever the caregiver, assuming he needed and wanted to be touched. He pulled himself away and hugged his car door.

"I wrote a poem that day after Mom broke all the dishes. It was called Dying Red Moon. 'In the light of day, I saw her red, I saw her sway, the strength you took away left her dead, left her, a dying red moon. In the dark of night, I heard her cry, misty sobs and sighs from her bed, you left her, a dying red moon.'"

I was silent. It was breathtaking, but to think a ten year old boy wrote that, left me silent, with tears welling in my eyes. "Why dying red moon?" I asked.

Will, cranked his window down, looked out at the water, and said, "She wasn't a whole beautiful moon anymore. It was like looking at something once strong, but only a piece of its former self. And she was angry. To me, she looked like a waning moon, but red, angry; Dying Red Moon."

I didn't know what to say. In the past hour I had learned so much about his family, secrets about his mother she didn't even know, and I couldn't stop thinking about how he'd pulled away from me when I tried to touch him. Quiet settled in. I was tense, but Will seemed comfortable. He was always comfortable in tense situations. He was a dark young man, but his sense of humor showered everyone within twenty feet of him with such sunshine, he became almost blinding. I had learned in our relationship that it was his way of dealing with hardship. It was a big part of who he was, who he'd become, and evidently who was pushing his way out. The lost boy, forgotten and unloved by his father, blamed for love lost by his mother, was beginning to realize who he needed to be. Again, after a long period of silence, he turned to me. My heart sank. My heart either sank or jumped any time he looked at me. I was yearning for acceptance from him, and I needed to be reminded all the time of his deep love for me. He was always amazing at showing it to me, but I was still a needy nineteen year old girl. My heart jumped because he was so incredibly beautiful. Inside he was pure and gentle; outside, he had spiral curls down to his chin and a smile that never ended. When he spoke I was lifted simply by the sound of his voice. He could be tender or gruff. When he sang, his voice sounded deeper with an edge his talking voice didn't possess, and I melted. My heart ached for him. He was reliving parts of his childhood he didn't even remember. He was hurting and I couldn't reach out and hold him, protect him and assure him that he was so amazingly wonderful; I couldn't imagine simply breathing without him. When he spoke, I wasn't sure I'd heard him correctly.

"I am just like him." He paused for a minute. "I don't want children. I can't do to anyone what he did to me. I can't do to you what he did to her."

I was dumbstruck. What was he saying, what did he mean? He wasn't like the man who left him so many years ago. He didn't even know that man; didn't know who he was, why he left, what made him tick. And why would he even say he didn't want children? I felt confused. The car got hot; I didn't even notice the tears running down my face until I felt chills running up my spine when he wiped them away.

"It's only fair, Nikki. I can't be with you. You've said over and over how much you love kids, and you want to be a mom. I can't be a dad. I don't want to be a dad. I'd be a horrible dad."

I couldn't breathe. I opened the car door and walked slowly, almost in a trance, to the shoreline and sat in the sand. The tide was rising, and I could feel the cool water hitting the backs of my legs. Will stayed in the car. I wasn't sure how the night got so turned around. How did I fail? Where did I go wrong? He'd shared so much of his personal life with me. He'd shared things I never expected him to ever share with anyone – with me. How could he sit there and tell me he couldn't be with me? What did he mean? My mind was going around and around in circles, my heart felt like it had stopped, and I didn't think I could ever feel such and live through it again. I felt Will's arms wrap around my shaking body. He was comforting me. We went there, to the beach, to talk about his dad. It was my place to comfort him in his hour of need, and there he was holding me while I cried and shook uncontrollably. Such care and comfort surely wouldn't be offered if he were in fact leaving me. With his arms around my shoulders, I laid my head in the crook of his arm and let the heated tears fall. I couldn't stop them, and I couldn't find words to speak. More silence overtook us, and my sobbing began to subside. Will was running his fingers through my hair and whispering something about sorry and okay. I couldn't hear his words. I lifted my head and looked up.

"WILL!" I exclaimed as I jumped up and out of his arms.

"Nikki, I'm sorry. I don't know wha..." Will started.

I grabbed his hand and pulled it closer while using my other hand to point to the night sky. We could see the faint glow of the flame at the Seaford power plant, but above the flame, I saw a perfect half-moon. A red half-moon.

"Dying Red Moon." Will simply said.

"It's a sign, Will. It's for you. For us. It's your dad telling you he's here now. Or it's a sign letting us know we are meant..." I couldn't finish. I didn't want to be selfish and finish my thought, my desire to let him know we were meant to be together.

Will let go of my hand and walked a few steps down the beach and sat down. He'd pulled himself away from me again. I hugged myself; losing his body heat was taking its toll on my body. Suddenly

I was shivering and cold and alone with a red half-moon hanging over me. I walked over to Will, instinctively, and put my arms around him kissing his back, then placing my cheek on his back as if to seal the kiss. I could feel his heart beating. A rhythm seemed to connect us. I couldn't love this man any more than I did at that moment, the moment I first lost him.

***

Sitting on the plane, flying above clouds hovering above circles of grain drawn on the ground below, thinking of that night, I realized it was truly the night I had really lost Will. We got back together after, of course, but it was never the same. Both reconnections were short lived before I was reminded again and again that Will was certain he wasn't the man I needed him to be. I resented the fact he'd made a choice for me.

Emily stirred next to me, Bella was sleeping with her head in Chris' lap, and Chris was dozing with his head against the headrest. He eventually woke when they announced we were approaching Denver. But the kids still slept until the plane started to descend, and their ears began to pop. I grabbed their sippy cups, asked them to settle down comfortably in their seats and watch the clouds come up to us. The girls were suddenly wide awake and happy to be in an airplane high above the clouds. We were almost home. Part of my journey was complete. Either things would go back to the same, or I begin to grow again and change my life for the better. We just needed to make sure we were focused on our lives, our marriage, and I needed to leave the past in Virginia where it seemed to be happy living life without me.

Chapter Eight

We really had no choice but to dive back into life. Chris went back to work, with long hours and late night work from home. Leaving the weekends to a busy schedule where he would try to cram a week's worth of house projects into two days, spend quality time with our children, and pay attention to me and our marriage. Eventually some of it was bound to slip. Our marriage and personal relationship was always first to go. We'd been in this cycle before. First we'd stop the morning and bedtime kisses. The flirting would gradually go away, and sex would, again, be nonexistent. Our girls were busy with the start of summer, play dates, play grounds, gymnastics, and swimming. The house fell apart every week and had to be put back together one piece at a time daily with a big weekend top to bottom cleaning. So went the weeks of summer. Fun at times, monotonous at others. And so was life. Day in and day out of cuteness from the girls. Bella was talking more. She'd started telling me she wanted to carry me, when she didn't want to walk. One day those words, "I want to carry you," would come out of her mouth as, "Carry me, Momma." I was reminded more and more of just how precious these times were with my babies, and they were changing daily.

Will called every Friday. I found it pleasantly odd he'd get married and then still have a need to call me weekly. We'd always been close, talking weekly for years, but I had imagined our communications would slow down with his new marriage as it did with each new pregnancy I'd had. There had been times our weekly call felt scheduled and processed. I knew on Friday afternoon, my phone would ring and it would be Will with his usual greeting, "Hey, there, Sweet Nikki Jay, how's my princess doing?"

I did force a major change in my life once we returned to Colorado. I decided the one thing I could do for my family was find time to take care of myself and do something I loved doing instead of living only around a revolving schedule of laundry and playdates. I had started painting again. My girls loved it, and I often did it with them because frankly, when else could I get time alone to paint? I'd stocked up on canvas and acrylics from the craft store, and I'd give the girls their own canvas with ideas of things to paint while I was set up on an easel near them doing one thing I used to do that made me feel complete and at peace. I was slowly redecorating our home with my own pieces and smaller canvases from the girls. Emily had outgrown Cinderella and had moved on to Aurora from *Sleeping Beauty*. Her canvases usually consisted of someone resembling a girl in a pink dress in a forest with trees, blobs of flowers, and blobs of gray bunnies surrounding her. I had so many of those pink art pieces, I started numbering them and giving them away since Emily's room was filled with them, and we had two in our living and dining rooms. Bella's canvas usually looked something like a dark gray or brown Van Gogh blob with thick lines of paint, but with so many colors on top of one another they just turn into one large dark color. It was fun though, and I felt more and more like my old self creating something outside of meals and clean diapers.

Will called one random Tuesday morning in early November. The girls and I were outside painting when the phone rang.

"Hang, on, Bell Bell," I said as I ran inside to grab the ringing phone. I was only slightly worried I'd come back to paint on every surface except for her canvas, but she'd been happily painting until she saw me moving toward the house. Then she suddenly needed me.

I knew it was Will after looking at the Caller ID. "Hey, Will, what's up? How ya doing?"

He spoke softly and sounded tired. "Nikki Jay. Hey, babe. I just wanted to say hello to you, hear your voice. Whatcha doin'?"

"Will, are you okay?" I asked. It was Tuesday early afternoon in Virginia, so I didn't think he could be drunk, but he was slurring his words, and his speech was incredibly slow.

"Yea, Princess, I'm A-OK! I've just had a cold or something, and I'm tired. But I was thinking of you today. I was going through some old things lying around the house. You know I have boxes of songs we wrote? Notebooks everywhere! It's crazy. Man, we wrote a lot of music back in the day, girl. I wonder why we stopped." I thought I heard a small chuckle. He knew why we stopped. We broke up. Life moved on without us.

"Will, I didn't write much. I may have written a few lyrics, but you were the song writer, not me." I walked back outside to the patio to see two happy children still painting on their own canvases. I was surprised to see Emily was not painting her usual princess motif. She was painting with green and brown. I smiled at them and sat down on a chair near the table where the girls were painting so I could keep a close eye on them. I wasn't sure what was really going on with Will, but I wasn't going to spend too much time away from my girls. I had grown to love our painting time together, and with winter coming soon, those outdoor painting days would be ending.

"Nikki Jay, do you remember when we drove up to Massachusetts? We were so young, with life ahead of us. We just got in the car and drove away. You stopped at a payphone outside of Washington and called your dad to tell him you'd be back in a few days. He was so mad, remember? But it was the best trip I think I've ever had. We saw things we'd never seen around here. How did that song go? 'Find your road and drive til dawn?'" Will grew quiet, but I could hear guitar strings in the background. He was picking up his guitar.

"Neila Lees. Yes, I remember her. Didn't we hear her in a bar up there or something?" I asked. I wasn't sure if I wanted to take this walk down memory lane with Will, but I was sure my creativity for my canvas had vanished. I felt sad suddenly.

"Yep. The North Pole -or something like that- I think it was called," Will said. He was tuning a guitar in the background. I wasn't in the mood for a concert or a walk down some lane I hadn't traveled in years.

"Will, what's going on? What are you doing? I don't remember the name of the bar. I remember Neila. I've listened to her a lot over the years. But why are you talking about all of this?" I watched Emily. She was painting a tree. I really wanted to sit with her and watch her paint, teach her technique, congratulate her for moving outside her normal theme.

"Oh, Nikki, I'm sorry. I guess I was just having a nostalgic moment and wanted to share it with you." Will voiced seemed melancholy. "What are you doing right now, Nikki Jay?"

"Well, when the phone rang, I was outside painting with my girls. Bella is getting really good at mixing colors to make a sloppy gray, but Emily has really moved me this morning. She usually draws with her paintbrush a pink girl, a princess, and green stuff all around, grass, a forest, I guess. But today I see a tree. I think it's a tree. And no pink at all. No princess. At all. Anyway, we were painting. Now I'm talking to you and watching them paint."

"Go paint, Princess. I'm so glad to see you getting back into something that almost defined you for so long. I remember summers when you'd get up and paint by the water first thing in the morning before you even had breakfast. Please don't stop. Go do it. And this time with your girls is so precious. I'm sorry, Nikki Jay, I'm sorry. I just got a little, I don't know, excited to find some of these things here in these boxes. It's been years since I've seen some of this stuff. But maybe one day we can take a walk down this lane again. Not today. I think I'm going to go take a nap. This is kicking my ass, Princess. This...cold." Will hung up without even saying goodbye. I'd heard a few cracks in his voice as he was talking and wondered if he'd been crying. Looking at old memories staring him in the face could be tough, but he's still a newlywed. I couldn't imagine going through old things from that time in our lives and feeling such sadness.

I almost called Will back, but I was on track with moving forward in my life, not backward. I missed those days. I missed Will. But with six months having passed since his wedding, I was able to almost laugh at myself when I thought of how jealous I was during those days in Virginia. I never would have admitted it then, but I was certain jealousy was what I felt and why I focused so much on Will and Rebecca and their relationship. I was completely jealous someone else had won Will over, and he wanted to give her something he never gave me. And I was even able to tell myself those feelings were absolutely crazy. I had talked to Chris about it a bit but never admitted I was envious of Rebecca and her relationship with Will. I tried to focus my conversations with Chris on how hard it was going back home to aging family and friends. When I was away for so long, I noticed it so much more, and it was harder and harder to go back. Chris recommended we fly my sister, her kids, and my dad out for a visit the following spring, so I didn't have to go back. I laughed. I could see the stress of adding five more people to our house, but then it couldn't be much different than the four of us encroaching on Dad's space. I told Chris I'd think about it. It would be a good way to share our lives with my family without the depressing views of an area I'd like to keep inside a little box in my head, unchanged.

Without a clear head, I couldn't continue my artwork, but I couldn't wait to sit with my girls and work with them.

"Emily! Show me what you are doing. I don't see a princess. Are you not doing a princess today?"

Emily smiled at me. For the first time since the abrupt end to my phone call with Will, I noticed Emily was covered in green paint. Her canvas was covered as well, but she had more on her body, face, and clothes than I could find on her canvas.

"Emily, I want to talk about your painting, what you've been able to do, all by yourself, and then I think it'll be time to clean up and take a bath." I sat down next to her on patio chair that appeared to have been spared of green paint.

"Mommy, I'm painting just the forest. Like the one in our backyard. See. Princess Aurora is not there. She's already at the castle with her prince. Mommy, what is her prince's name?"

I could tell we weren't going to talk about technique. I wanted so badly to teach her to paint her background and then the foreground, because it was clear to me she had started with grass, then painting what was behind the grass next, but then I realized I was talking to a four year old, and technique didn't matter as much as her love for doing it.

"Bella, I think it's beautiful. So, are you going to paint the castle next time we paint?"

"Mommy! I'm not Bella! You're a silly swan. The castle is right there," Emily pointed to a gray square in the middle of her painting. "The princess is inside. You can't see her, that's all."

"Is her Prince's name Eric?" I asked.

"No, Mommy!" Emily sounded frustrated.

"Honey, I don't remember his name. How about we go take a bath, and you can watch the movie while I finish cleaning up out here." I started cleaning up Bella's supplies before she decided to paint more dark blobs on her canvas.

"No, Mama. No, I paint," Bella started crying.

"Mommy, I want you to take me a bath. Bella, want Mommy to take you a bath too? And then we can watch Beauty!" Emily was very good at convincing Bella to do things she never wanted to do in the first place. And she was fantastic at being cute when she said she wanted me to take her a bath. She said it a lot when Chris was around. 'Daddy, no. I want Mommy to take me a bath,' was a common thing said in our house in the evening before bedtime.

"Yeah, Emmie take me a baff too!" Bella's mind had been changed. We'd go inside, take baths, get cuddly, watch a late morning movie, and find out which Prince saved Aurora from a life amongst birds and rabbits in a dark dreaded forest.

***

With the exception of Bella peeing in the tub just about as soon as she sat down, bath time was fairly uneventful. I'd learned to only fill the tub a little bit because she peed in every bath she took. It had become a routine with us. I'd fill it slightly, set her in the tub while Emily picked out toys, Bella peed, and I took her out, wiped her and the tub down and started over with fresh water. I could only hope it wasn't a routine I was teaching her for life. I could just see her in high school peeing in the tub before she bathed. I figured they wouldn't remember much of those times, and we had to do what we could to just get through them.

With clean babies watching a movie, I cleaned up the patio, paints, and drying artwork. I knew after a warm fall morning outdoors, the girls would probably fall asleep before the movie ended. I preferred those movie naps to be in the afternoon, but I figured I'd take what I could get. I stood on the patio looking at my canvas. It was all wrong. I'd let it dry and rework it. I could see it was not what I had envisioned when I started. But then the phone rang, and my mood drastically changed. Before I made any decisions about it, I needed to change my mood first. There was always the next day. Standing back a bit, I looked at it again. The mountains were a nice touch, but the lonely guitar standing upright on the beach wasn't right. What was holding it up? I could paint a guitar stand or a person to hold it, but I couldn't create magical non-gravity. What was I thinking? And why did I put a guitar there anyway? It was red and could have been something like a fire hydrant sitting in the middle of nowhere with no reason or purpose. A red guitar on a sandy beach with Colorado Mountains in the background. Where was my mind when I started that thing? I packed it up with the girls' to sit in the garage and dry overnight with a promise I'd get back to painting it. I knew something was lost in Will's phone call. What was he thinking, walking down memory lane so many years after our trip to Northampton, Massachusetts?

***

"Look, baby, there are churches everywhere! Rolling hills, little ones, see how they roll?" Will put his hand on my knee. New England was indeed beautiful. I thought I could see myself living anywhere among those little rolling hills. As we drove, we'd see little valleys, and then our view would be blocked by walls of granite along the interstate, only to open again to a green valley with little rolling hills. Each valley offered views of several chapels, all quaint with a different history we'd probably never know.

"This is going to be so great, babe," Will looked down at me for a brief second, squeezed my knee, and focused on driving again. "I've found this great little seafood place to eat dinner as soon as we get checked in to the hotel, but I think the Tavern at the hotel might be where we eat the rest of our meals. Or room service even. But look at the views here! We are going to want to get out and see this place. This is amazing."

I was looking. The little town of Northampton was beautiful. Character from ages ago oozed from the sidewalk cracks. I saw railroad bridges connecting the world to the little town from what seemed like all directions, waterways with small paddle boats that must have led somewhere but yet appeared to stay in place.

"Wow. This is a small town, but so different. Can we just move here? This is amazing!" I said before I really realized what had slipped out. We had decided to take a long weekend trip to a place we'd never been. I'd always wanted to visit New England, and Will simply said he'd be happy wherever I wanted to go. He actually said he'd be happy wherever I was, but I took it to mean I could decide and not that he'd follow me anywhere.

We'd only been back together for a couple of months and spring was in the air. I was nineteen years old and heading back to college classes for the summer term in a few weeks. Will wanted to get me out of town for a break and to show me I was still everything he wanted, and he was indeed everything I ever wanted. We were still so in love and ready to spend a long weekend together in a quaint little town away from those who didn't agree with our reunion.

Will pulled up to The Hotel Northampton, stopped in front of it and looked around for a moment. "Parking, parking. Where oh where is park-? Oh! Hotel parking," he was clearly talking to himself, but since he was able to resolve it himself as well, I just sat and stared up at the tall building in front of us. Five stories of old, beautifully crafted, brick lay in front of me. The building had two wings on either side of a brightly lit glass atrium.

As soon as Will found a parking spot, he started talking about the hotel. "It's almost 75 years old now, but even cooler than that, the guy who started this place had an uncle or something who started a tavern almost two hundred years ago...or more maybe. I think it was somewhere else, but the guy who built this place moved the Tavern here to this spot and built the hotel. There's a lot of history here, Nikki Jay. Let's get in there and make some of our own history. Why don't we?"

Will got out of the car and opened my door for me, bowing with his arm extended as if pointing the direction I needed to go. Butterflies filled my stomach. Will and I had spent a few nights together, but we'd never gone this far from home, and we'd never spent more than one night at a time together. I was getting nervous. But Will was so good at making me comfortable and taking the edge off for me. I looked like a young tourist walking in, looking up, and to each side, circling in place as I looked at the lattice woodwork details near the tops of the high walls. As I was looking the part of fascinated tourist, Will got us checked in and ready for our mini-vacation. He handed me a key to the room, told me which staircase to take up, and then went back out to the parking lot. I found our room and left the door propped open. Inside sat a queen bed and a private balcony with French doors. I opened them and stood on the balcony I learned sat just above the beautiful atrium below. The balcony was huge, and it took me a few moments to realize it was shared with other rooms. I was underage, so we wouldn't be drinking. There was no way I'd be outside making out with Will right up against the street. We could enjoy our breakfast out there, but that was about all I'd want to share with the people next door.

While I was on the balcony looking over the railing at the old stone church down the street, Will snuck up behind me, causing me to scream. People from the street looked up just as I backed away from the railing. "Will! I could have fallen!" I was livid.

"Nikki Jay," Will said as he pulled me closer to him. "I'm sorry, doll. I'm sorry. I didn't mean to scare you. And you know I would never let you fall. Unless you're falling for me." Will started singing and dancing with me right there on the balcony. "Fall for me, baby, why don't you fall for me? I won't let you fall but only for me. Baby. Fall for me, baby, fall for me," he started laughing then kissed me and whispered, "I'm sorry. Let's get ready for some dinner!"

I let him wrap his arms around me and then kiss me again before walking back into our room. I wanted to shower before we headed out for dinner, but after driving for almost nine hours, stopping for a fast food lunch and convenience store snacks, we were both famished. Will talked me into showering after dinner. His suggestion to shower together made my stomach flip over a few times, reminding me dinner was a necessity and showering with Will after dinner would be well worth the wait. Instead of walking around town just yet, we decided on dinner at the Tavern in the hotel. Will decided if we weren't too tired after dinner we'd explore a bit of town, but after dinner we decided exploring town wasn't as exciting as the prospect of exploring one another.

Our shower started with hot water pouring over us and Will placing bets.

"What'll ya give me if I can make it through this whole shower without kissing you?"

"A kiss!" I said while grabbing his face and pulling him closer to me. He smiled while I planted my lips onto his. Clearly he was serious. He wasn't kissing me back. "Okay, tough guy, I can play too. I'm not kissing you either. Not during the shower, and not after."

"Oh, it's on now, baby. No kisses for you! Nope, not a one." Will grabbed the little bar of soap and lathered his hands while he was talking. Then he turned me so I wasn't facing him, lathered my back and massaged my shoulders. His soapy hands moved from my shoulders and down my arms to my hands. He linked his fingers with mine and pushed his hard body against my back. "No, kisses," he whispered into my ear.

"Nope, not a one," I whispered back, arching my back toward his pressing body.

He continued his tease, letting go of my fingers and wrapping my arms around my stomach so he could explore further up. Within moments my hard nipples were between his fingers. His touch was gentle but firm. My neck relaxed, and I rested my head against his chest and let out a quiet moan. Without touching his lips to my body, he blew little kisses across my shoulders that sent shivers down my body. Holding my arms against my stomach with one arm, he pulled me closer to him, used his feet to spread my weakening legs and tipped my body forward slightly so his free hand could explore the areas of my body that were screaming for him. As soon as his hand and fingers found their place of yearning, I arched back again, with my head resting on his shoulder, this time because he was standing lower with his knees bent. I wanted so badly to feel his lips across my neck, my back, on my mouth. Not kissing Will was going to be the most difficult thing I'd done my entire life!

While I was leaning only slightly into his body, his free hand wrapped around between my thighs and found warmth and wetness not related to the hot shower we were standing under, and within moments my body was shaking uncontrollably from his touch and tears were streaming down my cheeks from the surprise pleasure. Will held me up because the shaking wouldn't stop. My legs were so weak I thought I may fall back into him, knocking us both down. After turning me around to face him, he pulled my face up to his and whispered, "No kisses for you."

"Who needs kisses after that?" I sighed, out of breath.

"You do. It's what you look forward to after I take your breath away. You do, Nikki Jay. You need kisses." Will said all of this while blowing little kisses on my shoulder. Each breath sent a shiver down my spine and gave me goose bumps as the water on my skin chilled me to the bone.

***

I stood outside in the cooler fall air thinking of our trip, and all that happened up there, all the music we made, found, and enjoyed together. All the plans we'd made to be together, to be one another's forever. Chills ran through my body as I looked at the paints I still needed to clean on the patio furniture. Bella wasn't as tidy as I had thought. Rubbing my arms in the chilly air, I remembered a sight from the trip, Will and I on a skinny river beach with his guitar propped up against a rock. Behind us were stone mountains. My painting. Without thinking about it, knowing about or even understanding it, I had begun to recreate a scene Will and I had made so many years ago. And then he called me and mentioned that exact time in our lives. I sat down on the patio, pulled my knees to my chest and cried. What was going on with my life? What was going on with Will? Why would I start such a painting in the first place?

After about ten minutes of crying, I started to sing one of his old songs to myself.

Oh, you gotta wonder
Where it all started
And you gotta wonder
Where it began
Why won't I
Let you in
Why am I building walls

For my sanity
I am
Building walls

Oh and sometimes
I wonder
Oh should I be angry
And should I
Question
If you
Hate me
Should I
Be angry
Or should I
Build up walls?

And I gotta wonder
Where you came from
And I gotta wonder
Why you are
Building walls

Will you ever
Let me in?
Are you
Building walls?
Or for your sanity
Are you
Building walls?

And sometimes
I wonder
Oh should I
Be angry?
And should I
Question
If you
Hate me
Should I
Be angry
Or should I
Build up walls?
Should I be angry?

It was a simple song, but it held so much meaning to both Will and me. He wrote it on the fly one night, sitting on the beach at his grandfather's house after we had an argument. It had been just a short little tune about how we both fought each other the same way, while blocking the other out. Will told me I built walls around me to protect myself. I listened to that for years, and I could see when I did it with Chris in our marriage. The same way I put things in little boxes in my mind, I put myself in a little box where I was protected from pain. I was certain I started my wall building defense when Will first broke up with me, and I thought I would die. From then on out, I knew how to protect myself from pain, from him, from feeling. It was the first time numbness became an emotion for me.

Shaking the chill from my arms, I stood up and walked inside to see my beautiful girls sleeping and a young princess walking through a dark tower on the TV. I was determined to not take my heart and mind back to a place I never wished to revisit. I wasn't going to build walls. I wasn't going to be angry. I wasn't even going to try to understand why Will called that day, a random Tuesday, or why he started talking about a past we no longer lived in. I curled up on the floor with Emily and Bella, turned the volume down on the TV and closed my eyes.

***

The North Star Bar was on a corner just outside of the little New England town. As soon as we walked in, Will, whispered in my ear.

"One of these things is not like the others. Your hint is, I'm it."

There were women everywhere. On second glance around the room, we did see a few men, but they all looked like they were employees.

"Well, we knew it was, what'd you call it? A 'lesbian town?' But this place is packed. There must be something going on. Oh, look. A merch table," I said as I walked toward a table with CDs laid out and T-shirt displays.

"Oh, I see," Will said. "Well, this could be cool. I should have brought my guitar, maybe they'd let me up there, too," he nudged my shoulder. "We'll take two CDs. Do you want a T-Shirt, Nikki Jay?" Will asked after handing the vendor a twenty.

"Will, we don't even know who she is. No, I don't want a T-Shirt."

"Baby, I don't care who she is. She brought out a huge crowd, and she's up there. Well, she's not up there...she might even be behind this table, I don't know. But she's got a gig, and I'm all for supporting anyone who will come out to a bar and play. Sure, you don't want a T-Shirt?"

He nudged me again, almost pushing me aside. "Medium or Large? What you do think?" Will was pointing to me as he was talking to blonde woman behind the table.

"They run big, I think medium would be fine," the woman told Will as she looked me over.

Will put the shirt on top of my head and smiled, "Hey, if she's turns out to be the next big thing, you can say you saw her when she was just playing bars."

"I'm not thinking along the lines of the next big thing," I said looking at her bright face plastered on the T-shirt. "But I was never really a fan of those big popular artists anyway. That's a face I could like. And she's playing a Gibson. Oh yeah, much better than a

pop star." I laughed and pulled him to a table close to the stage.

We ordered some bar food for dinner. Three appetizers and sodas to drink. After about twenty minutes the woman came on stage, with three guitars. She carried them all herself. No stage hands, just her. I was in awe again. I looked over at Will. He was smiling. I could tell he wanted to be up there with her, but he just watched from afar as she set up her three guitars, each on its own stand, then walked backstage again to get her mic stand and microphone. She was definitely grass roots. She handled all of her equipment, set up, and still managed to get up there in front of everyone who watched her set up and sing and pull music out of those guitars.

After she set up, we watched her tune each guitar with a battery operated tuner sitting on her knee. Will got antsy. This was where we were comfortable, watching a singer song writer in action, not just coming out of speakers on a stereo. I knew Will had been looking into bars hosting open mic nights, but Deltaville didn't offer anything of the sort. He'd have had to drive forty minutes to Yorktown at the least, but probably longer into Hampton or Williamsburg even to get decent gigs. I had tried to encourage him to do just that, but I sensed he didn't want to leave town much unless it was on his boat.

I rubbed his arm and said, "You can do this, you know. You're that good. I'd even come and set up for you. I could make it look like you have a crew and are too cool to have to set up the stage on your own." I smiled. He did his Will laugh grunt, "huh he he."

"One day, Princess. One day. For now, I just want to listen to what this chick has to say and then take you back to the hotel room." Will lifted my chin with his finger, "Don't you worry about me, Nikki Jay. I have the best audience any man could ask for." He kissed me gently while still holding my chin and then moved his hand to my knee and squeezed as he turned his head back to the stage.

***

"Bella. Bella, no, it's mine! Bell-Aaa! Mine. Doan NOT touch!" Doan. My daughter said 'doan.' I stifled a giggle through my sleepy haze.

I lifted my head. The DVD had moved onto special features, the making of *Sleeping Beauty,* and Emily was yelling at Bella, who was holding her soft blankie with a trembling lip.

"Mommy, she was taking my Aurora doll. The one with the magic jewel that lights up," Emily said to me while smoothing the doll's hair.

"Umm, okay, girls," I mumbled while getting to my knees and standing up with a feeling of loss and exhaustion overtaking me. "Emily, do you have the doll now?"

"Yes, but Mommy, she can't have her. She's mine."

"I doll. I doll, Mommy, I doll," Bella said pointing to Emily's doll.

"Come on, little one, let's go find you a doll. Don't you have Snow White somewhere?" I asked Bella, leading her up the stairs to her bedroom where I was sure to find many dolls thrown to the floor.

"Relly, Mommy, Relly. I'm a Relly," Bella said running into her room and picking up a blonde doll wearing a blue dress.

"Cinderella is a fun doll, Bella. She's a princess, too. Do you want to play in your room with Cinderella, or would you like to take her downstairs? She can meet Emily and Princess Aurora."

"Ohhh, she wants to meet Emmie. If Emmie be nice."

Holding hands, we walked back down the stairs to meet Emily and Aurora.

Chapter Nine

Will didn't call the next week or the week after. I started to worry about him and sent him a text just after Thanksgiving.

I hope your Thanksgiving was a great one. Funny stuff around here with my mother in law, of course and cooking with two little ones, but we had a good time. I'm thankful you're still in my life. Love ya.

I didn't get a response for another week. It was short and to the point. I looked at it for a long time picking apart words not there, wondering how I should feel.

Tgiving was good. Love you too, NikiJay

I knew it was just a text, but even my name was spelled wrong.

December and January came and went with no calls from Will and few texts. When he did text me, the text messages were short and to the point.

Merry Christmas
Happy New Year
Thinking of you
Hope U R ok
Sing a song for me
Kiss the girls

Finally the first week of February, I called him. Rebecca answered.

"Hello?" Rebecca said with a hurried voice.

"Rebecca?" I asked.

"Yeah, who's this?" She asked.

"Uh, it's Nikki Ford, Rebecca. Is Will around?"

"Oh, Honey, I'm sorry if I sounded short. This phone's been ringing off the hook lately. No, hon, he's not here today," her voice trailed off. "I mean he's not here right now. But I can tell him you called for him."

"Okay. Yeah, could you do that? Please?" My voice was soft

and slow. I knew something was wrong. Or not right. Something was off.

"Will do, honey. You take care now, ya hear?" Rebecca hung up the phone.

Chris took all of us to a fondue restaurant for Valentine's Day. The dinner was amazing. Having our young girls so close to two extremely hot melting pots was quite stressful for me. Chris didn't seem to notice. He spoke of work, talked to the girls about things they didn't know anything about, and ate like a king. I fished out meats from the pots the girls had put them in and left to overcook, tested meats they'd dipped but hadn't let cook yet, didn't get to eat much, and essentially was exhausted by the time dessert came around. For dessert, I asked for spoons and just spooned chocolate onto the girls' plates so they could dip their bananas, strawberries, marshmallows, and graham crackers on their own plates. It meant their cute red dresses had drips of chocolate running down them before we left the restaurant, but it also meant I could enjoy dessert without worrying about them touching the pot or heating element under the pot. With the cheese and bread appetizer and meat entrée, I think they'd enjoyed enough dipping to allow themselves to enjoy dessert from their own plates.

Will kept popping up in the back of my mind. It had been two weeks since I'd called, and he hadn't called me back. Our relationship had never been over text or email. We'd always talked over the phone. Our relationship dated back to a time before cell phones and Internet, and we'd never moved it to a texting format. But the last few times I'd heard from him were all text messages, and they were all short texts. I was starting to wonder if Rebecca had a problem with me. Or with our friendship. Maybe he was texting me to hide our relationship from his new wife. Maybe she hadn't told him I had called. I decided to call his cell phone next time and not the house phone.

It took me another two weeks to get up the nerve to call him. I felt so ignored. I hadn't heard his voice since November. Even after we broke up the final time, we'd still spoken quite a bit. I didn't think I had ever gone this long without talking to him. It had been almost four months since we'd spoken to each other.

The girls were napping. Emily had said she didn't want a nap, but after telling her I had a headache and needed to nap myself, she agreed to go to her room and play quietly. Before going into my bedroom to call Will, I checked on them both. Bella was sleeping soundly with her soft blankie snuggled next to her. Emily was sprawled on her bedroom floor with her Aurora doll in one hand and her Goon Goon bunny in the other hand. She had played quietly. And then, she'd fallen asleep.

I sat on my bed with the phone in my hand. I rubbed my thumb across the LCD screen on the phone over and over. I was nervous. Not just nervous. I felt like I was going to throw up. Like I was doing something wrong. Maybe he'd made it clear to me he didn't want to talk to me anymore. Maybe we weren't friends anymore. Maybe I'd pushed him away when he called that day and started talking about the trip up to Massachusetts. My mind wandered to the painting I'd started before he called. I had never finished it. Emily never finished her castle for Aurora either. They were all sitting in the garage still, where they'd spent the winter.

Looking at the phone again, I decided not to call him. He'd pushed me away. As busy as I had been over the years, getting married, having babies, moving to Colorado, and living my life, he'd always been the one to call me. I didn't know if it was his decision to stop calling me or if the decision making belonged to his new wife, but clearly he'd made a decision either way. He hadn't picked up his phone to call me. At least he hadn't dialed. Why should I? Instead of calling, I sat on my bed and cried. I'd finally lost a good friend, someone I had loved. Someone I had kept in my world as my world evolved and revolved around different people, my husband, my children. But he'd pushed me right out of his world. Six months into a marriage, and he had no space in his life for old friends. I looked at the clock. Chris would be home in about four hours. I had plenty of time to cry, feel sorry for myself, pull myself together, and get the girls and me dressed before he came home.

I fell asleep with the phone in my hand and woke about forty minutes later with dried tears on my cheeks. After washing my face, I looked at the phone one more time, then checked on the girls. Neither one napped much in the afternoon anymore, so if they weren't awake yet, they would be soon. Both girls were sleeping, so I freshened my makeup from the early morning application hours before and went downstairs to straighten up the family room and raid the kitchen for dinner ideas.

***

When Chris got home two hours later, the house was fairly clean. The girls were dirty from a random warm spring afternoon in the backyard. Dinner was cooking on the stove. I was still thinking of Will, but I felt as if the cry I'd had alone in my bedroom had helped me move on. It was becoming more obvious to me he'd moved on without me. I needed to do so as well. Without sadness, without anger, without emotion at all. If I didn't deserve a phone call to tell me he no longer needed me or wanted me as his friend, then he no longer deserved to have any control over my emotions. I needed to move forward with my life. Chris, Emily, Bella, and our friends here in Colorado. Will was never a part of my Colorado life anyway.

"Hey, babe. Smells good in here. What'cha cooking for dinner?" Chris asked as he walked in.

I walked up to him, stood on my tip toes, and kissed him. "Sweet and sour chicken, broccoli, carrots, and pineapple," I said to his lips as I ended our kiss.

Our first day of spring like weather ended with Chris and me sitting on the patio drinking a glass of wine watching the girls try to jump rope in the back yard. It was a pleasant ending to a stressful day, and I decided sitting there with my husband and children, I wouldn't invite stress and negativity into my life again. Will hadn't left my mind in weeks, and I realized it wasn't fair to me, my well-being, nor my family. If someone didn't want to be my friend, I was still good. Even if it was someone I still loved as dearly as Will. If his marriage was more important than maintaining our friendship, then I'd be happy he found something special to maintain rather than feeling sorry because I lost him somehow.

"I love you, Chris," I said and leaned into him for a kiss.

"I love you too, Nik. But I can tell something is bothering you. Another park playdate bad judgment today?" Chris asked laughing.

"No, we stayed home today. I didn't realize it would be so nice outside. It's been so windy and chilly lately. I haven't even thought of going to a park, but the girls would love it, I bet," I said, practically ignoring his inquiry of what could be bothering me.

"Nik?"

"What, Chris?" I was getting annoyed. I didn't want to talk

about it after talking to myself all day and working hard to push hurtful feelings away from my heart.

"Is it Will?" Chris asked.

"What do you mean?" I picked up my wine glass and gulped.

"Will. He hasn't been calling. I've noticed too, Nik. He used to call every week. Things like that don't go unnoticed, ya know." Chris sipped from his glass while watching me from over the wineglass.

I wiped a tear from my eye. "Yeah, Chris. He hasn't called. I've noticed. I tried calling him a few weeks ago. Rebecca took a message, but he hasn't called back. I actually haven't heard from him since November. He sent me a few text messages around the holidays, but that's it." I paused, drank some wine, refilled my glass, and then unloaded. "Chris, please understand. I know we went through these crazy emotions last year at the wedding, but it's not the same. He's been in my life almost as long as I can remember. If this is Rebecca...well, I'm just pissed. No. I'm hurt." I couldn't say any more. I had moved from hatred and anger to sadness and tears throughout much of the day. Once I opened the floodgates and decided I could feel something about it, I wasn't sure of anger or sadness, which emotion I should be feeling. So I tossed myself between the two. I knew I'd end up numb after allowing my emotions to fight one another. And then I'd have to let go. I'd have to let Will go, let go of a lifelong love and friendship I thought would last longer than any other relationship I'd ever have in my life. Numb felt better than letting go.

"Oh, Nikki. I'm sorry. I don't know what's going on," Chris looked ahead, and not at me. He seemed lost in his own thoughts. "Maybe it is Rebecca. Maybe after a year, he's ready to focus on his marriage. His new life." Chris sighed. His voice felt empty. Like he was leaving something behind. An opinion he didn't want to say to me. "You know, Nikki," he paused again. Chewing up words before he could spit them out. "Maybe he's got something going on. You know. Maybe he's just going through something."

"Chris. This is Will. He's called me for everything he's had going on. Every week for years, he's called me. I'm sure he'd want to tell me if something were going on." My mind started reeling through time after time of phone calls where he would tell me of a new job, a new gig at an open mic night, a new song, a new friend.

Rebecca. He didn't tell me about Rebecca until he proposed to her. Maybe their marriage was already on the rocks. The first year is the hardest, and after living so long paying tribute to his family at his grandfather's house, maybe those discussions about the cap to the toothpaste weren't going so well. I snickered, catching Chris' attention.

He looked at me, smiled, not knowing my thoughts, or maybe guessing my thoughts. "I'm just saying, give it some time. Maybe he's going through something and needs to do this one on his own." He finished off his glass of wine, got up, kissed my head, and walked into the house.

Sitting back in my chair, twirling my wine, I smiled. I didn't want his marriage to fail. Maybe he wasn't calling because they were having problems. Either they wanted to work them out on their own, or he planned to wait until she moved out of the house before calling me to tell me it just didn't work out.

Will had quoted a singer from one of the CDs we'd picked up on our Northampton trip a lot over the years. Sitting on my patio, I could hear Will saying, "Sometimes you've just gotta live your life, fight the world and what's coming." It was a line from Neila Lees' song, *What's Coming*. For years after that trip, and after the final break up, Will would end our call singing the line, "What's coming will tear us apart, but our love will always fight it." Over the years I stopped listening because I'd memorized every word and knew what was coming from Will at the end of each call. I usually focused on the tradition instead of the words.

Those thoughts made me smile. I finished my wine, took my glass inside, and then called the girls in from the backyard. Chris and I decided on some indoor family time.

Chapter Ten

Will never called me again. Rebecca called in late May. She talked to Chris for a long time. At first I thought it was his mother or a friend because he was speaking as if he were following up on a previous conversation. After a few minutes, he handed the phone to me.

"Nikki, sit down, please. Rebecca is on the phone. She needs to talk to you. I know what she's asked, so don't feel like you have to hang up and talk to me about it before you decide. You can call her back if you want to think about it alone, but you don't need to ask me. We'll work things out on this end. You just decide what you'd like to do. And," Chris handed me the phone. "I love you." Chris walked away, and took the girls upstairs. I just sat there with the phone in my hand wondering what was going on. Once I could hear Chris reading a book to our children, I picked up the phone, held it to my ear, waited a moment again, and then greeted Rebecca.

"Rebecca?" I said shaking. I knew something was wrong.

"Nikki? Hi, doll. How are ya?" Rebecca asked.

"I'm good, Rebecca. What's going on? Is Will okay?" Surely she didn't call me to see how I was doing. Surely my husband didn't just tell me I could decide something on my own without talking to him because he knew what was happening simply so Rebecca could ask how I was doing.

"Well, Nikki..." Rebecca grew quiet. When she started again, her voice was no longer solid. "We've been going through some things here. And Will..." she paused again.

"Will what?" I thought to myself, *Will was in an accident? Will was in the hospital?*

Rebecca continued with a shakier voice. "Will would like you here. To be with him."

"To be with him?" I asked in shock. "What the hell does that mean? You're with him. I'm with Chris in Colorado. Rebecca?

What's going on?" I was getting angry.

"Nikki. Will is sick. He's very sick. He has been for a long time. For years actually. But this time," she paused again. "This time, he's not going to pull through."

"What?" I asked.

"Oh, honey. I know it must be a surprise for you. He doesn't have much time. He'd like you to be here with him. Can you come out here? I can fill you in when you get here."

I couldn't answer. They wanted me to go to Virginia because Will was sick. What could I possibly do?

"Honey," Rebecca said getting my attention again. "Will is dying. He wants you to be with him."

"Uh," Dying? "Rebecca. I have to call you back." I hung up.

Part two

Deltaville, Virginia

June 2014

Chapter Eleven

Terrified and nervous, I walked into Will's bay house. He and Rebecca had been living there since their wedding just over a year ago. The last time I was this nervous to walk into this house was just after Will and Rebecca's wedding when they invited Chris and I over to talk and have a drink before we headed back to Colorado.

Rebecca told me over the phone once my plane landed in Richmond, Will had been pushing people away, not letting anyone do anything for him or stay with him for more than a few minutes. It sounded as if he was going downhill quickly. I was nervous and scared he wouldn't want me near him. I looked around, took a deep breath, and heard Rebecca say to Will, "Hey, Buddy, I brought a visitor." She was talking to him the way I talked to my four year old.

When I peeked into the room where he was lying in a hospital bed, he said weakly, "Nikki Jackson! Nikki Jay, Nikki, Nikki, Nik." Somewhere in his mind I was Nikki Jackson still, or again, but he also threw out his affectionate *Nikki Jay*, so I figured he couldn't be mad at me or Rebecca too much since he was being sweet.

Rebecca put her hand on my arm and said, "Just sit tight for a few minutes, I have to go grab his meds. It's almost time, babe, okay?" Will seemed to ignore her and just stared ahead.

Looking around the room, I noticed much was the same as it was when we were here a year ago, and not much different from when I was a teenager. Will's grandfather's mounted swordfish was in the same spot above the painted white brick fireplace. The couches no one ever sat on were white in color, pretty, but not as white as they had once been; salty air had discolored them, but I was a little taken aback when I saw the same furniture still here after all these years. I must have been through five couches myself and here these were still here from a memory I thought I'd never visit again. I stared at those two couches, one a full length couch, the other more like a love seat, placed facing one another in front of the fireplace.

As I stared, I recalled, or relived rather, a moment on those couches so many years ago. I could not believe they were the same couches.

***

"Nikki Jay," Will had said so long ago. "One day," he guided me by the elbow to sit on the crisp white couch his grandfather insisted no one ever sit on, though he was sitting on it each time I saw the older man sitting in this house. "One fine day. We're going to be out of this town. I'm taking you to a big city. Austin. You need to see Austin. Best music in all the country. I'm going to play on a stage in Austin. Even if it's just some crappy bar, I'll be up there looking into your eyes, and singing, not the blues, but the joys."

"The joys?" I asked giggling. "What are the joys?"

"You know, I won't be talking about crying into my beer or a thorn in my heart, but rather how my cup is filled, not with teary beer, but with love from a good woman." Will pulled my hair back behind my shoulders and kissed my neck. "You know I love you, Nikki Jay, right? Will you be my audience? Will you let me take you to Austin and make love to you through my microphone?" He grew quiet as my breathing grew louder. Not only were we sitting on restricted couches, but I was growing more excited by the second and had the urge to lie down on the pristine white couch and strip naked. I didn't have to move on any of my own urges because within moments, Will had my shirt over my head and was moving his kisses down from my collarbone to my breasts. Tickling each nipple with his tongue forced my hips to thrust into him. I let out a moan as my stomach rose and back arched. "I love you, Nik, you are the most amazing, most beautiful, most filling, and absolutely most wonderful woman I have ever known." Each word was punctuated with a kiss moving further down my stomach, and his sentence of love and praise ended at the top of my elastic waist skirt as he slid it off my body in one swift movement. Before I could even respond with my own words, he had my underwear pulled aside, his tongue working tickling magic and two fingers causing moans and sighs to exit my mouth instead of the words I wanted to say but couldn't manage to get out. I could hear him moan to himself as his knees hit the floor, and he wrapped my legs around his head. He placed his hands under my butt and pulled me closer, drinking me in. I couldn't think of the white couches or his grandfather anymore. I was entering a place I

thought of as heaven. A place where in my mind, I was in meadows filled with sweetly scented flowers, until the final flick of Will's tongue sent my mind to blackness, a dark black hole where I could see nothing and could feel only ecstasy.

***

That was then; so long ago. The memory of it brought on a tingle to my body and guilt in my heart. I looked over at Will, sat down on the floor next to the hospital bed where he lay. He still stared ahead. Rebecca had tried to prepare me, to warn me, but also practically begged me to be strong for Will. She had said, "Everyone breaks down as soon as they walk out the door. It won't be easy, but it isn't easy for Will either. I think he begins to push us away so we may have our own time to cry, away from him. Remember, he's pretty angry himself."

"Will...," I started and then stopped. I tried to cover a sob by covering my mouth with my hands. He didn't say anything.

Rebecca came back into the room. I felt some sense of relief to have company again. "Okay, Will, it's time for your meds, open up. I have some ginger ale here to wash it down." She handed him a syringe filled with a blue liquid, and I watched him put it in his mouth, push the syringe handle down, and make a sour face. He dropped the syringe to the floor and let Rebecca place the straw for the ginger ale into his mouth. "That's a good boy," Rebecca said. She was still speaking to him like I do with my small children. She pulled me aside and asked to speak to me in private. I turned and looked at Will. He was facing the wall next to his bed, seemingly avoiding me. I followed Rebecca out of the house and to the boathouse, where I saw a large armchair and a side table. Both looked out of place for a boathouse, but this was no ordinary boathouse for housing boats. It was a wooden structure connected to the dock, but it was more like what I would think of as a pool house. It had a small living area, open showers, and a mini kitchen with a large cooler for wines and a liquor cabinet. The boats were always at the end of the dock, never inside the boathouse, but everyone always called it the boathouse. On the table sat a box of tissues and an envelope.

"The letter is for you. Take as much time as you need," said Rebecca calmly and quietly, with a quick embrace, before walking out of the boathouse.

I hadn't had time to process anything I'd seen in his house or anything from the phone calls when I learned of Will's condition. Will was lying in a hospital bed. I knew he was sick, and I knew they had asked me out there to help out, but I never expected a hospital bed. I never expected a house stuck in a time from years before. When I had pulled into my father's driveway, his own house seemed to have aged another five years just in the year since I'd been home last.

I walked around the boathouse, smelling mothballs and memories. The scent of freshly lit fireworks came to my mind. On the Fourth of July during our first summer together, Will sent Brian out in the river with a boatload of fireworks, then set up a blanket on the dock. He'd gotten a hold of a four pack of wine coolers, and we sat there on the dock that led from this boathouse and watched Brian light each and every firework. We laughed a few times when we heard a yelp come from the water. Brian came back with a few new burns on his hands after a 'dud' chased him down the hill bringing us both to tears. Will rolled on the dock laughing.

***

Before I knew it, I was sitting in the chair, my mind walking down memory lane, but my hands held an open envelope. I flipped the flap open and closed with my thumb.

I pulled out the letter and looked at Will's beautiful handwriting. I paused for a moment, thinking about how my own handwriting has taken a dive over the years because I was always typing things out. I didn't have to hand write much anymore. Then I read.

My Dearest Nikki Jackson Ford,
Today is my wedding day, and I wish I was seeing you
at the other end of the aisle. I have always loved you.
I have always wanted this day. I have always wanted
to meet you at the end of this journey. I just never
expected this journey to take so many twists and
turns. I never thought my journey would end without
you. I couldn't bear it ending without you. If you are
reading this letter, there is hope it won't end without
you. If you are reading this letter, then it's because

my wife gave it to you.

I paused, looked out the window and let a tear roll down my cheek. What did he mean by, "I wish I was seeing you at the other end of the aisle?" I wondered if I could I handle reading more. Grabbing a tissue from the box on the table, I continued reading.

You might have a lot of questions, and I hope you can understand why I may not have all the answers, but I will try my best to answer what is most important, what matters most at this point in our lives. At the end of mine. You have a beautiful family, a loving husband, and good life. I'm not sure I could have given all of that to you, but I have wondered over the years if I've failed you or even myself by not allowing us to move forward, by not giving you a legacy, by not having children, by not allowing you to simply love me and live this journey with me. But these are decisions I have to accept, with a gracious but heavy heart. With that same heart, I let you go. I got your letter when Chris proposed to you; I got your wedding announcement in the mail, and smiled for you, with a tear in my eye. I got (and saved) every baby picture you sent of the girls. They sure were beautiful babies, and I can see your eyes in Emily, your passion in Bella, and I know Chris is a lucky man. I can only hope he knows just how lucky he is. I guess I could spend pages telling you how much I love you, how much I adore you, and how sorry I am that you are not going to say those two magic words I know you so longed to say to me so many years ago. I have found someone to say 'I do' to me this afternoon. She is special. But she is not you. And this is something she knows. Sure, we love one another. I don't think a woman could agree to go through this particular journey without some kind of love for me. She might even love me in ways I cannot reciprocate. But she understands what this journey is about, and what she will lose in the end. And she's still willing to say those two little words. Those vows, for better or for worse, in sickness and in health just might bite her in the end. She may have regrets, and she may need you to lean on when that time comes, but for now at least, she has agreed to say those important words and to take those vows.

You know, I'm going to back up and start this over. I wish I could change so much over the years. I wish I was mature enough to be who you wanted me to be, but I wasn't, and I knew I lost you when you got married. I also knew we had such a strong friendship and everlasting love for one another, we'd never really be apart. I sensed you weren't okay with our friendship all the time. I knew it was hard for you to talk to me at times, and I knew I pushed you away at times. I often did it to protect my own heart. When I felt we were getting close again, when we were laughing too comfortably, listening too intently, sighing too much over the phone, I would back away. I did these things on purpose. When we talked about getting back together years ago, I would have jumped at the chance. I was on my knees on the beach that day silently begging you to move back to Virginia, to move into my grandfather's house in The Hills with me. I wanted to wrap you up in a soft blanket, lay you down on the white couch and hold you there forever. You went back to Colorado and met Chris. I couldn't keep you from living life any longer. I wonder at times if we'd had those few years together, would they have been good years? Would we have married? Would we have children together? But I watched you walk away, get on a plane to Denver, and I let you go away and grow up into the beautiful woman you are today. And stunning you are. Looking at you the other night at the pool...I have no words. I wanted to stop time, pretend you didn't leave a husband and children at your father's house just a few miles away, and wrap my arms around you, make love to you, and beg you to be mine forever. Even if our forever wouldn't be long, I wanted to accept your hugs and kisses. I wanted to accept the present and ask you to run away from it all for a bit and be with me as long as you could be. You even laughed at me, questioning my intentions, right before my wedding. Rebecca knows if you ever knocked on my door and made the commitments I needed, I would walk away from her in an instant. I know it sounds cold and heartless, but it's true. And because I knew you wouldn't do it, it's easy for me to say how cowardly I'd become. I wanted to be selfish. I wanted to be in love with you again. Even if for just a short time. I wanted to hold you, wipe away the tears that are to come, and to live eternity knowing you love me back.

Look, I was stupid when I let you go all those years ago, and I was even more stupid letting you go back to Colorado where you would eventually start your life, create a family, and let your roots settle and grow. I was stupid not holding on to you when you were so young, pure, and beautiful. I can't change any of that today. Today I can tell you I love you more than life. You create the music within my soul. You are the one person, the one thing holding me together. Even with your own life separate from mine, you hold my heart. Without, it would fall into a million pieces, I would cry a million tears and would stop breathing. Loving you from afar has kept me alive. Knowing you are okay, well loved, and cared for will allow me to die.

I wanted to stop reading. I wanted to stop crying. I wanted to go back home to my family in Colorado, and pretend I never walked into this house of pain. I wanted to keep reading. I wanted to understand where Will was going with his words. I wanted to let him hold me forever. I wanted to walk back into the house, grab a blanket, and lay on the white couch and wait for him to climb out of his hospital bed and wrap his arms around me. But I read on.

Nikki, I am dying. I've been dying slowly for years.

After therapies, after doctors and surgeons and minimal hair loss, my body has decided it's done here. It's breaking down, piece by piece. I've talked to my doctors and told them I am not open to any more treatments, and it's time to let go. They tell me I may live another year without treatments. These treatments take a lot out of me. I remember you asking me why I missed the Austin Music Festival last fall. I gave you some lame excuse about work I knew you didn't accept. But it was a time when I was pushing you away. I didn't want you to know what I was going through. For months I went through treatments, I went to Georgetown University for experimental treatments. I let them poke and prod until I was too weak to even know of my own existence. My heart stopped twice during one treatment, and they kept bringing me back, fighting the good fight. Or maybe they were just making medical journals, and they needed their pin cushion to have a heartbeat for the tests to count. I don't know. But I do know I don't have any more fight left. It's not in me. It wasn't meant to be. I have been fighting this for almost five years now. Not counting the three times before. I know. I'm sorry. I know I never told you. Nik, I need you to forgive me. I need you to understand why I never told you. I needed you to be whole. I couldn't stand breaking any piece of you. I'm not a stupid man. I've done some stupid things, like letting you go. But now I know why I had to. It had to be fate. We weren't meant to be together. We weren't meant to have a family who I'd have to say goodbye to within a few years. Could you imagine what your girls would go through if Chris were going through this? What our children would be going through if you had the chance to say those two magic words you wanted to vow to me years ago. I think I was meant to not be with you because you can't be broken. You are here, and you are meant to be here for a long time to come. With your family, with your children. I am not meant to go any further.

I know you are angry. I know you all too well. Go take a walk. Go to the beach if the weather is nice. Go sit in my boat. I've asked for there to always be sunflowers on the dash for you. I know it's where you'll want to be with your thoughts. My guitar should be there too. Today is the last day I plan to play it unless I have a chance to play for you once more. Rebecca knows it belongs to you, but she has also promised to keep it out of the weather, and depending on the time of year you are reading this letter, she has promised to have it out there waiting for you. Go, take some time. Then come back, because I have more to say...

The rest of the page was blank, but there was another page with Will's writing behind it. I couldn't move. I also couldn't believe I wanted to obey something written in a letter over a year ago. He was right though, after reading all I had read, I needed to take a break. Will knew me so well. He knew I compartmentalized things, and when my main box was too full, I needed to walk away and put all the little pieces into their own little boxes. I needed to process several things. I needed to hide away any disappointment I had over lost love. I had just learned all I had to do was say the word and Will and I would have been together all those years. It was useless to even allow myself to feel anything about those facts. I was married, happily; we had two children, and there was no going back. After knowing of the life I had with Chris and my two amazing babies, I didn't even think I'd want to change the past to make the present anything but what it was. I had to box those things up and let them go. Will had always loved me. I'd always loved Will. I was okay with those things, and I couldn't think about what would have or could have been if I had not gone back to Colorado and met Chris. I just couldn't.

Before I knew it, I had boxed those things neatly up, with pretty little ribbons wrapped around ones I didn't need to mentally open for many years to come, if ever. And before I knew, I was standing on the sand in front of a boat. This boat was different than the one Will had years ago. And it wasn't in the boathouse, it was sitting on the beach, leaning slightly away from the water. I climbed aboard, finding footing along the backside. Inside I did find fresh sunflowers soaking in a yellow vase, and Will's Takamine G Series red guitar. It wasn't the guitar I was expecting to see. Will had played a Taylor for the past several years. I had expected to see the Taylor. But then the memory of him playing this guitar the year before for me and Chris crept into my mind. I had given him this very guitar for his twenty-first birthday. He was giving it back to me. I dropped to my knees and cried, burying my head into the neck of the guitar.

I sat there, my knees on the floor of Will's boat, my mind and my heart in the same boathouse so many years ago laughing with Liza and Will and Brian. Will's grandfather was setting the table in the dining room of the main house while Will explored the liquor cabinet in the boathouse. He'd said he had waited a long time to legally take his grandfather's liquor, and he'd let everyone know he was going to try it all. It didn't take long for me to follow him, and then for Liza and Brian to follow me. I walked up behind Will as he was standing in front of the liquor cabinet looking like a kid standing in front of a Christmas tree after Santa had paid a visit.

***

"What do you want to try, Nikki Jay?" he asked me.

"I'll have a Coke, Will," I said sighing. "I'm only twenty years old, not of age, not an old man like yourself." I put my arms around his waist from behind. He spun around on his heels so quickly, I barely noticed until his hand was cupping my chin, and his lips were finding mine.

"You are made of such purity, you must be an angel in disguise," Will whispered into my lips. Then he spun back around and grabbed a bottle of tequila from the cabinet, and started singing a Jimmy Buffett song.

"Ahh, Jimmy," I sighed, "Now it's a party. But I don't need the tequila. I just need to see you smile."

"I always smile, baby. When I'm with you, that is," he said in an especially cheesy way.

"But I want you to smile like never before," I said, grabbing his hands and pulling them up to settle between my breasts, while winking at him.

"Oh, Nikki Jay, you know I'm ready to smile, baby," his lips

126

were kissing my ears and tickling my neck. My whole body tingled. I loved how we could be playful with one another.

"Whoa, ho ho!" Brian said from the doorway. Liza was standing next to Brian with a smirk on her face.

"Busted!" she said.

"I wasn't suggesting smiles like that anyway, Will," I whispered to him. "I have something for you, for your birthday," I said louder so Brian and Liza could hear as well.

"That's the kind of present we came in here to stop. Granddad said to grab the light rum and a six pack of Cokes and head back to the house." Brian always seemed to call Will's grandfather Granddad. I loved the comfort he felt with Will's grandfather. I felt the same.

"The present I have is back at the house, Brian, and we are on our way," I said as I grabbed Will's hand and dragged him back to the cabinet for the rum and cans of soda.

Back at the house, Will's grandfather had dinner ready. Steaks cooked on the grill, roasted corn on the cob, grilled shrimp, and crab cakes. Liza had baked Will a cake, and Brian was doing rum shots by the minute until Will slapped Brian in the arm and told him to slow down.

After dinner, I brought a box out from a back bedroom no one ever used. It was a rather large white box, unwrapped, but with a big blue bow wrapped all around it. Will looked at it, and by its shape knew exactly what it was. He looked at it a few seconds longer, took a step toward it, a step back, and stuttered.

"B-b-baby. You didn't!"

"Get you a box full of rocks? Maybe I did!" I said to him, holding back laughter. I could tell he was really moved knowing I had gotten him a new guitar. He'd been playing an old Gibson, which was beautiful, but it was one he'd picked up at a garage sale years before and it wasn't in the best shape. He fell to his knees that day, opened up the beautiful red G Series Takamine guitar and cried. I remembered him burying his head in my hair and saying over and over how it was too much, too much money, too much thought. It was all he'd ever dreamed of... He just kept stuttering and crying and holding me, telling me how much he loved me, loved the guitar, could never thank me enough. It was a lot of money for a girl my age, but I didn't need handbags costing three paychecks. I drove

a used car that was paid off and made a few bucks every now and then helping out Liza.

His grandfather broke the tear fest by standing up and saying, "Well, son, let's hear it."

***

Will and Brian played guitar for hours. We all laughed and sang songs. I had one wine cooler. It was the best birthday celebration I'd ever been a part of. I came out of the memory sitting on my knees and crying into Will's guitar the same way Will had cried into my hair that night while sitting on his knees. He was twenty one years old at the time. Full of life, vibrant, young, beautiful, funny; very different from what he was today. And I loved him more than I could imagine I could love anyone. I thought of my children and how I couldn't imagine losing them. But for now I needed to compartmentalize the pain that came with losing Will – again.

I took one sunflower, gently grabbed the guitar, leaving the stand it was sitting on, and climbed off the boat. I had a letter to finish reading. My heart was breaking, but as much as I could box off the past into pretty little boxes inside my head, the present was staring me in the face. In my present life, my husband and children were 1800 miles away, and my old lover was lying in a hospital bed a few yards away, dying if I was understanding what I had read so far. Back in the boathouse, I leaned the guitar against the wall near the door, tossed the sunflower onto the chair as I walked past the box of tissues lying on the floor, and went to the fridge in the kitchenette. From the fridge, I took a bottle of spring water. I looked at the liquor cabinet for a moment, thinking I should open it and take a few shots of whatever was inside, but I'd never been much of a drinker. I figured my head and heart were hurting enough without any kind of depressant helping. I kept the water, skipped the liquor, and went back to the arm chair. This time I took the letter in my hands, put the box of tissues in my lap, and placed the water on the table. My hands shook as I opened the letter again and, the sight of Will's handwriting instantly drew tears from my eyes.

Nikki, I hope I know you as well as I believe I do. I also hope you took my advice and went to the boat. Yes, I remember that night, too. It was Saint Patrick's

Day, as my birthday always is, and we had so much fun. I remember it being a warm spring evening, but more than anything, I remember love. Love for you and for my friends and for Grandfather, who prepared and cooked this amazing meal for us. I remember holding that guitar and feeling magic running through those strings. It was amazing. I also remember you getting so sick after eating crab cakes! You may have blocked it out, but I remember holding your beautiful hair back as you puked off the dock. I know you were glad you stuck with one illegal wine cooler. Crab cakes. Who grows up in Deltaville and can't stomach crab? Only you, my dear, only you.

I can only hope I have conveyed my regrets, my complete loss and heart break, but also my joy in seeing you happy with a good life ahead of you. I think it's time in this particular journey to get to the point. If you are in fact reading this letter, you know a few things by now: I love you; I've always loved you; I'm grateful someone else loves you. I hope he can love you as much as you deserve. I'm getting married today. And I'm dying. As a matter of fact, if you are reading this and my dear wife has done as I asked, then I'm dying now. Sooner rather than later. So let me fast forward to Rebecca and explain her part in this; my life as well as my death. We met through a mutual friend, Bo, who will be marrying us this afternoon. Bo knew I was sick when he introduced me to Rebecca. I think he wanted me to have a good friend, maybe a girlfriend, and he probably wanted me to just get laid a lot. That's just Bo. Free love, live life to the fullest, and enjoy everything you have while you have it. Bo was actually heartbroken when I told him I was sick, and when I told him I planned to stop treatment all together, he cried like a baby. Rebecca has been in and out of my life as a friend, but not so much as a girlfriend. I know she loves me. But when she met me, she knew I was sick, so she can't bring herself to love me to her fullest. She also knows and has known for some time I am not going to be here much longer. She knows, much as you knew so many years ago, I cannot give myself fully to her either. I've wondered if I could, you know, if I weren't sick. Could I love someone the way I love you? I don't know. I know I never have, and I know I never will. But if I hadn't been sick, could I have? I just don't know. I do know I am loved, and I am lucky. Rebecca agreed to marry me because she's a good person. She knows this marriage won't last long. She knows she will be the one to sign necessary papers, to hold my hand, to be there, to give me medicines when the time is right. She has agreed to see me to my death, so I won't be alone. I know I have friends. You know I no longer have family. My friends have been here. Bo. Brian. They've been great. But I'm not sure even friends can do the difficult things ahead. So I'll have a wife. Rebecca has a large family, compared to my nonexistent family. They are many, but they don't have much. Once I am gone, she will inherit the house where I will die. My grandfather died in this house. It's been my house for so many years now, and I feel if Rebecca can give me those ever important vows, she can have the house in the end. You have my guitar. Brian has my Taylor. Rebecca will also have other things to give to you. Just simple things, like journals I've kept, copyrights to songs I've written. I've had some time now to clean house. When you look in on your life from the outside, you realize our lives are filled with so many things that don't matter. I've held on to the things that matter. First edition books, things belonging to my grandparents, the one thing my Dad ever gave me, a children's book. I sold or gave away all of my CDs and DVDs and books with no place in my life anymore. I have tried my best to get rid of clutter, but much of the clutter in the house will still take time to go through. There will be no liquor or alcohol of any kind in the boathouse or the main house. I don't need to fall back on old friends when I don't have medications. I have some hippie friends who have offered marijuana if I feel I need it, but I've told them to keep it away unless I ask for it. From my research, I may be asking for it soon enough. I guess what's important for you to know, is I've tried to tie loose ends and make this easy for everyone involved. Rebecca will be my caregiver, and Hospice will come in when I am ready for them. My hope is you will be here soon. If you are here, Hospice has already paid a visit. They promised Rebecca they will tell her when it will be time to call you.

Nikki, I've loved you for as long as I can remember. I know it's a lot to ask, I know you are in a loving marriage with another man, and I hope he's gracious enough to hold you up when you begin to fall. This will hurt. Even if you don't love me as much as I have always loved you, it will hurt. I know this because I know you. This is not going to be an easy journey. I've wanted to be selfish all these years and steal you away, lock you in my heart, and keep you forever. But I couldn't. And I'm glad I didn't. You have a better life today because I didn't. But I am asking you to please let me be selfish now. Will you be with me for this final part of my journey? Will you hold my hand and stay with me until I meet my end?

I don't know how to say goodbye to you. I don't know how to say goodbye to anyone, but I think I could manage with anyone but you. I've been told my personality might change. I may become bitter or angry. I may push you away, as I've done before. I won't want you to see me hurting or weak, but my body will hurt and my body and heart will become weak. It's during those times I ask you to hold on tighter and stay with me. Rebecca knows our story. She knows the beauty of us, and she knows how much I love you and how much I want you here. She will be

your support, and I hope you can be hers. For this, I love you both so very much. I will always be with you. When you hear an acoustic guitar, when you hear laughter, when you teach your children how to play music, please teach them on my guitar. I will be around. Sing my songs, play my music, open your heart to the breeze on open waters, and let me in. I will be there. I promise. I promise.
Forever,
Will

It took me a few seconds before I could draw a breath. I couldn't breathe, I couldn't see straight, I felt nauseous and dizzy, and my heart was breaking into a million pieces. Tears were streaming from my eyes in thick ropes instead of drops. I'd never hurt so horribly, and I knew if I agreed to stay there with Will and Rebecca, I would only hurt more.

Chapter Twelve

I don't know how long I stayed in the boathouse. My whole body felt wet once I moved. Maybe I had been sweating too, but I knew I had tears streaming down my face, dripping down my chest beneath my shirt, and snot covered my face. The tissue box had been emptied, and there were balls of tissue surrounding me on the floor. I didn't even remember sitting on the floor, but there I was, with Will's red guitar in my lap, a broken sunflower at my feet and wet tissue all around. After some time, I got up, left the guitar and mess on the floor and walked back to the main house. Rebecca was waiting for me in the kitchen. She had a tall glass of water. I noticed hers had ice, mine did not. I wondered what other things she would just automatically know about me. She also put on a pot for tea. I shook my head weakly. I couldn't speak, but I couldn't imagine stomaching anything right then.

"I know this is tough, Nikki. I also know you don't know me well, maybe not even as well as I may know you, but we need to find…no, we *have* common ground. Will. He brought us together. He believes not only can we bring him through this, but we can also bring each other through this." She spoke to me in almost a whisper.

"Bring him though this?" I raised my voice. "He's not coming through this, Mrs. Westerly. I'm not even sure I'm going to make it through this, not whole at least, but Will is definitely not going to come through this." I began to sob. With my elbows on the kitchen table my body shook. I felt claustrophobic. I lowered my voice and said to Rebecca. "I will do this. Of course, I will. I need to call my husband, I need to go see my dad, and I will be back. Is that okay?" I paused with another sob. "Do I have time?"

Rebecca put her arm around me, taking on the impact of my sobbing. "Honey, Will is dying, but this will be a process. We both know you have an amazing husband. We have both talked with him in the past few months. He knows why you are here. I'm sorry, we asked him not to tell you. Please don't be angry with Chris. Please don't be angry at Will. If you must, be angry with me. Will has some time. We think a few days, but this is not an exact science. Hospice has been here, and they will come by more often. They think three to five days. You'll probably want to stay a few days after. You can come and go as you wish, honey. I'll be here." It was the first time I noticed Rebecca's sweet and soft southern accent. She seemed very tender and caring. I think it was the most she had spoken to me since I met her at their wedding.

I couldn't speak, so I nodded and walked away from her, not looking back at the house as I got in my car and drove away. I couldn't think of a time I wanted to get away as quickly as possible, but the speed bumps still on the Stingray Bay Hills Road were as slow as ever, making the journey to my dad's house long and painful. When I pulled in, Dad was sitting on his back deck smoking a cigarette. He saw me pull up and stepped on his cigarette before walking down to greet me. I could see concern on his face. Instantly I knew Chris had already talked with him. Or maybe Will had talked to him before I arrived. I got out of the car crying as he wrapped his arms around me, allowing me to bury my head into his chest. He didn't say anything, he just stood there like a pillar, not moving, soaking up my tears into his shirt.

"Oh, Daddy. What am I going to do?" I asked.

"What you always do, hon, be there. Be there for him, spend some time with him, and say proper goodbyes."

"How?" I asked weakly.

"Nikki, I don't know how. But I do know Chris and the girls would love to hear from you. Why don't you go wash your face and call your family? They miss you very much." I could tell Dad didn't know what else to say. He was good at hugs, at standing strong, and good at offering advice, but if he didn't have any, he'd send me on my way until he could find a way to fix it for me. He knew this couldn't be fixed.

My phone call with Chris, Emily, and Bella was tough, but talking with the girls cheered me up. Emily kept trying to show me a picture she had drawn for me. Bella said a few short phrases and said 'Mama' a few times, but she was more interested in heading outside. Chris didn't have much to say. Just like the wedding over a year ago, he was strong, accepting, and understanding. At one point he just said, "Nikki, he's an old, dear friend. I don't know him well, so it's not my decision to make. I know your past with him, and he's told me enough to know he needs you. We are okay here. I have to head to Atlanta for some meetings in two weeks, so I can only hope you can be home by…" He stopped talking. We could both hear an understanding hanging between us. Will needs to be dead, and I need to be over this and on my way home before Chris has to go to Atlanta. Goodness. I didn't even know what to say.

"I'm sorry, Nikki. I've never done anything like this. I'm not sure what to tell you. If you want to stay out there, you can. If you want to come back home and live your life, you can do that, too. We all miss you. Dammit, Nikki. Nothing is coming out right. What do you want to do? You do what you need to do, what you want to do. We are okay here." I could tell Chris was struggling as well. I'm sure it was an odd feeling knowing your wife is on the other side of the country with an old boyfriend. And I couldn't think of a single time someone we knew had asked one of us to stay with them until they died. I tried to put myself in Chris' shoes. I'd never met any of his ex-girlfriends, and he had quite a few of them before me. I could never go to a wedding of theirs or be comfortable with my husband staying with them while they were sick. What kind of emotions would I be feeling spending so much time with Will? Would I come back a different person; changed because I'd lost someone I loved?

"Chris, I don't know what to expect. I don't even know what to do, but Will wrote me this letter…" I couldn't say anything more.

"Nikki? Nikki, are you there?" Chris asked.

"I'm here," my voice broke. "Chris, I can't expect you to understand. I think I need to be here. I don't know if I want to stay, but I think I need to. I hope you can understand. I will text, email, and call as often as I can. Please know I love you and the girls more than anything. I think I might be selfish here, but I'm going to stay. I love you. I gotta go."

"I love you too, Nikki," Chris said, and we hung up.

I took a shower, hugged my Daddy tight, and told him I loved him and I would be in touch, but I assumed I would be at Will's house for some time. I hadn't unpacked my bags since arriving in Deltaville. Everything was still in the rental car I'd picked up from the airport, so I just took it all over to Will's house, planning to stay there, or ready to come back to Daddy's house if I needed to get away.

By the time I rolled slowly over the first speed bump on Stingray Bay Hills Road, my eyes were dry for the first time in hours, and I was feeling unpleasantly numb. I found Rebecca in the kitchen preparing medications for Will. She told me I could give him his meds if I wanted and spend a few minutes with him if I was ready, and if he would let me. I thought, after everything, he'd better let me. But then I realized I wasn't even sure of what I would say to him. I was going through various emotions, I'd been thinking of all the things I'd read in the letter, and all I'd come to was none of it mattered then. Everything was just as Will had wanted it. I realized he didn't want to talk about the letter. He'd had the last word. What happened from then on was solely based on my decision to be there with him or to not be there, but in the end of someone's life, one doesn't just rehash years of hurt and pain. They hold on to what is important and don't let go of it until they no longer feel anything. Without ever asking me, I knew it was just what he needed, to hold on to me until he could no longer. Angry or not, I wasn't allowed to tell him how I felt about all the things I'd read in the letter. I wasn't allowed to ask why I didn't know until then he'd been sick for so long. I just had to be there for him and hope in the end I had no questions unanswered. Or at least none that mattered.

***

With instructions for the medications in my head, I entered the living room, avoiding the infamous white couch, and said to Will, "Hi, Will?" It came out as a question. I was nervous and saw for the first time since arriving just how frail he looked. His arms were so skinny, I could see bone; his skin was almost translucent. He smiled back at me.

"Nikki. Hi. I'm...you're here." He didn't speak clearly, so I wasn't sure if he wasn't sure what to say or if he was trying to express some emotion about my decision to be here.

Water fell from my eyes again, instantly wetting my face. "I'm here, Will. I'm here. I was here earlier. I don't know if you remember, but I..."

He waved an anorexic looking arm in my face, "I know." A quick glimpse of anger visited his face, and then he closed his eyes.

"Okay," I said. God it was so hard. I didn't know what to say.

Talking about the weather seemed fruitless. Talking about the letter might have caused tension, especially if I was right about his intentions to never be able to talk about it once I'd read it. So I just said to him, "Rebecca says it's time for your medicine. She let me bring it in, but if you want her to give it to you, she's just in the other room, I can get her."

He just took the syringe out of my hand and showed me he could do it himself. The medicine was a bright blue, and once he tossed the empty syringe onto the floor, I saw the same sour look on his face I had seen earlier. He rolled his head away from me for a few minutes while I just sat on the floor with my head resting on the side of his bed. I tried to find my strength the best I could, but tears dripped from my nose onto my pants. Will just laid there, quiet. By the time I could lift my head, he was asleep. I could see Rebecca standing in the doorway, so I got up quietly and went to her.

She put her arms around me and led me into the kitchen. "I made some hot tea for ya, hun," she said. I sat at the table with my hands over my eyes and just let the tears flow. I couldn't speak to her. I had so many questions, for Will, for Rebecca, and I just couldn't get anything out. Rebecca set a cup of hot tea in front of me, and I found enough voice and manners to say a quiet "thank you" to her. We sat in silence for several minutes until I heard a small knock on the back door. Rebecca jumped up, almost too quickly, saying something about windy. I listened for a moment and didn't hear any wind.

Rebecca was only gone for about two minutes before walking into the kitchen with another woman carrying medical supplies. Wendy was a hospice nurse, Rebecca explained. There would be three or four more I might meet, depending on the day and time of day we might need them.

"Well, well," Wendy said quietly with a thick Southern drawl. "Is this *the* Nikki?" She hugged me tightly, and keeping her hands on my shoulder while she pulled a chair next to me, she said to me, "Honey, I don't know if you know what you're in for here, but I do know you being here means the world to Will and to Rebecca here. You two can get each other through this, and we'll be here, too, of course, but just remember this is about making this as easy as possible for Will. This is his journey, and everything we do needs to be for him and his wants." I was crying, and Wendy grabbed me a tissue, didn't hand it me, but wiped the tear streaming down my cheeks and hugged me again. "Oh, Honey, I'm so sorry. I know how Will wanted this to be, and you have to know this is what he wanted."

Anger took over me. "To die? Will wanted to die?"

Rebecca stepped in. "Nikki, Will has known for a long time this was coming. He loved you, loves you, so very much, and no, he didn't want to die, but more than anything, he didn't want to die alone. And he especially didn't want to die without you. You are his blessing. You will be here." She paused. "If you want to be here, that is. You can be here for him, hold his hand, guide him through this; see him to wherever he is going."

"Where he's going," I started to say something, but lost myself in my own mind, my own thoughts.

***

"I don't believe in God." Will put his hand on my knee as the boat rocked gently on the calm river. The sun had set just moments before. We watched as the pine trees lit up before the sun fell beyond the horizon. "I could never grow tired of this sight. It's as if those trees wait all day for the sun's light to kiss them just before going to bed. But I don't believe God has anything to do with it. I think it just is. We are all made from space particles, atoms and energy, first formed in space near that very sun, and I think it just is what it is. God is something derived from many gods explaining everything man couldn't understand. Someone decided there were too many. The rain could finally be explained, so the god of water and rain was out of a job. That happened over and over until someone with an organized mind decided to organize all man's unanswered questions into one neat little box with one being supreme over it." I could tell Will had put a lot of thought into his atheist decision. I couldn't imagine having such understanding at our age. I grew up going to church on and off but also grew up never questioning our southern values, which included some sort of religious beliefs. I almost envied his tenacity to question the unquestionable.

"Will?" I was quiet, almost afraid to broach the subject and take the conversation any further. "If you don't believe in, you know, God, what do you think happens to people? You know," my nerves were taking over my voice, "when they die?"

"Oh, Nikki Jay, you're so deep." Will put his arm around me and kissed my temple. *"I don't know. I don't think anyone really knows, but I don't think we go to Heaven or Hell. I don't think I could stand to be anywhere animals aren't allowed, and we know enough about the core of the earth to know it's a bunch of heat, melted rock, and molten lava. No beings down there, with souls or without. Maybe we just go back to space. Maybe we simply rot in the ground six feet under and stop being, ceasing to exist anywhere. Maybe our souls do go somewhere, but maybe we have control over where we go. Maybe there's a Grand Central Station for souls, and we can choose to haunt loved ones, walk old battle grounds, or move on to places we've never seen or imagined before. But I don't think there's a puppet master up there controlling centuries of post-Earth journeys."*

I stayed quiet and shivered under his touch. *"Nikki, I've lost a lot of people in my lifetime. Friends, Mom and Dad, my grandmother. When you have losses like that, and no one comes back to hold you during a bad dream or cheer you on during a football game or just slam a door, it's pretty easy to be convinced there is nothing after this life. It's better than believing you're not worth them coming back for."*

"You never really told me about your mom and dad, Will. Will you tell me what happened?" The moon was sitting just above Will's head and darkness was starting to settle in. The river was still with no breeze, but still, I felt chilled.

"Dad gave up on her and Mom was soon to follow with giving up on me. And herself I guess. Dad left when I was little. I don't remember much of him, but I think I remember the smell of cheap beer. Mom had been sick when they first met. She went into remission, they had me, and then he left. She got sick again, and it cycled over and over. When I was fifteen, Mom's cancer came back, and though we all thought they'd caught it early enough, she only lasted a year. I learned later she'd had it when I was younger but pushed through it that time. Grandfather told me once that it was what had ruined their marriage to begin with. When mom died, I was in high school and was able to just live with my grandfather. This is the first summer I decided to stay at this house. Usually he lets me just stay in Richmond because that's where my friends are, summer sports keeping me busy, but this year, I decided to try out this slower

life ya'll have down here." Will put his hand on my cheek, turned my head toward him, and leaned in to kiss the tip of my nose. "I think so far, it's the best decision I've ever made." He moved his lips down and found my mouth. I had to take a breath after realizing I'd been holding it while he was talking. I knew the conversation was over. I wouldn't learn any more about his parents or his feelings on religion and God.

***

My mind met me back in reality, Will dying in the next room and Wendy and Rebecca talking about what a great idea it was to add blue food coloring to the morphine they had been giving Will so they could tell if he was taking all of it. I gathered it had been a clear liquid and that it was the blue medicine I'd given to him earlier. Morphine. I'd just handed morphine over to one of the strongest people I'd known without even knowing it was morphine. In the moment, I decided to learn everything I could from Wendy and Rebecca. I couldn't change the train he was to take when he got to his Grand Central Station, but I could make sure he arrived in one piece with his soul intact, and to do that, I needed to do everything he needed me to do.

"Rebecca, do you happen to have a notebook I could have? I'd like to take notes, keep track of his meds, and maybe we can make a chart of everything he's had and when he needs it again. I think you and I need to make a plan for ourselves for however long this takes." I couldn't believe I'd just said that. "I don't mean it like that. I just mean..."

"Oh, Nikki, I know what you mean. The past few weeks Will has been doing most of his medications on his own, but he is at a point now where we need to manage this more for him, and I think having a chart of some sort is a great idea. I'll go grab a notebook from the dining room. We have a lot to talk about still anyway, it might be a good thing for you to have something to write in anyway," and with that, Rebecca left, leaving me sitting at the table, a wet tissue in my hand, watching Wendy take inventory of supplies she was leaving at the house. I lost it again. Sobbing, I mumbled something to Wendy about going outside and left the house where Will and I spent so many days and nights falling in love; the house where he would take his last breath.

Walking down to the beach, I couldn't feel anything. Numbness was a feeling was I getting used to. Chris and I got through our daily lives together. We loved one another. Our girls were growing like weeds. But I spent each day surviving until bedtime, so I could do it all over again. I was numb to the world around me. Getting a preschooler and a toddler off to school dressed and clean each day was sometimes so much of a challenge, I was exhausted by lunchtime. When Chris was home on the weekends, we were packing home improvement projects and family time into two short days while I tried to clean all the laundry and manage as many errands and cleaning tasks as I could before the next week started. Survival. It's how I'd been living my life since becoming a mother to two amazing little people. It's how I lived daily...surviving to lunch time, pray for a nap time, survive until Friday evening when Chris would walk in the door exhausted from his work week, hoping he'd do something to help me survive. Living in survival mode makes one quite numb. Numb from the world's problems, neighbor's problems, and sometimes even numb to my own issues, but always aware of each moment with my children. I'd been living my life numb so for long, I wasn't even sure how to create feelings in my heart anymore. Unless numb was an emotion, I wasn't feeling any. While I was surviving until the next task or until the next day or the next week, Will was living life in hospitals, clinics, spending his days and nights possibly just wondering when he might die, how it might feel, what he would lose in the process. I knew nothing about survival. Tears streaked down my cheeks. They felt hot, and they hurt. Finally. Emotion. I could survive this. Will wouldn't survive this. First lesson learned, and first entry of my journal needed to be rethinking how I lived my day to day life with my children, my family, my husband, and my friends. I would survive, and I would be a different person.

Anger. Another emotion hit me. I wanted to scream. I did scream. I stood on the small beach and screamed. Years had taken much of the beach away. The sight of a smaller beach made me angry as well. Years gone by. Surviving to the next day. The beach wouldn't even survive much longer. Shit! Why was everything so hard? Fuck! I screamed again. There was nothing else I could do. Nothing to say, no one to say it to. I wiped my wet eyes and looked around. The beach was smaller, the boathouse looked as if it hadn't been painted in years, and paint was falling off in huge flakes. It appeared smaller too. I knew it wasn't possible, but maybe, just maybe the whole world was shrinking. I turned to look back at the house. Sinking to my knees onto the soft beach, I noticed even simpler but life affirming and depressing changes. The hinges on the latch door were rusted, and the door hung crooked. I imagined the only way it would sit straight was if the eye hook was latched. It, too, was rusted. The screens surrounding the porch had a few holes and looked dingy, brown, not the grey color they were when they were newer. The roof was missing a few shingles, probably from hurricane damage. At least one hits the area each year. I imagined Will trying to care for the home after his grandfather passed away. While he, too, was dying. It dawned on me Rebecca was going to have a lot of work ahead just to repair damage done from the ages gone by without proper maintenance. Sadness passed over me, and I let it flow. I was pissed. No, more than pissed. I wasn't sure what I was feeling, but it wasn't relief, it wasn't just sadness, it wasn't just anger. But I was feeling. It wasn't numbness. It hurt. Right in my chest, it hurt. In an effort to fight it, my heart flashed pictures of my girls to my brain, and all I could think of was how much they would have changed before I got home. Then I remembered Chris' trip to Atlanta and how I felt it all had to be over and, I had to be back home before he had to fly out of town. Like ships passing in the night. I could imagine the moment. "Hi, honey, hope all went well, see you on Friday," he'd say before heading to the airport. I'm sure it would be on a day when I had just walked in from a trip across the country with a new guitar in hand, dirty laundry, of course after the pesky task of watching someone I love die in front of me. I was feeling. Suddenly. All kinds of emotions were flowing. I sat with them. Imagined them all sitting next to me on the quiet, small beach. Anger, Sad, and Pissed Off all sitting next to me. I seemed to be missing Happy, Ecstatic, and Blissful, but maybe after everything, after learning to live beyond surviving each day or each minute even, I'd find them next to me instead. Laughter. I heard it. I looked around at no one; even Anger, Sad, and Pissed Off seemed to have left the beach. I didn't know who had laughed until I heard it again and realized it was me. Great. I had swapped all of the side by side emotions for Crazy. I was back to survival. I needed to survive this, and in order to do that, I had to leave all my emotions on this very small beach and head back inside. With all of my emotions, I decided to walk back up the weed filled yard to Will's house, leaving everyone else on the beach.

Chapter Thirteen

Wendy and Rebecca were still in the kitchen when I entered. They didn't say a word to me, but both gathered me in their arms and just hugged me. After a few moments, Wendy spoke first. "Honey, I want you to know everything you are feeling is normal, and we all deal with these things differently." My mind got defensive and wanted to say, 'these things?' But then I realized they probably saw me and my few emotions showing themselves all sitting in a row on the beach together, and maybe they'd decided I'd lost my mind or gained my nerve, so I didn't say anything at all. Wendy however, kept talking. After missing most of what she'd said, I finally heard her finishing with, "Mary will have books for you to take home. Just remember to let it out when you can."

"Thank you, Wendy. Who is Mary?" I asked trying to appear as if my mind weren't in the middle of an argument with her while she was talking.

"Mary is another Hospice nurse. They all have different shifts, and we will probably meet a few depending on when we need them and if it's night or day or the weekend. Will likes Mary." Rebecca was just as matter of fact as she could be, like she was just speaking of the sky being blue. I was simply reminded this was a job for these people. At some point they would not be there. They would be at home with their very alive families, watching TV or playing games with their kids while we sat there on death watch. Anger was talking to me again.

Rebecca and I spent the next few hours talking, crying, and even laughing a little bit. She shared some stories with me about the past year. We tried not to talk about the things I wasn't really aware of, the treatments, the days in the hospital, or the obvious, Will dying. She told some big fish tales, concerts, drives through the mountains, and even a road trip all the way to the Canadian border just because Will wanted to see how far away they could get before having to turn around and come home. He'd said he didn't even have any interest in seeing Canada, but wanted to see as much of the United States as he could. Rebecca laughed through the whole story and at how adamant Will was about simply turning around and heading home. It took them three days to drive to the northern border and back.

Before we knew it, four hours had gone by, and it was time for Will's medication again. "Would you like to do it alone this time, Nikki?" Rebecca asked me.

"No, let's do it together. I'm...uh...I don't know, Rebecca, I'm scared. I'm nervous. Let's go together."

"Come on, bud! You and me, we got this!" Rebecca grabbed my hand, and we walked to the kitchen counter, where various bottles were lined up. I stifled a giggle, and Rebecca looked at me like Crazy was here again.

"I'm sorry, Rebecca. I have two little girls. I couldn't imagine just leaving this many bottles...or even one bottle of medicine on the counter like this. I guess I'm just always thinking like a mom!"

"Nothing wrong with that, my dear. Nothing wrong with that! I can't even imagine just how much is here. Drugs, I mean. You know what some people would do to get their hands on stuff like this, and here we have it just sitting out on the damned kitchen counter!" We both giggled. Maybe we would make it through losing Will. And together even!

"Let me show you everything here." Rebecca picked up each bottle of the seven from the counter and explained each one and what it should be doing for Will.

We walked into the living room, where Will lay in the hospital bed sleeping. He hadn't been awake much at all since Wendy was here and he'd been given his last dose.

"He's going to be tired a lot. We've increased his morphine because of his pain just in the last two days, so he's sleeping more. But," Rebecca paused, "I guess for him, it's a good thing."

I sat on the floor next to his bed and put my hand on his arm. His skin remained the same gray, almost translucent, color. His body stirred a bit, and he moaned in his sleep. I whispered to him, "Hey, Will." I was afraid to rub his arm. His skin looked like it might just peel right off the bone. "Will?" I said a little louder. "It's time for your medicine. Will?"

He was very short with me when he woke up, almost yelling, "Owwww, wha?"

"I know you're in pain, dawling, I know. It's time for your meds, so the pain can go away. Okay, there, it'll be real quick like, and you can get back to sleep once we are done." Rebecca was all business, throwing in a little 'darling' that came out as 'dawling' with her southern accent.

"I just want to sleep!" Will yelled at us.

"I know, sweetie, I know. We'll let you sleep, but you need these meds first. Mary says these will help you feel better." I was impressed with Rebecca's sense of calm. Tears were flowing down my eyes. I wasn't sure I could ever give him these medications on my own with the same compassion and solemnity Rebecca had.

Will didn't say much else except something about ginger. I wasn't sure what he was talking about, but I saw Rebecca pull a can of ginger ale seemingly out of nowhere. She popped it open and stuck a straw in it and put it on the TV tray table near his bed. Rebecca put the two pills we'd gotten from the kitchen onto the table near his soda can and drew the syringe of blue morphine for him. With a frail arm filled with anger, he grabbed each pill. Sadly, it took him several tries to actually grip each pill, but he was determined to do it on his own. I watched him with tears still streaming down my cheeks, wondering if this was going to get easier, pausing in my mind, knowing it wouldn't get easier for Will. Each time Rebecca reached out to help Will, he'd wave her hands away and mumble, "I got it. I said I got it. I can do it!"

Watching him, I could see my toddler I'd left at home, saying to me, "I got it, Momma, I do it." I know I've heard in life when one dies, they are often much like they were when they were much younger; like a toddler who wants to be independent but can't actually do everything by themselves. Only Will was much too young to be at that stage in life. In his thirties, I thought he shouldn't be lying there in his home, in a hospital bed, dying. He should be helping a toddler of his own learn to do something on their own.

Once he took all three medications on his own, Rebecca took away the empty syringe, put the straw in his mouth, and told him to sip. He opened and closed his mouth like a fish out of water a few times and kept saying, "Yuck! Yuck," while shaking his head. Just like my kids did when they took medicines. Only my kids giggled because children's medicines actually tasted like cherry. I can't imagine his morphine was flavored like kids' medications. I jumped from my own thoughts when I heard him yell, "Leave me A-LONE! Why don't you leave me alone?"

Rebecca kissed his forehead and gently touched his shoulder, grabbed my arm, and led us back to the kitchen.

"He's not having a good evening," she said to me. "I know when you got here, you visited with your dad a while before coming over here. You are welcome to stay here with us if you'd like, or you can get away and stay with your dad if you'd like. He won't let me wake him in the middle of the night for his medications. He needs them. All of the nurses say he needs them, but he won't listen. He wants to take them when he's awake and already in pain, but what he's not really getting is the morphine has to build up in his system. It will only work if he's medicated all the time. He's not there yet. I mean, he won't let us give it to him every two hours like we are supposed to do. So he sleeps through the pain for a while, and then when he wakes up, he's in so much pain he can't handle it. Maybe you can talk him into a better schedule tomorrow, but I don't think he's going to want to be bothered any more tonight. The past two days I've had to blame Mary when he's a grump. He doesn't want to take his medications, but he seems to be more open to the idea of taking them if I remind him Mary told him to take them. He likes Mary. I think she's his favorite nurse." I could see tears in Rebecca's eyes. It hit me suddenly she was hurting too. Of course she was hurting. She'd spent the past year caring for Will, taking him to appointments, watching him hurt, loving him regardless of the fact he could never promise her forever. I grabbed her and wrapped my arms around her.

"Oh, Rebecca, I'm so sorry. I've been so selfish. This is all so new to me, and I've been in shock. You've been so wonderful to me. Patient with me. But you're hurting as well. Will is your husband. I know you love him. Oh, God. I'm so sorry." I was out of words. We just stood there holding one another, bonding over the pending death of a man we both loved.

After several long moments and more tears, Rebecca pulled back and said, "You are welcome to stay here, hon, but if you want to stay at your Dad's house tonight, it might be the best night. I don't know how long Will is going to hang on, but you might find yourself here more and more." She paused. "It might be good for you to get a break. Take a long bath, spend some time with your dad. Take a break from this house. Will's moods come and go. There'll be times he'll want you here and maybe times he won't. I don't know. But I can tell you he's changing. His personality is different. He's angry. Shoot, we're all pretty damn angry, I guess, aren't we?"

"Yeah, Rebecca. I think I will go to Dad's tonight. You have my number. Call me if you need anything. But also, if you need a break, want to go for a walk, get out of the house, please let me know, and I'll be right back here in minutes. I also think maybe you need some time here alone…with Will."

Once we offered a few more hugs and some promises to call if there were any changes or needs, I got into my rental car and started the drive to Dad's house. The world was different. The light seemed paler, speed bumps seemed higher and felt harder than ever before. Sounds seemingly stopped. I didn't hear birds, I didn't hear the waves hitting the beach the way they had done for millennia. I heard nothing. I felt nothing. Until I got to Dad's house. I could hear the sounds of singer songwriter music from the '70s playing from Dad's stereo when I pulled up. It was the only recollection of any sound I'd heard since leaving Rebecca and Will. Dad came out and met me on his big deck he'd power washed since I was there earlier. I just fell into his arms.

"Oh, Daddy, why is this happening?" I sobbed into his chest. "Why Will? Why am I here? Is this fair to Chris and the girls? I don't know what to think. I don't know what I am supposed to do. I don't even know if I can do anything."

My Dad always knew when to talk and when to say nothing. He said nothing. I was sure my questions didn't have any answers to them anyway.

When we got inside, I sat down, and Dad brought me a drink and sat in a big arm chair near me. "I don't know why he wants you here, Nikki. Love is something I was never very good at, so I can't tell you if it's the right thing to do, but I do know Chris and the girls are fine and will be fine without you for a little while at least. I've talked to Chris, and he's not sure what to say to you or what to do, but he thinks you should be here too, if it's what you want to do." Dad paused and turned down the volume on the stereo. "Nikki, if you don't want to be there, stay for a few days, visit with me and some friends, see your sister, and then head back to your family. You don't have to do this."

"I don't even know what to say, Daddy. Will wants me here."

"Nik, I was with Poppa when he died. It wasn't all pleasant. He was scared, I was worried. It's a sad thing. I just want you to think about it for a while before deciding to put yourself through all of this."

With those words, I lost it. I couldn't speak, I couldn't hear the music. Everything was at a standstill again.

"I didn't mean to sound heartless, Nikki. I love you and don't want you to have to go through all of this. Will has spoken to me a lot this past year. Maybe you don't know all of this yet, but Chris and I have known this was coming. We knew he'd ask you to come home. He asked Chris' permission before calling you. He told me not too long after the wedding last year."

"He told you what, Daddy?" I was shaking, and my words came out as a whisper.

"Well, Nikki. He came over here one day with a six pack of beer. He even told me he remembered I don't drink, but he thought it might be best if we 'crack a few,' is how he put it, and talk. I was a bit surprised. I haven't seen him much in years. I mean maybe around town I'd see him, but we've never said much more than a hello here and there over the years." Dad paused and took a drink of his soda. Before he continued, he got up and walked over to the stereo. I could tell by his inability to sit still he was nervous. This was a conversation he didn't want to have with me. But I had to know when he knew Will was sick, what he knew, and hope it could all help me find closure or answers to the questions I didn't even know yet. When he spoke again, his voice was softer and slower. "Well, he came in with a six pack. I think he drank a few, and I had two, so we managed to get through the evening. I even ordered some steamed shrimp, and oddly enough we even had a laugh or two."

"Daddy. You're not answering the question here. What aren't you telling me?" I asked.

"I guess I just don't know what you know and what you should know, Nikki. He never gave me instructions. He just told me he'd want you here, you know, when the time came." Dad's voice got even quieter than before.

"You're still not telling me something, Daddy."

"Nikki. I don't know what to say. He was sick. He'd known for years he would probably get sick. Or sicker, I guess. He told me how his mom had died when he was young and how he'd been very sick with a childhood cancer when he was a toddler. His mother didn't share much with him. I guess she never handled life very well anyway. He was sick again sometime after his mother died. Before he moved to Deltaville, I think. His grandfather knew enough to tell him it was the same thing that had made him sick when he was a baby, and it would likely come back. I think he felt like he was a walking time bomb. He didn't know enough about it. He didn't know what could happen, but it was a burden he'd carried with him since he was a boy. He knew he could never fall in love, have a family, have a wife. He knew he couldn't live a *normal* life. Honey, when you were together years ago, he decided he couldn't ever marry you. Because he thought he'd end up leaving you and maybe your children before you all were ready. I guess it was something he'd thought about since losing his own parents at such a young age." Dad paused again, went into a bedroom, and returned with a blanket and a box of tissues. "Honey," he started again, "He loved you more than anything. He told me he became mean to you before you broke up. Did he…did he ever do anything to hurt you?"

I took the blanket and tissues and didn't say a word. For the second time in a few hours, I was bowled over. My mind kept going back to the letter I read in the boathouse. I left it there, sitting next to the guitar, and I couldn't remember what it said. Some of what Dad was saying felt familiar, but it hurt so bad and so deep.

"Nikki?" I could hear my dad's voice, but it was faint. "Nikki, did he ever hurt you? What did he mean by those words? How was he mean to you?"

"No, Daddy. He never hurt me. I mean not in the way you're thinking. He broke my heart, Daddy. I loved him so much. I wanted to marry him. I wanted to have his children!" As I said those words, an image of Chris came into my mind, and guilt flooded my senses. I still loved Will. And I was losing him again. But truly forever this time. "Daddy, he left me. He told me we didn't want the same things. He told me he couldn't love me and give me what I wanted, what I needed." I was speaking quickly, and my voice was sharp. I took a deep breath and slowed down. "Daddy, it all makes sense now. He did love me. But he knew he'd probably die in the height of our lives. Daddy, if I'd married him, he would be leaving us, in my life now...with two babies." I knew what I was saying didn't make sense. I wouldn't have Emily and Bella if I'd married Will years ago. If we'd had kids they'd probably be much older because we would have started earlier in our lives. Instead, it took me years after our break up to meet Chris and more years to have a family. Anger overtook me again. I felt a wave of heat rush over my whole body. I stood up, threw the blanket to the floor and screamed, "Fuck him, Daddy. Fuck him." I cried. Falling to the floor, I hugged my knees and cried, my whole body shaking.

Daddy sat on the floor beside me and hugged me. Once I felt his arms around me, I started rocking. Finding a rhythm matching my anger, I rocked and sobbed and rocked some more, then I pulled away and said, "He chose my path for me, Daddy. I wanted to marry him, Daddy, and he decided for me it wasn't best. He took away what could have been the best years of my life. I was heartbroken for years. I couldn't date, I couldn't move on. He decided for me. Without me knowing why. He just told me he couldn't be what I wanted. Dammit! Dammit, Daddy. Didn't I deserve better? Why didn't he tell me and let me choose to spend all these years with him? What if he didn't develop this illness? What if it never happened? He never gave me the choice! Ugh! I'm so mad at him, Daddy. I'm so mad." I couldn't stop crying, and my words were becoming mumbled and not making sense.

"I knew it would upset you, Nikki. That's why I was hesitant to tell you all he told me." Daddy rubbed my back while I began rocking again. "He told me he loved you more than anything, and he wanted you to have a full life without having to lose him, who knows when, and he...," Daddy paused again. "He never wanted to put children through what he went through, losing his mother so young and then losing his father after not having him while growing up. Both before he was a grown man. Nikki, I think he thought he was doing what was best for you. Because he loved you so much. He loved you more than I knew, and I think he loved you more than even you knew. He broke up with you because he loved you, and he wanted you to find true love again and live a full life, with a husband and children. He knew you'd find love again. And his hope was you wouldn't lose it like when his father left his mother at the height of their lives."

"Didn't he think? Think about life? All we missed together? All we could have had? And Daddy, just because I haven't lost my husband to something like an illness that has haunted him for a lifetime, doesn't mean I won't lose him to other things, like a car accident, walking in front of a bus, a motorcycle accident, an airplane falling from the sky…" I was beginning to feel sick thinking of all the many ways I could lose Chris. And I was still pissed because Will took away all of my choices so long ago. "Daddy, Will could have been hit by a car the day of our wedding. If we'd had a wedding." I just stopped talking. The familiar feeling of numbness washed over my body again. My whole future had been essentially decided for me. Then it hit me. He chose Rebecca to go through everything, but maybe never thought I was strong enough to handle losing him myself. Yet he called me home to watch him die. He'd asked me to leave the family I'd created years after he broke my heart, so I could be here to watch him die. Feeling numb, I just let the tears roll down my cheeks.

Dad brought me two little blue pills and another glass of water. "It's headache medicine with a sleep aide. Nikki, you should get some sleep tonight. This isn't going to get any easier, I'm sorry to say. But you need to get some sleep. Before you go to bed, call your husband. It's still early enough, maybe the girls are still awake. You have a family who loves you. Today. Nikki, this is your life today. I understand how you must feel, but you can't change anything. You have a husband, a good one, I might add, and my two beautiful grandbabies. This will be hard, but you need to remember the life you have. Today. I love you, baby girl." He kissed the top of my head and walked down the hall to his bedroom.

After several minutes sitting on the floor, I swallowed the two pills, hoping they would bring a peaceful sleep. Once I took them, I got up, walked down to my bedroom, and called Chris.

"Hi, Mommy! I miss you so much! When are you coming home?" Emily sounded like she'd sucked on a helium balloon, but my heart sank again when I heard her little voice. Daddy was right. This was my life, and I had to come to terms with it. Here was an opportunity to permanently close a chapter in this book.

"Hi, sweetie! I miss you too. I'm so sorry I'm missing out on so much." I started crying again. "I really want to talk to you, baby, but is Daddy around? Can I talk with him for a minute?" I ignored her question about coming home, but knew she'd forget until we spoke again.

"Hey, Nikki," Chris said when he took the phone. "She knew it was Mommy calling and wanted to answer the phone herself. Sorry if it was a bad time, but she wasn't taking no for an answer."

"No, honey, it's okay. I miss you all so much. I want to talk to her more, but, well, I'm crying. I don't want her to think I'm sad. And, well, shit, honey. I don't know what to say now. I just want to cry. I miss you all so much, and now I want to come home."

"You can come home whenever you want. Are you ready to come home, honey? Do you just want to leave him to his wife and just come back?" Chris asked. "I'm sorry. I don't mean to be insensitive. I'm not sure what you want to do. But we are okay. You stay if you want." He stopped. I knew Chris well enough to know he just didn't know what to say and didn't want to dig a hole for himself to climb out of.

"Honey," I started. "I think I need to be here. I think I'd regret not being here, and it's not something I can ever change if I'm not here. I'm just now finding out a lot of stuff I didn't know, you know, like Will is dying, and it will be soon, and other things too. It's just been a rough day." I cleared my throat in an effort to stop the flow of tears. "I wish I could be there. I kind of wish this just never happened. To Will or to me. I'm trying real hard not to be selfish, understanding someone I once loved, I still love in many ways, is dying. This isn't about me right now, but it's so hard. I've been pulled away from those I love, but I chose to be here. I can't talk for long tonight, I'm pretty beat, and I want to talk to the girls before they go to bed, but I have a question for you."

"What is it, Nikki?" my husband asked.

"What did you know?"

I was left with silence. "I know, Chris, that Will talked to you. He talked to Dad too. But I don't know what everyone knew and when. I'm not even sure why it matters to me so much, but I feel so left in the dark."

Chris sighed, "Will called me about six months ago and told me he was sick. He told me he had known for years he was sick, he knew he would not recover, and he asked me if I would be alright with him asking you to come to Virginia to visit him. I think back then I didn't realize he'd ask you to visit when he was dying. I think

I figured he'd ask you to come and visit when he was well, he'd tell you about it, you'd say your goodbyes…I don't know, Nikki. I don't know exactly what he expected or what I expected. But I knew he was married, and I wasn't worried about you going out there for a visit. Honestly, Nikki, I'm not sure what to think now." Chris' voice faded. "We miss you, Nikki. And we love you, but you do what you need to do, and please tell me how I can help you. And tell me when you're ready to come home. I'll book everything."

"I'll let you know, Chris. Can you look into me driving the rental car back? I don't know yet, but I have his guitar to bring home with me," I paused. I couldn't think about getting back home just yet. "Look. I don't know what to do here, but I think I need to stay, for a while at least. I'm sorry this is disrupting our lives, your life, work. Chris, I just don't know what to do. But for now, I think I'd like to stop talking about it. I'm mad. I'm pissed actually, but hearing Emily's voice brought me back to life, and I think all I'm sure of is I need some sleep. Are the girls still awake, can I talk to them?" I couldn't end the conversation about Will quick enough. I just felt spent.

"I'll put Emily back on. Can you call Bella tomorrow sometime, she fell asleep watching a movie. I haven't moved her to bed yet, so I can wake her if you'd like, but…" I could tell Chris had his hands full with the kids and working from home. I knew he had lots of help, we had many friends step up and offer to keep the girls during the day when they could, but I also knew Chris wasn't accepting as much help as he could be. I reminded myself to make some calls and see if some friends could just force help onto him. We did have a lot of support if nothing else. Who was I kidding? We had a great life, great support, and lots of friends who were willing to do anything for our family and knew we'd do anything for theirs as well.

"Mommy! Are you coming home yet?" Emily had not forgotten her all important question after all.

"Soon, Ladybug, soon. I don't know when, but I think you might be able to go to Kayla's house for a big playdate soon. Would you like that? Maybe Kayla's mom can give you guys a special treat, like ice cream! And maybe, just maybe, if you try hard enough, you could draw me a picture. I bet you and Bella are changing so much while I'm away. Maybe you can draw a picture of yourself while I'm away. Can you do that, Em?"

"Silly Mommy. I already drew you a picture. But it wasn't of me. It was of all the butterflies I saw in my dreams. Mommy, they are blue and yellow and green and purple. They were so pretty, and I drew them all in my drawling." Emily was so sweet, and next to ladybugs, butterflies were a favorite for her to draw. At the age of four, she still put an L in the word drawing.

"I can't wait to see it, Emily. It sounds beautiful."

"Actually, Mommy, it's fabulous!" Emily's excitement was showing through the phone. I hoped with both of my girls I would be able to nurture art in their lives. I hoped it was something they would love forever, as much as I did for so long, but I also secretly hoped they would never give it up for anything, anyone, or ever become too busy to paint or draw the beautiful things in life.

"Emily, will you draw me a picture every day while I am gone?"

"Mommy, that's a fabulous idea. I think I can do that. I can help Bella drawl her pictures too. She just does squiggle lines, you know, but I can even write her name so you know it's from her. Daddy taught me how to spell Bella, B-E-A, Bella! See, Mommy, I can spell Bella! Isn't that fabulous?" I made a note to ask Chris where the word 'fabulous' came from. It was obviously a new favorite of Emily's in the days since I drove away from my wonderful, fabulous life to be with a friend 1800 miles away while he died. My mind was taking flight again.

"Emily, I love you so much. You are absolutely fabulous, you know. It would make me so happy if you could draw a picture for me every day, and even more so if you could help Bella write her name even. I love you, Ladybug," tears started falling from my swollen cheeks again.

"I love you too, Mommy." Then, Emily, my big baby girl was off the phone.

"Hey, honey," Chris was saying through the phone again.

"Hey," I said with the bit of energy I had left.

"Try to get some sleep tonight if you can. I'll text you anything we need, but we'll try to leave you be. You call when you can. I know Bella would love to hear from you tomorrow if you can call. Other than that, we'll be fine. Don't worry about us. We have lots of help, and we are okay."

"I know you are fine, Chris. I'm so sorry. I feel so bad. I guess this falls under the 'for worse' part of marriage vows. I definitely feel the worst I've felt, well, ever, and I'm so lucky to have you at that end. I'm just so sorry," I started crying again.

"Nikki, get some sleep. I love you."

"I love you too, Chris. Good night," I hung up. I couldn't even wait for him to bid me good night. It was almost too much for me to bear. The journey across the country, and finding out I was losing someone I loved, whether I approved or not, was taking its toll on me. I changed my clothes, leaving everything else in my suitcase, thinking I might not be sleeping there in the next few days. After washing what felt like gallons of tears from my face, I found my father in his room, hugged him without saying anything except wishing him a good night's sleep, and crawled into my bed. The next day would bring the sun and another day, and as I tried to teach my children, how I chose to deal with it all would determine how good or bad it would be. Drifting off to sleep, I tried to believe that. I knew I had no control over when Will would die, or how it would be for me or for him. There simply was no other way to deal with it except for crying, nonstop. I knew that was what was in my future, at least in the days to come. I reminded myself to ask Rebecca for a notebook so I could journal. I was learning not only a lot about myself, but also about how I want my life to be moving ahead. My life, with Chris and my children, whom I missed so very much.

***

Will was standing so close to me. I could smell him. I could feel his pulse running through my own veins. He was mid-calf deep in the water, and I was standing on a slippery rock. Covered in green algae, my toes felt slimy. We hadn't seen one another in a couple of years, so to have him show up out of the blue was amazing. Leaving Colorado was a tough decision. I was between jobs, between boyfriends, and ready to give up the good fight and move back to Deltaville. When my toes touched the beach, I felt right at home, but when the humidity settled in, I was immediately reminded why I didn't belong in Virginia. And then Will called. He'd heard I was in town; of course, everyone there knew everyone and everyone's business. In Denver, I knew about ten people and didn't care enough for any of them to know their business. Will and I had always stayed in touch, but we hadn't been extremely close for a few months. Though we talked weekly, I hadn't felt real close to Will recently.

He'd been dating a woman who stopped in Deltaville to visit friends and decided she'd stay a while. It wasn't like Will to date just one woman, since he'd made it clear to me relationships weren't for him, and that woman was nothing like him from what I understood. She was Wiccan and liked everything to be so very natural; eating from the land and all that. Will hadn't really changed since dating her, but the months he spent dating her, I hadn't felt close to him like I had in the years since our breakup. And there he was standing before me, breathing the same air. I hadn't been dating anyone in Colorado since my last fling, which was with someone I thought I could actually marry; only he was in the middle of a divorce and on a completely different plane than myself. While still in my twenties, I wasn't sure I could walk down the aisle with someone who had already done it. It might seem silly and mundane to some, like choosing not to be with someone because they hadn't washed their own laundry before, but I just felt like this man had been through so many life experiences I held sacred, and I wanted to share them with someone for the first time for us both. Maybe it was an excuse to walk away from another relationship because he wasn't Will. Maybe in my life it was that simple. I stood on the slippery rock thinking about all the reasons I couldn't come back to Deltaville. I couldn't live there. Not with Will and his witch girlfriend living in the same small town. I knew I wouldn't go anywhere in love or in life if I moved back home. Will spoke first after the long silence following our initial hugs and hellos. I was trying to be comfortable, to appear comfortable, but as he spoke, my feet slipped on the growing algae, and my butt landed in the water.

"What did you just say, Will?" I said from the water, laughing with tears in my eyes. My butt must have hit the rock on the way down.

Through laughter, I heard Will say, "I said, she's moved on to New York. But what I should have said is, these rocks are slippery. Don't you remember that? Or did dry Colorado dry that pretty little brain of yours?"

I tried to sound like I was hurting for him, gauging whether or not he was upset because his little witch had moved on without him. He was laughing at me with a hand held out to pull me out of the water. I grabbed his hand, caught him off guard, and was able to pull him down with me. Only he landed on top of me, pushing my back into the water as well. Will was a quick thinker and put his hand behind my head before it slammed into the rock I had just fallen from. We were in quite the precarious position, lying in the water, him on top of me, both wet and laughing, with no attachments except our past together. With his hand supporting my head, I was able to put my hands on his cheeks and pull myself closer to his lips.

"She's gone?" I whispered.

"Yes, the wicked witch is dead," he paused. "Well, she's not dead, but our relationship is dead. She moved to New York with some friends. Said something about living a real life in a real town."

I didn't even let him speak anymore, I put my lips closer to his while he pushed his down close to mine. When they touched, we both moaned. We were meant to be. This was definitely a sign or fate, or something. After the best kiss I'd had in years, we both laughed. He rolled off me, and I splashed him. We were like kids again, splashing in the shallow waters.

"You'll need something to change into. I can honestly say I don't have any women's clothes at my house, but I do have some sweats and t-shirts. Can you come up for a bit?" he paused again. "I mean, if you want to. I guess you have clothes at your dad's house you could change into," he started laughing again. "But then what will your dad say about you coming home all wet? Wasn't that his car you pulled up in? You can't go home all wet in his car. I can wash your clothes, but it'll mean you'll have to stay for a couple of hours. Do you have a couple of hours?"

"Will, you're rambling," I said and ran up to the beach.

"Oh, Nikki Jay," Will followed me and grabbed my waist before I got too far. "Rambling is what I do best when you are near." He kissed me again. It wasn't playful like before. It was long and filled with years of missed passion. His height dipped me back as he supported my weight in his arms. "Oh, Nikki Jay," he whispered. He didn't need to say anything else. Years of not being together had filled any void he'd had. Years of loving from afar, years of regrets we both had, years of never forgetting that exact feeling, that exact passion. One can't just forget that feeling when you are just meant to be. No words needed to be said, but yet there was so much to say, so much to acknowledge; like my flight back to Denver in two days.

***

I woke feeling guilty after dreaming all night of Will. I woke crying, knowing nothing in life was simple and, though I never thought I'd ever be in a position where I was with Will instead of Chris and had to choose one over the other, I was also quite pissed it was a choice I'd never been able to make.

Daddy had doughnuts and a cup of coffee waiting for me from the local convenience store. The store had changed names and hands, but did have better doughnuts than ever before. For me the change was just another reminder things subtly change but don't really change at all. I hugged Daddy, took a doughnut, and said, "You always know just what I need, Daddy. Thank you. You didn't have to," I stopped talking because I was fighting back tears and trying to hide my sorrow behind another doughnut.

"There's another dozen in there if you want to take them to Rebecca. You two might..." he stopped talking, too. I could tell he was going to make light of two women eating twelve doughnuts alone or something similar and then thought twice about it knowing what we were facing there. At her house. Where Will was still dying.

"Thank you, Daddy. I think I'll grab a quick shower and get over there," I paused, fighting back tears. "Umm, listen, I don't know how long I'll be there." I couldn't stop the tears from falling again. I was certain before everything was over I would just run out of tears all together. I wasn't even sure what I was trying to tell him, but whatever it was, it wasn't coming out.

"Honey, I'm not going anywhere. The only place I needed to go was to get you coffee, and that's done. I'll be here if you need me. If you need anything, you call me." He hugged me, kissed the top of my head, pulled away from me, and wiped my cheeks. There was nothing else to be said.

Chapter Fourteen

I barely noticed the many speed bumps slowing the drive on the way to Will's house. I was glad for the short delay in getting there. I knocked three times, then pushed the door open part ways and peeked in. Will was sitting up in his hospital bed and asked me to wait a few minutes before coming in. He mumbled something about the bathroom and waiting. I wasn't sure of everything he'd said, but took it to mean he didn't want me to see him walking away. I didn't see Rebecca anywhere. As I was pulling the door closed, I watched Will get up and shuffle towards the hallway. He was wearing a familiar robe and using a walker I hadn't seen earlier.

I waited outside the house sobbing for two minutes before peeking through the door again and walking in. The first thing I looked at was the menacing hospital bed. There was blood on the sheets. I tried to call to Will down the hall to see if I could change the sheets for him. I was crying again and grateful he wasn't in the room to see me. I looked for Rebecca. She wasn't in the kitchen or the living room or sunroom, and I didn't want to walk down the hallway. Maybe she was helping her husband use the bathroom in their bedroom. I looked around the smaller guest bedroom for sheets and found two paper bags with the Hospice logo on them. Looking inside I found what looked like pads for bedding. They reminded me of my babies I left at home, only the pads we used to put over their bedding were to keep the sheets dry in the case of a leaky diaper. These were for an adult who was somewhere in the house listening to a very loud clock winding down. Next to the bags, I saw some sheets. They had flowers on them, but looked like twin sized sheets. I took them out to the hospital bed and changed the sheets, balling up the old ones around the blood stained spots. Just as I was tucking the last top sheet in, Rebecca walked in from the kitchen.

"Hey there, honey, how ya doin' this mornin'?" She asked me. She seemed bright eyed and happy, while I was falling apart inside and out. "I'm a bit surprised Will even letcha in here. He's been quite the grump today. Didn't want any of his meds last night." Rebecca stopped talking for a moment, grabbed my arm and pulled me into a tight hug. "Oh, honey, I'm sorry. I'm rambling. This is hard on all of us. He has friends come and go, but he won't see them, he doesn't want to; he's pushed everyone away. But those of us allowed around, we cry. We cry a lot. We go outside, let it all fall down our blubbering faces, and then we come back and do what's needs doing. He needs us. He needs you too, doll." She walked me into the kitchen where she had a tea kettle starting to whistle on the gas stove. "I was just sitting in the boathouse doing my own crying. He yelled at me this morning. He still doesn't want to take his meds every few hours like he should, so when he wakes up, he's in pain and gets mad because he thinks the drugs aren't working. I can't get him to understand how it all works and all that stuff Wendy said about it building up in his system. He just doesn't get he needs to be on a schedule. You know, so he's not in so much pain."

"We'll just keep telling him, Rebecca, we'll just keep trying. Okay? I'm here. I don't want you to have to do all this alone. I'll talk to him too. Maybe I can be the bad guy here."

"Hell, honey, maybe he'll listen to you." Rebecca poured me a cup of tea.

"I didn't know where you were when I got here, but there was…there was blood on the sheets. Will saw me come in, asked me to wait outside, then he walked down the hall. When I came back in, I saw blood on the sheets. So I found some sheets in the guest room," I stifled a small giggle. "They were pink with flowers all over them."

"Oh, yeah, those pretty sheets. We have to make sure Will has the pretty sheets on. He'll like them, honey. Oh, he'll like them indeed." Rebecca started laughing too. The two of us sat at the kitchen table and giggled like two little school girls. Neither of us knew exactly what was so funny, but it brought out emotions we hadn't felt in days at least. So we laughed, laughed some more, then hugged, grabbed our coffee cups filled with hot tea, and walked into the living room.

"Yep, they sure are purty, Nikki Jay, purty they are!" Rebecca whispered and put her hand up to her mouth to silence the giggle that almost escaped. I put my hand on her back and agreed with a nod.

Pretty sheets. That's what Will needed.

It took almost an hour for Will to come out of his bedroom. In that hour, Rebecca and I took turns walking down the hall and listening for him through his almost closed door. It was clear he wanted not only privacy but also independence, so we left him alone to do whatever it was he needed to do. With his pace slow, he walked back down the hall wearing pajama pants and the same robe he'd been wearing earlier, only it was inside out. I looked at Rebecca, smiled in an attempt to keep a tear from finding my cheek, and then said to Will, "Well there you are." As soon as the words left my mouth I realized I sounded like he was just late for a movie date and felt instantly silly. I tried to fake a smile but knew I'd failed when yet another tear escaped.

"It's time for that crap, isn't it?" Will asked.

"Your medicine, Will. Yes, it's way past time to take your medicine. We need you to take it every few hours like Mary says to do, doll baby." Rebecca was very tender, but I could see the lines showing frustration in her face.

"Just go get it, Bec." Will returned her loving and tender care with a short statement. He was changing. For the first time ever I saw a deep true anger in him.

I stayed with Will for about an hour. Will even asked me about Chris and the girls. I wasn't sure if he heard my response, but it was the last time he and I had a coherent conversation. My mind kept going back to all the other things we could have talked about, but he started the conversation about my family, and I answered with no enthusiasm but instead in a very matter of fact manner. I told him about a project Chris was working on in Atlanta, preschool for Emily, and Bella's new words and cute phrases, like "Mommy, I want to carry you." I told him Emily had gone through that phase, too, when she would say 'carry you,' or 'hold you' when she wanted me to pick her up, and I told him Bella's new favorite food was potatoes, which she calls 'toepees.' It all felt very mundane, but comfortable because it was all about my daily life. Once he was ready to rest, I realized he probably didn't truly hear much of what I had said, but I still wished I had told him all the things I never got to say.

Will asked me to leave him alone after I told him all about my family. He was polite, but I could tell he was tired. Feeling groggy myself, I went into the guest bedroom where I found Rebecca changing sheets on the bed.

"Is he sleepin'?" Rebecca asked me as she was pulling the corners of a crisp fitted sheet onto the bed.

I walked over to the other side of the bed and pulled the other corners around the mattress, then helped her pull the top sheet up over the bed. "He looked like he was getting pretty sleepy there for a while, but I just kept talking. I guess I couldn't stop. But yes, I think he's out for a while."

"Well, we'll have to wake him in two hours. He has to take this stuff on time."

I could tell Rebecca was feeling something not good. Overwhelmed, angry, sad. I wasn't sure which, or all and more, but her speech was slower, and her responsibility was starting to show in her face. It hit me again the burden she'd been carrying for so long, and much of what I had focused on was me and how I was feeling, what I had lost so long ago, and what I was losing again so many years later.

"I'll go get a blanket, and then I think you should have everything you'll need in here to sleep. You'll need to sleep, you know. I also put a notebook in here and a couple a pens. Will said you like to write. Songs and such." Her voice faded again, and I could see tears forming in her eyes.

I put my arms around her. "First of all, I had no idea you were in here making a bed for me. I could have done that. I'm sorry you felt you had to make any accommodations for me. I appreciate it, but I think it's time someone care for you....you know, for a change. Have you had breakfast, coffee or tea? What do you need me to do around here? Is there something...I'm talking too much and not giving you a chance to answer." I paused, still hugging her. I could feel her relax and begin to sob against my shoulder.

When she pulled away, she sat on the edge of the bed and said, "Mary came by early this morning. She said she wasn't planning on it, but decided to stop by on her way home from her shift. We're not exactly on the way to anything out here, so I think she just wanted to check on me and Will. She said after today she's off for the next three days. She also told me if Will is still here by the time she comes back on shift, his time will be short. Then she said, he might not be here by then. I think she stopped by to say good-bye to him."

Rebecca paused again, sobbed a few times, then started again. "She told me I have to care for myself. She knows you are here, too. She sat me down and told me we, you and me, we need to take breaks, remember to sleep and to eat. I realized I don't really have anything much besides morphine and ginger ale in this house. What is wrong with me? Morphine and ginger ale!" She started laughing an almost sadistic laugh, but instead of cruelty in her, I only saw love and care for Will. Of course she had everything he would need in those days, but no one had been around to care for her. So her needs had gone by the wayside. She continued just as I was about to tell her I would go grocery shopping for the house. "I think Mary is right. Not only do you and I need to get Will through this, but we need to get each other through this, too. We need to be here for each other, you and me. And we need to make sure the other is eatin' and sleepin.' If you don't mind, doll, I think I might make a quick run to the market and pick us up some things." Her head lowered, and she watched her toes for a few minutes. I felt like I was watching one of my children ask if they could have three snacks, knowing the answer before the question even came out.

I sat on the bed next to her and put my arm around her. "Rebecca, I think it might do you some good to get out. But before I agree, please know you don't have to. I will be happy to go get some groceries. You can just tell me what you need, and I will stock this house with more than drugs and soda. But, if you want to get out, it might be good for you, and I will be right here. Will is napping and won't be waking soon. We will be fine. And I can call you if I need anything."

***

Will woke before Rebecca returned from the store. She had given me his medicines before she left and asked me not to wake him at the two hour mark, but if he woke on his own to give him his morphine and pills. The pills were stacking up. One was for nausea, one for sleep, one was a diuretic, and I couldn't remember what the last pill was for. I didn't remember so many the day before. It seemed Mary added some while she was visiting. Will was open to talking about taking the meds, and I got him to take the morphine, but he argued about the rest. Probably because some were new, and he wasn't aware there was a new regimen in place for him. I couldn't imagine someone making so many decisions for me and understood his need for independent decision making about his care. I was able to talk to him about the timing of the morphine to control his pain.

"Will, I didn't get to meet Mary, but she said you really need to take your morphine every two hours. It needs to stay in your system to work all the time."

He interrupted me, his voice rising, "I don't want to wake up to take anything. I finally get to sleep, and someone is waking me up right away to take something to make me sleep. I don't get it. I don't want to wake up to take some damn medicine!"

"The morphine isn't to help you sleep, Will, it's to help with pain. If you let more than two hours pass, then it starts to wear off, and then when you take it again, you are already in pain. It has to build back up in your system before the pain goes away. So can we try to take it every two hours now? Today. Will you try today?" I felt myself begin to get defensive, my tone went up an octave, and I felt like I did when disciplining my daughters. I caught myself before I spoke again. One thing I did at home with my girls was lecture until I thought they "got it" or until I'd heard myself talk long enough. Will thought about it and told me he would take the medicine then, at midnight, and at 4 o'clock in the morning. I wasn't sure how he came up with those times, I wasn't even sure what time it was while we were talking, but I thought it was maybe early afternoon, and Will's times didn't make much sense. I agreed as if it was the best plan ever, noting he wasn't quite agreeing to every two hours.

Will sat up in the hospital bed. It took him several minutes to maneuver himself into a position where he was comfortable, or where he'd at least given up moving around so much. He took a shaky hand and reached out for the medicine. My hand was shaking as well. Will grabbed the syringe with the dyed blue morphine inside. I almost dropped it before he had a hold of it. With conviction, Will put it in his mouth and then struggled to push the plunger down the barrel, but after a long minute, he had all the morphine in his mouth and changed his struggle to swallowing. Before he got it all down, I had a can of ginger ale with a straw threatening to bob out of the top in my hand. He gave this awful taste look and took the can of ginger ale from me before dropping the syringe to the floor. Like a small child, he made several noises letting me know just how nasty the medicine tasted. We sat in silence for a few minutes before he looked like he was going to lay down with the soda can in his hand, and without taking his other pills. I started to say something to him, but the sound of my voice made him jump, and he reached out to the TV tray near the hospital bed, grabbing recklessly for the pills. Ginger ale was sloshing out of the can onto the carpet. Will seemed out of control, angry, and not quite...all there.

"Will?" Tears were streaming down my face, and I was having a hard time finding my voice, but I tried again. "W-Will? Will!"

"I got it, Nikki. I got it, but I took these today. I know I took them already. Didn't I just take these?" Will was confused, and confirmed for me what I had been thinking. I needed to create a schedule with what meds he needed and what he actually took and when.

"Will, I think you did take them earlier," I put my right hand on his arm and my left reached out for the can of ginger ale. I noted to myself to empty some of the can next time before I gave it to him. I was stumped; I didn't know what to say. I felt like the first time I was home alone with Emily after she was born. I was away from doctors and nurses who knew exactly what to do if something happened, if I dropped her, if she choked or swallowed something, if she couldn't be consoled. I was alone with Will, responsible for his care, for giving him his medicines, the correct doses, at the right time. He wasn't exactly willing, and I didn't know what to do about it. I didn't want to argue with an adult who should be able to take some simple pills.

"I'm sorry, Nikki. What did you just say? I don't remember." Will sat there on the edge of his bed, looking down at the pills in his hand. I was sitting on the floor in front of him, looking slightly up at his face, his handsome face with chiseled cheeks appeared hollow with too much skin. When he glanced at me, my head dipped down to stare at my lap, where tears fell.

I tried again. "Will, Mary says you need to take them again. Now. With the morphine you just took."

"I took them. I know I did. You're trying to make me take more. You're going to get into trouble. You can't make me take more. It will make me..." Will paused. "Where's Chris?" Will's face seemed lost. He wasn't all together there with me.

"Chris is at home, in Colorado." I couldn't stop crying. Had

Will just accused me of trying to drug him, do harm to him…overdose him? I didn't give up. "Mary was here earlier. She gave you some new medicines to take."

Will was quiet for a moment and then looked down where I was sitting on the floor in front of his feet. He tilted his head to the left like a dog with a question. "Can you repeat the question?" He asked me. Then he looked up and raised his voice, making me jump in my own skin. "I don't remember what you asked, what did you say?" I wasn't even sure if he was talking to me. I remembered my father talking about losing Poppa a few years earlier. Daddy and his father were never very close, but my dad was with him for weeks before Poppa passed. Daddy said he spoke to people who weren't there. He'd argue with the people who were there about the people who weren't there. Or at least the people the living couldn't see. Poppa talked about a baby someone left on the floor. Of course there were never any babies around the house while Poppa was taking his long journey to Heaven, but there were times when he'd speak fondly of the baby, concerned someone would step on it, and there were times when he'd resent the baby and everyone else around him because no one was caring for the baby, and all it did was cry. No one ever asked Poppa why he didn't pick up the baby and move it or soothe it even. It was just something everyone accepted. I wasn't sure if Will was going through some kind of dementia and talking, yelling at someone not there in the room with us or if he was talking to me in that manner.

"Nik. I'm sorry. I'm fuzzy. I don't know what you asked me." He was stuck on some question he thought I'd asked.

I tried to hide my tears, but it was pointless. My dry cracking cheeks would just have to take more. "I didn't ask a question, Will. I just…I'm just trying to tell you it's time to take your medicines." I paused again, wiped my snotty nose on my arm, an action I was never inclined to do, even after my husband had taught our children at early ages they didn't ever need tissues as long as they had clothing. Clearing my throat in effort to find strength and voice, I said to Will again, "Mary said to take these medicines. Even if you just had them, Mary said it's time to take them again." I told my first true lie and broke into motherhood with my long lost lover. "Mary just called, just a few minutes ago. I talked to her. She told me it's time," my voice was shaking. "It's time now, Will. Mary needs you to take your medicine."

Will bought it and put all the pills in his mouth at once. The thought of a newborn baby choking on something on my watch flashed through my mind again. In a split second, I was on my knees with the ginger ale can in one hand and my other hand holding the straw in place so it wouldn't bob around in the carbonation and miss Will's mouth when he needed it. I held my breath while I watched his face change as he swallowed each pill in his mouth. He let me hold the straw up to his mouth while he took the pills and once he was done, he waved my hands away and fell back onto the bed.

"I'm shorey, Nnn, I don't know..." Will said to me. It sounded as if the morphine was kicking in, making him drowsy and slurring his words. I didn't know what he was trying to say, but I thought he was trying to acknowledge he was aware. Aware, at least, he was falling apart. I felt like he knew me, he knew he had medicines to take, but he wasn't sure if it was time to actually take them or if I was trying to push them on him too early.

I put the soda can down and helped him move his legs and feet into place on the bed. I couldn't believe he let me help him get comfortable. Let me get close to him. I held his drink for him, his straw up to his mouth, then I was able to move his legs from an awkward position where he left them sitting while the rest of his body lay back. I smiled, made a small triumphant sound, and felt a huge sense of gratitude. He had let me in. And he didn't die. He let me get close to him, even if only for a moment, and we had made it through something that would normally seem so small but felt like climbing Everest. New confidence built in me as I watched Will drift off to sleep. But the overwhelming positivity filling my heart was sucked dry once he was asleep, and I could hear his breathing; rattled, slow, and shallow. I went from feeling like I felt the first night he kissed me, when I could practically feel our hearts beating through the palms of our hands to feeling like I just found out my best friend, my lover, my partner, my future was dying before my eyes.

After a long while, Rebecca walked in with a paper bag filled with groceries in one hand and a twelve pack of ginger ale in the other. Will was sleeping peacefully, and I was in a ball on the floor in hysterics.

Rebecca rushed to put the groceries down and ran over to me.

On her way, she looked at Will, doing the same thing I did every night when I went into my children's rooms before I went to bed myself, watching his chest for movement, for breath, for life. After looking at Will, and hearing his breathing more than seeing it, she dropped down to me on the floor and put her arms around me. "Nikki," she whispered. "Are you okay? What happened? Is Will okay?"

I realized she didn't know if I was crying because I failed at caring for him while she was gone or because for the fifty thousandth time it was hitting me, the reality of the situation I was in, the reality of the situation Will was in, and this woman in front of me, comforting me...Will's wife. The room began to close in on me, and I felt cold.

"Will is...Will is fine. Oh, shit, Rebecca, I don't know how to say it. He took his medicine just about fifteen minutes ago. He took them all." I stopped talking, pulled my arms around my stomach, then sat up and stood up in one move. I had to move, I had to get out of there. "Rebecca, I know I break down at every turn. I'm sorry. Maybe I'm not built for this. Maybe...I think I just need to get out for a little. Are you okay if I get out for a bit?"

Rebecca stood next to me and tried to comfort me again, but I pushed her away and walked out the front door. Once outside, I fell to my knees, took my phone out of my pocket, and called someone I hadn't spoken to in more than ten years.

Kristy was at Will's house in less than ten minutes. I wasn't sure where she was living, but it didn't seem to take her any time to get down the road with speed bumps bigger than the best waves around. Before I had the strength to pull myself up from my knees, Kristy was doing it for me. With strength and control, she had me to my feet and her arms around me in a matter of seconds. She didn't say a word; she didn't need to. We had a history that melted years in seconds and one which never required words. After a few moments of not speaking, and with Kristy trying to control my sobs and shaking body, she folded me into her little car and drove me away, taking each speed bump carefully, as if I might break with each bump.

After several tense minutes, Kristy pulled into a little bar in town. When I was growing up, the bar was a grocery store where I held my first real paying job. Amazingly enough, after years and years, I walked through the same doors expecting to see racks of canned goods and fresh bread, but instead saw smoke hovering two feet above several tall tables, a quiet live band, and a table full of old friends awaiting my arrival. After only two steps into the bar, I was swarmed with people. The sun was still shining outside, but inside the smoke hovered and the lights were off. There were hugs, questions about my children, where my husband was, how long was I staying. For a moment I felt a sense of relief. There were so many people there who loved me and wanted to see me. Kristy headed to the bar and brought back two bottles of Coors Light for herself and me.

"Aww right, step back, e'eryone. Step. Back." Kristy always knew how to take hold and control a crowd. It was one quality that made her one heck of a cop. "Now," she said calmly and quietly with the tiniest bit of condescension, "Nikki Jackson Ford is here. But she's not here for you." Kristy paused again. "You. Are here for her. Some ya'll may not know, but she's here alone. Without her husband and those cute little kids she has back in that mile high city. She is here to watch someone she loves. That someone she is watching is dying. And she ain't taking it so well." She paused again as if she were waiting for all of it to sink in. There were a few oohhhs and ahhhs and some ohs from the small group, but I could tell a few already knew I was in town and exactly why I was in town. A few raised their glasses and someone said, "To Will." The group repeated the toast and the chatter of the group commenced. One at a time or in groups of two, people came to me to give me a hug or say hello. I felt like I was in a receiving line at a funeral. That brought more tears streaming down my face.

I found out some people were already hanging out at The Sand Bar before Kristy got my call, but the ones who came out just to see me, Kristy had arranged as soon as she got off the phone with me. With modern technology, she was able to send out a group text and voila, instant company to make me smile or sing sad country songs with. That wouldn't have happened years ago.

I spent the next three hours talking about my life at home, my children, which was the easiest thing for me to speak of, and I listened to gossip about everyone I remembered, those I didn't remember, and some I was pretty sure I'd never even known to begin with.

At 6:00pm, with the sunlight still shining outside and half the room having a bit too much to drink, I turned to Kristy, a dear old friend who dropped whatever she had on her afternoon agenda and managed to get a group of people together with no notice, and asked her to drive me back to Will.

"I left without telling Rebecca. You probably don't know Rebecca; she's Will's wife." Now it was time for Kristy's head to turn sideways like a pup with a question. I was sure most people in town knew Will had gotten married, but Kristy lived a different life. She lived and worked in town, but stayed out of town to date and stayed out of town gossip. She was pretty high up on the list of people I adored and top of the list of people who never liked Will and never forgave him for breaking my heart. I realized with the gathering she had planned for me, to lift my spirits, I hadn't had the chance to tell her about Will's letter, why he asked me to be there, and more importantly, why he broke my heart so badly to begin with. "I left just after he took his last medicines, but I didn't write anything down. It's almost time for his next round, and I don't want Rebecca to be there for those alone." I started crying again. Kristy pulled me closer and gently wiped a tear before it fell from my cheek.

"Sure thing, Squirt. Let's get you back." She made an announcement to the people still gathered nearby our table about us leaving, instructed everyone to say their goodbyes, thanked them all for coming, then took off to the bar to pay our tab. I hugged again, listening to everyone's sympathies and struggling to get through many names of people I just couldn't remember from my early years living in Deltaville.

Kristy pulled into the circular drive way at Will's house, got out, and opened my door for me. She took my hand and helped me out of the car and had her arm around my waist pulling me into a deep, meaningful hug before I could even take a breath. She whispered in my ear, "You are not alone. I am here. You have so many people here who love you and care for you. And I'm one of 'em, Little Shit. I love you more than you'll ever know. And I'm here for you. Always." I tried to laugh at her calling me 'Little Shit.' It was a nickname she'd had for me since we were in high school. High school was also the first time she'd told me she loved me.

"I know, Kris. I know. And I can't thank you enough. You

showed up here like magic, no questions, just whisked me away to drink away my sorrows and solve my problems, even if only for a moment, and remind me of how much you care. I can't thank you enough. Really. Look, I didn't know half of those people at The Sand Bar this afternoon. I'm sure they don't know me either, at least not anymore, but it was a good break. I really appreciate you doing that. I have no idea exactly how you did it, but I've never really understood how you managed to do most things."

I hugged Kristy, turned, and walked away. I knew I'd be seeing her again. I'd either call because I needed a friend, or she'd just show up – because I needed a friend. She'd also know exactly when to do it, too.

"Anytime, Nikki, anytime, my dear. You call me if you need me. I'll be here." I could hear her talking as I walked into the house and gave her a last wave goodbye.

I hesitated just inside the doorway for several minutes, listening, feeling like an intruder and not wanting to face what was inside. A wave of guilt washed over me. At the first really difficult moment, I ran like an abused puppy dog, leaving Rebecca alone with Will.

I tiptoed inside, pausing every few steps to listen for talking, breathing, or crying, expecting all of those sounds to come from various places in the house. I heard nothing.

Nothing made me worry. As I turned away from the foyer and into the living room where Will was now living in his hospital bed, I did hear breathing. Short, shallow breaths coming from the bed. I looked around in the semi darkness for Rebecca and didn't see her. Like I did with my children in my own home, I stood in front of Will, watching his chest heave up and down with each slow breath. I could hear his raspy lungs and the work they were doing supplying oxygen to his body, but I had to watch his body working, too.

"He told me not to wake him up for his medicine," Rebecca was standing in the hallway. "He's getting angrier. He just won't do it. He just won't take them on time."

"You know, I was thinking, Rebecca. This is the last thing he can control. We want him to be comfortable, not in pain. We want this to be easier for him. But it's what we want. Maybe we need to do what he wants." I followed her down the hallway. "I don't want to treat him like a child, but I've been reading a lot of parenting books as I'm challenged every day with new things, from my four year old especially. She tends to pick up things from kids at school. Things I never thought she'd do." I shook my head. I was getting off topic. "Anyway, we're learning the one thing she really wants is control. We tell her what's for each meal and tell her to eat it. There were years when I just walked into her room, got some clothes out of her closet, and got her dressed. I give her a bath, tell her when it's time to get out...anyway, we've been giving her choices. I give her two choices each morning of outfits to wear to school and on weekends let her choose on her own. She's been happier making her own choices. We make sure we give her options we are happy with, but in her little world, she's in control." I couldn't stop the tears from falling from my face. I missed my little Emily and Bella so very much, and the path I was going with my thought sharing session with Rebecca was getting more difficult. But I continued, "Will...Will is running out of time to make those choices for himself. I think..." I had to stop talking to give myself some air and time to calm my heart down. I was on the verge of hysterics again. "I think he needs to make these decisions. On his own. If there's a time when...when..." Rebecca put her arms around me and cried with me.

"I see what you're sayin', doll. I see. I think you're right. It's hard on us to see him hurtin', but if he wants to sleep, let's let him sleep. We can give him the damned morphine when he wakes." We stood there in the hallway for a long moment crying with each other, empathizing with one another, until Rebecca pulled away and said, "Let's get some rest while he's sleeping." I know it's early still, but isn't that what ya'll do when your babies are little? Sleep when they're sleeping?"

"Good night, Rebecca. I'll be in the guest room. If you need anything, please wake me." I turned to walk away. "Not just if Will needs anything, but if you need anything. To talk, to cry, to just sit and have company. I'm here. Okay?"

She nodded and walked down to the bedroom down the hall. I watched her turn to what I remember was once an office when Will's grandfather owned the house. It wasn't the master bedroom. I wondered for a minute if she couldn't sleep in the master bedroom without Will. Or maybe she had her own room during these times. It didn't matter. What mattered was I'd spent my afternoon in a bar and hadn't called Chris or spoken to my children all day. I was tired.

Chris would be awake because he averaged about five hours a night starting around 1am. But I didn't feel like talking. I just sent him a simple text message telling him it was a rough day, and I loved them all, then I got ready for bed. As I was brushing my teeth, I searched my makeup bag for a sleep aide. It was my only hope for sleep.

Chapter Fifteen

Thanks to modern medicine, I was able to get a few hours of straight sleep. But when I woke I felt off. Something didn't feel right. I was scared. I grabbed my phone, thinking of the girls, and sent Chris a message. I didn't want him to worry or think I was crazy for waking scared for no reason, so I just simply wrote, "Give the girls kisses for me. Hope all is well. Love you."

Chris replied immediately with, "They love you too. Off to a playdate soon. Syrupy waffle kisses coming your way. From them, not me." Then a second text from him said, "I'd love to kiss you, too, but not with maple syrup all over my face. That's all I meant."

My family was fine. The girls were okay. And awake. But I still didn't feel right. I brushed my teeth, pulled my hair up in a ponytail, and walked down the hall towards the room where Rebecca was the night before. I knocked gently, and she opened within seconds. She was dressed just like I was, in pajamas, but comfortable, hair up, awake but not ready to face the day ahead.

"I hope I didn't wake you. I just...I feel off," I said to her. "I don't know what, but something doesn't feel right."

"Let's go check on Will. Together. We can do this. I don't feel anything but worn out, honey, but let's head out there and hope he's awake and ready for his medicine. He didn't wake you at all did he? I slept pretty well, so I figure he slept all night."

We walked down the hallway and into the living room. Will's hospital bed was empty. I knew something wasn't right. I felt it. Where the hell was Will?

Rebecca called out, trying to control the worry in her voice. "Will? Will, where are you?" She was walking toward the hallway on the other side of the long ranch style home. That side was always formal dining, parlor, and a work shop for Will's grandfather. We heard mumbling coming from that side of the house.

The two of us walked down the hallway like two young girls

visiting a haunted house. I realized we were holding on to one another like something was going to jump out at us and make us pee our pants. We were both scared. When we got to the old parlor, the double doors were pulled to but not entirely closed. I spoke this time. "Will. Rebecca and I are here. Are you okay? Do you need anything? What are you doing?" After the third question, I realized I was on the verge of tears and starting to nag by asking question after question without giving him a chance to respond to the previous questions. I peeked through the opening in the doors and could tell there was another room off to the side.

"Is there another room back there? I don't remember..." I didn't finish getting into how well I once knew the house.

"Yes, hon, there's a bathroom back there. He's used it since he started resting in the living room. It even has a shower. I think he started when, well, I think he just didn't want to bother me if I was sleeping down in the other end of the house. I'm sure he's okay. Let's just go wait for him in the living room."

I could hear some more mumbling, only louder than before, but still not very clear. I raised my voice a little louder, knowing he was behind another door which was pulled to but not fully closed. "Will, we're going to wait in the living room. It's time for your medicine, so when you're ready, come on out, and we'll get it all ready for you."

I heard two loud bangs and jumped to open the parlor doors. Before I was able to get in, Rebecca put her hand on my arm and whispered, "Walker." Will must have thought I was coming in. I don't know if it was because my voice sounded louder or if Will thought I had entered the parlor already, but he had shuffled his walker around in the bathroom to try to get the door closed. Will was trying to maintain control. And his modesty.

We turned and walked away down the hall and back into the living room. We sat in the chairs in the living room, neither of us bothering to get up to prepare Will's medicine I told him we'd have ready once he returned. Neither of us wanted to talk about Will or medicine, so we talked about the wind overnight, the weather, my children, life in Deltaville. We talked about a lot of things and a lot of nothing in ten minutes before we got quiet. The air felt heavy.

"It's been a while, where is he?" I asked Rebecca. Rebecca just sat there. I could see fear in her eyes. We had no idea what we had ahead of us. I walked down the newly scary hallway to the parlor door, peeked in, and then opened it up a tad more than I had before.

"Will, you okay?"

I heard a mumble I was certain had at least one cuss word hidden in it. Then he clearly stated in an angry voice, "I'll be out in a minute!"

Walking back down the hall, I felt defeated. I looked at Rebecca, and just simply said, "We should get his meds ready. And since we're both here giving him meds, and he's fighting it, let's create that chart we'd talked about. Then we can…well, I was going to say we can show him how often he's getting them, but I don't think he cares. At least we'll know what he's had and when. Now he's on more meds, it might be easier to keep track of." I wasn't sure why I was over explaining the chart. It made perfect sense. We weren't medical professionals, and hell, even professionals had charts to keep track of medicines. I was hurt. Will had just yelled at me, and I was dealing with it the way I dealt with most things. With endless words.

Rebecca and I got the medicines ready and started a chart. On the chart, we wrote the time, 8am, and we wrote four medicines: Oxycodone, Morphine, the laxative, and the anti-anxiety meds. These were the medicines he was to take this time around, then in two hours we'd drop the laxative but give him the other three. If he wasn't sleeping well, we'd add a heavy prescription sleep aide, even if it was morning. After we talked and planned, we were glad we'd had the conversation and made a chart. We wondered how Rebecca had kept track of it all before the chart. We actually laughed a little while making the little chart, but once we were done, a heavy quiet settled over the room. We'd been talking another ten minutes since Will last yelled at me and told me he'd be out in a minute. Rebecca looked at me and shook her head.

I ignored whatever it was she was trying to tell me and darted down the hallway. Dark. It was a dark hallway. The air felt denser in this hallway. Maybe it wasn't a well-used area of the house, but it felt weighty each time I walked down it. When I got to the parlor doors, I didn't pause, I walked in and quietly walked to the bathroom door that still wasn't fully closed. I peeked through the doorway at Will who was on his hands and knees on the tile bathroom floor. I didn't want Will to know I was so close to him. I knew he was in trouble, but if I rushed in there, I'd be in trouble too, and I knew I couldn't lift him off the floor on my own.

I quickly and quietly ran down the hall into the living room and told Rebecca where Will was, on his hands and knees. For the first time I realized the two of us were really alone, and though it might be difficult to watch over him and give him medications, we weren't equipped for just any scenario. Rebecca got on the phone while I went back to the parlor door and stayed put in the hallway catching my breath. Will didn't have to know I'd seen him. He'd be irritated, but I figured I'd just let him think I was nagging him to come out again.

Trying to control the worry in my own voice this time, I asked through the parlor doors, "Will, are you okay? Do you need help?"

Will was pissed. "I'll be out in a little while, dammit!" While he was yelling at me, I slipped back into the parlor and peeked through the bathroom door. Will was still on the floor, but he was now laying on his back instead of on his knees. He was also naked.

Without thinking much, I ran out to the living room. Rebecca was in the foyer looking out the front windows. "We need help," I said to her.

"I've called Brian. I know. I know I didn't tell you he's here. He's staying at my old house. Will had been pushing him away, so he hasn't been around much, but he's here to help. Will and us. Is Will up yet?" My heart broke again, into another million pieces. How many pieces were in my heart, and how many more would fall out at my feet before the nightmare was over?

"He's not up. And he's going to be harder to help up. He's on his back now. And Rebecca? He's naked. I'm sure he's not going to want me in there."

"He'll have to let Brian help him. He won't let me in there either."

We needed another person. If we had to carry him out of the little bathroom, we'd need another person. I called my dad.

Brian showed up before my dad got there. Rebecca had walked into the parlor to secretly look after Will. When Brian got there, we hugged, said awkward hellos, and I updated him. We decided the first thing he needed to do was protect Will and his modesty. I figured the banging I had heard earlier when I first raised my voice to let Will know we were waiting for him was when he fell. If so, it meant he'd been on the floor for more than thirty minutes. Those thirty minutes Rebecca and I spent shooting the shit, wasting time on simple topics, prepping his meds, and creating a chart, then giggling over it. I knew at that moment Brian was going to have to stay with us. If Will needed to use the bathroom, shower or dress, he'd be more likely to allow Brian to help than us; even his own wife.

I walked with Brian to the parlor where we found Rebecca sitting against the wall opposite the bathroom, but not in the light of the doorway. I sat with her and put my arm around her. Brian walked into the bathroom slowly, knocking on the door as he pushed it open enough to get in, then pulled it to again. We could hear him talking to Will.

"Hey, man. Whatcha doin' on the floor? I'm going to cover you up with your robe here, okay? And then when we get you up, we'll get this robe on you, okay, Willy Nilly?"

Willy Nilly. It was a name Brian used to use when Will was being a pushover when it came time to choose an evening with his girlfriend or his best friend. I wasn't sure it was appropriate with Will lying naked on the floor, but silently smiled at the sentiment.

I sat there against the wall, feeling the old style large baseboard digging in my lower back. It wasn't the first time I was void of emotion. I wasn't even numb. I just didn't have anything. I was nervous and scared, but those feelings were separated from the others I'd felt the past day. This was our responsibility, and we had to make decisions, all the right choices. I felt like my body didn't have time for emotions, but fear was creeping in anyway.

My dad walked into the house whispering my name. I walked out to him, hugged him, but didn't fall into his arms like I normally would have. There was no time for me, my emotions, or my needs. Will needed my Dad. Brian needed help. My dad hadn't seen Will much over the years. The last time they saw one another, Will was having 'the talk' with Dad, and now Dad was there to be part of this process. I quietly filled Dad in before we walked into the parlor room, and then he walked in the bathroom to help Brian and Will.

Rebecca and I held guard at the baseboard on the edge of the room. We could hear voices, but we couldn't really tell what they were saying. After a few minutes, I heard Will say, "I can do it!" Again, my life as a mother with young children flashed into my head. Will was angry and strong willed. He couldn't accept he had been stuck on the bathroom floor for almost an hour now, and there was no way he could have gotten up alone; or he would have by now.

More voices, questions, my dad and Brian bantering back and forth. I assumed they were coming up with a plan, but what I couldn't understand was why they just weren't getting Will out of the bathroom.

Ten minutes into their conversation, I heard a scream. Rebecca and I both jumped. It was worse than we thought. Was he hurt? Did we miss something? We had just assumed he was too weak to get up, but with a couple of guys on each side, he should be up and getting comfortable in the bed in no time.

More moaning came out of the bathroom. Another scream, and then Dad came out. He looked like he was beat already. Whatever he was seeing was affecting him like I'd never seen before.

"Girls, I'm afraid Will's skin is so sensitive it hurts him to be touched. We tried lifting him, Brian with a leg and an arm and me with a leg and arm, but he hurt. Then we tried getting under his arms, but he screamed again. He's in a lot of pain."

Rebecca started shaking through her sobs. I put my arm back around her and looked at Dad. No time for emotions, this was serious business, and I'd felt sorry for Will and for myself long enough.

"Dad, if I can get a blanket, can you roll him onto it?"

"Maybe, honey, I don't know. I'll try. Go get a blanket, and I'll tell Brian the plan."

I kissed Rebecca's forehead, squeezed her arm, and left the room. On my bed was a burgundy blanket. When I crawled into bed the night before, I was thinking I'd sleep all night every night if I had a blanket as soft. I lay in bed with it wrapped around my body before I got hot and needed to fall asleep. Its warmth filled my body, covered me, rose from under and soaked into me. I was looking forward to using it again that night. But Will needed it. More than anything, he'd need something soft on his sensitive, translucent skin.

I wrapped it around myself as if I were wrapping Will's arms around me while I walked down the two hallways leading to the parlor where Will lay waiting for something healing. I unwrapped myself and handed it to my Dad.

"I think it might be better for Will if you two gave us some

180

space. He's really hurting. He's still naked, but with the robe covering him. Well...it just might be easier for you and for him, if you left the room for a bit. We're going to try to get him out of the bathroom, but I'm not sure how far he'll let us take him." Dad looked at us sympathetically, but also with conviction. Rebecca and I had to leave and let the boys do their jobs.

I wasn't sure just how they managed to get Will onto the blanket, but Rebecca and I heard a lot of moans, crying, and screaming while they did it. I stood in the hall with my arms wrapped around Rebecca, each of us feeling hopeless, and poured all my positive energy into the ever so soft burgundy blanket. I willed it to provide comfort for Will, to warm him, protect his skin, and help him to relax. Each time I thought of the minutes reaching over an hour he lay on the floor alone, cold, hurting, and unable to help himself, my body shook and tears dropped onto my cheeks. Rebecca looked scared. When Dad stepped into the hallway and told us to come into the parlor, we looked at each other and paused, not knowing what we'd see. On the floor, Will was lying on a meadow of burgundy. His robe, also burgundy, was somehow on his body, not just covering him, but wrapped around him, providing comfort, warmth, and restoring his modesty. He looked serene. Calm even. Comfortable. Like he could just throw on a movie, pop some popcorn, and enjoy an evening of ease in his own home. Only he also looked frail. Tired. Older. His arms were thin, bearing saggy, almost translucent skin. His once thick head of hair with curls spiraling down to his ears and face at one time was also thin and wild, like he'd gone for a long and leisurely drive with his head out the window. His face was hollow and had aged several years. He was looking older than my father. He reminded me of his grandfather. It was like looking into a scrapbook of a man who was born long ago. None of him looked like Will. Not my Will.

I blinked away tears. No time for emotions. We had business to take care of there. The four of us talked about how we would get him out of the parlor, down the hallway, and into his hospital bed in the living room which now seemed miles away. We were standing over him talking about him as if he weren't there, right in front of us. It hit me he was probably lying down there, grateful, but embarrassed and worrying about the responsibility we now carried – for him. I dropped to my knees and started rubbing his hair like I did with my children when they were not feeling well. I didn't want him to feel like we were treating him like an old piece of furniture we needed to maneuver down closed spaces. He was my friend, Rebecca's husband, my old lover, my one time future, and he needed to know he was not a burden. He was still loved, and we'd do this as respectfully as we could. He was weak, too weak to move, tired from the trauma in the bathroom, probably in pain from not taking his medicines overnight.

After much thought and discussion, we decided to roll the corners of the blanket a bit and each grab a corner to carry Will down the hallway. We wanted to make sure we didn't touch him in any way. The blanket would protect his skin, and we hoped it was indeed strong enough to hold his light-weight body as we carried him. We all picked a corner, Rebecca and I at his feet and the men at his head. The rational thought was if Rebecca and I were to drop him, his head would be protected. We made our way through the parlor and gently turned the corner out of the room and into the hallway. Again I was certain I was blocking all emotion, but then, while looking down at Will, one of my tears dropped onto his robe, spreading into a dark circle. I looked up at Rebecca. Her chin was quivering, she was biting her bottom lip, trying to keep her emotions detached from the task at hand. Our eyes met, and we both lost composure. I knew Will could hear our sobs now. Rebecca's face was red and wet, her tears spilling onto her sleeves. The look we gave one another said the same thing: our hearts were breaking. This was a man we both loved. The look also said we were both committed to him, and it meant being committed to each other as well. It was exactly what Will had wanted.

Walking down the hallway, the air felt heavier than ever. Will moaned more the longer the journey to the living room took. Once we finally made it to the living room, we gently lowered him to the floor. It wasn't much space as the height we were carrying him had dropped over the time it took to get down the hallway. We talked about getting him onto the bed, but in the end, decided he was too tired, we were too tired, and lifting him that high was quite a risk. We decided to leave him on the floor until the hospice nurse came by for her morning visit. We figured it would be about an hour or more before then, and we all could use the rest.

Rebecca and I unrolled the blanket and sat next to Will, both near his head. Suddenly I felt intrusive. I looked around, and Dad was sitting on a chair nearby, Brian was sitting on the floor near Will's feet. I got up a few times and paced the room, feeling like I could hear an EMT nearby saying, "Give him some room!"

I walked to the kitchen, brought his medicines out and said to everyone, "He's been through a lot. It's way past time for his medicines. I think we should try to make him more comfortable with some morphine, maybe the others." I looked at Rebecca for help. I was trying to get Brian and Dad to back off, step away or go away, but goodness, they had just helped us out for the past two hours, and I just wanted them gone. I didn't know how to say it. "Maybe we can just give him some room?" I ended with a question of course.

Dad walked outside, probably to smoke. I didn't think he'd leave the house just yet, knowing we'd need to get Will up onto the bed, but he knew how to take a hint. Brian moved to the couch on the other side of the room.

The room grew quiet, and Will drifted off to sleep. Rebecca took the medicines back to the kitchen. We decided we'd wait until the nurse arrived for those too.

After a few minutes, he woke, angry. "I don't want to be here. I want to sleep. Just leave me alone!" He was looking right at me.

"You don't want to be where, Will? We didn't think it was a good idea to try to put you in the bed. I'm afraid we'll hurt you." I was shocked. He'd yelled again – at me.

"Stop talking to me like I'm a child! I want to go to sleep, dammit!"

Rebecca chimed in this time. "Will, it's time to take your medicine. Maybe you can take it and then go to sleep. You haven't had any in a long time, and moving you out of the bathroom was hard your body. Will you take some medicine?"

"Stop talking about me like I'm not here!" Will was still looking at me. I wasn't even talking. I didn't think I could even muster up words if I had to. I was bawling again. Caring for him was extremely difficult, but having him yell at me, be angry with me was even harder. I thought I was doing the best I could do, the best we all could do. For him. But he was still angry.

I got up, went to the kitchen, splashed water on my face, and came back with a box of tissues and his syringe of morphine.

Kneeling down next to him, I held it out and looked at Rebecca for help. I'd forgotten the ginger ale. She read my mind. "Can you pour some out first, Rebecca?"

She nodded, grabbed a tissue from the box I had, and walked into the kitchen.

"Will, can you take some morphine? It'll make you feel better, and it might even help you sleep." I could tell the tone of my voice was different, raised an octave.

"I'm not a child! Stop talking to me like I don't know anything!"

I knew I had to make a conscious effort to not talk down to him. These were still his choices after all, and I was trying to talk him into doing something I wanted him to do.

Rebecca came in with the ginger ale, and Will tried to move toward her. He winced and gave up. "Fine! Dammit. I'll take the damned shit tasting shit."

I moved to put the syringe into his mouth for him, and he snatched it out of my hand. "I'll do it!" He said, acting much like a toddler wanting to do something on his own for a change. He struggled with the syringe plunger, just as he had done the day before, and then he handed it to me. It was a huge step in accepting his own limits. I put it in his cheek and slowly squeezed the liquid into his mouth. Rebecca was quick to follow with the straw from the ginger ale can. After some noises of disgust, Will grew quiet and looked peaceful.

"Hey, girls?" Dad was standing in the doorway of the living room and foyer. "Someone's here."

"Hospice, Dad. It's probably the hospice nurse. Can you let her in, please?"

Wendy walked in and looked at Will on the floor, wrapped in a burgundy robe and lying on a big burgundy blanket. She looked at Rebecca and then me. "What're ya'll doin'? Having a picnic in here? A slumber party?" she sounded almost cheery.

We quickly told her the story, leaving out the painful details, of Will's trip out of the bathroom.

Wendy sat on the floor next to Will. "Well, well, Mr. Will. Didn't you just get yourself in some predicament? It is quite the quandary we have here. How ya feeling, dawlin'? You doing okay?" While Wendy was talking to him, she took Will's vitals and rubbed his arm, which made me flinch knowing just how sensitive his skin was, but Will didn't seem to mind. He smiled at Wendy. She looked at Rebecca and me and simply said, "So we'll just have to get him up into his bed, then."

"We carried him out here on the blanket, but we're not sure if we can lift him high enough to get him on the bed. He just took his morphine, so hopefully it will kick in pretty quickly, but he's hurting." I wasn't sure how to handle the task.

Wendy looked around. "I think the men can handle it. I'll show you how to wrap him so he's secure, and it's easier to lift him." She walked around Will, pulling the blanket up around him. As she walked around, she rolled the blanket on each side. Will was covered, with only his head sticking out. He looked like a papoose, or a burrito. After she had him covered and the sides rolled, she rolled each end of the blanket tight. Now he resembled a Tootsie Roll. Looking at my dad and Brian, she said, "Now if each of ya'll could get on each end, you should just be able to pick him right up and lift him high enough to get up on the bed. The girls and I will walk along-side of him as you get him on. We can put our hand under him if we have to, but after hearing how much his skin hurts, I only want to do it if we have to. Okay, girls?"

Rebecca and I got up and moved out of the way of the men, but stayed right next to Will and Wendy, offering our arms if they should need help lifting Will higher. My father was sixty-three years old, but he and Brian managed to lift Will higher than we all had before and slowly walked him to the hospital bed. Once they got him on the bed, Wendy worked on getting Will freed from the tight candy wrapper he was in. "He might get hot, but we'll wait a little while before removing the blanket from under him. He might move around enough in his sleep, and we can get it out easier then."

I sat on the floor next to his bed for a while after he'd settled down. Dad came by and hugged me quietly, then left. We didn't have to say anything. I could tell he was touched, hurting even, and his hug told me I didn't even have to give him thanks. It could wait, and who knew what else I might need to thank him for later. Rebecca came over and sat next to me. She held a coffee cup in each hand. "It's almost one o'clock, hon, we haven't even had coffee today. Or breakfast. Or lunch. We're not doing a fantastic job taking care of ourselves, are we?"

I took the cup of coffee. "Thank you so much, Rebecca. I had no idea it was that late."

"Wendy is just checking our supplies, and calling in his status to the central nurses' station. She reminded me to eat and told me to tell you the same thing. We'll be not much better off than Will if we can't care for ourselves too."

"You're right, Rebecca. You are right. I'm sorry this morning was so difficult. But hey, we made it. Will is no worse for the wear. Well, shit..." I didn't know what that meant, but I felt my foot being inserted into my mouth.

"He isn't, doll, he's okay, and we are doing the best we can. For him. He has to know that." Rebecca put her hand on my knee, tilted her head, and smiled at me. She was right. I was watching every word I said because it bothered me if it wasn't entirely true. The truth was Will was not okay. He was not ever going to be okay again. But I knew what Rebecca meant. He hadn't died yet, and hopefully when he did, it wouldn't be naked on the bathroom floor. We had salvaged his dignity for him, and we'd continue to do whatever we could to make the transition as easy as possible for Will. And as long as we could give him that, he would be okay.

"I think since he's napping, and since Wendy is still here, I'll go shower and get dressed. I'll be quick so you can do the same if you want. Unless...you can go first. I'm sorry, I should have offered for you to take a break." I was hesitating again and feeling selfish for wanting to shower.

"No, doll, you go shower. I'll sneak one in when you are done. I'll check on Wendy and then just sit here with Will for a while. Go relax. Why don't you take a minute and call your family? I know you haven't had a chance to really talk to them much. Those sweethearts must really miss you!"

Tears welled up in my eyes again. The whole situation was tough enough for me. Add being away from my family, and I could hardly manage to smile. "Thanks," was all I could muster.

***

Calling my family was almost as tough as the rest of the morning. Their tiny little voices fill my ears and pulled and tugged on my heart.

"Mommy! At the park today, I held a frog! We have frogs now. They were poles, but now they are real frogs. But they are still small.

186

Are you home yet?"

"Hi, Sweetie. I miss you guys so much. I hope to be coming home real soon, but it will still be a few days. Did you name the frogs?"

"No, Mommy. Frogs don't have names! Here's Bella. Byyyeeee."

"Love you, sweetie." I was talking to air.

Bella in her little tiny helium filled sounding voice told me Emily sang a 'granola-bye' to her to help her sleep the night before. "She didn't know the zoo song, like you do, Mommy, so she sang me a Granolabye song. When you home, Momma?"

"I don't know, honey. Soon." I could hear the change in her words already, and I'd only been gone a few days so far. "What's a granolabye, honey?"

"She said, 'gra-no-la-bye-gra-nola-bye, go to sleep'." Bella was singing me the lullaby her big sister had made up since I wasn't there to sing to them.

The next voice I heard belonged to Chris. "Hey, hon, we're just getting home from a playdate at the park. I've got a meeting over the phone, so I was hoping to get them set up with a movie after lunch and maybe some naps. They aren't napping well during the day, so we've resorted to watching Toy Story over and over. Sorry to put them in front of the TV so much, but they do fall asleep. How's your day going? What's the word?"

I didn't even know how to respond after my morning, but I really missed my family, and felt extremely guilty for leaving Chris with his work from home schedule and two small children. "We're not having a good day here, babe, but I don't think I want to talk about it now. Listen, you're busy, I'm sorry I'm putting this all on you. I'll just touch base with you later."

We said our goodbyes, and I found the usual comfort in a hot shower with tears streaming down my cheeks.

After an hour of showering and slowly dressing with little makeup and another pony tail, I walked back to the living room to find Will's hospital bed empty again. I looked at Rebecca and Brian who were sitting on the couch together. A question formed on my face, but Rebecca shrugged her shoulders and shook her head.

With a sigh, we started the last twenty six hours of Will's life.

Chapter Sixteen

"Where is he?" I asked Rebecca and Brian.

Brian spoke. "He got up, moaned a little, cussed at us, and walked with his walker down the hallway to his bedroom." Rebecca looked scared and angry even. They were both looking down the hallway I had come out of. Will had passed by my bedroom on his way to his bedroom.

"I'm surprised you didn't hear him," Rebecca said. "He banged the walls quite a bit on his way down. After he got quiet, I walked down there, and he was in the bathroom. After this morning, I'm surprised he's even trying again. He yelled at us a few times while he was trying to get up, wouldn't let us help him, and he walked away. I gave him a few more minutes and went back in to force help on him before...well, I just didn't want to go through all that again. But he was laying on the bed when I went back in. He's still there. Sleeping."

"Oh, goodness," was all I could say.

We all just sat there, not knowing what to do, what was coming, nor what to say to one another. After a few minutes, I realized Rebecca never got the shower she wanted and with Will, her husband, in their bedroom, she actually might not want to shower in there and risk waking him.

"Rebecca, I'm sorry. I should have been here. I called the kids and Chris, and then took a long shower. There should be plenty of hot water though, so if you don't want to go in your room, you can use the shower in my room." My room. Open mouth, inset foot. This was her house after all, how was it my room? "I just mean..."

"Oh, honey, I'm okay. Don't worry about it, I'll get showered soon. Thanks, doll." She sure did have a way of making me feel better about being there with her, in her house...with her husband.

Will napped for hours. Time seemed to stand still at times, and it seemed to fly by at other times. My watch was still set to Colorado time, so there was always the chance I had looked at my watch on one occasion and a clock inside the house on another and felt like two hours had passed rather quickly. Either way, we were on death watch, and we all knew it. Brian was there to stay, but no one made plans with him. Did he have a tooth brush, where would he sleep, how long would we all be there, together, waiting?

Every ten minutes or so one of the three of us was up, walking silently down the hall, checking on Will. We were determined to make sure he didn't try to get up and walk alone again. It just wasn't worth the risk of him falling again. There were times when Rebecca and I would sit in the room on the floor just looking up at Will on the bed. He'd rolled quite a bit in the hours he'd been there. We had been sitting with him on and off in his room, watching him sleep, just to keep watch. We'd watch him roll around, from side to side, then completely turn around and lay sideways on the bed. He'd managed to roam around the whole bed, so we stayed close, and if we weren't in the room, we checked on him often.

"He's goin' to fall out of the bed!" Rebecca said.

"I know, I don't know how he's moving so much. We should try to....I dunno, is there something we can put alongside the bed? My two year old has a railing alongside her toddler bed, you know to keep her from falling out. I wonder if we can do something like that." I looked around the room and saw big pieces of furniture and two night stands only about two inches taller than the bed itself. "Do you have extra blankets? What if we put the night stands against the bed and cover them with blankets so he can't hit them too hard if he rolls into them? I don't know if they will keep him from falling out of bed, but...well, it might help. "

We stood together, side by side, looking at Will move around more. I was amazed at his strength. For a man who was so weak, he managed to push his body all over the bed. We both moved at the same time to get the nightstands placed along the side of the bed. Rebecca opened the closet and handed me a comforter. I tucked it around the night stand, leaving room between the night stand and the bed, then padded the empty space with more of the comforter. Will moved sideways again, inching himself so he'd turned 90 degrees, lying sideways on the bed with his legs just below his knees hanging off the bed. I had to grab the nightstand I was setting up and tilt it outward so he didn't hit it with his feet. That moment was the first time I saw the tumors on his legs. I'd assumed Rebecca had been looking at them for however long he'd been sick, but the first look for me was shock. I understood why he was being so modest. His body had done more than thinned. His body was being eaten alive. I suddenly felt like I was intruding. I put the night stand back, squeezed Rebecca's arm, and left the room.

At five o'clock, Kristy and three other old friends gently tapped on the front door. Each one was carrying a large aluminum container filled with food. All I could manage to do was tilt my head, put my hands over my mouth, and cry – again.

"Rebecca, I don't know if you know Kristy, but she's a friend of mine. She and a few other friends brought us food."

Rebecca jumped up from the couch and hugged Kristy like she was a long lost friend come home. "Thank ya'll. Ya'll so sweet! Wow! Brian, look at this!"

I led them into the kitchen with their fried chicken, mashed potatoes, salads, and pasta dishes. Before I could even say more to Kristy, she was back outside bringing in bags filled with paper plates, bread, cold cuts, cheeses, fruit, and bottles of water and soda. Clearly she didn't know how long we were going to be there, but she knew somehow we weren't going anywhere either.

"I ran into your dad at 7-11. He told me something happened this morning. He didn't tell me what, but after yesterday and all, well I figured you wouldn't be heading out to stock up on food anytime soon. We won't stay, but you just tell me what you need, and I'll be here. You know that. I'll be right here." Kristy hugged me and pointed her head to the door while looking at the friends she brought with her as their cue to head on out. Their task was done, and they were leaving. I thought it appropriate as well, but just didn't know how to thank them.

The smell of food reminded us we hadn't eaten much that day. The three of us got paper plates, plastic ware, plastic cups and filled them up with soda and fried chicken and macaroni and cheese. We started to relax. Sitting around the little breakfast table in the kitchen, we even shared a few laughs. It felt good. Food, drink, companionship. It all meshed.

"It's been a little while since we've been in there, we should be with him." Guilt was taking over me. We'd been eating real food, a meal. And talking and laughing. Not talking about the events of the day, not even talking about Will.

Brian spoke up, "No, he's okay. You need to eat. Look at the two of you. You haven't eaten all day, have you?"

Thump!

We all stopped eating, looked at each other, and then jumped up. "I just said we should be with him. Dammit! We sat here and ate. Dammit!" I felt bad for saying it as soon as it came out. Brian had encouraged us to eat, because he knew it was best for us. No one knew what happened, no one knew what could have happened, but we all knew we'd let our guard down.

The three of us ran down the hall and into Will's room. One of the nightstands was tipped over on the floor, the comforters pushed off the bed and the other nightstand, and Will was sitting there with his legs hanging off the bed and his walker near him with one hand on it. His robe was open, his modesty beginning to diminish.

"Where ya, goin', Will?" Rebecca asked. He just moaned and pushed her away. I got next to him and put my arm around him. He felt like an older man. A much older man.

He yelled at us, "Leave me alone! I need to get up!"

"Okay, we'll help you get up," I said.

He flopped back onto the bed.

We didn't leave him again, but we did watch him several times roll around the bed, yell out something unintelligible and then sleep peacefully for a while. After another hour, or five hours, who knew, he rolled sideways on the bed again and began another stage of agitation. He moaned, grabbed at the wall and his headboard over and over. He inched his way to the edge of the bed. For the second time, he got his legs over the bed and was determined to get up. Sounds of fury escaped his mouth. I stood next to him. He pushed me away. His strength was astonishing.

"Aaaahhhhhhh," he said. He was angry. With his life, lack thereof, with us, with God even. He was very clearly angry. And frustrated.

Giving in, he fell back on the bed again. But within minutes, he got agitated again. It was a cycle. Rebecca and I would get close to him, Brian standing off near the doorway if we needed help. Will would push us away, yell at us and then fall backwards onto the bed again. Rebecca and I talked quietly after one cycle.

"He was in the bathroom when he fell this morning. He rushed to the bathroom in the afternoon and yelled at Brian and me on his way back here." Rebecca was thinking out loud.

"That was several hours ago, Rebecca. Do you think he needs to use the bathroom?" I looked over at Brian for help on the topic and maybe help getting Will into the bathroom. Brian nodded his head at me, but stayed where he was.

"Will, do you need to use the bathroom? We can help you get up. Brian can help you into the bathroom. You can't get up on your own. You can't get up, Will. Because we can't help you back up if you fall down," I said to Will.

Brian left the room, and I looked out the doorway wondering why he'd left us. He was our best bet of getting Will to the bathroom. It was only twenty feet or less away, surely with all the strength Will had shown, moving around the bed, with help from Brian and his walker, he could make it that far and back.

Brian came back in with a plastic urinal hospice had left. "I saw it in the room with all the supplies earlier. I knew what it was, but never thought he'd be using it."

Will was sitting up again, trying to stand. I sat next to him, and he pushed me away. He had so much force behind that push, I was almost willing to let him get up and try it. I wanted to say, 'If you're so strong...,' but I didn't. Instead I said to my lost love, "Will, I have a urinal in my hand, and I will hold it, if you need to use it. Brian and Rebecca are here, Brian can help you hold it, if you'd rather. Or Rebecca. But you can't get up. Will, you just can't get up."

Will just yelled at us and fell back onto the bed. Again.

Eventually after a few more cycles of anger, sitting up, pulling himself up with his hands on his headboard, he relaxed and fell asleep. And then he peed in the bed. More dignity gone for Will. I felt so awful. We had stopped him from visiting the toilet. We'd taken away his choices. We'd broken our own promises we'd made to ourselves.

But we knew it was what was best for him. It had to be. If he had gotten up...If he had fallen again...

Rebecca looked at me. We were both crying. "Honey, it's okay. If he'd fallen, he could have broken something. If he broke his leg or somethin'...well, he wanted to be here, in this house. He doesn't want to go to a hospital. We did the right thing. Will ya help me change the sheets?" She started laughing. "If we can get him to move now."

I tried to encourage Will to slide or roll to the side of the bed closest to the wall, the side he'd been avoiding so far in his trips all over the rest of the bed. It took me time, but I got him to the other side of the bed. We put new sheets on the wet side of the bed.

"Bed pads!" Rebecca said so quick, I almost didn't know what she'd said.

"Oh yeah, we should put those on the bed. But...," I was thinking. "If we put them on top, we save the sheets if he goes again, but the way he's moving, he'll just move them around too." I looked at Will, at the new sheets we had on half of the bed and the old sheets rolled up in the center of the bed. "Can we just put them under the sheets? If they get wet, then we have to change them again, but at least the mattress isn't wet, so we can get new sheets under him, and he won't be on a wet mattress." I wasn't even sure if I was making sense. I just knew the pads would be moved around with each roll Will made across the bed.

"Okay, can you slip them under the part you already made?"

Brian must have been listening because he was standing in the doorway with a stack of them. I took two and slipped them under the new sheets. I was still thinking it just didn't make sense to get the sheets wet and have to change them again, but otherwise, I knew the pads would just be in a ball, irritating Will or on the floor useless anyway.

It took us another hour to get the other side of the sheets changed. We didn't bother Will unless he was moving on his own. Keeping him off the wet side in the center of the bed was a challenge, but Rebecca was able to sit on the new side while he inched his way over, and I took off the old sheets and pulled the corners of the new clean sheets around the mattress. Brian was there right away to take the old sheets, and we could hear him starting the washing machine. It was good he was thinking ahead. I wasn't sure how many sets of sheets they had and how long we could keep the cycle going.

Chapter Seventeen

Will slept peacefully for a while. Rebecca and I gathered blankets and pillows for us from the other rooms and camped out on the floor next to Will's bed. We kept the medicines in the kitchen with the chart and would take turns every two hours getting morphine into his system. He hated when we woke him, but when he slept, it was mostly peaceful and, we hoped, pain free. According to the chart we kept, every four hours he got oxycodone and other things as well. I was so glad we'd decided to do the chart. I lay there in the dark wondering if Rebecca was thinking about being in their bed together. She must have been heartbroken, watching her husband up there in pain and complete discomfort lying in their marital bed alone, while she lay on the floor only near him. But then I also remembered in a selfish way the conditions of their marriage. Sure maybe they were in love, but I knew Will couldn't commit his whole heart. He never could.

Will cycled again. He grew agitated, moved a lot, rolled, grabbed his headboard pulling his body up with one weak thin arm, and bent his knees, inching himself around another ninety degrees. This time, instead of stopping at ninety degrees, his body kept turning. On his back, he'd pulled up to the headboard, with his head hitting the wood, then he spun himself a full one hundred eighty degrees until his head was facing his footboard. With his knees still bent, his feet were now touching the headboard, but it proved to be a problem when he tried to straighten out his legs. He laid still for a bit. Rebecca and I both sat up.

"Is he in the middle of the bed?" I asked.

"No, he's closer to this side, but I don't think he'll fall off. I don't think we'll be sleeping much. But at least if he falls, he has us to cushion his fall." She giggled quietly. It was nice to see we could still be human in this complete inhumane scene. We were still living and laughing, and that was a huge part of being alive. I was glad to see her able to find humor amongst all this pain.

I tried to stifle a giggle. "Let's just hope he doesn't fall." I wondered if he could hear us, if he was sleeping still or was just still. As soon as I hoped for no falling, Will's legs pushed against the headboard and his frail body went sliding down the bed, his head now heading toward the footboard. With such force coming from his legs, his body turned, and his head ended up off the side of the bed. He was looking at Rebecca, teetering between the comforts of the bed and falling on top of us. Rebecca and I both bolted to him. I stood next to his chest, willing it to stay on the bed, while Rebecca gently held his head, standing next to his chest to steady him. I was afraid to touch him. But he needed to slide back onto the bed.

"Will. You're going to fall off the bed. You can't move this way anymore," I was stern with him; almost angry myself.

"Will?" Rebecca tried to get his attention as well.

I wasn't even sure if he was aware of us, knew where he was, what position he'd allowed his body to put him in, nor what to do about it. "Will, the only thing I can think to do here is to help guide your body back onto the bed before you scooch too far off to this side. I know your body hurts, but I hope if I just slip my arms under your robe, you won't feel much. Rebecca, can you help lift and guide his head at the same time?"

"Sure, hon, let's go slow, okay? Will, you tell us to stop if we need to, okay, baby, tell us to stop." Rebecca was crying too. I didn't even realize tears were streaming down my cheeks until they began to drop onto Will's robe. Again. Crying was so second nature in those moments, we weren't even aware it was happening until the tears begin to fall on us or onto Will.

"Okay, Will. Here we go. Hey, when we're done with this, we'll get you some more medicine to help you sleep and help with any pain I cause here. I'm so sorry, sweetie, I'm so sorry. I'm going to move you now, one...two..." I slipped my arms under him, heard protest coming from him, and then lifted him as if he were just a sack of soft laundry and slid him closer to the middle of the bed. Once Rebecca had his head positioned on top of the bed and not hanging off, she and I looked at each other and sighed. We noticed Brian was standing in the doorway once Will was positioned safely on the bed.

"Everything okay? I heard voices. I must have fallen asleep, but

I'm here if you need anything."

"We're okay, Brian, thanks. Will was just moving around again and well, he tried to head dive off the bed." Now it was my turn let out a little giggle. "I'll go get his medicine. I think it's a good time for it." I squeezed Rebecca's upper arm and left the room. I did feel relieved, like we'd mounted another hurdle and passed through it with very little problem. At least for us. Who knew how much pain we'd left Will in. Something was tugging in the back of my mind again. Will was agitated. He'd been moving in his sleep again, waking easily. He probably needed to pee. I remembered the pattern and hoped we'd handle it better this time, then wondered how many chances we'd have to make it right for Will.

When I got back to the bedroom, Rebecca had his head resting in her lap just slightly elevated. He took his morphine with no problem and sipped some old ginger ale then yelled at us to leave him alone. Rebecca got up and moved to the door. We'd agreed there was no need for him to know or think we'd been lying on the floor near him all night. He'd feel like a bug in a glass jar. Violated. I put my pillow next to Will's body in an effort to keep him from rolling off the bed while we were out of the room. Then Brian and I followed Rebecca out the door. Brian reminded us he was just on the couch if we needed anything. I could tell he was not only giving us our space, but also having a very hard time dealing with all of this himself. Rebecca and I stayed in the hallway until Will stopped moving and quieted, then we placed ourselves back on the floor next to him. He was still lying in the same position, his head near the footboard. We were awake, unable to sleep for a while, but we remained quiet. Moments passed when I could hear Rebecca sniffle. I found myself doing the same. We just laid side by side; our arms linked; our lives linked. We both grew quiet. I was not sure how much time had passed when Will's moaning woke us, but we both sat up, not knowing why he sounded so horribly wounded. After jumping up, I realized I was looking for Will at the head of the bed, and it took me a moment in the dark to orient myself after waking from sleep but also to find Will. Of course he wasn't at the head of the bed, he'd been turned around before we all fell asleep. But I couldn't really see his body at the foot of the bed either. Will had fallen into the rather small crack between the foot of the bed and the footboard. He was laying sideways again and would have fallen to the floor had it not been for the footboard. We had no idea how we'd slept through all the moves he must have made to get into the position, wedged between the mattress and the footboard, and we had no idea how'd we'd get him out.

"Oh my God," was all I could muster.

"Will? Will, baby, how the hell'd ya get all the way down there?" Rebecca was already near the foot of the bed, trying to get his head up. I ran around to where the bed was pushed up against the wall and tried to see where his feet were. They weren't too far down, he was wedged, but not close to the floor. While I was on that side, I flipped on the bathroom light so we wouldn't irritate him too much, but so we could see a little bit. With the bit of light provided through the bathroom door, I could see just how wide the space was. It was definitely wide enough for him to fall to the floor if time and movement allowed. It appeared the bedframe was not actually attached to the footboard. There was an old wooden trunk at the foot of the bed leaning against the footboard. Yet another problem to face, something that may have been prevented, had we only been able to Will-proof the room before the journey started. Every time I thought of all the things we'd learned along the way, I put those thoughts in a little box as if to save them for the next time it were to happen.

"Rebecca, I think I'm going to kneel on the trunk. We need to try to lift him out. He's not all the way wedged in like I thought at first, one of his legs is up on top of the mattress, so we just need to get him to move that one while we get his upper body and other leg out. Maybe Brian could..." I looked over at the door and Brian was standing there, waiting for instructions of his own.

"I'll get his upper body if I can get under him, Nik. You stay near his feet, and see if you can get his leg out." Brian walked over, held the footboard up against his body, and pushed the trunk out of the way just an inch or two so he could wedge himself between it and the footboard and still get a good grasp on Will's upper body. I watched him bend over and put his hands and arms under Will's shoulder and ribs. He nodded at me, looked at Rebecca, and we all lifted Will out of the tight space. It wasn't as difficult as I had expected it to be, but Will screamed as soon as we all started moving him. We all paused, and for a moment, I was afraid we'd drop him back down. But he managed to move his upper leg and pull on the sheets with his exposed arm to get himself mostly unstuck. Just when we thought he was out, and we'd just have to update his medicines, fix the footboard so it didn't happen again, and wait for the next event, Will screamed. Louder than before.

"I...leg! Ahhhh." Will put his face into the bedding and moaned. At second glance, I realized he wasn't fully out of the empty space. One leg was still stuck. And that leg, at least in the semi-darkness, looked much bigger than the other leg. With Will fairly secure on the bed, Brian moved the footboard out of the way, thank goodness, his foot wasn't between the balusters of the footboard, while I, as gently as possible, lifted Will's swollen leg back onto the bed. He was secure again. Rebecca was soothing his hair, whispering to him while Brian and I moved the footboard back, secured it tighter, and pushed closer against the bed with the trunk. He was secure. But he was lying sideways across the bed again and already getting irritated with us. He started reaching for the footboard in the same grasping way he had reached for the head board earlier. He was trying to pull himself up. The first time he pulled on the footboard, we all saw the trunk push outward at least an inch. That was how he had created the gap he'd fallen in earlier. Only then we had all been sleeping through it. Again, I was struck with awe at his speed and strength. Within a few seconds he'd had the lower part of his body turned, his head up against the footboard leaving the three of us all glaring at him.

"Whatcha doing, Will?" I asked. He was still on a mission and still maneuvering himself pretty quickly. In just a few more seconds, he had his head on the other side of the bed, near the wall, and his feet were dangling off the bed near where Rebecca was sitting. Right where his head had just been when she was smoothing his hair back trying to comfort him. He managed to do all of this with the help of the footboard. It was lower than the headboard, so he was able to get more leverage and pull his body around more easily. It only took a few more seconds for him to flip himself over on to his back, and inch his way to the edge of the bed using the footboard again to pull him along.

"Whoa, big guy, where ya going?" I regretted it as soon as the words came out. I was just shocked it all happened so quickly. He was sitting on the edge of the bed. He looked worn out, like the trip there had drained him of any and all energy he'd had.

Rebecca quickly got up and moved to his left side while motioning me to sit between Will and the footboard, blocking him from using it to stand up. She got firm with him, but I could hear so much love in her voice. "Where ya goin', Will? You can't get up. If you get up, you'll fall down. We've been over this with you before. If you fall down, you'll get hurt. If you get hurt, we'll have to call an ambulance to come and get you. If they come and get you, they will take you to the hospital. Do you want to go to the hospital, Will?"

Will was irate. He pushed us both, yelling at us without using words. He turned away from Rebecca and turned in my direction. I knew it was my turn to be firm yet loving with him as Rebecca had just been. Before I could say anything, Will grabbed my face and pushed me away. I had so much respect and love for this man, and he'd just pushed me away from him – using my face to do it. I immediately got up and started crying. Rebecca looked at me with the strength I couldn't gather, and said, "Nikki! Don't. Sit down and stand up to him. He can't get up. He can't fall into the footboard again. He doesn't mean to hurt you. Please don't take this personally. He needs to you to love him, and to do that now, we have to be firm. He cannot get up." Rebecca gave me strength and energy I had lost in this fight. I realized I was about to give up. On Will. On myself. On the task. I had fallen into a young woman again. The one who let Will push her away so many years ago. Only this time I was willing to walk away from him. Will was angry with me. I hated that. But Rebecca was right. This wasn't personal. I wanted to curl up in the corner with a blanket and just cry. Instead I joined Rebecca and Will back on the bed. I held firm in my spot between Will and the footboard he'd used to get himself in that position.

"I love you, Will. We love you. We are here to help you, but we can only do so much. We can't get you up off the floor if you fall again, Will, please don't get up." I said it, but I cried with every word leaving my mouth. I knew he was listening to me because as soon as I was finished I felt his weight leaning against me. I almost sighed in relief until I realized he was trying to push me off the bed.

"Lay down. Leave me alone!" then all he had were mumbles. He pushed me again. Harder. I wasn't sure if he was trying to get me off the bed or if he was trying to lay down himself.

"No, Will, you have to lay down the other way. We need your head at the top of the bed because you fell into the crack between the mattress and the footboard before. We can't let that happen to you again." I leaned into him just as hard as he was leaning into me. I held my breath the whole time I fought because I was so afraid of hurting him. Breaking his thin skin or hitting a tumor on his leg or wherever else they may be would be devastating to us all.

Will eventually fell back onto the bed. And peed. I knew it. I had forgotten, with all the trauma with the footboard and quick movements from Will, plus the hand in my face pushing me away, he seemed to have this pattern. He'd move and become irritated when he had to pee. Rebecca just looked at me and sighed. Then she said, "He'll be out for a while now. We should have given him his medicine. I'm sure if it's not time now, it will be soon."

"Well, we have to change the sheets again. He's starting to smell like pee. I think we should try to clean him up a bit too. I don't want him to itch. Brian?" Brian was no longer standing in the room with us. I didn't know when he'd left, but he was gone.

"I'll see if the other sheets ever made it into the dryer. I'm not sure how many more we have for this bed." Rebecca left the room too. I went into the bathroom and ran the hot water, found a wash cloth, wet it with warm water, let it cool a little bit, and then went to go clean an old lover's naked peed on body. Probably something his wife should be doing, but, what the hell. Rebecca came back in the room and said Brian was just putting the other sheets into the dryer. It seemed he knew what was coming as well, but since we'd all fallen asleep earlier, they never made it out of the washer.

"How about this. Do you have two top sheets? Maybe I can make two sides of the bed, we can put pads under each side, and then when he goes again, we can try to get him to the other side. It is already dressed with a pad and a clean sheet, or half of one at least." I was thinking of all the mom tricks I had tried when my little Emily had the stomach flu the year before and couldn't keep her bed clean for more than an hour at a time.

Rebecca looked at me like I had said something completely crazy; maybe I had. None of us had gotten much sleep. Who knew what I was saying, but I did have a plan in mind. Will hadn't moved, so he was still lying on the side of the bed with his legs hanging down. I knew that wouldn't last long without discomfort, but I thought maybe I could make the other side of the bed and the top end of the side he was on, and then only have one quarter left to make. If

I did it in parts and pieces, he'd be ready to move by the time I was ready. Rebecca tossed one top sheet into the room and told me she'd be right back with another. I got to work on the opposite side of the bed. I was terrified Will would just slide to the floor while I was away from him, but before I could worry too much, Rebecca was back and standing right in front of him just in case he'd fallen.

"Were you able to clean him? I don't smell urine anymore," she said.

"Just a quick wipe. His legs were wet. I tried to get under him. I think his robe might still be wet, but I don't know. We'll just have to let that go." I had the wall side of the bed made with pads underneath. I was coming around to the top side of the bed when Will's body started to slip downward.

"Oh no. No no no, Mister! You ain't going nowhere!" Before I could even react, Rebecca had his legs in her arms and was scooting his body backwards. He was able to roll a bit on his own once his legs were fully on the bed. All of the worry and within a few moments, he was resting on the clean side of the bed. I quickly rolled the wet sheets and put a new top sheet on the wet side of the bed with bed pads placed under the sheets. But on that side I also placed the bed pads on top of the clean sheets with them tucked under the other top sheet to keep them in place. I hoped Will wouldn't notice them, and if he wet the bed again, we wouldn't have to irritate him more by changing the sheets. Over time, the seam I created between the two top sheets irritated Will, but each time he moved I was able to straighten and move it around to smooth it out keeping the top bed pads in place. I had high hopes for this new plan I had in my head for his bed.

Will was comfortable again. The bed was clean, dry, and somewhat protected. We didn't get his medicines into him, but he was resting. It was after midnight, so we decided to let him sleep and the next time he woke, one of us would get the meds ready. Until then, we rested too. As a mom who nursed two kids for over a year each, and whose children didn't sleep through the night until after they stopped nursing, I was feeling cynical about sleeping. I knew Mommy's Law, much like Murphy's Law, said as soon as I fell asleep, Will would wake up. It had been like that for years in my house, at least with my children. And would we actually sleep anyway?

I did eventually fall asleep, but only after lying in the dark, staring at the ceiling, watching the seconds tick by on Will's Epoch clock. I noted the numbers once and tried desperately to figure out what day and time it was, but I knew nothing about Epoch time. I thought I wouldn't be able to turn my mind off, shut down and fall asleep. I kept seeing Will all those years ago, his curls hugging his beautiful face, his smile, his half laugh always coming before a full blown laugh, the way he'd make fun of the way I said, "go head," instead of go ahead, and the way he'd laugh at my own silent laughs. He'd make me laugh so hard no sound would come out of my mouth, but my body would shake so hard he thought I would pass out from non-laughter. My mind did eventually fade out, and my body gave in to sleep.

When I woke again, the numbers had changed on the Epoch clock, but I had no idea how much time had passed. All I knew was Will was standing above me looking down at me and Rebecca, who was sleeping next to me on the floor. I jumped up, "Will! Rebecca."

Rebecca was already moving before I said her name. We were both at Will's side in a split second. But we had no idea what to do. Here was a dying man with no strength standing next to me, and I couldn't muster the strength to do what needed to be done. We laughed later about how we should have just pushed him backwards back on to the bed, but we never could have done such a thing. It may have turned out better than trying to let Will walk to the bathroom. He mumbled something about his walker, and we tried to talk him out of using it.

Brian was standing in to doorway with the portable urinal in his hand. "Hey, Buddy. I have the urinal right here, how about you leave your walker there and I'll just..." his voice cracked and faded. "...I'll just hold this for you."

"I have to piss, dammit, and you can't stop me." Will was very clear with his words after the mumbling moments earlier.

Will grabbed the walker from Rebecca and me with more strength we than we could find in ourselves, and he took two steps towards the bathroom. He stopped, took two more, screamed, and then took two more. He was doing it, shuffling towards the bathroom. I walked next to him, looked at Brian, and nodded towards the bathroom. Brian walked to the bathroom door to help Will inside while Rebecca and I walked next to Will and his walker.

I figured if he was determined to pee in the toilet, we should let him. Will took two more steps. Paused. And fell to the floor. He was about four steps from the bathroom door. He fell very close to a huge, heavy dresser. My stomach sank. I fell to my knees next to Will, who was on his stomach moaning.

"Rebecca, he hasn't had his medicine. Remember, we skipped..." She stopped me with a hand signal and ran out of the room. Will had fallen. He was determined, but he was still weak. I was sure he was in pain before he fell. What were we thinking? We should have pushed his ass back on the bed and given him medicine, knocked him out, and let him pee in the bed again. In trying to let him have his dignity and pee where he wanted to pee, we put him at risk of breaking something and having to go to the hospital in an ambulance. I was in shock. Again, I didn't know what to do beyond cry and apologize to Will. Rebecca came in with his meds and a small glass of ginger ale with a cut straw. Will was still on his stomach, but he'd grown subdued; almost too quiet. I put my hand on his back, thinking of all the times I did the same to my babies when they were sleeping and were turned over or too quiet, to make sure they were still breathing. I could feel Will's frail body moving under my hand. "Will, Rebecca brought your medicine. I think if we can get you on your back, we can get it into you. You need it, sweetie. You just fell, and if you're not hurting now, well, you will be...well, I'm sure you are now. Can we get you to roll over toward me?"

I think Will knew exactly what I was saying, so he put his arm in front of his chest and rolled to his side. Only he was going the wrong way. He couldn't get over to his back because he'd rolled away from me and up against the trunk at the foot of the bed. "Will? Can you use the other hand and roll this way? We can't get you on your back, the trunk is there."

"I am!" Will yelled at me. Only he wasn't.

"Brian, maybe he can stay there and roll onto his back that way, if we can move the trunk," Rebecca said. "Just remember the trunk is pushing on the footboard, so we need to make sure it doesn't pop out and hit him." Rebecca and Brian wedged a pillow against the trunk and Will's backside and pushed the trunk out of the way. Gravity took over, and Will thumped onto his back and moaned as if he'd been dropped.

"Good thinking with the pillow," I said, "The trunk might have scratched his skin, and he's so sensitive. That's why I didn't want to try to roll him myself. I couldn't imagine that thing scraping against him. Oh, man. I didn't even think about the trunk scratching him when you mentioned moving it. Oh, my God, what are we going to do now?" I was rambling again, my mouth spewing all the random thoughts swimming around in my head.

"Well, we get some of this into him, that's what we do." Rebecca sat next to me with the loaded syringe in her hand. "Come on, Will. I have them all ready here, and then you can have some ginger ale."

Will took the meds with no problems this time. I guess after skipping a dose, standing up on his own, walking half way across the room, and falling, he was ready for something to take the edge off. He took his meds with little noise and no protest, took one sip from the straw, and plopped his head down onto the floor.

We all sat there, Brian, too, who usually left Rebecca and me alone with Will once things were under control, in silence, all looking at Will. Will kept his eyes closed for several minutes. He seemed calm, and I wondered if he still had to use the bathroom. There was no way of getting him in the bathroom without hurting him, and no way he would allow any of us to help him use the urinal. I decided to let the thought go and just be prepared for any accidents he may have. Rebecca seemed to read my mind and left the room to gather more bed pads. She handed me two when she came back, and I laid them out on the floor where I thought Will might roll if he were to move again. She put the two she'd kept for herself on the trunk.

"He can't be comfortable," I said quietly. "Maybe we should try to get a blanket down so he has a softer surface. This carpet," I said as I rubbed the same carpet from so long ago, "might be scratchy on his skin."

"I'll get it," Brian left the room. I knew he'd be coming back with the same blanket he'd helped carry Will in earlier when Will had fallen in the other bathroom on the opposite side of the house. At least it was a fluffy soft blanket.

While Brian was gone, I felt tears well up in my eyes again. I watched Rebecca gently move Will's thin hair away from his face. She was so careful not to touch his skin.

"The bed," I said.

"I know," Rebecca looked at me and smiled. "We finally got it all set up, bed pads under the sheets in all the right places, sheets on all sides, ready to sleep in, and no one to sleep in it."

"Yea, that's a bit ironic, huh? We did work hard getting the bed all ready for a good nap," my voice cracked. "…and here he is, on the floor. But I was thinking the hospice bed. Do you think we can bring it in here, into the bedroom? If we can get it set up, it has the rails on it to keep him from falling out, and well, I don't know. I can't imagine it's any more comfortable than," my voice cracked again as I was thinking about their shared bed, "his own bed, but maybe it would be better than the floor. If we can get him back up, that is."

Rebecca looked down at Will for a moment, then looked at me. Brian spoke from the doorway before Rebecca could respond. He had the fluffy burgundy blanket in his arms. "It's just a roll away type bed. I think if you two can handle the bedding, I can get it folded and in here."

"I think it's worth a try," Rebecca said. "The sheets on that bed are fairly fresh. We just might want to put some of those pads underneath. But how do we get him in the bed?"

"I don't know, but let's just get it in here and set up before we worry about it," I told her.

Rebecca and I didn't move. Neither of us wanted to leave Will. Brian brought the blanket over and dropped in to the floor near where I was sitting, then walked out to see what he could do about the bed. Deciding to leave Rebecca closer to Will, I got up, spread out the bed pads she'd brought in and then spread much of the blanket Brian brought in on top of them. No matter how we handled it, Will would have to work his way onto the blanket before we could move him. Once the blanket was in place, I took the side closest to Will and touched his skin with it. It was so very soft. I wanted something comforting against his skin. I knew our touch was too harsh for him. Rebecca and I both sat there with Will and his extraordinarily soft blanket crying silent tears.

***

"Are you cold?" Will found me sitting on the beach near my house.

"Yes, it's getting chilly at night now. Fall is coming. But, look," I said, pointing to the water. *"Jellyfish are still out. The water must be warm enough for them. If the wind would die down a bit, I think I'd be okay. But yes, it's chilly out here."*

As I spoke, Will was placing a blanket around my shoulders. He stayed in place behind me, squatting, hugging me through the blanket. The blanket was soft and warm, but I got more warmth from his body heat and just having him near me.

"I don't want you to leave, Will. I don't want summer to end." I had been sitting on the beach after a short run. Running always helped me clear my head or think through things I needed to work out on my own. It hadn't helped. When I got to the beach, I sat down, pulled my knees to my chest, and with my chin resting on my knees, felt hot tears run down my face. I was in love with a boy from the city. Something I always said I would never do was fall for someone who lived here or came here to vacation. I'd made it through high school without attaching myself to the local boys. I knew it would be disappointing to my family, but I never planned on staying in a small town. I wanted sidewalks, stop lights, people I didn't know, more than one grocery store, neighborhoods, coffee shops; I wanted a city. I couldn't screw up my dreams by falling for some boy who would come there every summer and then go live his real life somewhere else.

Will hugged me through the blanket once more and then came and sat beside me. He put his left arm around me and pulled me into his warmth. *"I'm not leaving. I think I'm going to stay here and help Grandfather out this winter. I hadn't told you because I wasn't sure how you'd feel about me being here full time."* He paused looking at me. My heart was fluttering. How did I feel? *"Nikki Jay, my grandfather can use some help. He's told me of some of the marinas could use some winter help too, so I can make some money. If you don't want me to stay, I don't have to, but..."* he paused again and looked away from me at the water. I followed his eyes to a fishing boat coming in from a morning catch. What he said next almost caught me off guard. I was so engrossed in watching the boat maneuver around the buoys, I almost missed it all together. *"So it seems, Nikki Jay, I'm in love with this beautiful girl, and I can't imagine even being an hour and a half away from her. I'm hoping she can love me back as much as I love her."*

Silence. My heart beat faster. I pulled the blanket around me tighter as the wind picked up more. Staring at the boat, another tear fell from my eyes. Did I just hear what I thought I heard? Did Will just say he loved a girl? A beautiful girl? Me? I looked at Will, who gently wiped a tear from my cheek.

"I love you, Nikki. With all my heart I love you. I adore you in fact." Will grabbed the blanket where I'd had it bunched up between my hands and pulled me to him. I managed to whisper between kisses and tears. I loved him too.

***

Back in Will's bedroom I wrapped the blanket around my hands. Sitting next to Will, feeling every emotion I've ever felt but allowing none to surface, all I wanted to do was keep him safe and comfortable. The burgundy blanket felt like such a small offering, but it was all I had to offer. I couldn't get him off the floor, I couldn't take his pain away, and I couldn't even force death to take him any sooner so the suffering would end for us all. I only had a soft and warm blanket. But Will wasn't even on it. I didn't know how long it would take us, but I vowed to myself if he died on this floor, he'd at least have the comfort of his blanket with him. We had to get him to roll away from the trunk and onto the blanket, even if we never got him into the bed.

We heard Brian coming down the hall with the hospice bed. Rebecca got up to make room. She cleared the blankets and pillows we were using on the floor next to Will's bed, and Brian wheeled the hospice bed into the space.

Since Rebecca was up with Brian, helping him set up and prep the bed with appropriate bedding, I stayed on the floor, closer to Will. After setting up the bed, Rebecca came to the floor where Will and I were lying side by side. She laid down next to us. Will was still far from the bathroom, where he'd wanted to go over an hour ago, sleeping peacefully, so Rebecca and I decided to get some rest. Brian stayed in the room with us, resting on the bed made after hours of trying to get dry sheets covering the whole mattress. All was quiet for some time. Then Brian tossed two throw pillows our way, away from Will, and before I drifted off to sleep I noticed another clock in the room instead of the Epoch clock I knew I'd never fully understand. It was 2:34am. It had been a long night and was not going to get any shorter, even as the minutes ticked by.

Chapter Eighteen

At 3:16am, I woke to Will moaning. Rebecca was leaning on her elbow watching him. In the thirty minutes of sleep I had managed, I'd moved over slightly, and Will had followed. He was almost a foot closer to the bathroom door, with part of his body on top of the burgundy blanket.

"Owwww," Will moaned.

I sat up. "Will?" I looked at Rebecca, and we both looked at the bathroom. We were certain it was his bladder waking him again. Will gathered more strength during his nap, and rolled his whole body over from his right side, onto his stomach and then from his left side to his back. He was now even closer to the bathroom. I scooted myself backwards until I bumped into the tall dresser next to the bathroom door. It was a massive, beautiful piece of furniture made of dark cherry wood with ornate legs and long feet resembling lion's paws. I was sure it was an antique; probably starting with Will's grandparents. I rubbed my back where I'd bumped into the corner of the dresser and crossed my legs trying to get as comfortable as possible sitting upright in the middle of the night. I was quite used to being awake in the middle of the night, but I usually had a healthy child to care for, not a dying cancer patient. I usually had a soft and warm glider to sit in where I could put my head back and snooze while my babies rocked with me. Shaking my head, I took my heart and mind away from those thoughts. It was selfish of me to think I should be any more comfortable than I was. I was still more comfortable than Will, who was still trying to roll or scoot across the blanket. And it was too hurtful to even think of my children back home with my husband, sleeping soundly or not. They were left alone so I could be there with someone I'd loved so much so long ago, while he died. My children certainly didn't ask for that, and my heart was breaking enough without thinking of the disappointment they were facing back home. Will started using his legs to push his body, headfirst, towards the bathroom door. He was moving fast, with power I couldn't imagine he could possess. Within moments, his head was dangerously close to the corner of the dresser. One more push and his head was under the dresser, pressing against the lion leg. Just as I did with my children, I put my hand between his head and the corner of the leg. If he pushed again, he'd hit my hand and not split his head open on the hard wood. With my other hand, I grabbed the pillow I'd used during my last nap. I tried to shove the pillow under the dresser so Will couldn't get under there anymore, but he was adamant and yelled at me.

"Will? You can't go under the dresser. You could get stuck. You could hit your head," I started crying. I looked up for Rebecca, who was already next to Will pulling the blanket that had rolled with him out from under his body. She was wincing for fear of hurting him too.

Will pushed himself again, but miraculously he'd lost strength in the leg that had forced him under the dresser, and using the other leg was able to inch his head out from danger. He was still very close to the dresser leg and the sharp corner, but he was at least out from under the dresser, and safe for the moment from getting stuck underneath a large piece of furniture. One push with the other leg, and he'd be right back under there.

"NO!" Will just yelled. Then he grew quiet again. I wasn't sure why he was yelling, but my mind went back to why he was so adamant about getting out of bed to begin with. I positioned myself between Will and the dresser in hopes he wouldn't be able to get under there again. I kept one hand resting gently on the back of Will's head. His hair was so thin, but baby soft, like it must have been when he was much younger.

The room was quiet again, and when I looked at the clock it was almost 4am. Will had been on the floor for hours now.

"I've been thinking about what we should do," Rebecca said. "I don't think the three of us can lift him into bed. And I'm not even sure how long it's been since we gave him his medicines last. We seemed to be on a schedule, but then, well we just aren't anymore." She was crying again. I wasn't sure if she'd ever stopped, actually. I wasn't sure any of us would ever stop crying.

"We can call my Dad again, but I think even with him and Brian, we won't be able to lift him onto the bed without causing some pain," I said, looking at Brian, who was sitting up on the bed.

"I've been thinking maybe we should call hospice," Rebecca spoke quietly. I realized I had leaned on her knowledge and experience with Will over the months he'd been declining, and wanting to call hospice showed me a weakness in Rebecca I wasn't ready to face. I felt my stomach churn. More feelings I had to suppress because I couldn't handle reality as it tried to surface. I wasn't sure what calling hospice meant. Would they insist on an ambulance, would they bring four gentle but burly men who could lift him onto the bed, would they tell us it was over, just let him die on the floor? Putting my head down, I sobbed. Just sobbed. Rebecca left the room to call hospice.

Martha, the overnight nurse, was there within the hour. She came into the room after her quiet knocking at the front door got Brian's attention. Will had been quiet since his last outburst an hour before. He'd pushed himself against my crossed legs, and I was feeling blessed because he was so close to me, but I was also unwilling to move away from the dresser and its sharp edged legs. Part of me was hoping he chose to be so close to me, but the part of me grounded in reality wasn't even sure if Will knew I was there anymore, much less right next to him, trying to keep his head from splitting open.

Martha sat down next to me and Will motioning Rebecca to sit with us. Will was still sleeping, so she looked around at us, smiled, and said, "It looks like it's been a rough night? How long has he been lying here like this?"

I thought right off the bat I wasn't going to like her. She had no idea what we'd been through those past few hours. I was wrong. Before she even allowed us to answer, she began checking Will's vital signs. She was tender, she was quiet, and the look on her face told me she knew everything we'd been through. After checking vitals, she asked if Rebecca and I could talk with her in the living room while Brian waited with Will. But before we went, she spoke to Will in a loving and calm voice. "Will, darling, I'm not sure how you got to this floor, but I can't imagine it's very comfortable much at all. Now, we're gonna get you up, but not just yet. Is there anything else I can do for you right now?" She placed her hand near his arm without touching him. I could tell she knew he was hurting, and a simple touch would be excruciating for him.

"Yes," Will said clearer than anything he'd said all night. "I want you," he said while he put his hand over my face and pushed on me, "to get THIS away from me, dammit."

I put my hand up, but didn't grab his hand. He kept his hand covering my face for a moment while I stifled a sob, then pulled away from me. I just got up, but since I was worried Will would still hit his head, I made Brian sit where I had been sitting and slowly followed Martha and Rebecca out of the room.

"His time is near, my dears. He won't live much longer," Martha said quietly. She put her hand on both of our arms for comfort, as if the pressure of her hand on our arms would take away the pain her words brought us. We knew our situation couldn't last forever, much longer even, but we didn't feel the need to hear it out loud. Martha asked us a few questions about the past few hours, and we all decided we needed to get him into the hospice bed. Just as quietly as she shared unwanted news with us, she left the room, leaving Rebecca and I hugging and crying into each other's shoulders.

We were somber as we walked back into the bedroom. There'd be plenty of time to cry together, but we knew we had to help move Will to the hospice bed Brian brought in the bedroom. Martha helped us make another bedroll, and we all lifted him up and, as quickly and quietly as we could, placed him over the flower sheets on the hospice bed.

Rebecca checked the sheets on their bed, looked at me and said, "Well, the bed is all set, with nine pads, clean warm sheets, and no one to sleep in it."

I looked down at the bed and sighed. "We'll sleep in it. And hey, we can even pee in it if we need to." She laughed, and we hugged again. Rebecca and I were bonding. She grabbed my hand and pulled me down on the bed, where we both lay with our heads at the foot of the bed; exactly where we'd fought Will not to lay for what seemed like hours.

Brian and Martha were in the kitchen. Will was breathing. Long but slow breaths. He'd inhale deeply for longer than I was sure I could inhale, then he'd make no sound exhaling. There were times I wasn't even sure he was exhaling.

Rebecca and had I started to drift to sleep when Martha popped her head in. She smiled, then walked over to Will where she started working again checking vitals, listening for longer than normal at his breathing and heart rate. She whispered to us, "He's not here right now." And then she came to sit on the bed next to where we were laying. Still whispering, she said to us while holding onto our hands, "I'd like to talk away from him normally, but he's not with us right now. There will be stages of death you will watch him take. He may not respond to you again, but he may. He may get up again, exert all of his energy, and fall again. Or he may open his eyes and look at you, or he may squeeze your hand. There's no way of knowing. And there's really no way of knowing if what I believe is true, but I'm sure with the morphine he just had and the exertion of energy he's put in this night, he's at least unconscious if not visiting elsewhere. Now, I can't get into religion with you, but I think no matter what you believe, we go in and out, here and there, wherever it might be, until our body is done and fully shuts down. Maybe he's visiting a light, maybe he's saying hello to loved ones, maybe somewhere in our minds we know to come back every now and then to be with the ones we love. The ones we'll be leaving behind. You might see that. But his time is near, my dears. He won't be with us much longer now. I'm very sorry I can't say more to comfort you. I hope you can care for yourselves, care for one another, and remember what you are doing here is to see him to wherever he is going."

She didn't say another word, just looked at us. Both of our faces were covered in silent tears constantly flowing. Martha got up, retrieved a tissue box from the other side of the room and kissed the tops of our heads before she walked out. After a few moments, I could hear her talking to Brian, but Rebecca and I never saw her again. That woman was tossed into our lives, said some profound things to us, kissed our heads, and walked right back out of our lives. Her words would always be with me, and I think I would remember them if I were ever with a loved one during a similar kind of journey.

Rebecca and I lay on the bed together holding hands, crying in silence. At 7am, I sent Liza a text message, "It was a rough night."

She replied, "Should I come?"

"Yes, you should come soon. Please call Dad."

Liza showed up within twenty minutes. She hugged us and told us she'd be around all day if we needed her. She brought me a cup of coffee and Rebecca a cup of green tea from the 7-11 down the street.

"Your dad says he'd rather remember Will the way he was, not the way he is now."

I think I was the only one who saw the irony in his choice of words since Dad didn't really like Will when we were together, but I figured they'd developed some kind of friendship or tolerance over the years living together in the same little town. I also thought maybe carrying Will in the blanket may have been a bit traumatic for my father. It certainly wasn't easy for any of us. Including Will.

"I didn't think he'd want to be here. I just wanted him to know." I hugged Liza and cried again.

The house filled over the next hour with friends. People brought food into the bedroom, and people stopped in to give Rebecca and me hugs and to say hello. The town was on death watch. No one spoke to Will. I don't even remember anyone else looking at him. Rebecca and I wouldn't leave his side. Liza and Brian came in together after a few hours, looking like they'd had a long talk together.

"We're going to stay in here with Will, girls, and we want you to go take a break." Liza said so timidly I felt she was asking permission.

"I'm not leaving him," I said firmly. "But you can go get my phone, I'd like to put some music on and maybe check my messages. It's in the guest room."

I didn't move an inch or look at anyone, but I saw Brian slink out of the room. Liza sighed and left, and Rebecca looked at me, took my hand, and said, "I appreciate you being here. I think I might take them up on their offer and take a shower."

"Oh, honey, it's fine. I'm okay. They don't need to stay in here. I'll stay, and Will is...Will is fine." How could I say Will was fine? Did I mean Will was dying just the way he should be? Will was not trying to walk across the room, and hey, look it had been hours since he'd even tried to pee, in the bed or not. I just smiled. "Why don't you go get something to eat and take a shower? Maybe I'll grab a sandwich after you take care of yourself. Maybe I'll try to nap for a bit."

Rebecca stood at the side of Will's hospice bed, stroked his thin skin a moment and walked out of the room. Liza passed her on the way in with my cell phone, a bottle of water, and sandwich for me.

I took the bottle of water from her hand and nodded toward the end table Will had pushed over several hours ago. Looking at it, I remembered it was the last time I had eaten, and none of us finished our meal. It all seemed so long ago. We'd all been through a rough night, and I couldn't help but think we'd all grown a lot too.

I looked at the clock as Liza found a home for the sandwich she knew I didn't intend on eating any time soon. The epoch clock was the only one I could see while watching Will, and it said 1402109182. I hadn't a clue what all those numbers meant. Liza quietly left the room, leaving me alone with Will, my thoughts, and a clock that couldn't communicate with the likes of me. The silence was deafening. Will would take those long deep breaths, inhaling and wheezing, and then he'd grow silent. I started counting the seconds. One...two...three...four...five...my phone was in my hand. I opened the bright pink cover and saw it was 2:47pm. Saturday, 2:47pm. I found the Pandora app on my phone and played my *Singer Songwriter* station. It was a mix of music from the 60s and 70s. Music Will and I used to listen to together. Usually when I started the station, it started with a simple folk song. I laid on the bed, tears streaming down my face. Several seconds had gone by again before I realized I was counting the seconds again between Will's breaths.

Six...Seven...Eight...Nine...Ten...Eleven...Twelve...Thirteen ...Fourteen...Fifteen...

Sixteen...Seventeen. Inhale

I found lack of sound and the counting relaxing, and I was able to lie on Will and Rebecca's bed looking across the space to Will breathing in his hospice bed. I remembered the conversation we had with Martha earlier; another thing that seemed lifetimes ago. Since getting Will into the hospice bed in his bedroom, he hadn't moved. He hadn't struggled to get up to go to the bathroom, his sheets were dry, and he hadn't opened his eyes at all. For the last several hours his mouth had been wide open and dry. The thought got me up looking for Vaseline or something to soften his dry lips. I found a tube of lip balm on the bathroom counter and went to his side, sitting up on my knees on the floor next to the bed.

"Will?" my voice cracked. "Your lips are very dry. I'm sorry we didn't notice before. But I'm going to put this on your lips." I couldn't stop the crying while touching his lips. "I'm so sorry, Will, I'm so sorry." I was not even sure what for, but God, my heart was breaking. Yet I couldn't feel a thing. Not a thing. Maybe it was emotion overload, I didn't know. I didn't know what else to say, and the music coming from my phone didn't allow room for me to speak. The song from the little speaker seemed to fill the room, leaving no space for thought, movement, or motion. Except, I saw it! Will's little finger moved. It lifted ever so slightly. Paul Simon played over Pandora Radio and brought Will back to me, to his home, to this world, even if only for a moment. He flickered here and then left again. I sat there holding his hand, singing the song as hard as my cracked tear-filled voice could. And when the song ended, I began counting again.

Inhale

Six...Seven...Eight...Nine...Ten...Eleven...Twelve...Thirteen ...Fourteen...Fifteen...

Sixteen...Seventeen...Eighteen...Nineteen...Twenty...Twenty-One. Wheeze, inhale.

The moments between his breaths were getting longer. His mouth hadn't moved at all, it was still wide open, but not as dry as before. Staring at his hand, I willed it to move again, and I began to think I had imagined it, but I was certain he'd moved. Maybe I was dreaming, but no matter what, I would believe I saw it. I just wished I had felt it too, but my hand was on his lips, trying to bring him comfort. I knew I was right. I had to be right. He'd moved. Maybe he was responding to my touch. Maybe he was responding to the moisture on his lips, but I liked to believe he was responding to a song that meant a lot to us in our relationship so long ago. He was letting me know he was still there and not ready to give up just yet. Or ready to leave maybe, because there was no fight really, the giving up had already taken place. I heard other artists we had enjoyed together so long ago playing on the radio. James Taylor, John Denver, Carole King, Jim Croce all filled the sad space through my phone. I started talking to him. I couldn't lay back down. He was here, and I had to feel him again.

"Will. Will, if you're still here..." I could no longer keep my voice from cracking when I spoke. "I'm glad you came back. I know you did. I just know it. Thank you. Thank you for coming back. For giving me a chance to see you again. Oh, goodness. Thank you, Will, for even asking me to be here. For everything, for telling my dad, for working this out with Chris, for needing me to begin with.

For all those years of friendship and true love. That's what we had, true love. The kind of love that didn't need nurturing, building, coddling. We had that. It just was. It was free. It was pure, and it's what I long for again. I'm sorry for all of those years I've missed. I'm sorry we both gave up. I wish you hadn't been so selfless and let me decide my own fate, my own future." I took a deep breath and realized this was it. Emotional overload was coming to a head, and I was getting it all out. I was angry. Pissed off. At God, at Will, and myself. Maybe even at Chris because he wasn't everything I'd dreamed of. I was hurt. I was losing not only a lover I'd never stopped loving, but also my best friend. The one person I could call night or day and empty my heart to, dump everything that lay on my shoulders, and cry or laugh until my face hurt. I put my head down on the thin mattress, leaving my hands on his arms. Music was still pouring out of Pandora. Music we'd fallen in love with, and the music that became the soundtrack of our love together. Emotions filled the air.

One…Two…Three…Four…Five…Six…Seven…Eight…Nine …Ten…Eleven…Twelve…Thirteen…Fourteen…Fifteen…Sixteen …Seventeen…Eighteen…Nineteen…Twenty…Twenty-One…Twenty-Two…Twenty-Three…Twenty-Four…Twenty-Five…I had taken three breaths in the time Will took his one long inhale and slowly, silently, let it out.

"I could probably go on forever, Will. Thank you. But," it took me one…two…three seconds to find my voice again and stop the sobs from overwhelming my speech. "But you don't have forever. So I think I need to say a few things before forever comes for us." I sobbed again, took three more seconds to find my voice and began again. "We'll be okay, Will. Rebecca will be okay. You picked a good one there. She really loves you. She's hurting, but she's also brave. She's amazing. I'm not sure I could have ever walked into this knowingly. She did. But she'll be okay, too. I'll be okay. I have two beautiful children, Will. You saw them. I miss them so much. It's so surreal to think of my life in Colorado. With my children, with Chris…my family. I feel like I am exactly where I am supposed to be right now. Here, with you. I can't even begin to imagine the emotions I will go through once I drive away from here, unable to call you to keep me awake, to laugh at the random chickens I see on the side of the road in West Virginia." I paused to allow more tears to surface. "I wish you could laugh with me. Chickens on the road in West Virginia. Who else is going to ever get that? It was just you and me on that road trip." I couldn't control the tears anymore. I lifted my head more, looked at Will's open mouth, moved my eyes up to his closed eyelids, and watched. I was hoping to see movement, recognition, something I might see if he were sleeping and dreaming.

"Do you remember that, Will? How in God's green Earth did we get your Volkswagen up and down those West Virginia Mountains? What the hell were we thinking? This is a great idea! Let's drive to bumfuck West Virginia just to see what's it's like out there, have lunch, and drive back! We were lucky we didn't have to wait for my dad to drive seven hours to rescue us! Oh, man! That just reminds me of all the stupid shit my kids are going to do – and get away with! Hmph." Silence took over me again. Will inhaled.

One...Two...Three...Four...Five...Six...Seven...Eight...Nine ...Ten...Eleven...Twelve...Thirteen...Fourteen...Fifteen...Sixteen ...Seventeen...Eighteen...Nineteen...Twenty...Twenty-One... Twenty-Two...Twenty-Three...Twenty-Four...Twenty-Five...Twenty-Six...Twenty-Seven...Twenty-Eight. Wheeze. The death rattle. Wasn't that what someone had said the day before? Had it just been the day before? I was so tired. Saturday. 3:24pm, 1402111461.

John Lennon was playing from my phone. "Will, I guess I just need to say we all love you. I love you. Rebecca loves you. Brian loves you. The people in this town all love you. I don't even know who is here, but I know people have been coming by all day. I think they want to show you respect, so they haven't been coming in here, but they love you. They also want Rebecca and me to know they are here for us. We will all be alright. We will. We will miss you so much, but we'll be alright. We'll move forward. We'll think of you each and every day, maybe even every second of every day, but, Will? You can let go." I said it. I knew I had to. I wasn't sure what Will needed to hear. Or if he was even listening, but I was done talking. I gave him permission to let go, but all I was really saying was to myself – he could let go.

One...Two...Three...Four...Five...Six...Seven...Eight...Nine

...Ten...Eleven...Twelve...Thirteen...Fourteen...Fifteen...Sixteen ...Seventeen...Eighteen...Nineteen...Twenty...Twenty-One... Twenty-Two...Twenty-Three...Twenty-Four...Twenty-Five...Twenty-Six...Twenty-Seven...Twenty-Eight. Inhale.

I kissed his cheek, gently smoothed his thinning hair back away from his face. I could still see his curls. He looked so much older than he really was. Cancer was a bitch indeed. It took away his dignity, his beauty, and it was taking him away too. A tear of mine dropped onto his face. He didn't flinch. More fell from my cheeks. I wiped them from his grey, almost translucent skin, and kissed him again before laying back on the bed and starting to count again.

One...Two...Three...Four...Five...Six...Seven...Eight...Nine ...Ten...Eleven...Twelve...Thirteen...Fourteen...Fifteen...Sixteen ...Seventeen...Eighteen...Nineteen...Twenty...Twenty-One... Twenty-Two...Twenty-Three...Twenty-Four...Twenty-Five...Twenty-Six...Twenty-Seven...Twenty-Eight. Inhale

One...Two...Three...Four...Five...Six...Seven...Eight...Nine ...Ten...Eleven...Twelve...Thirteen...Fourteen...Fifteen...Sixteen ...Seventeen...Eighteen...Nineteen...Twenty...Twenty-One... Twenty-Two...Twenty-Three...Twenty-Four...Twenty-Five...Twenty-Six...Twenty-Seven...Twenty-Eight. Wheeze and inhale. I thought next time I should maybe count how long it took him to actually inhale. I was counting the silence before he exhaled, the time his body was just doing what it naturally did. Survival mechanisms automatically kicking in because he was still alive. Next time I would count how long it took him to take an entire breath while his lungs were filling.

***

One...Two...Three...Four...Five...Six...Seven...Eight...Nine ...Ten...Eleven...Twelve...Thirteen...Fourteen...Fifteen...Sixteen ...Seventeen...Eighteen...Nineteen...Twenty...Twenty-One...Twenty-Two...Twenty-Three...Twenty-Four...Twenty-Five...Twenty-Six...Twenty-Seven...Twenty-Eight...Twenty-Nine...Thirty...Thirty-One...Thirty-Two...Thirty-Three...I sat up and stared at Will. Thirty-four.

***

Thirty-four seconds. Rebecca walked in the room just as I was flying off the bed to Will's side.

"Nikki? Why don't you take a break?" Rebecca said to me as she came in.

I looked up at her, horrified. Thirty-four seconds. I didn't know how many had gone by since I stopped counting, but I did know his wife missed his last breath by that last second.

"I..I…" I fell to the floor.

"What?" Rebecca came running over to me.

"Thirty-Four seconds," was all I could say.

Rebecca looked at Will. She couldn't tell all the things I could tell. His breathing had been so silent for so many hours, she couldn't tell.

"I was counting his breaths. He was taking so long," I sighed, sobbed, buried my face in my hands. "He's gone. I counted to thirty-four, and I knew. Rebecca, he's gone."

She fell to the floor next to me and started crying as hysterically as I was. Both of us sat staring at Will. Watching. Waiting. Listening. To nothingness.

"Kenny Loggins," I said looking at my phone. "*Celebrate Me Home*. On the radio. Rebecca, I'm so sorry. You should have been here. I should have come to get you. I had been talking to him. I told him we all loved him." My body was shaking, but I had to tell her about his last few moments. "I told him we would all be okay, and he could let go. I should have waited until you were here to say all of those things. I'm so sorry." I just kept my face in my hands and tried to calm my own breathing. "I played music for him. I don't know what he would have liked, so I picked a station of artists we used to listen to together. Rebecca, I think I saw his finger move once when one song came on. I talked to him, and then I thought I'd just ramble on and on, so I laid down and started counting the time between his breaths again. He'd gotten to twenty-eight, but once he got to thirty-four, I just knew."

Rebecca was crying so hard she was shaking as much as I was. I felt responsible. Like I had pushed Will right off his death bed and into Heaven.

She put her arms around me and smoothed my hair. "Oh, doll, you don't need to apologize. It's okay. You were here. He wasn't alone. He was with someone he loved, someone who loves him.

That's what he wanted. I knew when I took a break I might miss something. I guess I didn't think it would be this quick. Now. This afternoon, but I knew it could happen at any time. And," she lifted my face with her hands to look into my red runny eyes, "You played him music. I don't know why none of us thought about playing music to begin with. It must have brought him such comfort. But once you were alone and all was settled and quiet in here, you were able to give him what he needed. Music took a journey into his soul, doll, and it helped his soul journey right on out of here too. You did that for him. And Kenny Loggins! What a blessing that one is. He loved that song." She let out a small laugh.

I hugged her back and got up. I kissed Will's cheek, touched those curls for the last time, and looked at his wife. "I'm so sorry," I said. "I'm so sorry. The least I can do is leave you alone for a bit. I'll let everyone know." I stopped at the door and said, "Unless you want to let everyone know. I'm so sorry, Rebecca, I feel like I am taking every opportunity away from you. How about I just go sit in the guest room, and you talk to all of your guests when you're ready."

Rebecca nodded. Her tears were falling harder than just moments before. I walked around the hallway trying not to peek into the spaces of the house that held so many people waiting the news of Will's passing. It reminded me of a maternity ward waiting room, everyone patiently awaiting news of new baby arrivals. Only no one was there to welcome life. We were all there to say goodbye to an entire life, to a friend, to someone we all loved. I fell onto the bed in Will's guest room and sobbed. It was over. He was gone, in thirty-four seconds.

Chapter Nineteen

The next several hours were a blur. People gave us hugs and condolences. People I must have known at some point in my life told me to let them know if I needed anything, and then all the people left the house. Once the house was empty, I couldn't think of one single person I recognized from my past life there other than Liza, and I noticed Kristy lingering in the background. I kept thinking of all the times I hugged someone who had used my name in our conversation, yet I didn't know anyone. I didn't belong there. It was obvious. My life there ended with Will, and I needed to start thinking about those who did await me back home in Colorado.

The house was just regaining its silence when the funeral caddy pulled up. I had almost forgotten Will was still lying alone, on those flower sheets in a hospice bed in his own bedroom. I made myself scarce after sitting with him for a few minutes. I'd said my goodbyes, given him permission to leave me, to leave us, and for us to move on, so I had nothing to say to his body. I kissed my fingertips and placed them on his forehead, then walked away. From the guest bedroom, I could hear the funeral director talking to Rebecca and Brian about how they would handle the body. At those words, my tears gave up the fight to stay within my eyes and fell down my face in torrents, like a welcomed spring rain. They were going to dress Will and move him out on a stretcher. Then he'd be gone from his house, the place he loved. He'd be buried at Philippi Church in town, where he'd purchased one plot and had already ordered his headstone. It would have song lyrics from a song he'd written imprinted on it, but I wasn't sure which one or if I'd even recognize it after all those years apart. I imagine he'd written a lot of songs. The house grew quiet again, and I assumed the funeral director was in Will's room, while Brian and Rebecca were probably in the kitchen. If they were, the medicine log and all the medicines were sitting right in front of them on the small kitchen table as if they needed yet another reminder of the past several days. I sent Chris a text to let him know Will was gone, but I still wasn't sure when I'd be heading home. Then I quietly cried myself to sleep.

After sleeping only two hours, I woke with a dry nose and puffy eyes. I quietly walked out into the living room where Rebecca was sleeping on the couch and Brian was sitting in a chair staring out into space.

"Hey, you," Brian said. "Did you get some sleep?"

"I guess I did. More than I thought I would, I guess. How are you feeling? You should find some sleep too. Do you want to go lie down in the room I was in?" I rubbed my eyes and reached for a tissue box nearby.

"No, I'm okay. I'm, uh…" Brian sighed. "I guess I'm spent. I'm exhausted, I'm sad, and I'm angry. I don't think I can sleep. Do you want something to eat?"

Brian was the unsung hero of the whole situation, and his role was truly coming to light in that moment as I looked at him. He had been with us when we needed him, gave us space when we needed it, did the manual labor us girls needed a man to do, and I wasn't sure if we'd even asked him how he was doing.

"Brian? Do you want something to eat? You've taken such great care of us, and of Will, and, well," I started crying again. "I don't think we've properly thanked you. If we ever said the words, it wasn't enough. What can I do to care for you right now? Do you need some food? Some coffee, a soda?" I wiped my tears from my eyes and cheeks and walked over to the chair where Brian sat.

"I don't want to eat, but thank you, Nik. Thank you." He put his head back and closed his eyes. We all felt the same; spent, exhausted, sad, angry, and probably unable to process anything with any sound reason.

I picked the other straight back chair in the room and sat down with my phone in hand. I had only texted Chris earlier to tell him the news, but I hadn't checked my messages since. Chris had responded with, "I'm so sorry, honey. We miss you a lot around here, maybe hearing all about Goon-Goon will lift your spirits. Call us when you can. We are all home." Looking at my watch, I realized it was about dinner time in Colorado, so I quietly walked back into the guest room to call my family.

"Mommy!" I heard as soon as the phone was answered. This

time the tears welled up in my eyes began their journey down my face.

"Emily, hi, sweetie! How are you?" It was all I could get out before sobbing. I had left my children to watch a man die. In that moment, I wasn't sure which hurt worse.

"Mommy. We went to the toy store! Daddy bought Bella a new blankie! She can't find her soft blankie, so I got a new Bunny! Oh, Mommy, she's so pretty. See her? She's all fluffy and pink and look at her long ears. Oh, Mommy, I just love her so much. And she's Goon-Goon's new bestest friend in the whole wide world. They play together all the time. They are so funny. Goon-Goon just laughs at Flip-Flop all day long. Goon-Goon is a girl you know, Daddy keeps saying 'him!' I have to tell HIM all the time that Goon-Goon is a HER, and now she has a new best friend."

There were several seconds there I was glad Emily went on and on because I couldn't find my voice again. I'd never felt so far away as I did in the moment my daughter was trying to show me her new stuffed bunny over the telephone.

"Did you say the new bunny's name is Flip-Flop?" I asked Emily.

"Yes, Mommy. She has flippy floppy ears, but I made it shorter and named her Flip-Flop. Isn't she so pretty, Mommy? When are you coming back home? Before bedtime?"

"Oh," my voice squeaked. "I bet she's beautiful, honey. I'm not sure when I'm coming home, but no, not before bed time tonight. I'm sure it will be soon though, maybe a few more days?" I had no clue when I was going to leave Virginia and begin the 1800 mile drive back, but I was certain it had to be soon.

"Honey, I love you so much," I couldn't stop the tears from flowing. It hurt being away from her, and it hurt talking to her. "Is Daddy nearby, can I talk to him? And will you please give Bella a big hug from me?"

"Sure, Mommy. Bye, Mommy, miss you!"

"Nikki?" Chris started with a soft voice.

"Hey, Chris." Everything I had left my body the second I said his name. I couldn't speak again. There was no sound, no emotion, no feeling, my senses weren't coming to the surface. My mind and body didn't register a single thing. No dust particle in the air, no breeze whispering through the house.

"Nik?"

Heartbeat.

Thump. Thump.

Thump. Thump.

My senses were starting to come back to me. I couldn't hear my heartbeat, but I could feel it. A beating reminder I was still among the living. Without Will.

"It's done. He's gone," I whispered to my husband from 1800 miles away.

Chris sighed. "I'm sorry, hon." He sighed again. "I'm not sure what else to say. Are you okay? How about Rebecca? How's she doing?"

"Chris, I can't talk right now. I have to go. I love you. I'll call you later." I hung up. Just like that, I ended a conversation with my husband without waiting to hear his response or giving him a chance to say goodbye.

Chapter Twenty

The hours belonging to the next two days seemed to fly by at times and stand still at others. I spent the rest of my days away from Will's house, trying to help Rebecca from the comfort of my father's house. It was nice to spend time with my family. Natalie was very kind, and brought meals to me and Dad. Nana asked a lot of questions I didn't want to answer. But mostly I sat in quiet with my dad.

"When is the funeral?" my father asked one morning while we were having coffee on his back deck.

"It's tomorrow," I said calmly and quietly. "Dad?"

When I looked up, I could see him looking at me. "Nikki, I'll go with you. If you'd like me to, that is. I know Chris can't come out here for a funeral. You probably shouldn't be there alone anyway. I guess his wife will have her family around."

"I talked to her. I think they are a little upset at her. She just told them about the marriage arrangement. I guess they don't think she should have married just so someone isn't alone when they die. They think she should have married for love."

"I married for love. It wasn't all it was cracked up to be," Dad laughed. My parents' marriage hadn't survived much beyond my own toddlerhood. Mom lived in Florida. We didn't see her much. Dad had raised my sister and me, and his family was always around. Mom was some corporate big wig, selling south Florida real estate.

"I married for love, too, Dad," I said. "It's been a great choice for me. I actually don't think I could do what Rebecca did. She actually loved Will. Maybe he loved her, too. But she knew what she was getting into." I paused and thought about the past few days. I thought about my last statement. "Well, maybe she didn't know everything she was getting into. But she knew she wasn't getting into a lifelong marriage. Shit. Did I just say life long? She was with Will for the rest of his life, wasn't she?" I dabbed my wet eyes, thinking of Rebecca. I'd had such dislike for her over the past several months, thinking she'd pushed Will and me apart.

"Yeah, maybe she didn't know how it would all end, but she did sign up for something the rest of us aren't privy to; knowing our spouse will die, and it will be sooner than anyone would be ready for. I guess there is some nobility there." Dad plucked a cigarette from his shirt pocket and twirled it between his fingers.

"Will you go with me, really?"

"Of course, Buttercup. I don't have a suit though. And you know I hate funerals. So if you are okay with me just wearing a button down, I'm good with driving you up there and standing with you. I'll even iron the shirt," He got up, squeezed my shoulder and lit his cigarette as he walked away. Even without my children around me, he wouldn't smoke in front of me anymore.

"Shit!" I exclaimed.

"What?" Dad turned around at the bottom of the steps to see what had gotten me. I was sure he was thinking some very tiny spider had crossed my path or something similar.

"I need a dress. I'm going to run down to Newport News real quick. I'll be back for dinner," I said. But then I laughed. Real quick and going to Newport News from Deltaville didn't connect somehow. Newport News was an hour away. But at least I was alone and knew where the mall was. A simple black dress should be fairly easy to find. Maybe I'd have a chance to stop at Dunkin' Donuts on my way back. They were Dad's favorites, and I was Dunkin' deprived in Colorado.

I watched Dad walk around his property just so he could enjoy a smoke alone. Then I called Chris and my girls.

"Mommy. Volcanoes killed the dinosaurs. Daddy got me a new dinosaur book, and there's a picture of them right inside. It was a volcano. I remember the man at the museum told us it was a spaceship!"

I laughed. My girls were growing so quickly, changing so fast, and I was on the other side of the country missing it.

We spoke for a few more minutes, and I told everyone while they were all on speaker phone I would leave the day after the funeral. I'd take the rental car across the country and drop it off in Boulder. I flew out and figured I'd fly back home, but I hadn't counted on having things to bring home with me. I promised my girls I'd be home within four days. Chris wanted me to promise to stay at least one night on the road.

"I love you all, and I'll see you all real soon, okay?"

More tears streamed down my face. I hadn't expected to be there so long, and I hadn't expected to not talk to my babies several times a day. The past few days I'd only spoken to them once. I needed to get back to my life, but something nagged in my mind. I had my own journey to make across country. Right after I watched some strangers put Will six feet under.

Chapter Twenty-One

Dad and I showed up at the funeral home about fifteen minutes before services were to start. The funeral home had a separate room for family, and I had been on that side of the room more over the years than in the public room. The family room had angled wooden slats so people inside the room could look out into the main room where guests spoke at a high podium, the casket lay in waiting, and the crowd dabbed their eyes with tissues. But the way the wooden slats tilted, the public audience couldn't see the family. It was built for privacy. Wives often cried so hard their makeup would run down their cheeks, and they'd be rushed out a back door to freshen up before greeting the crowd. Rebecca decided not to use the family room. I was happy to know of her decision beforehand, as I had been afraid she'd ask me to sit in there with her. But then I wondered who else would be there in the private room. Will's family were his friends. Local people he'd grown fond of over the years. Once his grandfather passed away, he had no other family. No cousins, no one to leave a legacy, no one to sit behind the privacy wall. Except his wife.

Rebecca was in the receiving room when we walked in. She hugged us, asked us to sign the guest book, and told us where she would be sitting. I walked into the room and thought my knees would give out. I sank about an inch before Dad grabbed my arm and led me to a seat about three rows behind the first row where Rebecca had indicated she'd be sitting. Neither of us were sure if she'd told us because she wanted us near her or if she told us so we didn't take her seats. I hoped her mother or someone from her family would be here for her and decided if no one sat in the front row, then Dad and I would move up there to be with her. Despite what her family thought of her decision to marry a man she knew was dying, she did something for him not many people could do. And it was damn hard. She deserved company and support at this time.

Once we were seated, I started looking around. His casket was sitting in the front of the room. I imagined our flowers were up there amongst the several standing near the casket. Chris had ordered flowers with my name and his name on the card. I would have forgotten otherwise. On either side of the casket almost hiding behind two large arrangements were easels with large photographs of Will. The one on the left was Will on his grandfather's boat. It was from a more recent time. He looked older, but full of life. Smiling with a ringlet of hair touching his nose as he looked up for the photographer. I wondered if Rebecca had taken the picture before his skin had gotten hollow and thin. The picture on the right hit me like a ton of bricks. The last time I had spoken to Will over the phone, he was going through a box of memories. Pictures, notebooks filled with songs never finished, journals, movie stubs, and maps. He must have found the picture himself and requested it be used for this purpose. It was a picture I had taken in Northampton, Massachusetts. Will was on the beach with his red Takamine guitar, strumming, singing, likely thinking of the singer we'd heard in the Northampton bar and how she was making it happen in her life.

***

"A-Mazing! She was amazing! Did you hear that song? What was it, 'climbing mountains in life?' Weren't we saying something about those mountain walls along the interstate on the drive up here? What did she say about the paths we take down the mountain? Damn, I couldn't be so poetic while describing the view from the interstate. Oh my God. She was amazing." Will was spinning in the street. If it had been raining, I could say he was dancing in the rain, but as it was it just looked like he was spinning around in the middle of a road.

"I heard her too, Will. She was very good. I think that song was called What's Coming...or was it What's Next? And yes, it was beautiful." I was laughing at him, but also wondering if he was on a natural high or if someone had slipped something in his drink.

Will stopped spinning so suddenly, I thought he'd topple over. "Nikki Jay. My beautiful Nikki. I am inspired!" As he shouted, he ran across the road, skipped up the curb, and lifted me up from the waist all in one gentle movement. "I am inspired. Tonight I will

230

make love to you as an inspired man. I will pull you up and over those walls of stone into oblivion. And tomorrow, we write. We can do this, Nikki. We can get up there on a stage and harmonize together." He spun me around then stopped my momentum by grabbing my waist again. "We have such great harmony, baby. We can do that, you know."

Will seemed to find a new breath of life in this new found excitement. We'd seen several great bands on stage before, but the level of energy coming from Will was a first for me to witness.

The lovemaking shattered records that night; Will performed more than twice. We both fell asleep with smiles on our faces and new life in our chests. After a Tavern breakfast the next morning, Will asked me to wait downstairs while he went upstairs to grab his guitar. With the heavy hard case in his hand, he also skipped down the stairs and into the hotel lobby. "Let's go, baby!" he said and pulled my elbow with his free hand.

I had no idea where we were going or how Will knew how to get anywhere other than the hotel and the bar we'd discovered. But once we and the guitar were safely buckled in the car, he started driving in a different direction from the one that led us into town. After about ten minutes of driving, I could see water, a train track bridge, and a small beach. He pulled over into a makeshift dirt lot and jumped out.

"Grab the blanket, if you want to sit on something, Nik." He grabbed his guitar, searched the console and between seats for two pens, and grabbed the notebook he carried everywhere. They all looked the same, a black and white composition book, but he filled them so quickly he almost never had the same one twice. I had seen several office boxes in his house filled with them. He'd been writing and journaling for many more years than I had known him.

Will beat me to the beach as I went back to get a couple of bottles of water and my camera. Once on the beach, I could see him setting up in the sand, a new determination written all over his face.

"I brought the blanket, why don't you and the guitar sit on it, so you don't get sand in the sound hole, goofball," I said to Will laughing. He was like a kid on Christmas, and I was left not knowing Santa had arrived yet. I spread out the blanket and sat down, rolling the bottles of water out of the way. Will sat near me, strumming and humming along.

"We are writing today, but bear with me, baby Nikki Jay. I'm not going to sit here and write in one spot. I feel I need to move around, baby. These walls are talking up here. That bridge up there. Look at it. It speaks to me. You relax, I was just thinking of this hook and rhythm."

He just stopped talking, hummed along to his constant strumming. G, C, D, typical folk song chords. I just watched him from one fingering to another. Then he stood up, pulled a capo out of his pocket, clipped it on the neck of the guitar, and started strumming again as he walked away. He walked slowly stopping every few moments to look at his fingers, nod his head, and then move on along the small beach. As he turned a small corner, and paused for a look at his fingering, he was almost facing me, but I could tell he didn't have clue I was watching him. He was in a world alone with his guitar. I picked up the camera and took a picture. We didn't know for weeks until I took the time to get the pictures from our trip developed what an amazing picture that one was. I wasn't sure how I did it, but I managed to capture his excitement, nervousness, and personal will to get through the writing journey he'd just started a few steps down the beach. It was a perfect picture. After I snapped it, he leaned the guitar against a rock and ran over to the blanket, picked up his notebook and pen, then ran back. While he was running toward me, I took a picture of his lonely guitar on the beach. Behind his guitar I could see those stone walls showing themselves way beyond along the interstate miles away. I also took a quick photo of Will as he looked up at me with his notebook in hand but his pen still six inches away. He was alive and filled with energy only he could turn into something magical. I let him do it. I sat back, grabbed a bottle of water and kept my camera close by while he traveled the beach writing.

***

I came back to current day when I heard the booming words, "Life and death are one as the seas and rivers are one." Someone I didn't recognize was at the podium starting the service. I had been staring at the picture of Will I had taken so long ago, losing myself in his ecstatic smile and the spiral curl that had fallen into his face. I gave the photo a smile as if it knew my feeling by my expression and then looked for Rebecca in the front row. She had two people sitting next to her. I hoped they offered enough support for her. I was feeling as if I should have been there next to her for some reason, but I didn't want to assume she needed me. It wasn't she who requested I even be there at all over the past few days. That was Will's request. I figured now Will was gone, she should be around those she loved, not just those who loved Will.

Brian got up and said a few words about music, how they used to write, play in boats along the shore for anyone who would listen, and how Will had fallen in love with a little town, a girl from the little town, the people in it and decided the little town was where he wanted to spend the rest of his days. He thanked those people there who had supported Will and Rebecca over the past year and those who had supported Will for the many years before. It made me wonder how many people knew Will was sick and for how long local folks knew before I knew.

There was a small graveside service at Philippi Church in Deltaville. The funeral home moved all the flowers to the church and were setting the last one in place as Dad and I walked up. There were six chairs under the green canopy. Dad and I chose to stand out in the sunshine with most of the rest of the crowd. From where I was standing, I could see my name on a beautiful flower arrangement. It wasn't one of the huge graveside arrangements. It was a pot filled with lilies on a tall stand. Chris had thought ahead and gotten an arrangement Rebecca could take home. I smiled at his ability to multi task and think about the big picture. From 1800 miles away, trying to work from home and take care of two very demanding little girls, he was still able to think about what Rebecca might like instead of simply filling a grave side with so many flowers people from the road could tell the plot was new.

Rebecca came to me after the very quick ashes to ashes dust to dust speech. "Nikki." She looked down, wiped an eye with a balled up tissue she'd had in her hand. My hands we also holding two wet and very used tissues. I just hugged her. She didn't need to say anything beyond my name.

"Nikki. I can't begin to thank you enough. I didn't know what to expect, doll. I didn't know it was going to be like that. All I knew was he wanted you here, and he did everything he could think of to make sure that happened. He told me once after talking to your husband on the phone he'd tried for years to live his life unselfishly, but he was trying his damnedest to be selfish and get his Nikki Jay with him while he died."

She put her chin on her balled up fists, sniffled, paused to gain composure, and then shook her arms out on front of her. "He had a lot of requests, actually. I know you have the letter. And that guitar is yours. But there are other things at the house he wanted you to have. He," she paused, took a deep cleansing breath and then continued, "he left me a list and left the same list with his lawyer. I have it all boxed up in the boathouse. I wanted to give it to you the day I gave you the letter, but he wanted you to have some while he was here and the rest after he was gone."

"Rebecca," I said, trying not to cry. "Slow down. First. I'm trying to take this all in. Will gave me his guitar. I don't need anything else. The rest is yours." I felt Dad's hand on my back. I also felt uneasy, so I wasn't sure if he was trying to steady me or trying to tell me silently to shut up and let Rebecca talk.

"Hon, it's yours. You do what you want with it. I think it's stuff from when you and Will," she paused, looked down, wrung her hands together, "when you and Will were together. One of the boxes says MA on it. At first I thought it was something from his mother, but now I think it means Massachusetts. I don't know. You can do what you want, toss it all if you'd like, but it's yours. Yours and Will's. And he's not here anymore." A sole tear streamed down her cheek.

I took her hand in mine, "Of course, honey. I know everyone is planning on coming over after they leave here. Maybe I can stay later, help you clean up after everyone is gone, and then you can give me the box."

"Boxes," Rebecca said as she walked away toward her car.

"Boxes," I said as I looked at my Dad. "How about if I take you back to your house, and then I'll head over there. Unless you want fried chicken and potato salad and whatever else people bring to these things, I can only imagine you don't want to be there."

He nodded at me, leaned down to kiss the top of my head and said, "You're right. But a plate of fried chicken doesn't sound too bad. Maybe you can bring a plate home if there's enough. I know you're all shrimped out from dinner yesterday, so make sure you get something to eat for yourself."

Chapter Twenty-Two

I dropped Dad off at his house, ran inside to freshen up my makeup after another afternoon of crying, and then headed back down the road with too many speed bumps. About halfway down the road, I realized I didn't have any food to bring. I stopped for several minutes at one speed bump, wondering if I should turn around in someone's driveway and head to the store or to Molly's to get a tray of food. After staring out at the water for a few minutes, I decided to keep driving. In this case, Rebecca wasn't a family the community was trying to feed after everyone left. Rebecca would probably be the only one in the house after the reception. It was part of her deal. She married Will, was his caregiver before he died, and for all she did for him, she got his house. I just drove ahead. I was a part of this experience, too. And I was going back into that house for the last time. Going in the house again wasn't going to be easy. I feared walking out with boxes of Will's belongings just might break me. My new Takamine guitar was still here along with Will's memories and whatever else he wanted me to have.

I parked at the pool, stood along the slick fence covered in green algae or mold and stared beyond the pool toward the Chesapeake Bay. I couldn't control the tears flowing freely from my eyes. I knew I had to walk down to Will's house, but what I really wanted was some time alone to reflect. Find a door I could close on the experience, the life out there, and on Will all together. Instead I heard a door close behind me and someone quietly walk up to me.

"Hey, sweetie, I saw you and your Dad at the service today, but I didn't want to bother you. How ya doing, hon?" Liza said with her arms out, ready to embrace me as soon as she got to me.

I didn't say anything in response, just let her take me into her arms as I sank to the ground. So much for fresh makeup. I let loose. I'd had Rebecca. I'd had Brian. I'd had my Dad and Chris over the phone, but for the first time in days I felt comfort in someone I knew so well and let everything I'd held in out to breathe for the first time since pulling into town.

"Oh, Liza," I said as I looked up. "I know you came by with food for us. I didn't even get to say hello then. I cannot believe everything I've been through. No. I can't believe everything that's happened these past few days." As I sobbed, my whole body shook. Liza sat on the moist ground with me practically in her lap and held me. "He's gone, Liza, he's gone. And I haven't spoken to him in months." I paused. "No. He spoke to me when I first got here. And he pushed my face and told the nurse to 'get this away from me.' Meaning me of course. I can't believe all that's happened. I can't believe he's gone. And I can't believe I'm heading back to a life I created, one I love, and I will never hear his voice again. Liza, he's gone."

I let my sobs do the speaking for me. And Liza, being a woman who had known me for years, knew to just be there for me. We sat for about ten minutes, and then I laughed. "My butt is wet."

I looked up at Liza, who was wiping a silent tear from her cheek. "Mine has been wet since we decided this was a good place to set it, my butt that is. Nothing's ever really dry out here, you know that."

We looked at each other, mascara running, cheeks red, lips swollen, and laughed. Liza laid back into the grass and laughed harder. "This is what you need to get out, Nikki. Let it out. Laugh. Be free. Will is free. Free from cancer. Free from pain. Be free, Nikki. Free to laugh." Liza sat up with two handfuls of grass and threw the grass in the air above our heads.

I laughed, but then got up, shook out my hair, wiped off the back of my dress, and held out my hand to Liza. She took it, still giggling, and got up. "I guess we should head on down to the house then, huh?" Liza said. With that, we started walking. I didn't look back to the pool. I knew I'd never look at the same pool again. But I also knew my memories didn't lie in a chlorine pool with mossy stumps around it and a moldy fence. My memories were with a salt water pool, young adults, and laughter. That pool only made me sad. The pool in my mind made me smile. The salt water pool where Will still smiled a young vibrant smile.

I held the door for Liza when we got to Will's house, feeling happy I'd run into her. Other than Brian, I wasn't sure who else I'd know there. I assumed Rebecca and Will had their own circle of friends. I hadn't lived here for many years, and of course I was still hoping Rebecca's family was among the crowd I saw gathered in the sunroom.

"Hey, Rebecca," I said as I walked up behind her. She turned, and I hugged her.

"Hey, sweetie. I want you to meet my mom. I know she'd like to meet you. Oh, I'm so glad you are here." Rebecca took my hand and led me across the room. I smiled to myself. Her mother was there. I hoped she could see what I saw in Rebecca, a woman I barely knew, and feel some pride for what she did for another person. My love for Will was never ending, but I hadn't been in a position to marry him for years. In the end, he was with his wife, a woman who cared for him, took him to treatments, hospitals, doctors' appointments, and probably did various things at home none of us would know about. I may have seen the end of Will's journey, but it probably wasn't the worst of it. Rebecca was the one there for those difficult moments. The private times we'd never know existed. Except I knew, because I saw so much more than I ever thought I'd see.

"Mom," Rebecca called quietly in a group of people talking together. "Mom, come here," she beckoned.

"Hi, sweetie," Rebecca's mom said as she walked over to us and put her arm around Rebecca's waist. She smiled at me and nodded in a quiet hello.

"Mom, I want you to meet Nikki. She was a very good friend of Will's and has been with me the past several days. I don't know how I would have gotten through all of this without her."

"Hi," I said, with a weak smile. I wasn't comfortable with everything Rebecca had just said about me, and I didn't even know the woman's name, so all I could come up with was a simple greeting.

"Well, hello to you, my dear. I do think Rebecca has mentioned your name to me. Nikki, you say? I'm Gina. It's such a pleasure to meet you. And thank you for being here for my Becca. I'm sure she needed a good friend during this time. Do you live around here, dear?"

"No, ma'am. I live in Colorado. I grew up here, and met Will when we were teenagers. We've been...we were friends for a long time," I said quietly again. I hadn't said ma'am to anyone since I was probably eight years old. Clearly I was nervous, but I had no idea why. I also didn't know what Gina knew about me. Or about Will for that matter. It took me some time to develop respect, care, and almost love for Rebecca, but I sensed I would never find respect for her mother.

"Well, Colorado sure is a long ways away. Surely you didn't just come out here for this, didcha?" Gina looked down at me through the top of her glasses. She reminded me of a school teacher scolding her student in a condescending way.

"Mom. Will wanted her here." Rebecca saved me from punching her mother and having to explain anything to her. Yes, I left my husband and two small daughters 1800 miles away to come and watch my ex-lover die.

"I'll be leaving tomorrow. I'm very sad about Will. But I do need to get back home." I hoped it would be enough for her to move on from the conversation. I didn't want to give her the benefit of seeing me cry over Will and know I had a family back home. I could just hear the berating she'd give me for having feelings and Rebecca for allowing someone else into her web of a deceitful marriage.

"Oh, I see," Gina said. "Now, dahhling," Gina's attentions were now directed to her daughter. "People are bringing food over. You know, that's what they do for families after funerals. Do you have someone in the kitchen setting up?"

"No, Mom, I don't. I haven't been able to see beyond my face lately. I've been greeting pe-"

Gina cut her off. "Well, people need to eat, my love. I'll go put things out for people to eat. Once they eat at these things, they usually head on home. And I'm not staying down here tonight. So I'll need to be heading back to Alexandria within a couple a hours, you know." Gina walked away for what appeared to be playing hostess after funeral visitation.

"Sorry, about her, doll," Rebecca said to me. I could tell by one meeting that Rebecca's mother had spent a lifetime cutting her daughter down. "She's in her own little world most days. And her world consists of art gallery openings, charity events, and country club dinners. She has no idea what the people of this town do, how they survive without a stoplight, and I think she even wonders why we all bother getting out of bed in the morning if we don't have the poor to serve like she does with all of her extravagant charity events. Of course she wouldn't know what the poor looked like if they kicked her in the chin and asked her for a can of soup." Rebecca laughed. I suddenly liked her more. In different circumstances, we could have been friends.

I laughed and hugged her again. "I hope we can stay in touch, girl. I'm liking you!" We both laughed, then hugged again acknowledging it was not only good to laugh but also okay.

We walked around the sunroom saying "hello" and "thank you" to people we saw. As much as I hadn't wanted to play the supportive role for Rebecca earlier at the funeral home, after meeting her mother, I found I fit right into the role and was pretty good at it too. After about fifteen minutes, Gina brought us both plates filled with macaroni and cheese and fried chicken with a buttery southern biscuit on the side. I didn't see a single vegetable, and it so felt good. This was what we needed, down home southern comfort food. We took our plates into the formal living room and each sat on a white couch. I laughed, causing Rebecca to turn toward me with her plate in her lap and a questioning look on her face. No one else was in the room, so my laughter felt completely inappropriate and loud.

"What?" Rebecca asked with her head cocked to the side like a puppy.

"Oh nothing," I started but then changed my mind. "Well, these couches. They were forbidden back in the day. When Will's grandfather was here, this was a parlor like room where no one was allowed to be. I always wondered if something had happened in the room, because I couldn't imagine not using an entire room in the house."

Rebecca laughed again. "Oh my! I had no idea! I read in here all the time. Will never said anything. But," she took a bite of macaroni and cheese, then laughed again. I was afraid the white couch was going to have a yellow stain on it. "Come to think of it, I never saw Will in here either." We both laughed again. We were cleansing. And it felt good. "I think it's my new party room." More laughter. "No, I probably won't party, I'm not a party kind of girl, but it is close to the kitchen, so maybe it will be my new living room. I can put the TV up there," she was looking around the room through a square she'd made with her fingers. "I don't know," she said, putting her hands back on the plate balanced on her lap. "I just know it won't be a room off limits." She looked down at her food. I could tell her mind was wandering.

"You okay?" I asked.

"Yeah. You know. I hadn't really even thought about it. I don't know what I'm going to do with this house. I love this town. I love the house. So I'll live here. For a while at least. It's only worth about $200,000. Don't get me wrong, I'm not complaining, it's nice. But for waterfront, it needs a lot of updating, so it's not worth the price of waterfronts in the area. If I decided to sell one day, it would be enough to get me going, but I think I'll stay." She took a bite of her chicken, then looked up at me as she wiped a tear from the corner of her eye. "You know I was a waitress when we met. I haven't worked in almost two years. I'm set up okay, financially, you know. But I don't know what I'll do for work when I have to go back to it."

"Oh, honey," I leaned forward and put my hand on her knee almost dumping my plate onto the white couch. "Oh, shit!" We laughed again. Once I was composed, with two hands on my plate, I continued. "I haven't worked in years either. I guess giving up my career was easy because I traded it to become a mom, but if something happened, I'd have to go back, too." I stopped and looked at her. "I'm sorry. I…I'm just…well, I mean, I still have Chris, of course. I'm sorry. That was a callous thing to say."

"No, doll. It wasn't. You can relate. I understand. I don't know what I'd do if I had kids. But I don't, so in a way, my situation is easier than if you were to lose Chris. It's just me here. The house is owned outright. I just need to keep up with it, pay utilities and taxes, and I can live here as long as I want, I guess." We both got quiet. Hearing about Rebecca's financials wasn't top on my list, and I think she finally felt the discomfort in the air. Maybe one day we could be good friends, especially after all we shared during the time we shared Will. But at the moment, I didn't want to know personal things about her and Will. She broke our silence with, "He really loved you, you know. He talked about you a lot."

I wasn't feeling much more comfort with that line of dialogue. I didn't want to hear about how much Will loved me, cared for me, or missed me. My reality was he'd hurt me a lot over the past several months of his life, and then I went there only to learn not only was he dying, but he knew years ago he wouldn't live a long life and didn't want me in the position his wife was in now, a widow.

"Look, hon," Rebecca started. "I like you. I knew I liked you before I ever met you because Will talked so darn much aboutcha. But I know it'll take some time before you really know me. Maybe we can talk on the phone. Maybe we can email. And maybe when you come out here to visit your family, we can have dinner together. I'd like to stay in touch with you." She paused to look down. "But I understand if you don't want that. You just remember if you ever have any questions about Will, well, questions I can answer, you just ask 'em. Okay. Promise?"

"I promise. Thank you, Rebecca. Really. Thank you. I'm sorry I'm not ready to really open up just yet. I may not at all. This is my past that has been locked up for so long." I wiped my mouth with the napkin hidden under my plate. The fried chicken was good. I needed to make sure I made a plate for Dad before I left. My appetite hadn't returned just yet. My stomach had been feeling weak for days, like anything I was planning on eating was working its way out before I even put it in my stomach. I hadn't been sleeping well and had been through what I thought to be the most difficult thing I'd ever done. I was sure some distance would heal my tummy issues, but at that moment a few bites of chicken and macaroni surrounded by rich cheese was plenty for me.

"Come on, hon, let's go put you in the boathouse with those boxes. I can help you load your car. And we can't forget the guitar too. But I want to make sure you at least see what these boxes are. You can stay as long as you'd like if you want to look through them, but if you just want to look and then go through them in Colorado, well that's fine too." She got up, took my hand, and started walking me toward the kitchen where we left our plates with Gina to clean. Then she led me out the kitchen door to the backyard and down to the boathouse. The lights were on, but no one had decided to gather here.

"I have them behind the bar, over there. Three boxes. And a note with a list of things Will wanted to make sure I gave to you. I'm gonna head on back up to the house. If you need anything, you holler. K?" Rebecca hugged me and walked back out to the yard and up to the house. I watched her until she closed the kitchen door behind her.

I sat in the same chair I'd sat in just days earlier to read a letter Will had written me. The box of tissues was still there. I looked around, sighed and got back up and headed behind the bar. Behind the bar there were three small office supply boxes with lids. The first one had MA written on it and the other two were blank. I dropped to my knees and opened the MA box. Inside were three notebooks, papers, guitar picks, the hotel receipt, a T-shirt from the North Star Bar, and a Neila Lees CD. I just closed the box, picked it up, and carried it to the chair. I glanced at the other two boxes, lifted their lids at the same time and saw things I didn't want to look at; CDs that looked blank, but I was certain they contained Will's music, cassette tapes and thumb drives, guitar tablature books for song writing and more. There was a small ukulele in one box, too many notebooks to count, envelopes, a wooden box I recognized as the keepsake box Will used to put shells and movie ticket stubs in, and at the bottom of the box, songbooks for singer songwriters. Paul Simon's collection was on top of the stack.

"I can't go through this stuff here," I said to myself. "God, Will, what did you want from me? What am I supposed to do with this stuff?" I carried both boxes and stacked them on the chair, then I sat on the floor and grabbed the box of tissues. My eyes weren't exactly dry, but they weren't leaking tears uncontrollably either. Leaning against the chair, I put my head back and sighed. My time with Will had come down to thirty-four seconds and three boxes filled with memories I had let go of over the years. I had my own boxes, in my basement, in my head, and in my heart. But I hadn't opened a box of memories in any of those places in years.

"Oh, Will. I miss you so much," I said to no one.

I stayed with Will's boxed memories for about twenty minutes, wiped my eyes, and walked outside. Sitting on a stand near the door was the Takamine guitar. I strummed my thumb across the strings along the neck, and headed to the house.

Rebecca and Liza were in the kitchen cleaning up. The house was fairly quiet.

"Oh, honey, I was about to leave, but I wanted to say goodbye," Liza said, wiping her hands on a kitchen towel. She hugged me and said, "I'm sorry, sweetie. I know it's hard. I'm gonna miss him too. Don't be a stranger, hear? Don't you go back to Colorado, to those beautiful babies of yours and forget all us locals. We think of you, you know. We miss you. You keep coming back here to visit us, ya hear me?"

She didn't even let me reply. She silently hugged Rebecca, left her towel on the counter, and walked out.

"Did everyone leave?" I asked.

"Yeah, with a three o'clock funeral, I guess it gave everyone time enough to come over here for some dinner and then head home to bed," Rebecca laughed. "Even my mom had some charity thing in the morning and started her drive up north. I bet having Starbucks with a girlfriend and tipping the barista is considered charity for her. She probably writes it all off," she laughed again. "Oh, my goodness. My family." She finished wrapping the plate she had in her hand with plastic wrap, held it up for me to see and said, "For your Dad. Believe it or not, I've gotten to know him a bit this past year. I bet he'd like some dinner, huh?"

"Hmph, yeah, he would. Thank you. Can I help you clean up?" I asked.

"No, doll. But let me help you with those boxes, and there's a case out there for the guitar. Let's get it all packed up for you," she put her arm around my shoulder and led me back out to the boathouse.

She carried two boxes and I carried one box with Dad's dinner sitting on top and the guitar to my car. After loading, we stood next to the pool where I'd parked, just staring out at the bay. It was quiet enough to hear the rhythm of the waves hitting the beach. By that time it was high tide, bringing the waves closer to the rock wall that helped to stop the land from eroding around the area.

"Honey, I don't even know what to say to you. How can I thank you? How can I say good-bye to you?" She shivered, hugged her arms, and I watched a tear fall from her chin.

"I feel the same way. I can't thank you enough. I don't have the words to form to tell you how special this experience was, how much I love and respect you for what you did for Will, and how much it meant to me, keeping me alive in his life. I just..." I couldn't find any more words.

"Will you try to stay in touch with me? Call me and ask me anything. I might not have the answer, but I might."

"I will. I promise." I turned to get in the car. "And, Rebecca? If you ever find yourself west of the Mississippi...well, if you ever find yourself in Colorado at least, you have a home there. You are welcome. And we'd love to have you."

"I just might have to take a trip out west." She turned and walked toward the house. I started the car, then sat and watched her until darkness swallowed her image. I could see the lights on at the house I'd probably never visit again. The lights were on along the dock as well, and though I couldn't see them all, I could see the ones at the end and the boathouse that held ghosts of two young people falling in love, writing songs about it, and singing their hearts out. I wondered what others ghosts lived there. Will's cancer lived there. He knew, even back then, he wouldn't live to see middle age. After holding his life's last breath for thirty-four seconds, he let everything go. Maybe those ghosts went with him.

Making a three point turn in the grass near the pool, I turned around and didn't look back. I took every speed bump at a good enough speed to keep moving forward. I feared if I stopped and slowly rolled over a bump, I'd roll all the way back to Will's...Rebecca's house and would want to walk through each room, touch his bed, feel the carpet, sit on the white couch, look at the pictures along the mantel. I couldn't go back anymore. I knew I had to move forward.

Chapter Twenty-Three

Saying goodbye to Dad, Natalie, and Nana, though I didn't see much of any of them on my trip, was difficult, but quick. Dad helped me pack my rental car before we'd gone to bed the night before. I got up at six o'clock in the morning and ate a bagel with black coffee. As I was getting into the rental car, Dad asked what was in the boxes, and all I could say was "Will." Will was not in the boxes of course, but everything I could ever have of Will was in those boxes. We all stood in Dad's driveway and hugged, said all the right things, and I promised to call from the road and once I got home. Home. To Colorado. To Chris. To my babies, Emily and Bella, who I desperately hoped would remember me once I got there.

I drove out of Deltaville on the same road I had driven in. I passed all the familiar sights and noted the few new ones, wondering if they were here the week before, the year before even, and if they'd last long enough to be there when I came back. I'd never come back for just Will, except to see him and Rebecca exchange lifelong vows to be together until death did they part. The next time I went there it wouldn't be for Will, but I knew I'd never come that way again without thinking of him. Deltaville will never be the same for me again.

Within a few minutes I was out of the area, traveling up the county towards the interstate that would have taken me to the airport I was originally to fly out of. As it stood now, it would be the same interstate that would take me all the way to St. Louis, where I would then pick up I-70 west to Colorado. I'd done the cross country drive many times before, and many times alone. It usually took about thirty hours. I wasn't sure how long it would take, but I'd promised Chris I'd stop for the night somewhere.

The first few hours went by without me singing a single song. The rental car had satellite radio, and I listened to mindless talk radio until I had to stop and pee just outside of Charlottesville, Virginia.

Charlottesville was home to a lot of well-known musicians and celebrities. It was also home to an indie record store that had consigned Will's first demo CD once Will decided to try to get out into the music world. It was the only piece of music he put out into the world. Not too long after he got three stores to stock his CD, we broke up. Sitting in the Burger King parking lot, I suddenly remembered he'd been feeling down just before the store took his music. I wondered if he'd been sick and had started giving up on life then. Just after he'd spent a few days in bed, pushing me away and telling me he didn't feel well, he broke up with me for the final time.

I thought about going into the little record store while I was in Charlottesville to pick up a few CDs to listen to on the drive, but I couldn't bear to do it. Satellite radio would have to hold me through the whole trip. At least it wasn't AM/FM. I couldn't imagine there were many radio stations accessible in the mountains of West Virginia. After using the restroom and buying a soda at Burger King, I left Charlottesville and the memories of the beautiful town. I continued along I-64 for several more hours, but had to stop again just over the West Virginia border. Driving through the western mountains of Virginia made my eyes water. The hills rolled along, bright green, dotted with red barns and green tractors. I wanted to pull over along the interstate and stare out into the immense scenery, but I couldn't bring myself to stop. For the first time in the drive west, I started to feel again. My heart opened. Out of it poured a wealth of emotion. I started crying, I banged the steering wheel, and I pounded my left foot into the floor board. Finally I stopped at the Welcome Center and got out of the car as if a bee were buzzing around my head inside the car. I was breathing so heavy I thought I might hyperventilate.

"Breathe, Nikki," I said to no one as I paced in front of the car. "Just breathe." I slowed my pacing down as my breaths slowed. "In and out," sigh. "In through the nose, out through the mouth." I repeated my mantra until I felt calm enough to walk to the rest rooms. Once inside, I rinsed my face in the sink and went back outside and sat on a bench near the car. I always hated rest areas. I usually tried to stop at exits with fast food restaurants when I traveled. I was at a Welcome Center, not just a rest area. It was nicer than a rest area. It had statues, a large grassy area, and several maps showing West Virginia. I took it all in from the bench. Then I sighed and walked to the car.

I sat in the driver's seat for a few moments, then got back out and opened the back door. The boxes were staring at me. I opened the box with the MA written on it, grabbed the only CD inside, then opened another box and grabbed a handful of unmarked CDs, closed the lid, tossed them on the front seat, and got back in the car.

"I have to get home," I said to no one again. No one was there. I was on a journey, across country, through my mind, and into my heart, and I would have to travel alone.

I started the car and got back onto the interstate. Voices over the radio bickered about military spending, a war too long running, and other points in politics. None of it struck me as anything I was interested in feeling anything about at the moment. After switching to a comedy channel, I allowed myself to laugh. Every few miles or so I glanced at the CDs sitting on and sliding across the passenger seat. I couldn't put them on. Not yet. But I would need to. Sometime in that car, on my journey, I would need to put them on.

I went through several comedy channels on the drive through West Virginia. I laughed out loud, let my heart relax, and felt nothing. West Virginia required focus while driving through the mountains, and the hours seemed to pass with much more ease than I had going into the state. Kentucky hit me in a decent mood. As I drove, I watched the scenery, the stones sticking out of the small hills along the road reminded me of home.

"Colorado." I said to no one again. "Rocky Mountains. Rocks, stones, landlocked. I'm going home again. Finally."

No one replied.

Kentucky brought me one bathroom break and a cup of coffee. While sitting in the parking lot sweetening the bitter coffee, I stared at the CDs spread out across the passenger seat. They looked like a deck of cards, all fanned out on the seat.

"Aces wild," I said to no one again as I put the car in reverse and backed out of the parking lot. It did dawn on me I might be losing my mind. I had gone from talking to myself to talking to a pile of CDs I thought were a deck of cards.

The satellite radio was changed to a channel playing singer/songwriter music from the '70s. I sang along to every song for over an hour until the DJ started talking too long and my mind began to wander back to Stingray Bay Hills, Will's house, Rebecca, and everything that lay before me on the road ahead. My girls had probably changed so much I wouldn't recognize them. I thought it would probably take me days to see all the new things they did and said. I stayed in my mind for a while, tuning out the radio, and thinking of my girls and Chris.

The last time I talked to Emily, she told me they had seen a car accident in town and there were fire trucks everywhere, but also some police cars too. She was so excited, but then said, "Mommy, I guess they didn't have a potty chair in their car like we do!" It took me a few moments to realize what she was talking about and how the conversation had gone from a car accident to a potty chair. But then I realized to my four year old, an accident meant not making it to the potty in time. I laughed, asked her about the fire trucks, and she picked up the conversation again. I couldn't imagine several fire trucks coming to our house each time she didn't make it to the potty on time, but in her little mind, an accident was just an accident, and if it happened to bring fire trucks, then well, maybe everyone needed a potty chair inside their car. Kids are amazing. I smiled through Indiana thinking of my girls. I could see their little smiles. The way Bella's hair curls right at the tips. Emily's little fingers wrapped around her sister's smaller hands as if she was the biggest kid in the world and would do anything to protect her baby sister. It was June. Emily would be turning five years old soon. She would be heading to Kindergarten in the fall. Christmas would come, Santa would shower them with gifts, stuffed bunnies, maybe a doll house for Bella, books for Emily to begin reading. Life would go on indeed. Without Will. We'd all move on. We all had purpose. Mine had been my family for the past several years. My husband. My girls. They needed their mother. And after being away so long, greeting death in the face, even if it wasn't my own, I knew more than ever, I breathed for them. I needed them more than I ever knew.

The rain started just a few miles into Illinois. I was getting tired. I'd been on the road for over twelve hours and had only munched on a few treats from Starbucks and a fast food lunch. I was craving some vegetables and fruit. Anything fresh and not processed or fast. I decided to stop at the next exit and grab a salad for dinner and call Chris.

"Mommy! Daddy said you're home!" Bella sounded like she had sucked on a helium balloon. Her voice sounded so small, but at the same time, she sounded different. Bigger. Older even.

"Hey, Babydoll! I miss you so much! I am not home yet. But I am coming home. I think I should be home tomorrow. Maybe around dinner time. Maybe you and Emily can help Daddy make all of us a special dinner. Can you do that?" My heart filled. I smiled, I felt alive. I was going home. I was going to see those babies, and I wasn't going to leave them again for as long as I had.

I got quiet. I was feeling again. Happiness. Sadness for being so far away, for being gone so long. I couldn't speak. And no one was on the line.

"Bell? Bella Boo...are you there?" I was talking to no one again.

A few minutes went by, but I didn't want to hang up. I could still hear household noise. I was still connected to my family. Tears streamed down my cheeks, and I hadn't even realized they were coming from my eyes.

"Hey, hon, are you there?" Chris picked up the phone.

I sniffed. "Yeah, I'm here." Suddenly I was wiping my cheeks as if he was looking at me.

"Sorry about that. I was in the kitchen, and Bella set the phone in her bedroom. I guess she was done talking. How's the drive? Where abouts are you?"

"I'm in Illinois. I just got here. I think if I remember correctly Illinois isn't a long drive. I'm getting tired, but I just ate a salad from a deli I found, and I grabbed some apples and a banana, so I think I'm going to go a few more hours. Maybe go until bedtime so I don't have any down time in the hotel. Maybe I can roll in and drop into bed. Can you look around online for something about four hours away and book it?"

"Sure. I'll go do it as soon as I get the girls' dinner. We're doing something easy tonight, and tomorrow I'll cook something good for you. Sorry, hon, but let me go so I can get them food and then get you a hotel. I'll call you with an exit about four hours away and a hotel confirmation."

"Okay. Thanks, Chris. I'll wait to hear from you. Try to get me as close to St. Louis as possible. Well, I don't even know how far away that is. I guess it's probably more than four hours. I wish I could get on the west side of St. Louis so I don't have to go through the city first thing in the morning."

"I'll take a look at a map, see how far away you are now and get back to you. I love you, Nikki."

"Love you too, Chris."

"Stay safe, I'll call within the hour." And with that, Chris hung up. Before the phone clicked off, I could hear him calling Emily. I would have to find a way to thank him, to recognize all he'd done those days I was gone. I had no idea how I would ever convey my appreciation to him.

After some healthier foods and a large bottle of water, I was ready to put in a few more hours of driving. I felt energized. My family was waiting for me to come home. I had a place to go where I was loved. And needed. I was feeling validated. I was feeling something. Finally after feeling numb for so long, I was feeling something. Smiling, I reached down and blindly grabbed a CD off the seat next to me. I pressed Load on the CD player, inserting it while driving away.

Will's voice filled the car. My heart sank, but I smiled. I thought how much I would like to sit in a quiet room on the floor with my eyes closed and have his voice fill me. But I was driving, so eye closing wasn't an option. But I knew I could let his voice in.

Chris called me back within the hour, "Good news, hon. Four hours takes you beyond St. Louis. I can get you to Columbia, Missouri. There's a Hampton Inn there waiting for me to call back and confirm. Without stops and traffic, it's about four hours. Can you manage, or do you want me to look for something closer to you now?"

"Book it!" I was excited. I'd have a bed. I'd roll into it before midnight, hopefully find sleep and the next day I'd be home.

"Check check, Nik. Gotta go call them back. Call me if you get tired beforehand, otherwise, call me when you get there and get checked in. Love you."

"Love you too. Thank you, Chris."

I hung up the phone and turned up the volume on the stereo. Will was singing songs I had never heard. He'd laugh in the middle of the song and say something like, 'Huh hehe, try that one again,' then start it over. It sounded like a fun recording done at home. I wondered if the discs were labeled with dates. I had no idea when this was recorded, I just knew they weren't songs from years ago, and they weren't the few songs from recent years I'd heard.

Listening to Will's voice was mesmerizing. I drove in silence as his voice filled my heart through the speakers in the rental car. Before I knew it, I could see the lights of St. Louis ahead. When the CD ended, I picked up another and loaded it into the player. I realized then the car had a multi-disc changer. I don't know how I missed it earlier, but I wasn't ready for the CDs I had with me anyway earlier. Maybe in the morning I'd load up six discs and let them carry me to Boulder.

I was mesmerized in another song I didn't know when it stopped suddenly, and I heard Will speak my name.

"Nikki Jay. This one is for you," the disc said. I had listened through the city and almost missed my exit to interstate 270. I had almost forgotten the interstate runs north through the city or south through the city or around the city. I couldn't remember which one to take. It had been years since I'd driven that cross-country drive. Quickly I decided to take I270, and it carried me back to I70. The change from I64 to I70 was a milestone. Interstate 70 would take me almost to Boulder. After leaving St. Louis, I looked at the clock and realized I'd been driving just over two hours. I was half way to my hotel. It was time for a bathroom break, my banana, and a bottle of water.

I found a fast food restaurant at the next exit, ran inside to use the bathroom and then bought an order of fries. Not the healthiest choice, but I hated just using the bathroom, and fries were tasty, even if not healthy. In the parking lot, I ate the fries, then peeled the banana, and drove away again. I didn't realize until I started seeing signs for Columbia that the CD player didn't start again when I started the car. I had been listening to satellite radio again and singing along to songs from the '70s for almost two hours.

The hotel was easy to find right off the exit. I parked the car, stood in the parking lot staring at the back seat filled with boxes and wondered if they'd be stolen overnight.

"Ugh!" I said to no one again, grabbed a bag with some overnight stuff, pajamas, and one outfit for the next day, slammed the door as if to dare anyone nearby to go near the car and walked inside the hotel. My room was on the third floor on the backside of the building. That told me they weren't a busy hotel since I'd had reservations for just a few hours and got the quiet side of the building.

Before I could even get my cell phone out of my bag, it rang. I dug through my purse looking for it and managed to answer before Chris hung up.

"Hey!" I said, almost out of breath.

"Hey, you," Chris said. "Where are you? Getting close to the hotel?"

"I'm actually getting close to the bed. I just got to the hotel, and I'm beat. I don't think I realized just how tired I was until I got out of the car and in sight of a bed."

"Oh, good. I'm glad you made it. And it looks like you made good time too. Hey, I won't keep you. Why don't you get some sleep and get on home to us, okay?" Chris sounded tired himself.

"I think I will wash my face, brush my teeth, as long as I packed my toothbrush, and head to bed. Are you and the girls doing okay?"

"Yes, babe, everyone is fine. We all miss you. Get some sleep, and we'll see you tomorrow."

"Yep, tomorrow!" I perked up a bit, but then decided I was too tired for perky. "Okay, sweetie, I'm going to head to bed. I love you."

"'Night, babe. I love you too. Call me in the morning when you hit the road. I'll let you know where to meet me to drop off the rental car."

"K. Goodnight." I hung up and laid back onto the bed, rubbing my eyes.

***

"I'm so tired," Will put his head down against my shoulder and snuggled.

"I am too. That was a long day. But beautiful. The weather was perfect. Thank you for taking me out on the water today. It feels like forever since I've been out there."

"Nikki?" Will looked at me. He was crying. "Nikki. I took you out there today to enjoy space with you. To ride the sea inside your eyes. But everything is still as it is. I can't be the man you need me to be."

I was crying too. I knew what was coming. He took me out on his boat because I had shown up at his house and just asked him to take me sailing. So he did. I wasn't sure if we had anything except a salty breeze in my hair and on my skin, but as soon as we got on the boat together, it felt natural. Real. Normal. We worked side by side getting the sails up, pulling and tying ropes, and then we sat down side by side and enjoyed the quiet of the bay.

"Will, you are everything I've ever wanted. Everything. You are beautiful. You are smart. You are funny. You are amazing. I love you so much." I paused to wipe my nose and catch my breath. My chest hurt so badly. "I love you so much it hurts. It hurts me, Will, to see you hurting. I know you don't want this. I know you love me. I can feel it. Tell me, Will. Tell me you still love me." I was feeling desperate. "Tell me, Will. Fucking tell me already." My voice was raised. I stood up, filled with hurt and anger. "Tell me. I know it's true."

Will stood up next to me, and put his arms around me. "I love you, Nikki Jay. You are my princess. You are my world. You fill me with summer and sunshine on the coldest of days."

He sat back down and pulled me down with him. With his elbows on his knees, he held his face in his hands. His whole body was shaking. "I'm sorry, Nikki. I never should have done this today. I wanted to be with you just as much as you wanted to be with me." Will looked at me, then turned his head and looked at the floor between his feet. "I won't be here long enough to give you the life you want, Nik. I just won't be able to do it."

***

I sat up, jolted. I was still wearing my clothes, lying on the hotel bed. But there it was, in the front of my mind. Will tried to tell me. I walked away after he said those words, but I never thought about them again. I had known he would just keep telling me he couldn't be the man I needed or wanted him to be, but he actually told me that day he wouldn't be around long enough to be the man I needed in my life. I thought he just didn't want to be married and have children, and I knew we were too young to make those decisions.

"He told me. He told me he wasn't going to be here long enough to give me what I want. He thought he wouldn't be living long enough to give me children when I wanted them, or raise them with me. He knew. And he told me. I didn't hear it. Oh my God, Will. Did you send that dream to me? How in the world did I remember after all this time?" I got up and paced the room, found a clock, and realized it was only just after midnight. I had slept only just over an hour. I was wide awake. Aware. Mindful. For years it had been staring me in the face. And I ignored it.

"But I don't know what I would have, or could have done about it. Would you have stayed with me if I told you I would have, could have been the wife Rebecca was for you? Would you have stayed with me if I told you then I would be with you the day you are taken away from me and every day until then? Or did you need to live life alone? At least without me. Dammit, Will. What did you want from me? Why didn't you make it clearer? Why didn't you tell me you were sick, and you didn't know how long you could be my love? Shit. None of us knew how long we'd be here. I could..." I fell to my knees on the hotel room floor and buried my head in the bed. I couldn't get my last thought out. I could die myself before I got home to my babies. As true as it was, I couldn't say it out loud.

"Dammit!" I yelled. I figured the hotel probably had no guests near my room since I got a decent room with almost no notice, but I decided then I needed to get back to bed, and with the help of a sleep aide, hopefully get a good night's sleep.

Chapter Twenty-Four

The next morning, I woke with a clearer head. I showered, attempted some makeup so I wouldn't scare my children when I finally got to see them, and hit the road. About thirty minutes into my drive, I called Chris to let him know I was on my way home.

Satellite radio kept me occupied for a few hours. I switched from comedy channels to 70s folk rock radio channels and just drove. I didn't sing, I barely laughed. I just drove. My mission was to get home. I wasn't processing. I wasn't crying. I was ignoring any feelings surfacing. I drove for hours. Kansas passed by one field at a time. Cows watched me pass. Clouds moved toward me and then away from me. Cars and trucks passed me carrying drivers with problems of their own, lives they were living, loved ones they were going to or driving from. I just drove.

Hours into my drive, getting closer to Colorado, my hand moved up to the stereo without me evening thinking of whether I was going to switch to coffee house music or to another comedy channel. My fingers switched to the CD player. Will's voice filled the air. The pressure changed inside the car. My breathing changed. I found myself sighing after holding my breath through much of the song. The next came on, and I listened, allowing emotion back into my world. Will's songwriting always filled my arms with chills that ran down my spine and into my soul. A tear escaped my eye and ran down my cheek. I didn't want to allow emotion or feeling into the car. My mission was to get home, the hundreds of miles, to my family.

The song ended, and Will spoke to me.

"Nikki. Nikki. I love you," the stereo said to me.

I looked down at it as if to see a face smiling at me and spiral curls falling into blue eyes.

"I wish I could be with you right now," the stereo continued in Will's voice. "I wish I could sing to you in this very moment. But know this, my love. Know I am with you. I am always with you. When you hold your children, when you cry, when you love, I can feel your pain. I can feel your love. I can feel your anger. I am there…with you…always."

The car slowed to a crawl on the interstate. Cars passed me by, maybe wondering if I'd had car trouble. After a moment, I pulled to the shoulder and continued to stare at the stereo. Will was still talking, but with a voice that cracked every few words.

"Nikki. I want to apologize. I need to apologize to you. I am sorry. I hope you can forgive me. I never should have let you leave. I shouldn't have let you go. I pushed you away for so long, and I should have known it wouldn't work. Not with us. We couldn't be far from one another."

Tears were streaming down my face. My breathing quickened, my chest heavier.

Will continued, "I think I failed most when I let you go, but then pulled you back in, over and over. I told myself not long ago, if I had let you go…I mean really go…not remained friends over the years, you'd have forgotten about me, forgotten how much you loved me, how I loved you, stopped caring for me. And you might not be hurting so much right now. I am sorry I couldn't do that for you. I'm sorry I kept you close. I'm sorry I ever let you go to begin with. I'm sorry I didn't believe in you, in us, in our love and how healing it was for me. I didn't want you to face today, a life without me, so I was hurtful to you. I tore us apart. I walked away and kept pulling you back in. I'm sorry I lied to you."

I wiped my cheeks and looked at the stereo with curiosity. Lied to me?

"I would have loved you to the end of my days – I did love you to the end of my days – I would have loved to have had children with you. I would have walked you down the aisle. I would have given you a family, if only I had been given time. I'm honored to have been here, in your life, for as long as I have, but I wasn't meant to be here. I wasn't meant to carry on. I want you to do something for me."

I stared at the stereo. Will's voice cleared, paused, and continued. "Look around you, princess. Look at the biggest thing you can see. Go ahead. Look." His voice got quiet.

I looked around the car, my body shaking, my face and neck wet from tears. Then something outside the car got my attention. Looking outside, I was awed. All around me were wind mills. A wind farm. Steel wind mills stood in every direction, surrounding me as if showing power, wisdom, and strength. They stood hundreds of feet up into the warm air, with blades spanning over a hundred feet. I had missed them while driving. I looked in awe. The farm spread out along both sides of the interstate.

Will had been talking again. His words caught my attention again, "...don't let the obstacles in life stand in your path. Go around them, above them or through them, but don't let them control you." I got out of the car and stood alongside, staring up and out across the land. Hundreds of wind mills looked back at me. A few spun their blades slowly as if waving to me.

Will's voice continued from the stereo, "Please go, Nikki. Go live your life to the fullest. Love hard and fierce. Don't fear. Talk it out with those you care for, and don't let anyone into your life who cannot offer you something. In turn, don't offer anyone something you cannot give, but don't let time scare you into not living. Time is borrowed. Time is never certain as much as we think it might be. Time will not be controlled. Make choices that empower you. Never think about leaving this world wondering what may have been different if..."

His voice paused. I stared across I70 in the middle of Kansas, with a wet face, matted hair, tears, and sweat running down my chest, wondering if I could do any of what he asked of me. I could forgive him. I had to. Could l walk around obstacles? Could I live and love fiercely without fear? I was so scared. In that moment, I was terrified.

"I love you, Nikki Jackson. I will always love you. And I will be there with you. Always. Thank you for always loving me back."

Guitar chords filled the space. The air became lighter as the strumming grew faster. Will's voice came back in song.

Stranded in my life
Wanting to bring you home
Could you slip inside
My suitcase
And will I ever see you again

On that sunny Saturday
When I looked into your eyes
That's when I knew
I would wake up
Next to you

And can you tell me
Do you believe
In destiny
Do you believe in fate
I do believe I could have had you
But instead I chose to wait

You take care of yourself
And the world watches over you
Never had the nerve now
To dance with you
That day in the rain
Wanting to play
Where you just stood
How could I wane

And can you tell me
Do you believe
In destiny
Do you believe in fate
I do believe I could have had you
But instead I chose to wait

Then it happened again
Flight 267
Chicago to Denver
I pulled you back in

Sleeping while I stare
Give me one reason
For this
Change of season

Let me tell you
I believe
In destiny
I believe in fate

Do you know you could have had me
But instead
I chose to wait

Stranded in my life
On that sunny Saturday
Your eyes pierced my skin
And I only wish
To stay

The rocks along the side of the road dug into my knees. Gravity had pulled me down during the song. I didn't have the strength to get up, to carry on, to drive home. My own will had escaped. The hurt in my chest was brutal. My body hurt. My cheeks itched from the tears drying in the Kansas sun. I grabbed the bottom of the door frame and pulled myself up to the driver's seat. The stereo was quiet. Will was gone. He wasn't coming back. His voice wasn't going to say anything different than it had said before. I couldn't bring his voice back to answer questions, to get him to say something different. He was just gone.

I sat in the car, on the side of I70 West in Kansas next to an enormous wind farm and cried until my body couldn't produce anymore tears. Until my head ached. My heart ached. My soul felt empty. Slowly something awakened in my body. My heart filled with love. Joy almost seeped in. I began to feel content. I was comfortable, in my own body, with my emotions. Sitting on the side of the road with enormous stalks of steel looking down on me, I began to feel again. I sensed excitement coming to the surface over seeing my girls and my husband who all awaited me at home. I had a life to live, people to love. And Will had asked me to go do it. It dawned on me, he'd asked me years ago to go do it. He blamed himself for not letting me go, but I was holding on to him all those years. I treasured our years together, the friendship we'd created after hurtful breakups. It took us years to regain trust, set boundaries, and exude happiness for one another as we moved in different directions. But we'd remained close, not just because of Will, but because I was wanting to hold on to any chance I could have with him again. It hit me sitting on the side of the interstate with the huge powerful machines lurking at me. I had lived my life with a just in case, just in case things didn't work out with Chris. Just in case something happened to him, or to our marriage. I would always have Will. I had been living my life very similar to the way Will had lived his. But instead of letting someone go because I couldn't live life to the fullest for long, I was holding on to someone in case I didn't live life to the fullest. I owed Chris a better marriage. I owed him more. I owed our family a chance to live and grow together. I knew I would go back to Colorado then and live my life filled with love, passion, and a better understanding of who I used to be.

I wiped my cheeks, swallowed water, nodded a goodbye to the machines I'd bonded with during my time there, wiped away the rocks embedded into my skin, and pulled back out onto the interstate.

I was ready to go home. I was ready to see my children. I was ready to face life. To live and to love with everything I had. Will would always be with me, but I carried new found confidence that I would continue in the world, my world, with him in my heart. I had a good man to go home to, a man who loved me, and just wanted me to love him back.

Epilogue

"Mommy, let's go! Daddy and Emily are already inside!"

I waddled into the art gallery in Downtown Boulder. There was a big sign with my face plastered on it staring down at me. I read the small bio next to the sign.

Nikki Ford, Boulder, Colorado
Nikki considers herself a 'small town' artist, focusing on
landscapes and still life. Nikki works in Acrylics.
When not painting, Nikki teaches weekly art classes at
Small Hands Preschool in Boulder.
She and her husband have two children
And are expecting their third in early June

Thirty Four pieces are
For sale tonight.
Background music was composed
And written by Will Westerly

"Does it read well?" I asked Chris as I walked up next to him. "The bio? Does it read well?"

"It's fine, Nik, it's fine. It'll be a little outdated soon though," he said as he rubbed my swollen belly. "That little guy may just make a May appearance, you know."

"I sure hope so!" I said as I rubbed my lower back.

"Mommy, did you say Willy Woo is coming now?" Emily asked. She'd been calling the baby Willy Woo since we decided we'd name him after Will. I smiled down at her.

"Maybe, Baby Girl, maybe. Soon enough." I placed my hand over Chris' as he rubbed my belly. Bella stood on her tip toes while she and Emily rubbed my belly too. I smiled thinking of Baby Will's namesake. He would always be with me. With all of us. And we would go on.

"I can't wait to see Will for the first time," Bella said, as we all felt a kick.

~The End~

Acknowledgements

I would like to thank my family. My husband, Jeff, and my children. You are each a beautiful gift I treasure each day. It may have taken me time to get through this process, but I couldn't have written this novel without your love and support. To my children, I hope as you grow, you'll find you enjoy writing as much as we all enjoy reading together. I love you all so very much. Thank you for always being you.

I have had countless support in friends and other family members. I could never begin to repay you, but I can thank at least some of you here. May it be enough to bring a smile to your faces. Michelle Croxton, Lisa Schulist, Susan Teabeault, Laura Miller, Diana Buscher, Elaine Haislip, Christina Martinez, and Anne Mellichampe. As Beta readers, you've given me support, found errors, and offered me more hugs, coffee, and wine than one writer should need. Thank you all for your continued support and help. Melanie Glenn, you picked this up in the eleventh hour, and gave it new life. Knowing my bad writing habits and my patterns, you were able to see things I couldn't see. Every word you touched made *34 Seconds* better. I hope to continue to learn from you for many years to come. Thank you for your support from the beginning of this process as well as the rescue near the end of this process. John Harman, Melanie Glenn, Charles Cooper, Kristy Webb, Laura Hirsch, Anne Mellichampe, and Robin Atwood, I would like to thank you all for your help, opinions, ideas, and creative energy. Each of you has offered support, advice, thoughts, and opinions at varying points in this process. They were all invaluable for me, and you are amazing for supporting me every day. Thank you.

I would also like to acknowledge the family I had before I had my wonderful husband and amazing children. Michelle Croxton, your input, and more than anything, blessing to be who I am, write what I feel, and share it with the world means so very much to me. I love you, look up to you, and adore you. For my mother, Marlene Rennie, thank you for being here for me. I love you. And to my father, Woody, I made you a promise, and I'm proud to say I've kept it. I will keep doing what I love to do. Thank you for your love and support over the years. I miss you and wish you could be here to read my words. I have cousins, aunts and uncles and grandparents, too, who have offered love, kindness, and support over the years. Virginia and Lorraine, thank you for always being around. Stella was my grandmother. She was an amazing woman, and Nikki's Nana was based on the many things I miss about her. I hope Nana's silly ways can help keep our Stella alive for many years to come. Thank you all – for being you, and you, for being amazing.

Finally, to the many Indie Authors out there. The journey of writing is a personal journey. However, without the support you all have given, I might be reading this all alone. Valerie, Kai, Rik, Stephen, and the many wonderful people at IAG, thank you for creating such a venue. For those who have walked before me, thank you for laying the path, I will try to sweep up the dirt I brought along as I pave way for those after me. Katharine Grubb, Eric Johnson, Jessica White, Michele Mathews, Sabrina Ramoth, and many others in the 10 Minute Novelists group, thank you all. You are fun, bright, and you all make me smile, which brings words to paper. You've helped me with blurb writing, imaginary foods with zero calories, and helped to keep my sanity throughout this process. Eric, thank you for pushing me further, even when I didn't want to be pushed.

Rik Hall and Kai Wilson, I came to you both in a time when I knew I had done everything possible to be ready and asked you to help me get this out to the world. Only I wasn't nearly as ready as I thought. I revised again. I edited again. I sent revisions. I sent edits. I asked questions when I thought I had the answers but questioned everything. Thank you both for your patience, for your professionalism, and for your help.

A quick note on Deltaville, Virginia. Though this novel takes place in Deltaville, I've taken some liberties on the layout of a real town. Deltaville does exist, and it is a stunning place to be. It's small, quaint, country, neighborly, and quiet. I challenge you to visit by car or by boat; you won't be disappointed. Talk to the locals, they have stories about the area from centuries ago. Eat at the local restaurants, and be sure to get some local seafood, especially the blue crabs and the hush puppies.

Another thing I encourage, is to research and support your local Hospice organization. Losing a loved one is not an easy journey. Hospice nurses and staff are not only trained to care for the terminally ill with respect and dignity, but they also care for the survivors. They offer many services in various localities, please utilize them should that time come in your lives. They are invaluable, and I thank them for being a part of my own journey.

John C. Harman created the beautiful artwork and cover for this book. He's an amazing man, good friend, and a fabulous artist who continues to learn more about his craft each and every day. Be sure to check out his portfolio at www.johncharman.com

Dayne at Dark Star Publishing edited this book. I learned so much from him. Thanks for everything. Dayne can be found at www.darkstarpublishing.com where you can see his writing projects as well as services he offers.

Melanie Glenn offered copy edits and line edits. She has been a school teacher for 21 years, which meant, for me, she hasn't forgotten those grammar rules that used to come easy but often hide from my writing. She read this book in one night and sent me edits I needed to make it complete. She even pointed out more bad habits of mine. I am constantly learning from Melanie.

Rik Hall formatted this book. I appreciate his knowledge, experience, and patience. He's formatted more than 700 books. Rik has a Masters degree in Education and has been involved with publishing for more than 40 years. Rik can be found at: www.WildSeasFormatting.com.

Best to all~
Stella
July 2015

About the Author

Stella Samuel is a busy wife, mother, and a lover of anything summer. When not working on a new novel, she might be found reading several books at a time. She resides in Colorado with her family and two Saint Bernards, where she enjoys running and hiking and just about anything done at home with family. 34 Seconds is her debut novel.

Stella can be found at www.StellaSamuel.com
On Facebook at www.facebook.com/writerstella5?ref=hl
And on Twitter at www.twitter.com/WriterStella